Rickety Stitch

—— AND THE GELATINOUS GOO ——

THE MIDDLE-ROUTE RUN

Created and Written by
BEN COSTA & JAMES PARKS

Illustrated by
BEN COSTA

ALFRED A. KNOPF
New York

It is an age of ashes. The gleaming empires of old have faded into obscurity, leaving a tired world riddled with dungeons and ruled by fiends. With trade roads host to brigands and mighty castles neglected, goodly folk are left to huddle in remote villages, where the tales of a golden age lie all but forgotten . . .

Chapter 1
In the Weeds

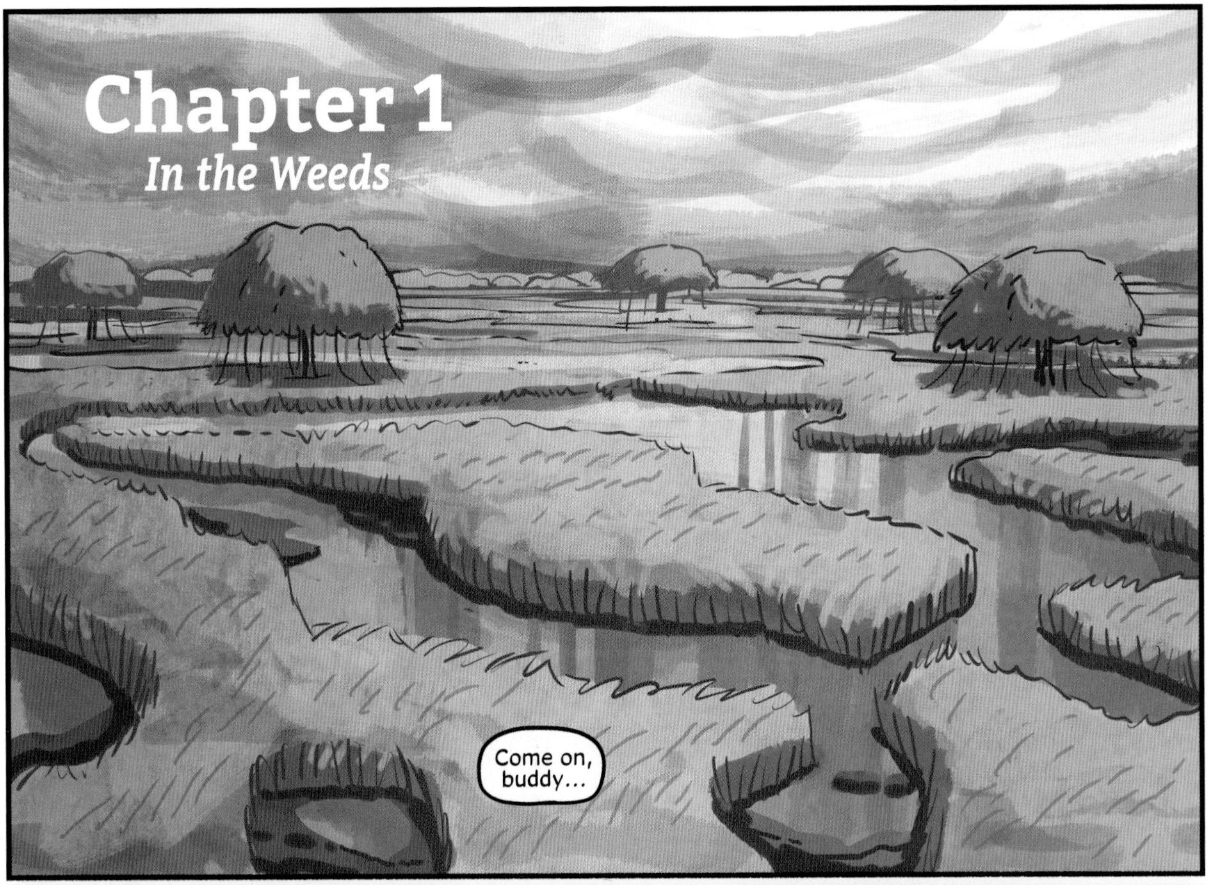
Come on, buddy...

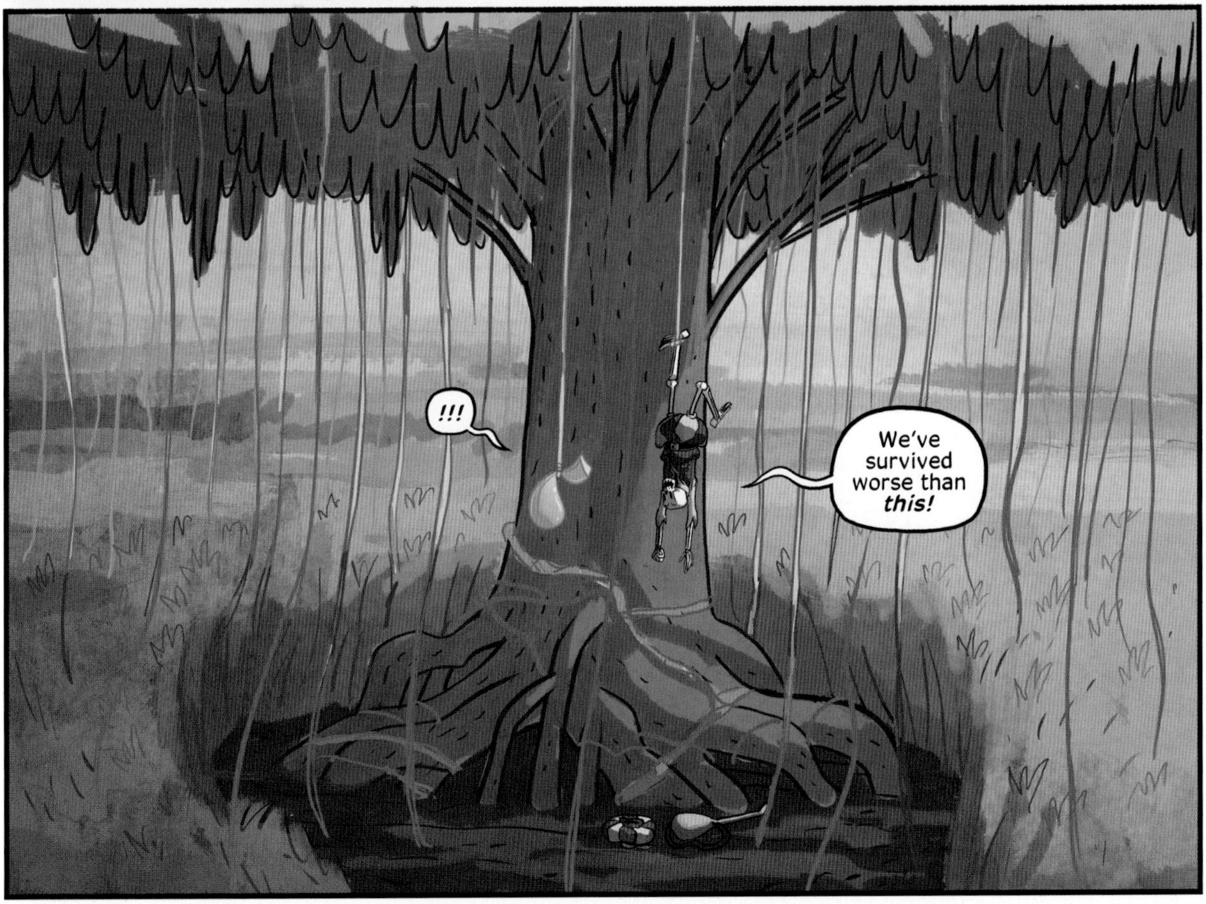
!!!
We've survived worse than *this!*

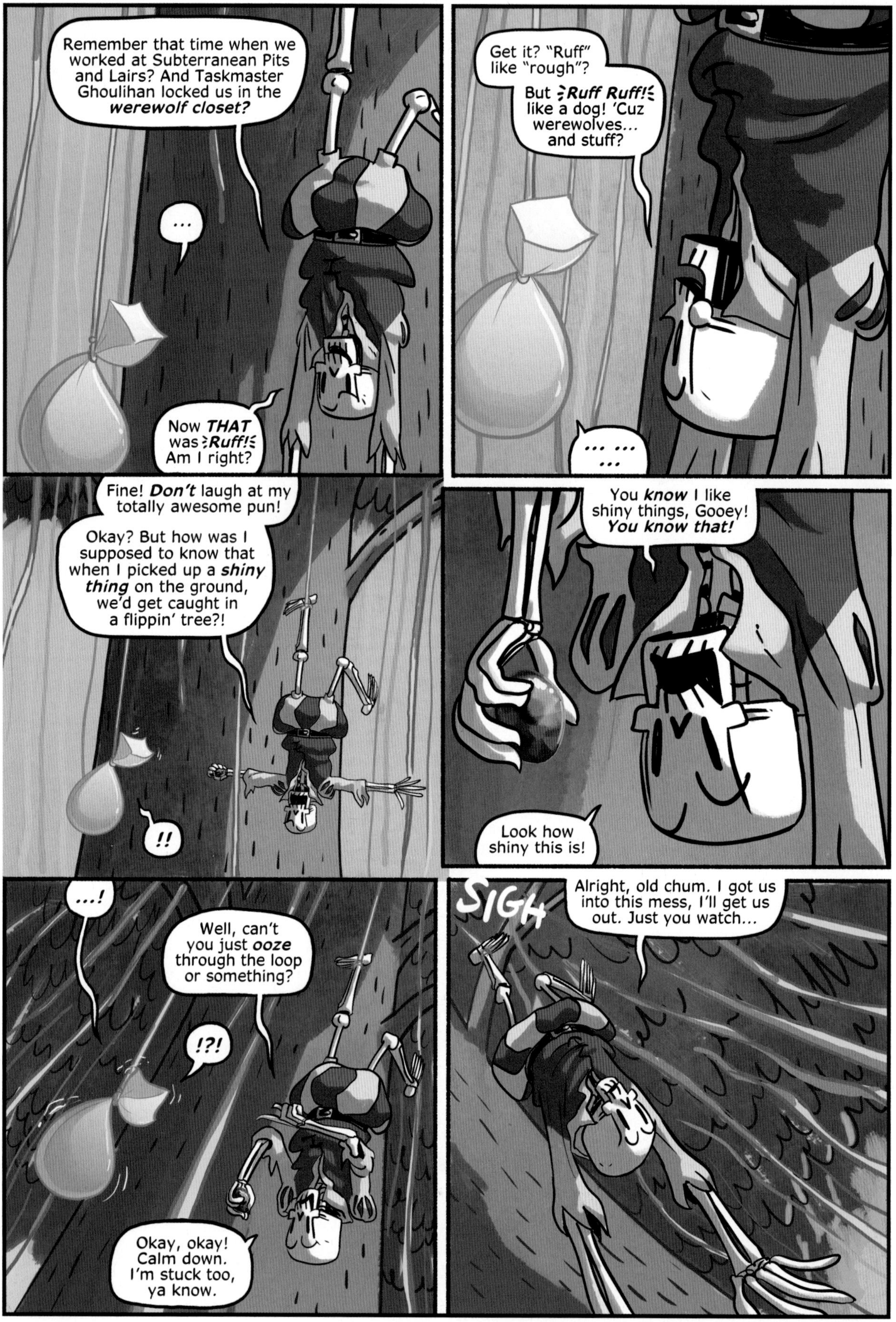
Remember that time when we worked at Subterranean Pits and Lairs? And Taskmaster Ghoulihan locked us in the ***werewolf closet?***
...
Now ***THAT*** was ***Ruff!*** Am I right?
Get it? "Ruff" like "rough"?
But ***Ruff Ruff!*** like a dog! 'Cuz werewolves... and stuff?
... ...
Fine! ***Don't*** laugh at my totally awesome pun!
Okay? But how was I supposed to know that when I picked up a ***shiny thing*** on the ground, we'd get caught in a flippin' tree?!
!!
You ***know*** I like shiny things, Gooey! ***You know that!***
Look how shiny this is!
...!
Well, can't you just ***ooze*** through the loop or something?
!?!
Okay, okay! Calm down. I'm stuck too, ya know.
SIGH
Alright, old chum. I got us into this mess, I'll get us out. Just you watch...

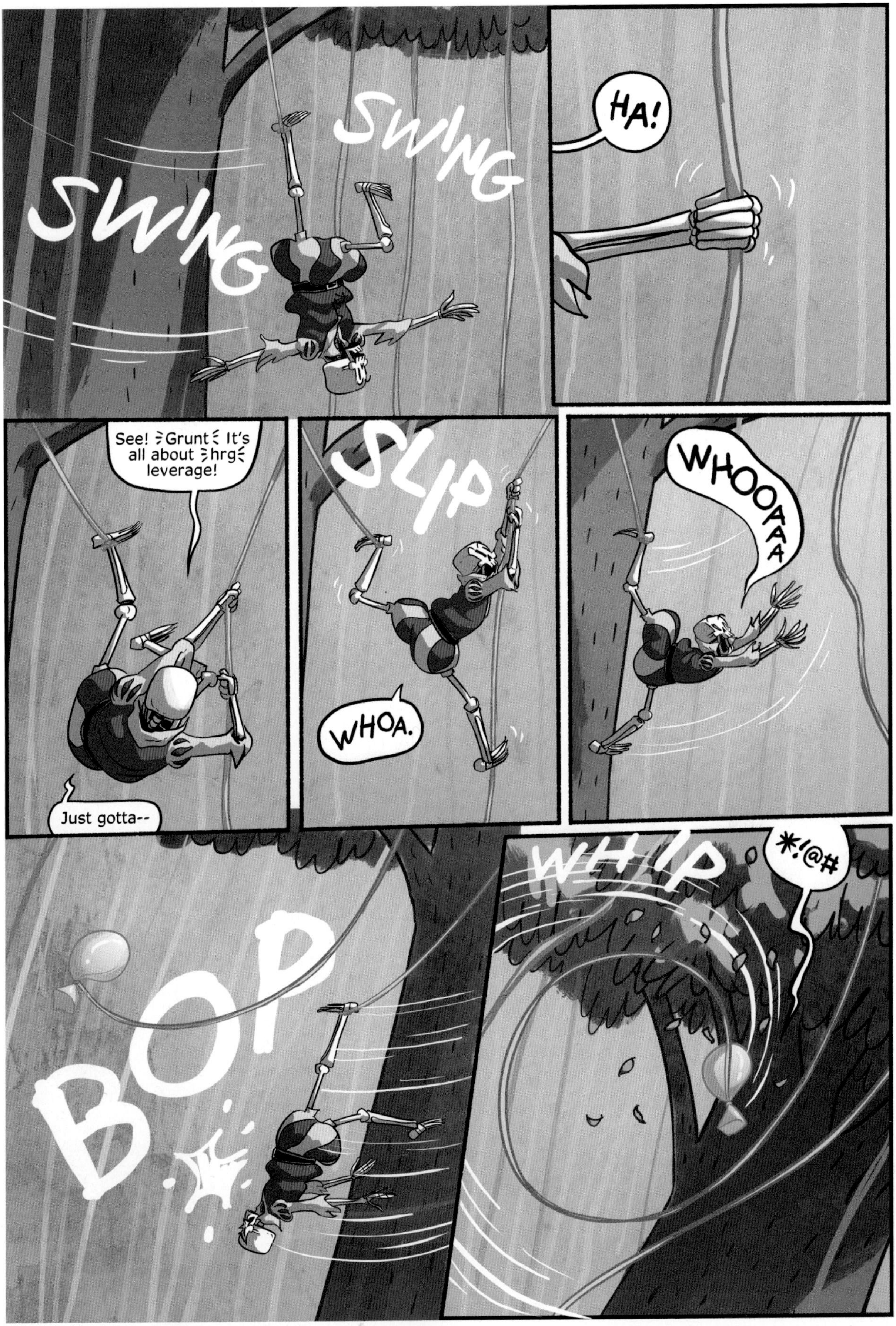
SWING
SWING
HA!
See! ⁓Grunt⁓ It's all about ⁓hrg⁓ leverage!
Just gotta--
SLIP
WHOA.
WHOOAAA
BOP
WHIP
*!@#

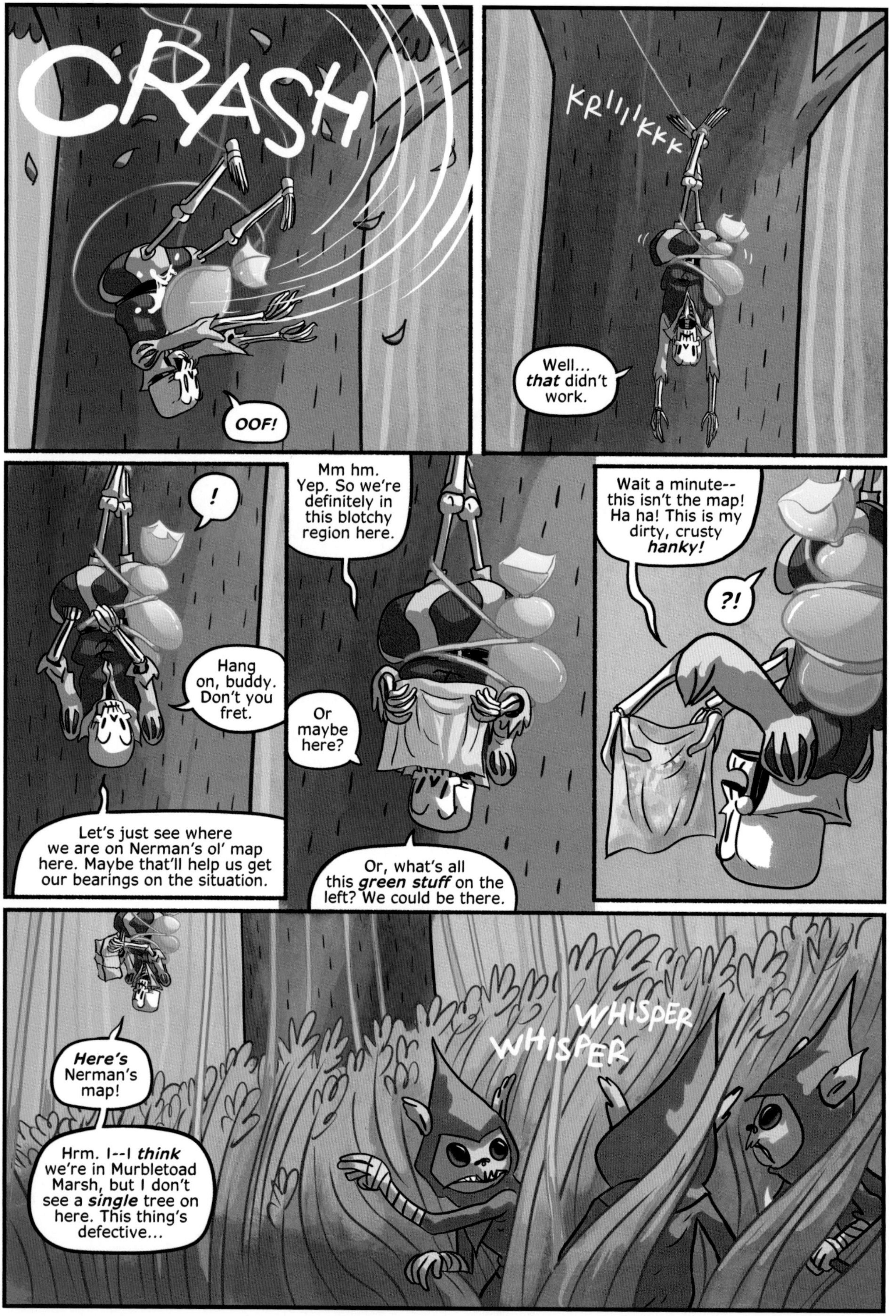
CRASH
OOF!
KRIIIIKKK
Well... *that* didn't work.
!
Hang on, buddy. Don't you fret.
Let's just see where we are on Nerman's ol' map here. Maybe that'll help us get our bearings on the situation.
Mm hm. Yep. So we're definitely in this blotchy region here.
Or maybe here?
Or, what's all this *green stuff* on the left? We could be there.
Wait a minute-- this isn't the map! Ha ha! This is my dirty, crusty *hanky!*
?!
Here's Nerman's map!
Hrm. I--I *think* we're in Murbletoad Marsh, but I don't see a *single* tree on here. This thing's defective...
WHISPER
WHISPER

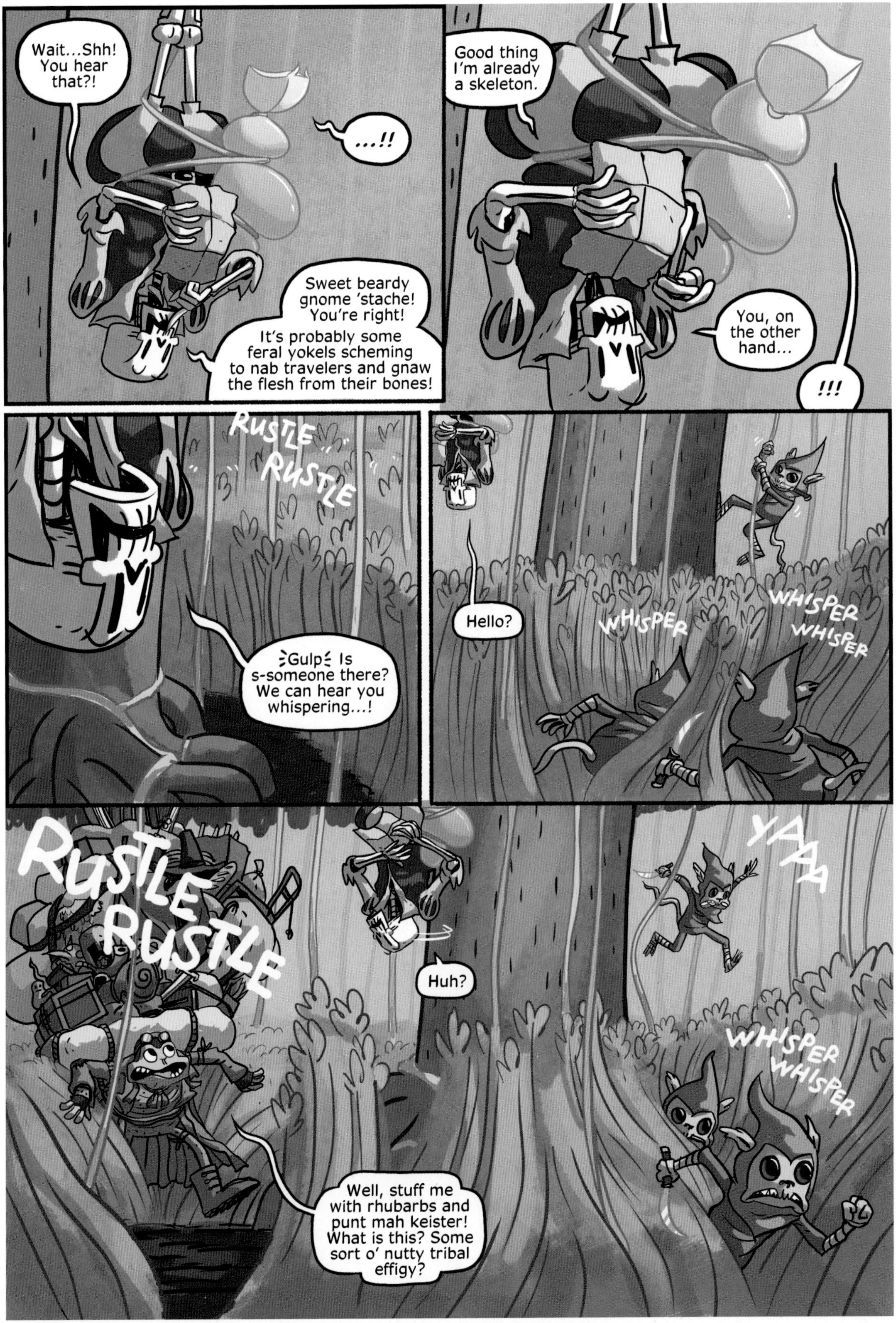
Wait...Shh! You hear that?!
...!!
Sweet beardy gnome 'stache! You're right!
It's probably some feral yokels scheming to nab travelers and gnaw the flesh from their bones!
Good thing I'm already a skeleton.
You, on the other hand...
!!!
RUSTLE RUSTLE
Gulp Is s-someone there? We can hear you whispering...!
Hello?
WHISPER
WHISPER WHISPER
RUSTLE RUSTLE
Huh?
YAAA
WHISPER WHISPER
Well, stuff me with rhubarbs and punt mah keister! What is this? Some sort o' nutty tribal effigy?

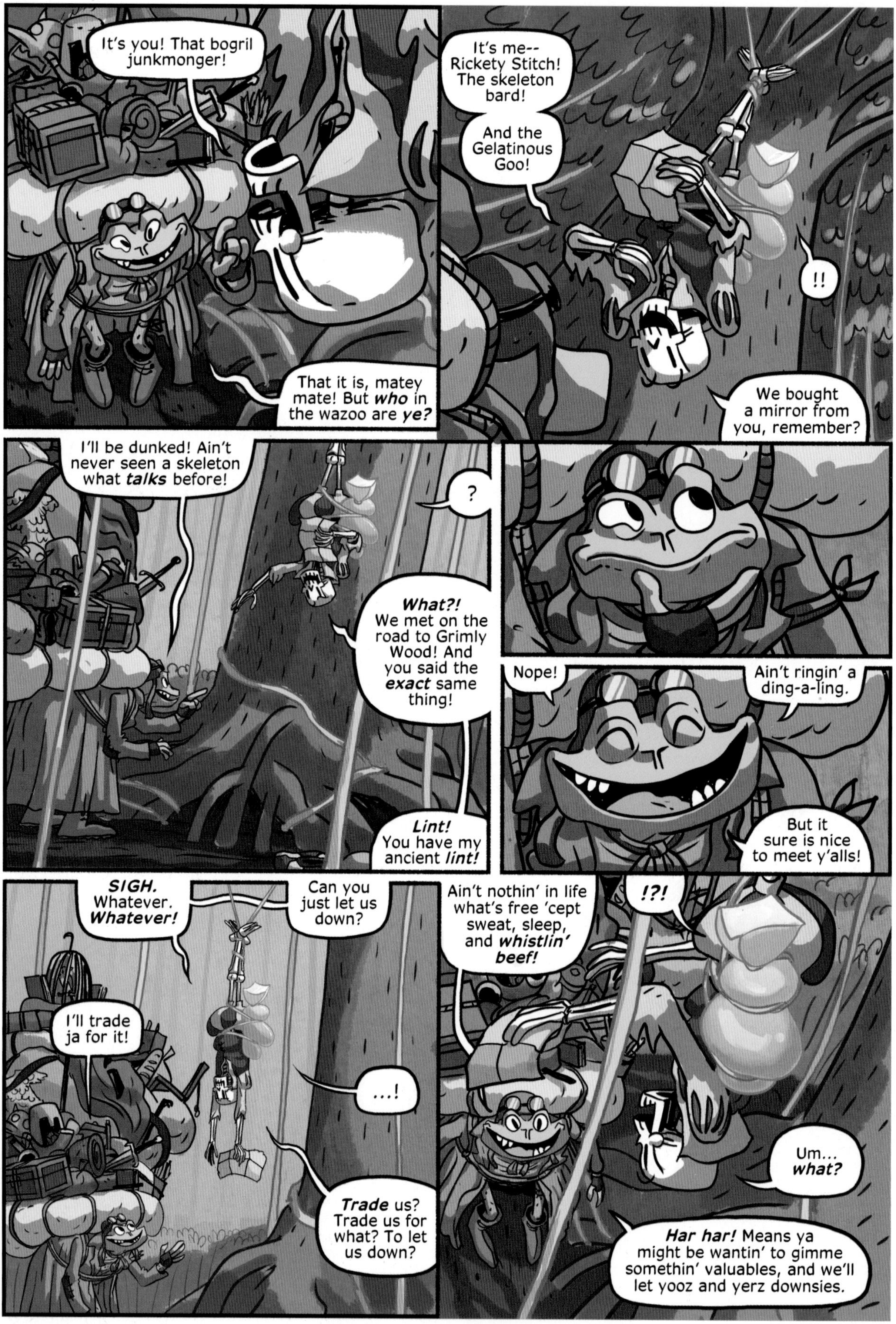
It's you! That bogril junkmonger!
That it is, matey mate! But *who* in the wazoo are *ye?*
It's me-- Rickety Stitch! The skeleton bard!
And the Gelatinous Goo!
!!
We bought a mirror from you, remember?
I'll be dunked! Ain't never seen a skeleton what *talks* before!
?
What?! We met on the road to Grimly Wood! And you said the *exact* same thing!
Lint! You have my ancient *lint!*
Nope!
Ain't ringin' a ding-a-ling.
But it sure is nice to meet y'alls!
SIGH. Whatever. *Whatever!*
Can you just let us down?
I'll trade ja for it!
...!
Trade us? Trade us for what? To let us down?
Ain't nothin' in life what's free 'cept sweat, sleep, and *whistlin' beef!*
!?!
Um... *what?*
Har har! Means ya might be wantin' to gimme somethin' valuables, and we'll let yooz and yerz downsies.

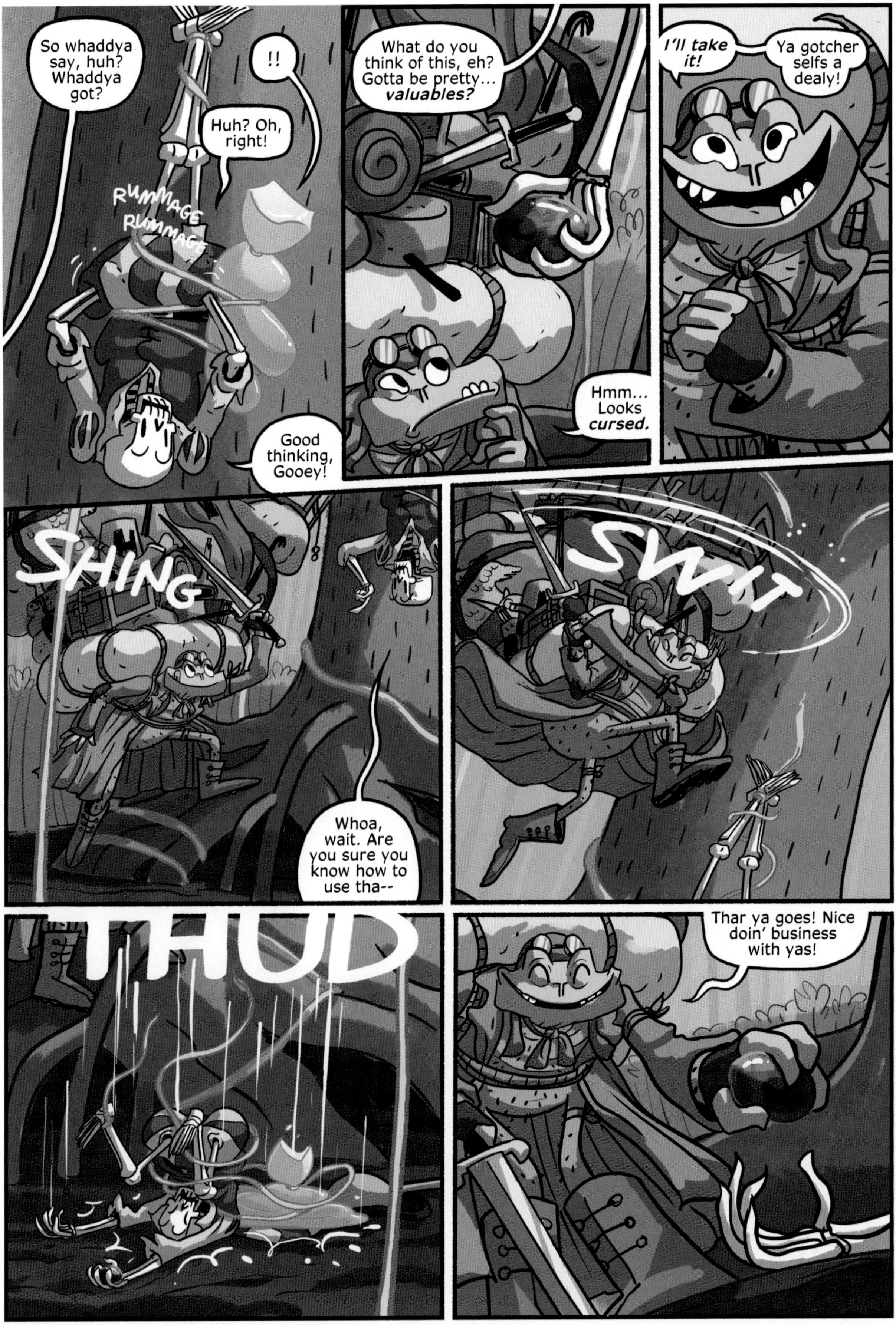
So whaddya say, huh? Whaddya got?
!!
Huh? Oh, right!
RUMMAGE RUMMAGE
Good thinking, Gooey!
What do you think of this, eh? Gotta be pretty... *valuables?*
Hmm... Looks *cursed.*
I'll *take it!*
Ya gotcher selfs a dealy!
SHING
Whoa, wait. Are you sure you know how to use tha--
SWIT
THUD
Thar ya goes! Nice doin' business with yas!

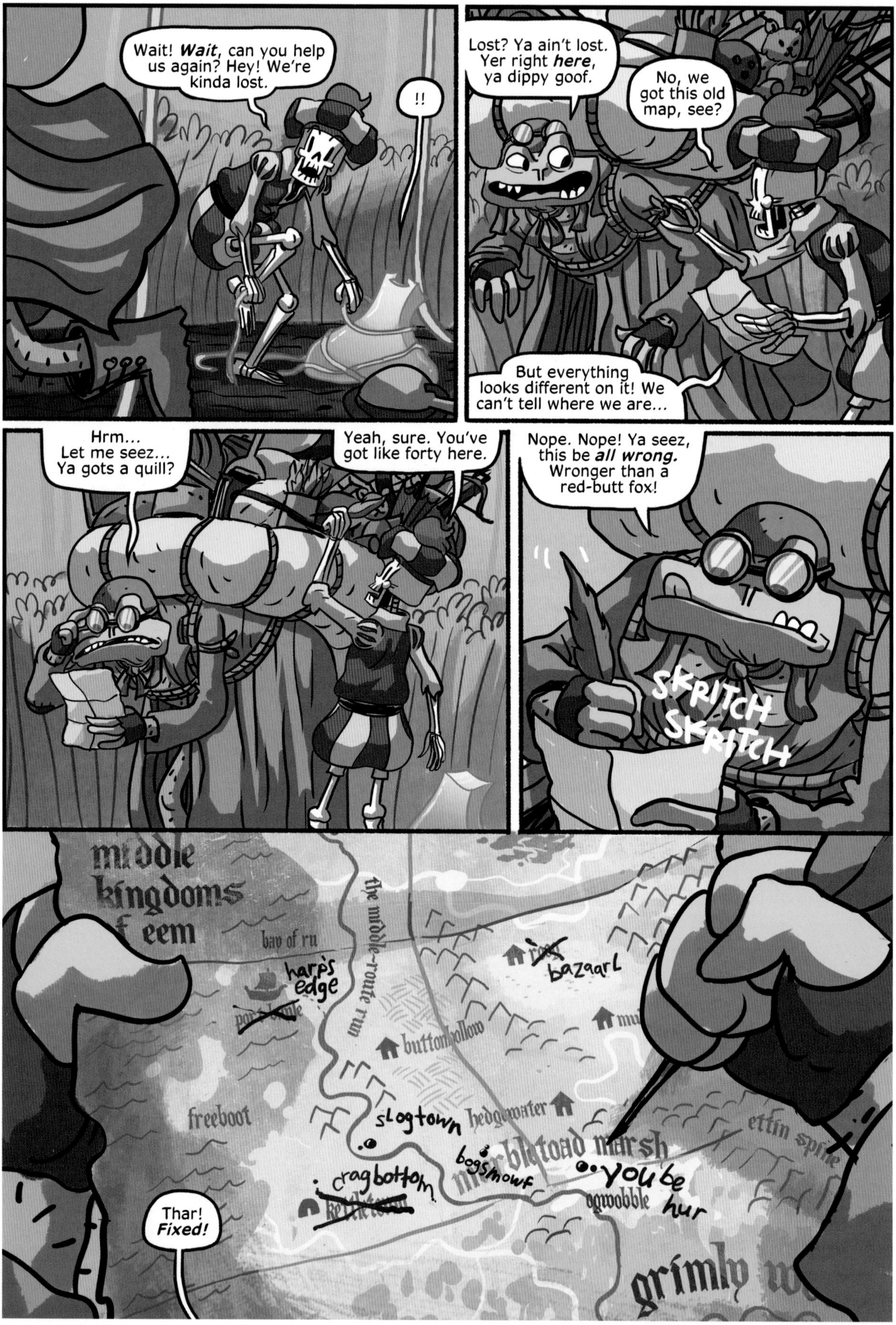
Wait! *Wait*, can you help us again? Hey! We're kinda lost.
!!
Lost? Ya ain't lost. Yer right *here*, ya dippy goof.
No, we got this old map, see?
But everything looks different on it! We can't tell where we are...
Hrm... Let me seez... Ya gots a quill?
Yeah, sure. You've got like forty here.
Nope. Nope! Ya seez, this be *all wrong.* Wronger than a red-butt fox!
SKRITCH SKRITCH
kingdoms
bay of ru
harp's edge
the middle-route run
bazaarl
buttonhollow
freeboot
slogtown
hedgewater
ettin spine
bogsmowf
you be hur
cragbottom
ogwobble
Thar! *Fixed!*

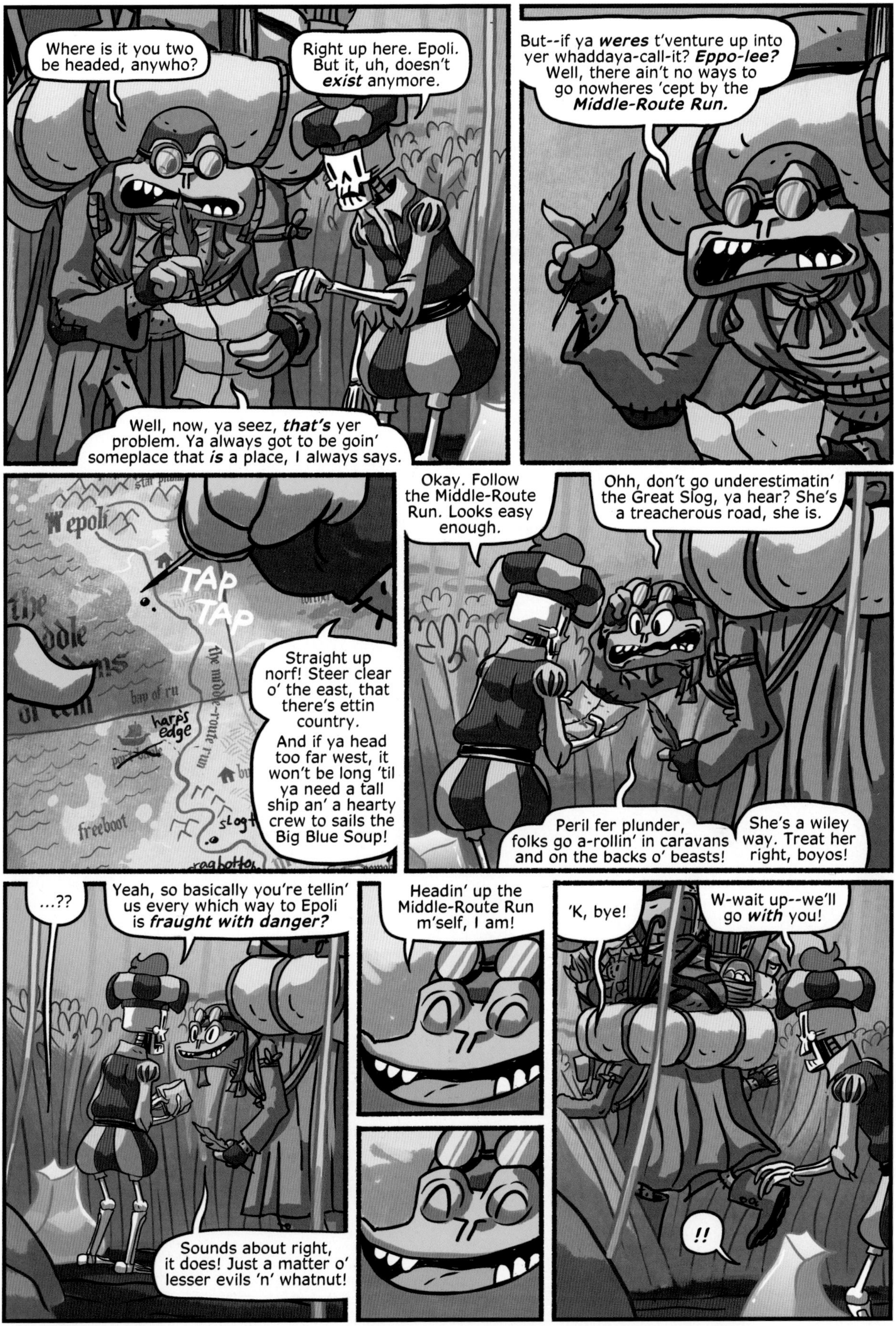
Where is it you two be headed, anywho?
Right up here. Epoli. But it, uh, doesn't *exist* anymore.
Well, now, ya seez, *that's* yer problem. Ya always got to be goin' someplace that *is* a place, I always says.
But--if ya *weres* t'venture up into yer whaddaya-call-it? *Eppo-lee?* Well, there ain't no ways to go nowheres 'cept by the *Middle-Route Run.*
epoli
TAP TAP
the middle-route run
bay of ru
harp's edge
freeboot
slog
Straight up norf! Steer clear o' the east, that there's ettin country.
And if ya head too far west, it won't be long 'til ya need a tall ship an' a hearty crew to sails the Big Blue Soup!
Okay. Follow the Middle-Route Run. Looks easy enough.
Ohh, don't go underestimatin' the Great Slog, ya hear? She's a treacherous road, she is.
Peril fer plunder, folks go a-rollin' in caravans and on the backs o' beasts!
She's a wiley way. Treat her right, boyos!
...??
Yeah, so basically you're tellin' us every which way to Epoli is *fraught with danger?*
Sounds about right, it does! Just a matter o' lesser evils 'n' whatnut!
Headin' up the Middle-Route Run m'self, I am!
'K, bye!
W-wait up--we'll go *with* you!
!!

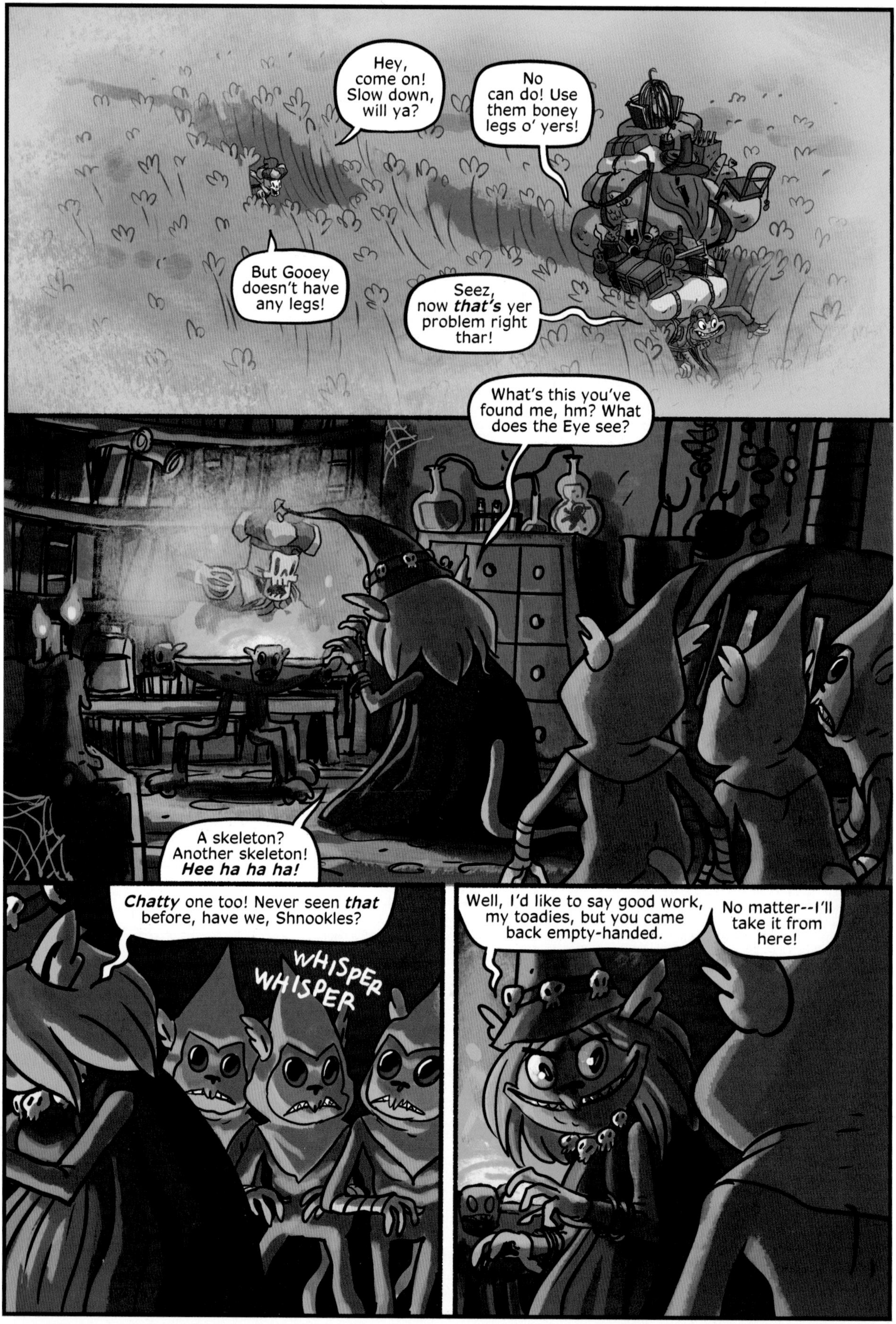
Hey, come on! Slow down, will ya?
No can do! Use them boney legs o' yers!
But Gooey doesn't have any legs!
Seez, now *that's* yer problem right thar!
What's this you've found me, hm? What does the Eye see?
A skeleton? Another skeleton! ***Hee ha ha ha!***
Chatty one too! Never seen *that* before, have we, Shnookles?
WHISPER
WHISPER
Well, I'd like to say good work, my toadies, but you came back empty-handed.
No matter--I'll take it from here!

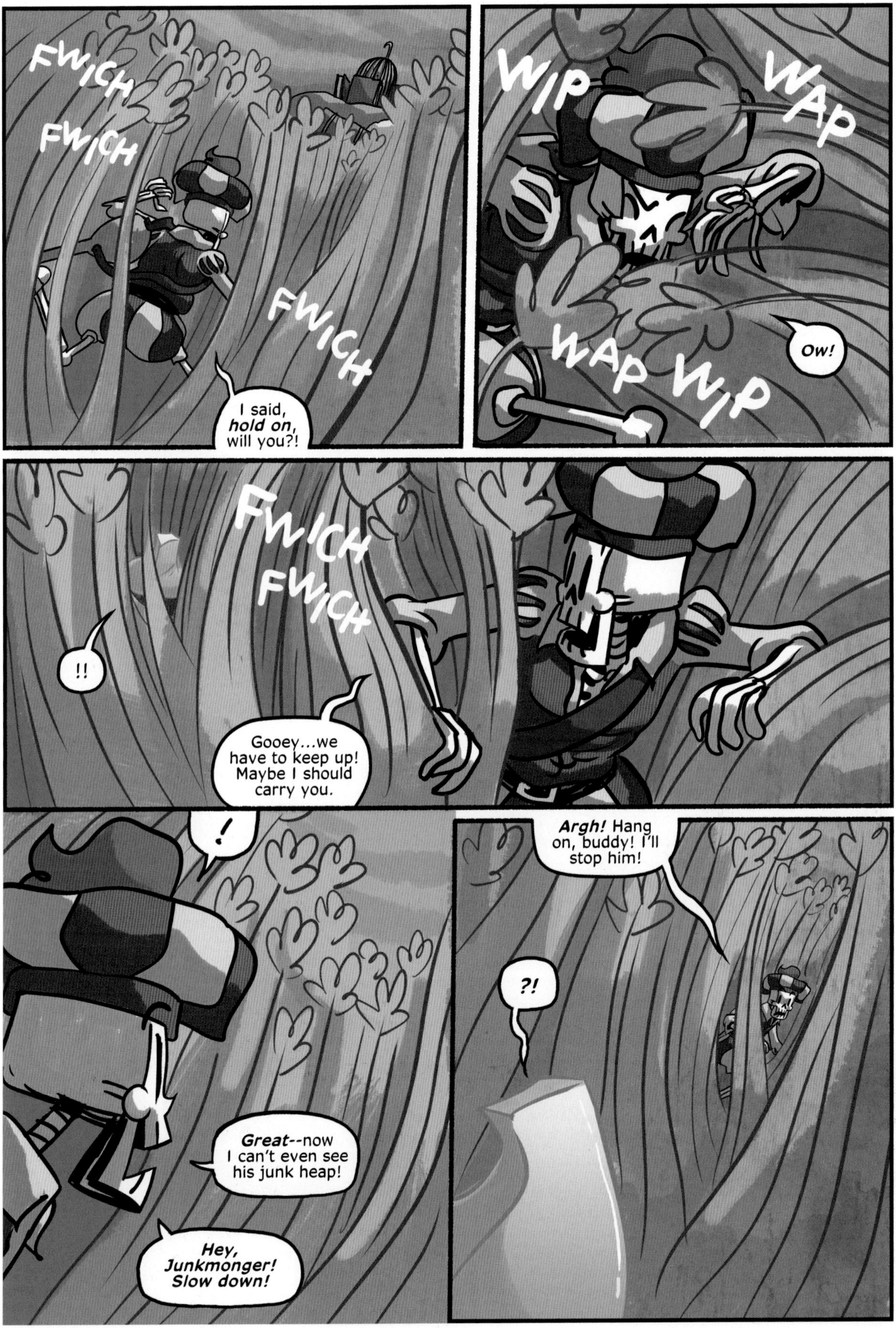
FWICH
FWICH
FWICH
I said, *hold on*, will you?!
WIP
WAP
WAP WIP
Ow!
FWICH
FWICH
!!
Gooey...we have to keep up! Maybe I should carry you.
!
Great--now I can't even see his junk heap!
Hey, Junkmonger! Slow down!
Argh! Hang on, buddy! I'll stop him!
?!

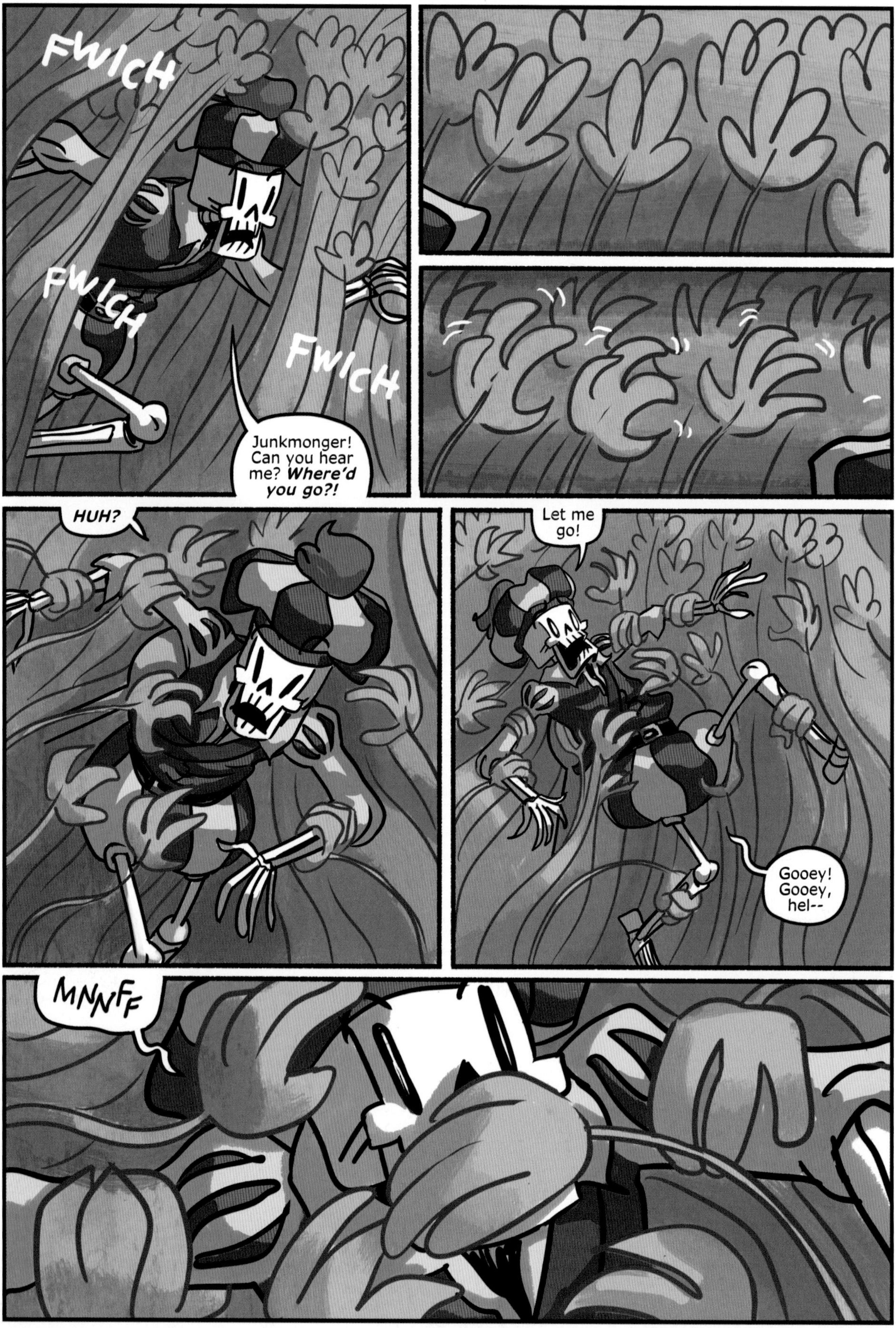
FWICH
FWICH
FWICH
Junkmonger! Can you hear me? *Where'd you go?!*
HUH?
Let me go!
Gooey! Gooey, hel--
MNNFF

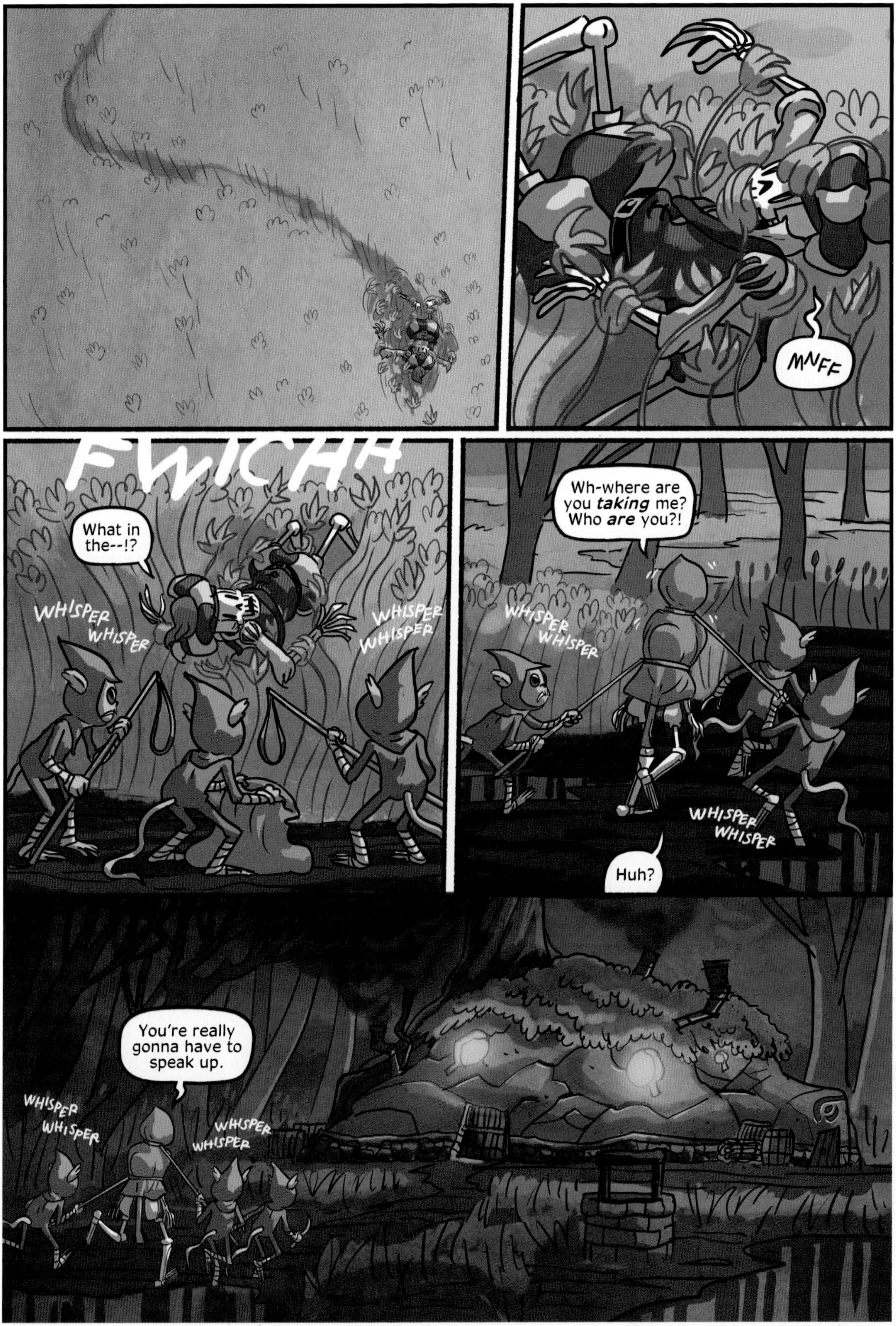
MNFF
FWICHH
What in the--!?
WHISPER WHISPER
WHISPER WHISPER
Wh-where are you *taking* me? Who *are* you?!
WHISPER WHISPER
WHISPER WHISPER
Huh?
You're really gonna have to speak up.
WHISPER WHISPER
WHISPER WHISPER

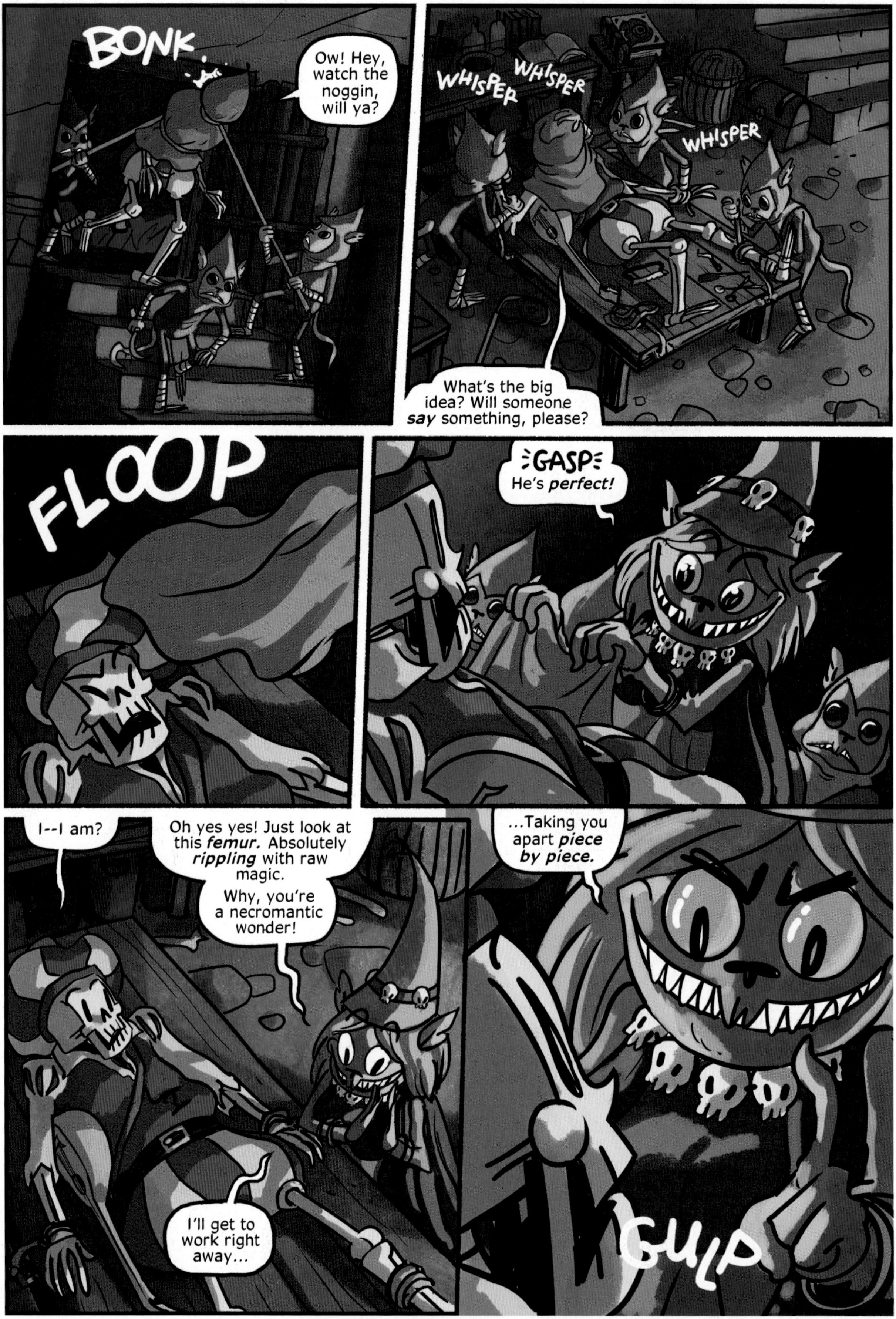
BONK
Ow! Hey, watch the noggin, will ya?
WHISPER
WHISPER
WHISPER
What's the big idea? Will someone *say* something, please?
FLOOP
GASP
He's *perfect!*
I--I am?
Oh yes yes! Just look at this *femur.* Absolutely *rippling* with raw magic.
Why, you're a necromantic wonder!
I'll get to work right away...
...Taking you apart *piece by piece.*
GULP

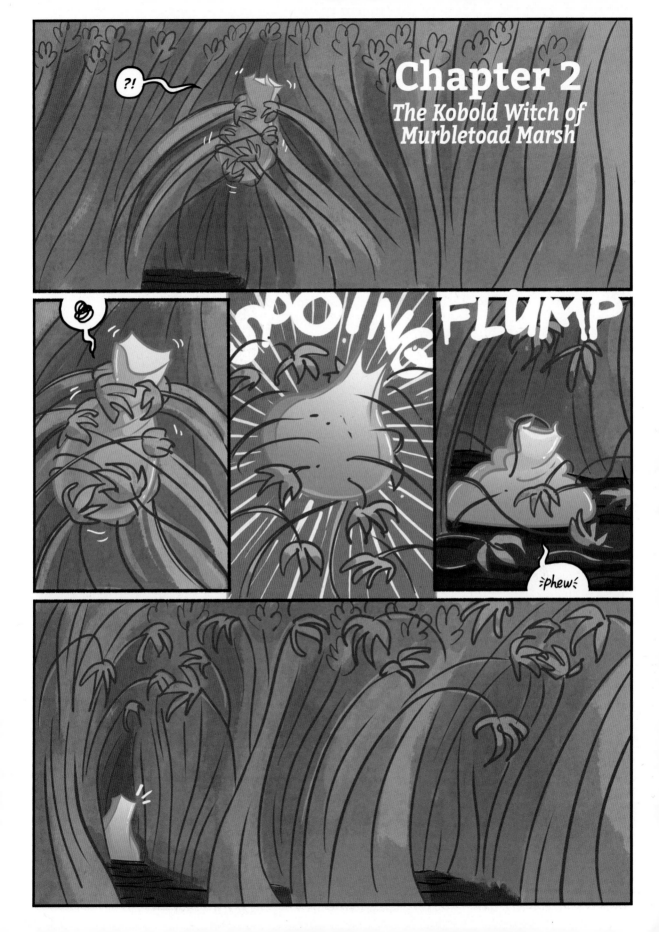

Chapter 2
The Kobold Witch of Murbletoad Marsh

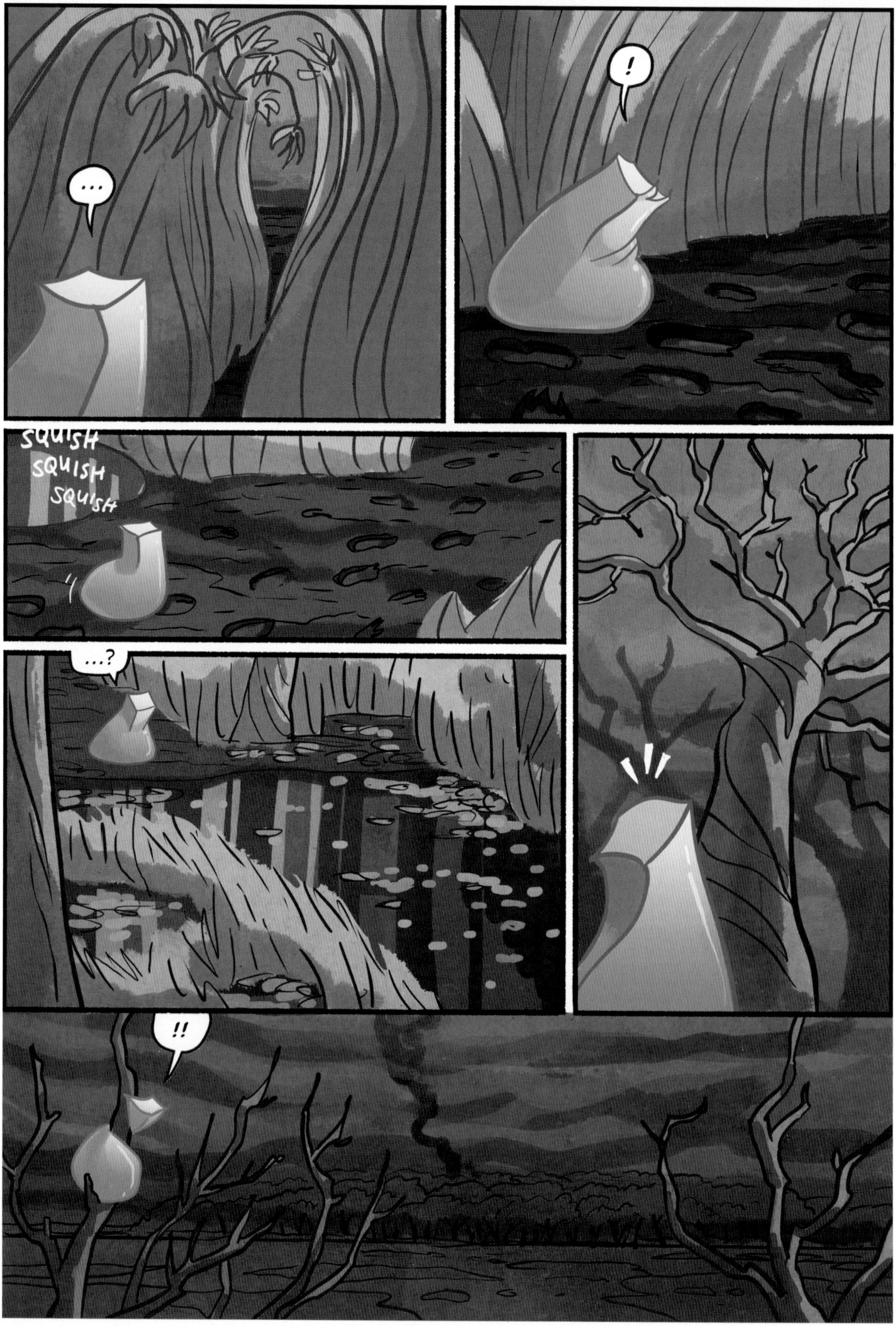
...
!
SQUISH
SQUISH
SQUISH
...?
!!

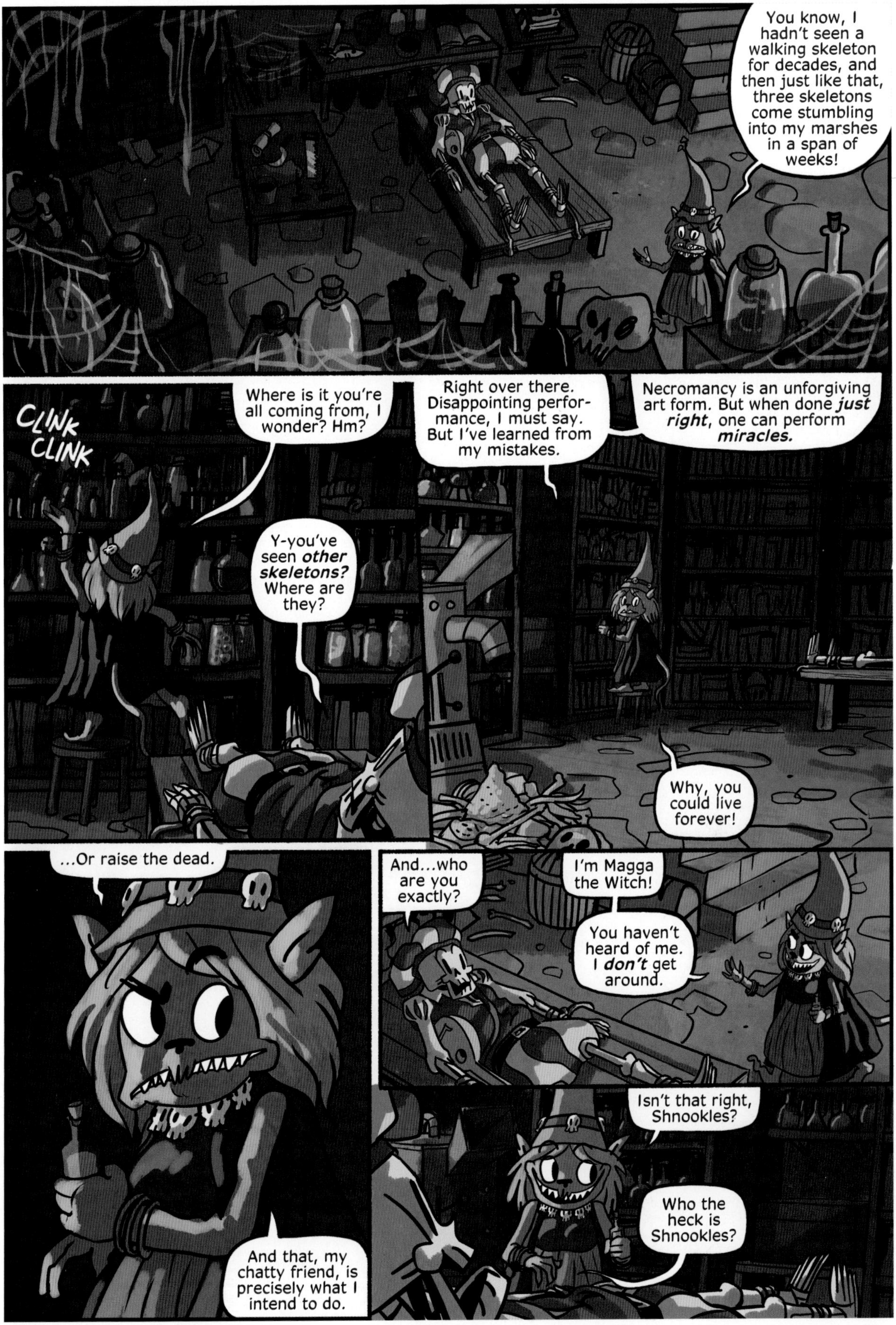
You know, I hadn't seen a walking skeleton for decades, and then just like that, three skeletons come stumbling into my marshes in a span of weeks!
CLINK CLINK
Where is it you're all coming from, I wonder? Hm?
Y-you've seen *other skeletons?* Where are they?
Right over there. Disappointing perfor-mance, I must say. But I've learned from my mistakes.
Necromancy is an unforgiving art form. But when done *just right*, one can perform *miracles.*
Why, you could live forever!
...Or raise the dead.
And that, my chatty friend, is precisely what I intend to do.
And...who are you exactly?
I'm Magga the Witch!
You haven't heard of me. I *don't* get around.
Isn't that right, Shnookles?
Who the heck is Shnookles?

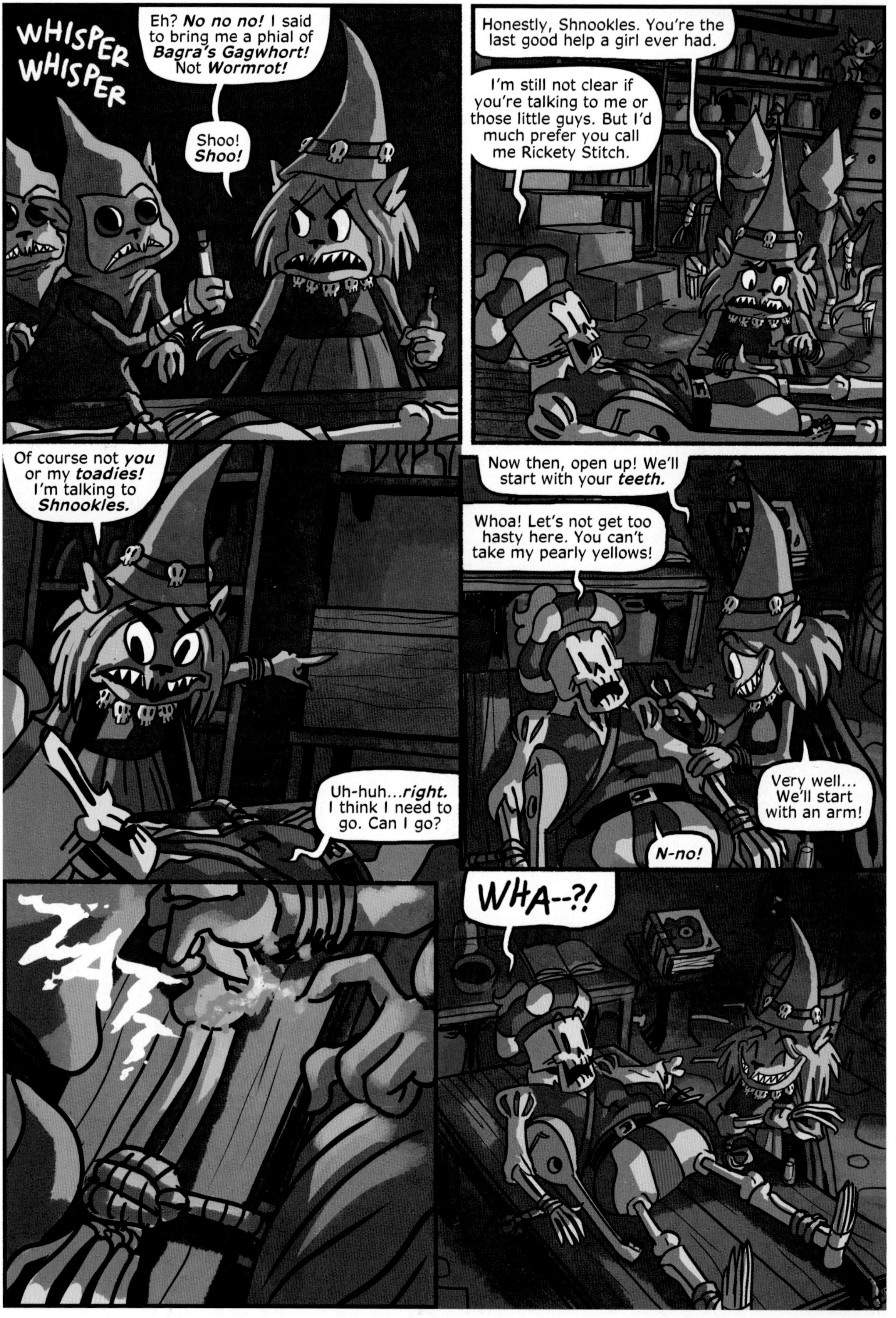
WHISPER WHISPER
Eh? *No no no!* I said to bring me a phial of *Bagra's Gagwhort!* Not *Wormrot!*
Shoo! *Shoo!*
Honestly, Shnookles. You're the last good help a girl ever had.
I'm still not clear if you're talking to me or those little guys. But I'd much prefer you call me Rickety Stitch.
Of course not *you* or my *toadies!* I'm talking to *Shnookles.*
Uh-huh...*right.* I think I need to go. Can I go?
Now then, open up! We'll start with your *teeth.*
Whoa! Let's not get too hasty here. You can't take my pearly yellows!
Very well... We'll start with an arm!
N-no!
ZAT
WHA--?!

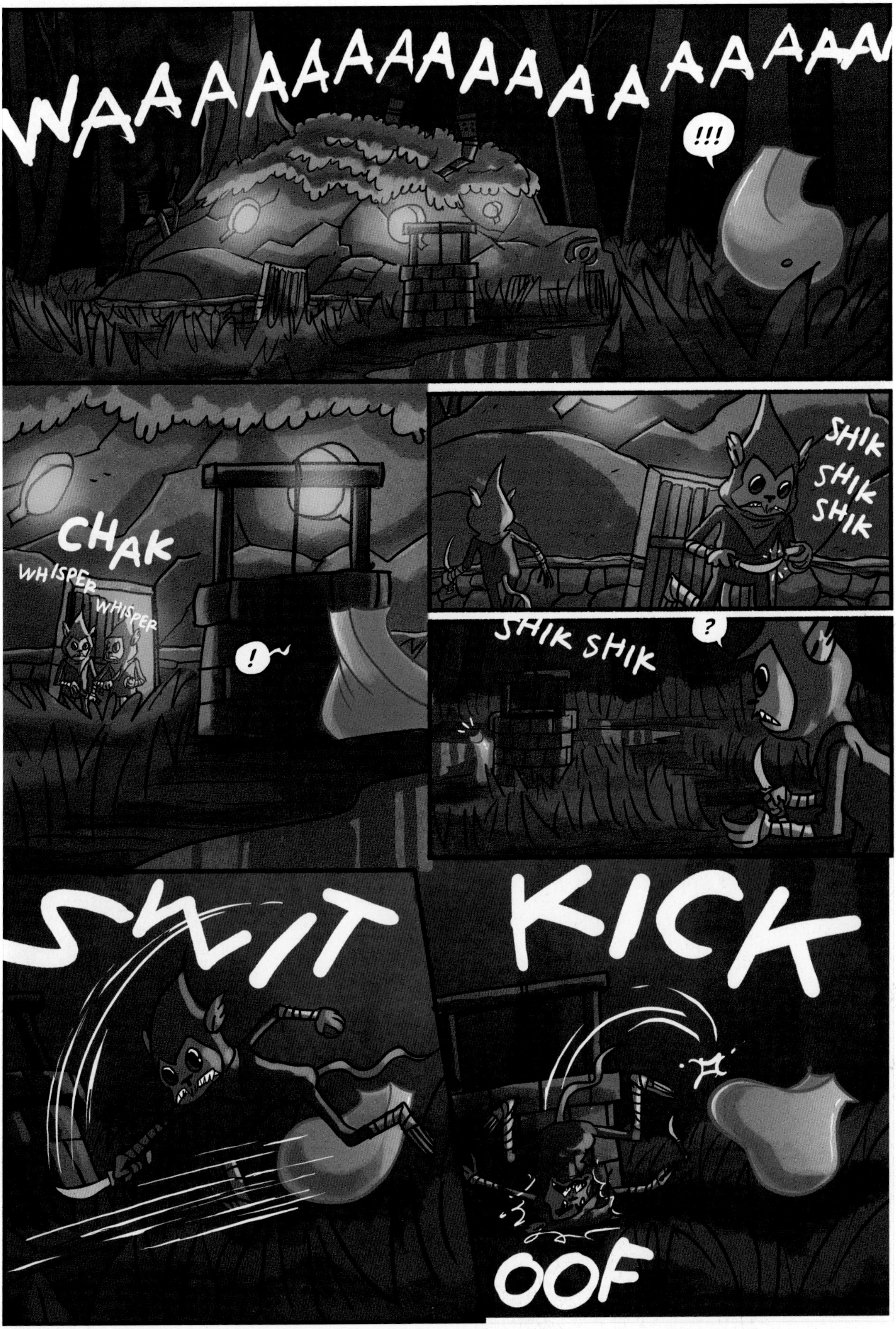
WAAAAAAAAAAAAAAAAA
!!!
CHAK
WHISPER
WHISPER
!
SHIK
SHIK
SHIK
SHIK SHIK
?
SWIT
KICK
OOF

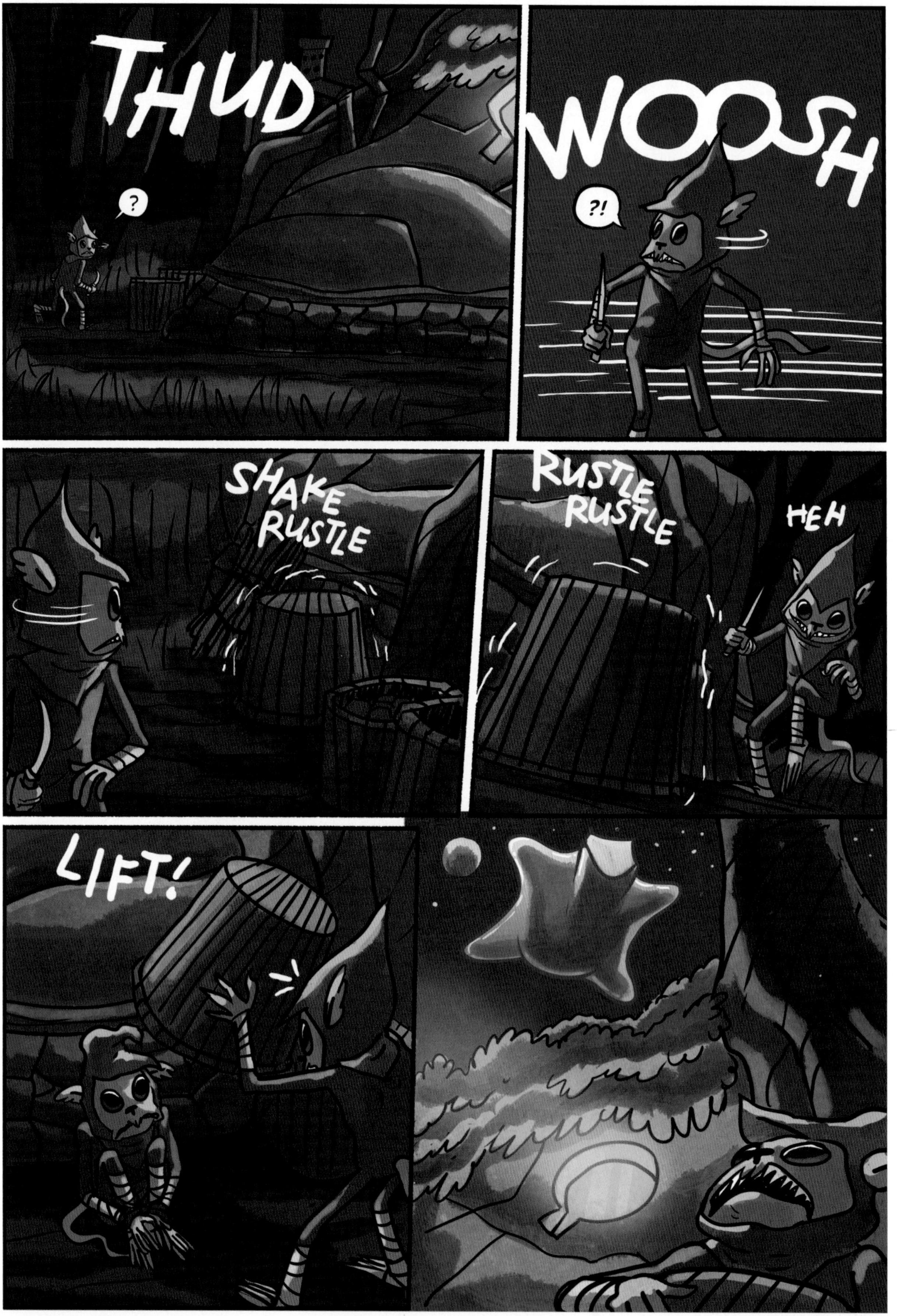
THUD
?
WOOSH
?!
SHAKE
RUSTLE
RUSTLE
RUSTLE
HEH
LIFT!

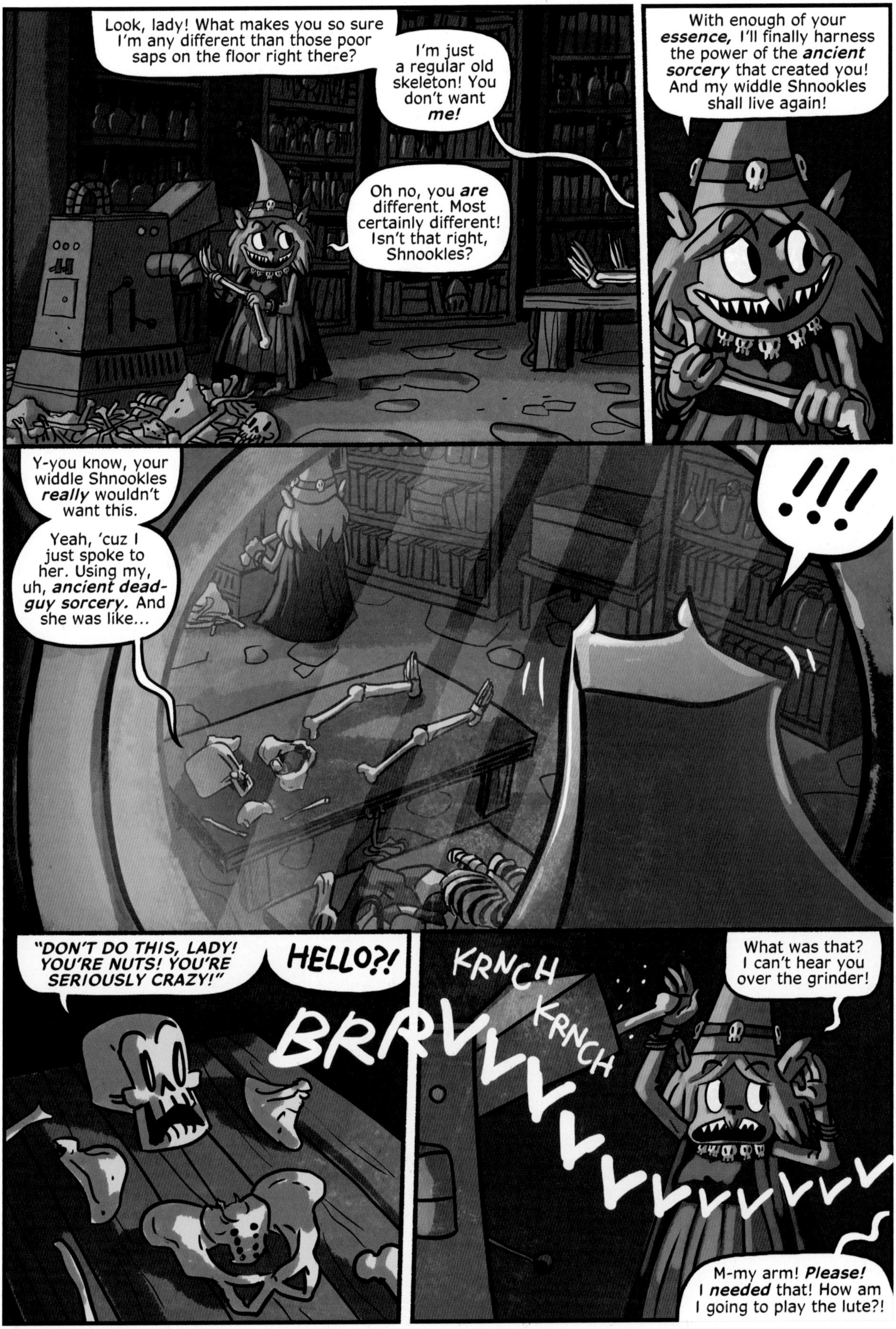

Look, lady! What makes you so sure I'm any different than those poor saps on the floor right there?
I'm just a regular old skeleton! You don't want *me!*
Oh no, you *are* different. Most certainly different! Isn't that right, Shnookles?
With enough of your *essence,* I'll finally harness the power of the *ancient sorcery* that created you! And my widdle Shnookles shall live again!
Y-you know, your widdle Shnookles *really* wouldn't want this.
Yeah, 'cuz I just spoke to her. Using my, uh, *ancient dead-guy sorcery.* And she was like...
!!!
"DON'T DO THIS, LADY! YOU'RE NUTS! YOU'RE SERIOUSLY CRAZY!"
HELLO?!
KRNCH
KRNCH
BRRVVVVVVVVVVVVVV
What was that? I can't hear you over the grinder!
M-my arm! *Please!* I *needed* that! How am I going to play the lute?!

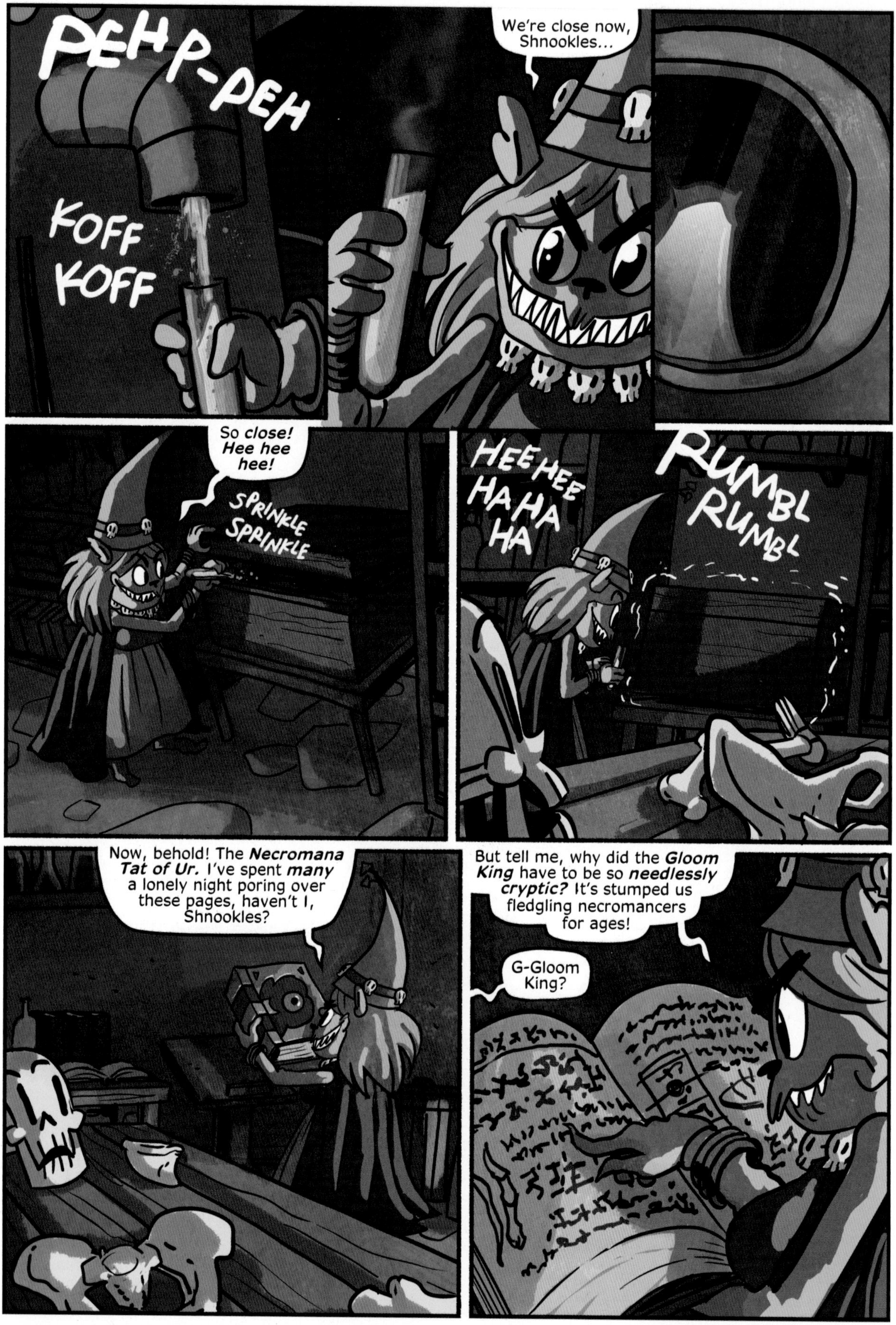
PEHP-PEH
KOFF KOFF
We're close now, Shnookles...
So *close!* ***Hee hee hee!***
SPRINKLE SPRINKLE
HEE HEE HA HA HA
RUMBL RUMBL
Now, behold! The ***Necromana Tat of Ur.*** I've spent ***many*** a lonely night poring over these pages, haven't I, Shnookles?
But tell me, why did the ***Gloom King*** have to be so ***needlessly cryptic?*** It's stumped us fledgling necromancers for ages!
G-Gloom King?

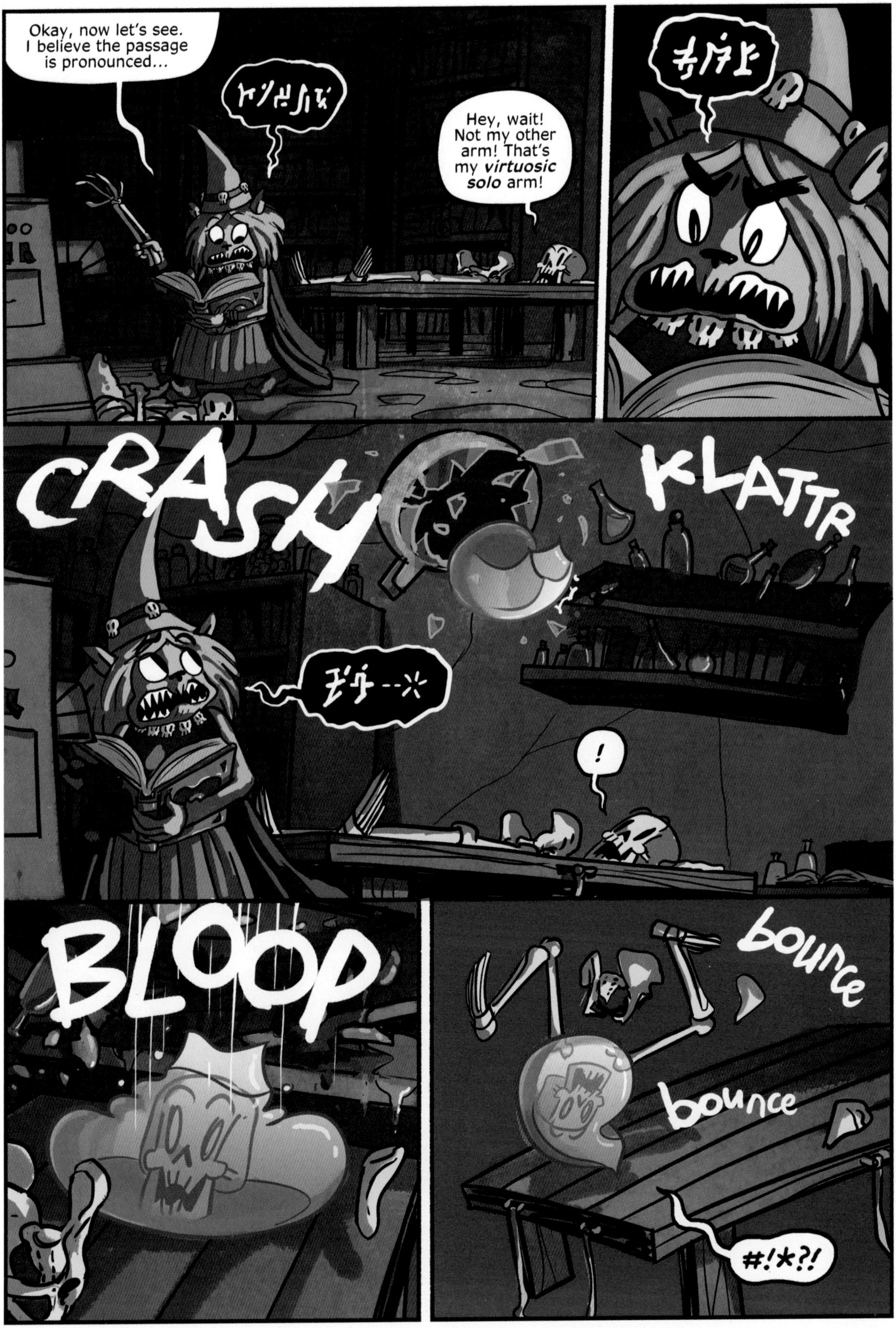
Okay, now let's see. I believe the passage is pronounced...
Hey, wait! Not my other arm! That's my *virtuosic solo* arm!
CRASH
KLATTR
!
BLOOP
bounce
bounce
#!*?!

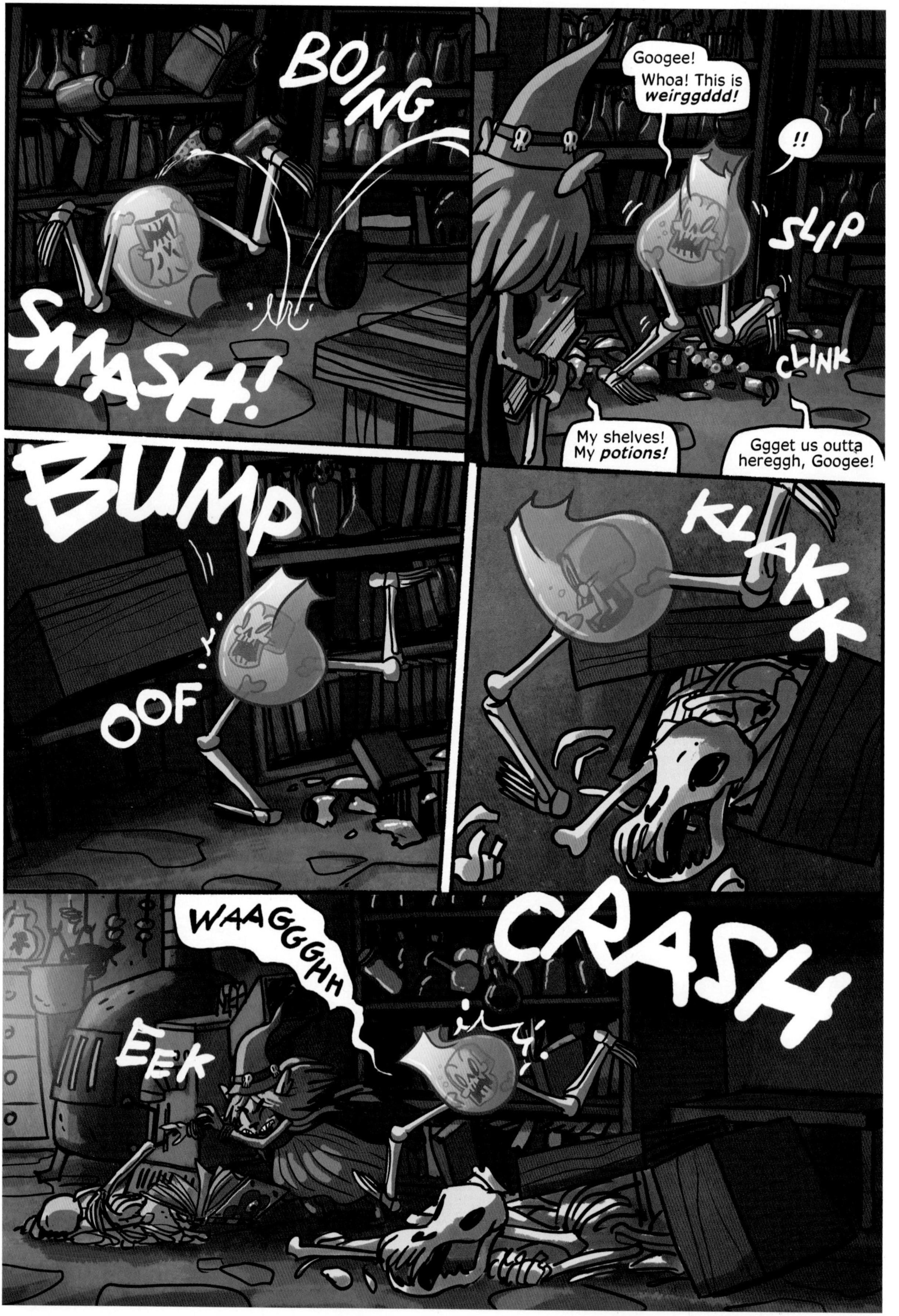
BOING
SMASH!
Googee!
Whoa! This is *weirggddd!*
!!
SLIP
CLINK
My shelves! My *potions!*
Ggget us outta hereggh, Googee!
BUMP
OOF
KLAKK
WAAGGGHH
CRASH
EEK

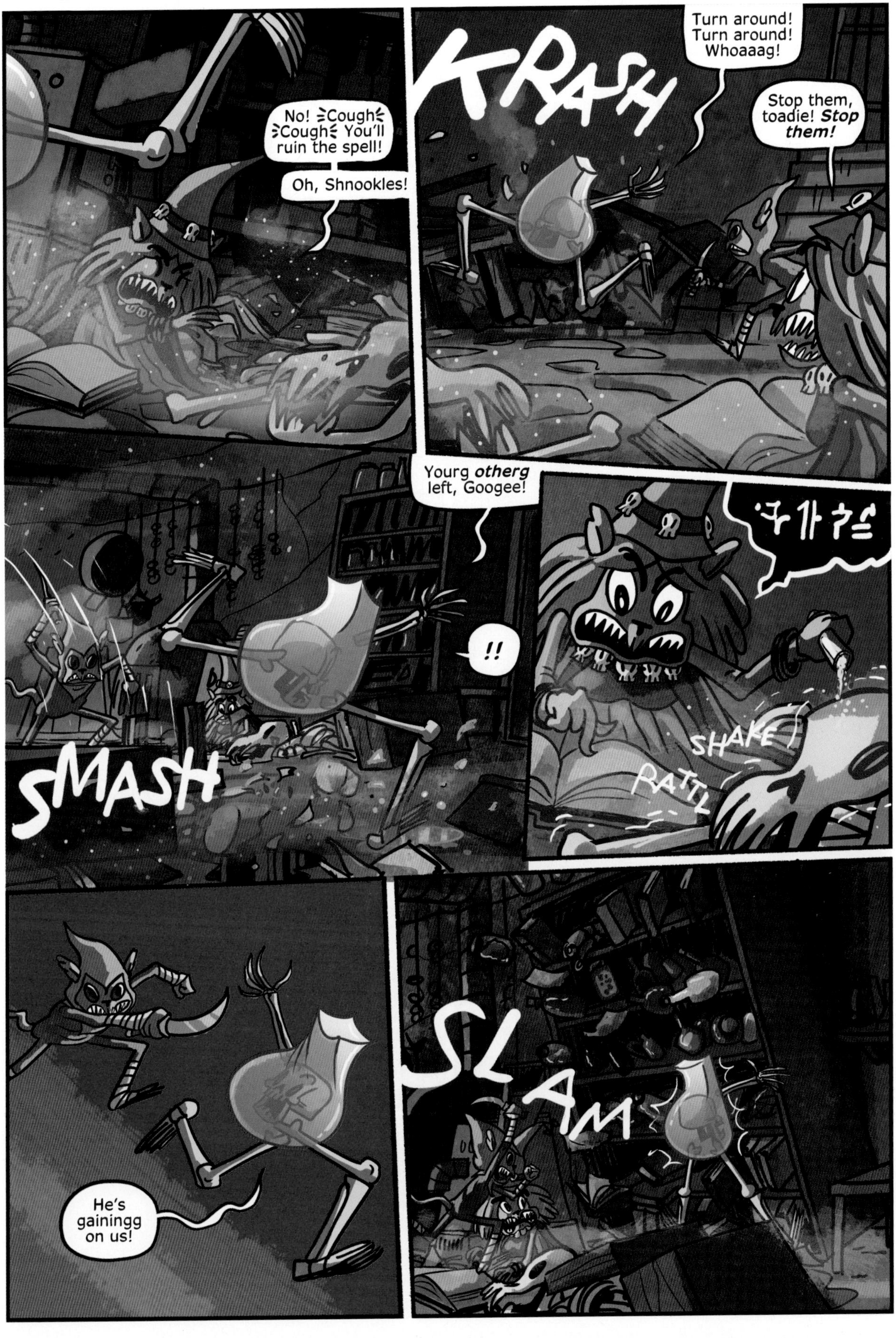
No! Cough Cough You'll ruin the spell!
Oh, Shnookles!
KRASH
Turn around! Turn around! Whoaaag!
Stop them, toadie! ***Stop them!***
Yourg ***otherg*** left, Googee!
!!
SMASH
SHAKE
RATTL
He's gainingg on us!
SLAM

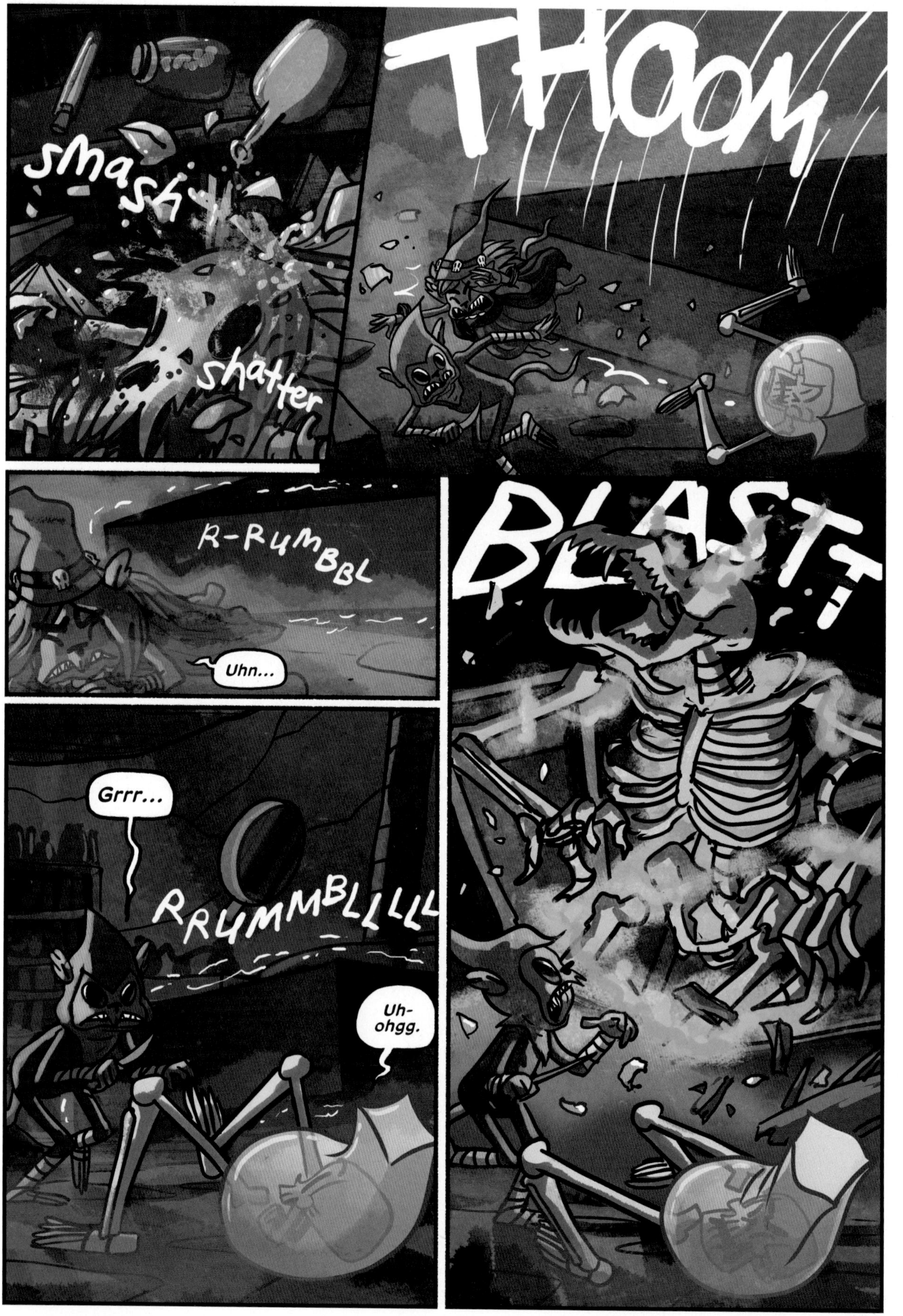
smash
shatter
THOOM
R-RUMBBL
Uhn...
BLASTT
Grrr...
RRUMMBLLLLL
Uh-ohgg.

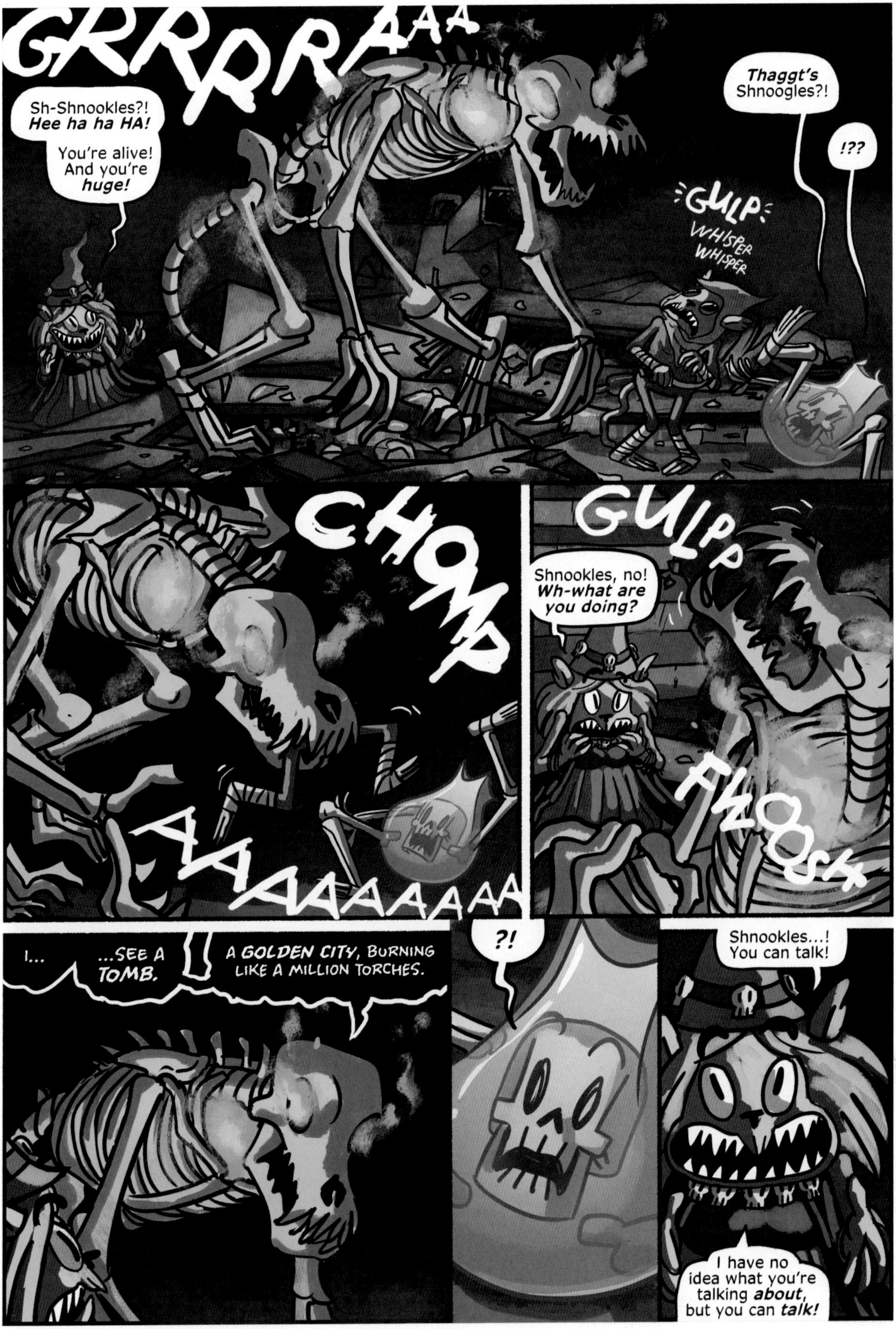
GRRRRAAA
Sh-Shnookles?! *Hee ha ha HA!*
You're alive! And you're *huge!*
Thaggt's Shnoogles?!
!??
GULP
WHISPER WHISPER
CHOMP
AAAAAAAAAA
GULPP
Shnookles, no! *Wh-what are you doing?*
FLOOSH
I...
...SEE A TOMB.
A GOLDEN CITY, BURNING LIKE A MILLION TORCHES.
?!
Shnookles...! You can talk!
I have no idea what you're talking *about*, but you can *talk!*

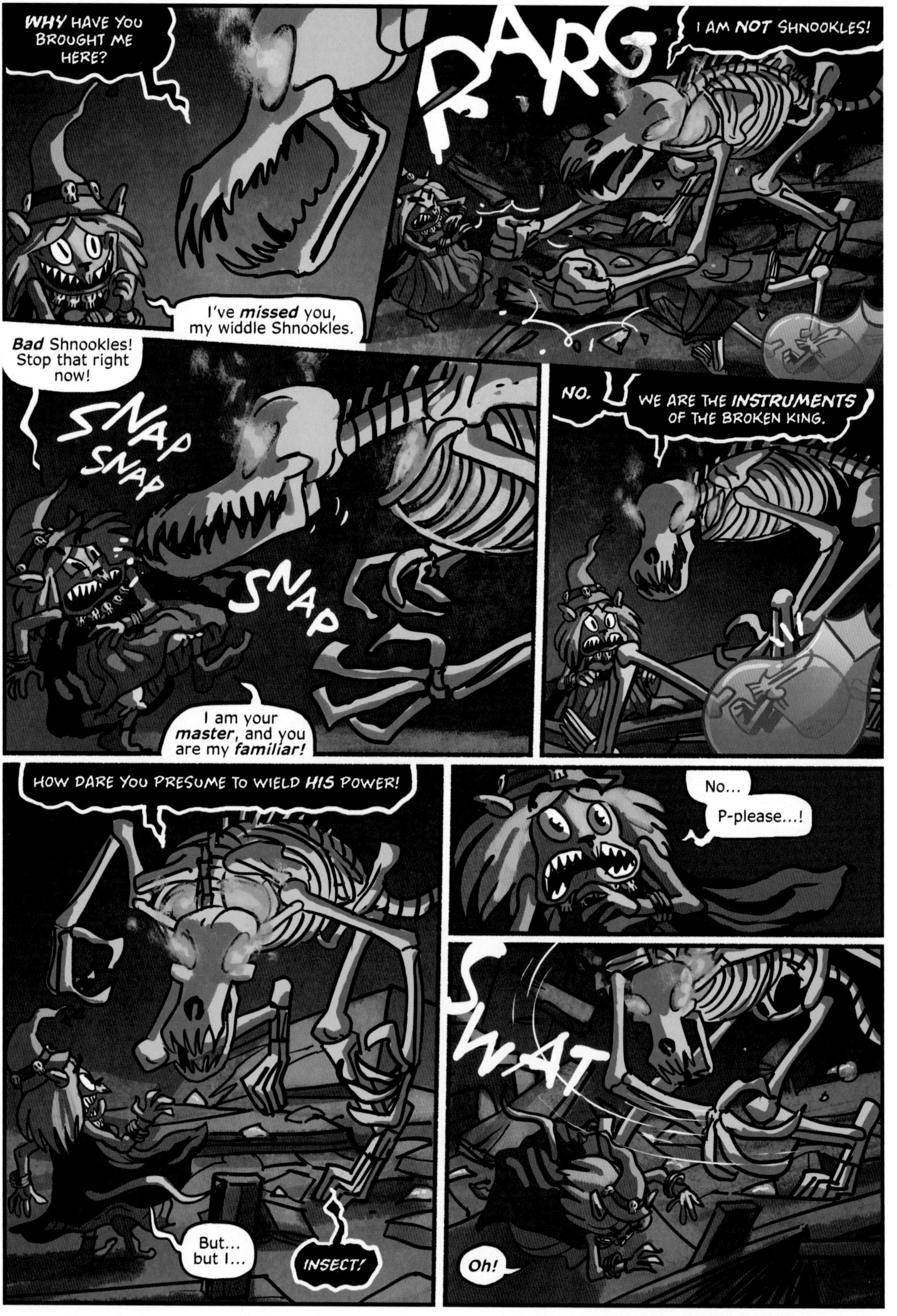
WHY HAVE YOU BROUGHT ME HERE?
I've missed you, my widdle Shnookles.
RARG
I AM NOT SHNOOKLES!
Bad Shnookles! Stop that right now!
SNAP SNAP
SNAP
I am your master, and you are my familiar!
NO.
WE ARE THE INSTRUMENTS OF THE BROKEN KING.
HOW DARE YOU PRESUME TO WIELD HIS POWER!
But... but I...
INSECT!
No...
P-please...!
SWAT
Oh!

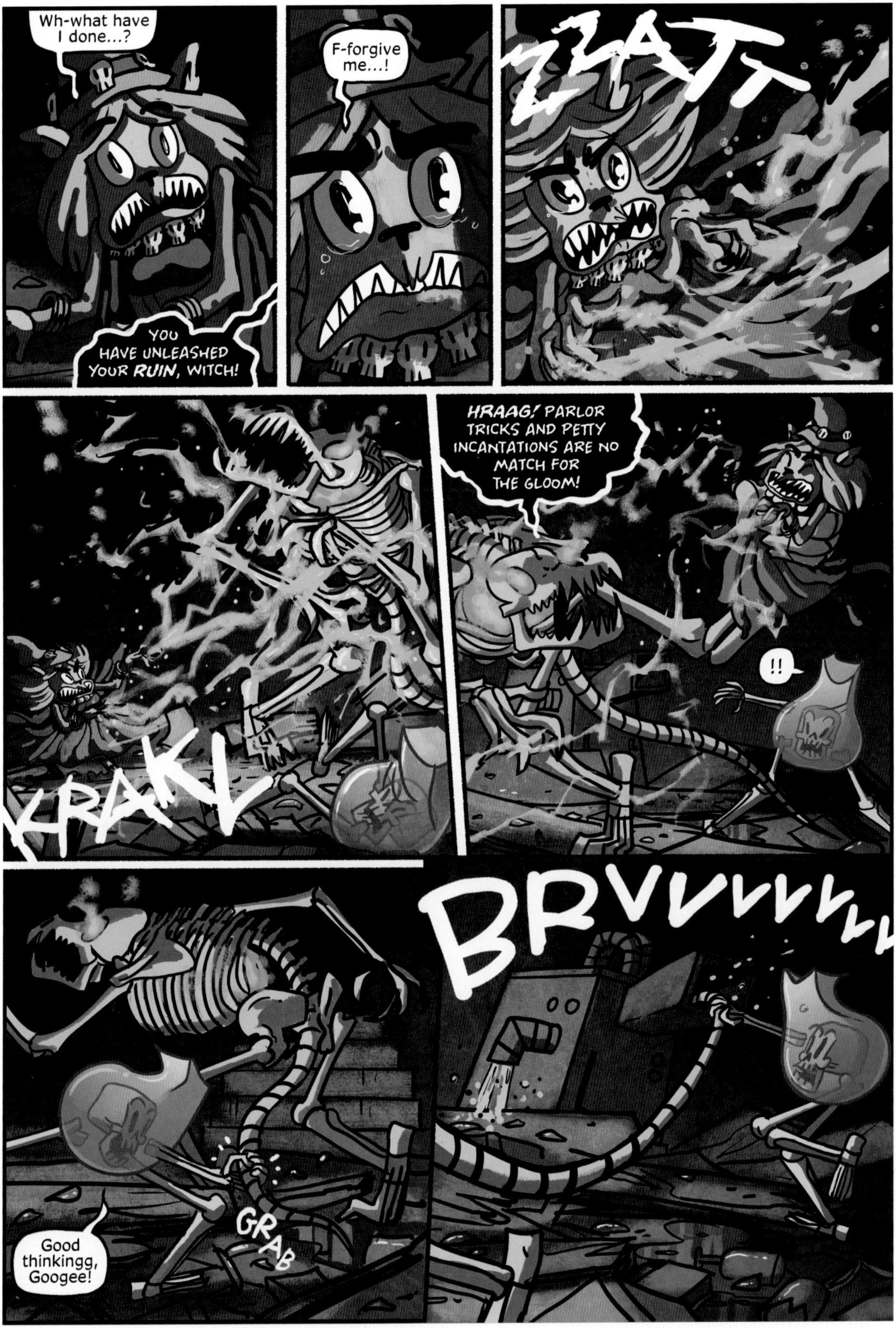
Wh-what have I done...?
YOU HAVE UNLEASHED YOUR RUIN, WITCH!
F-forgive me...!
ZZATT
KRAK
HRAAG! PARLOR TRICKS AND PETTY INCANTATIONS ARE NO MATCH FOR THE GLOOM!
!!
GRAB
Good thinkingg, Googee!
BRVVVVVVV

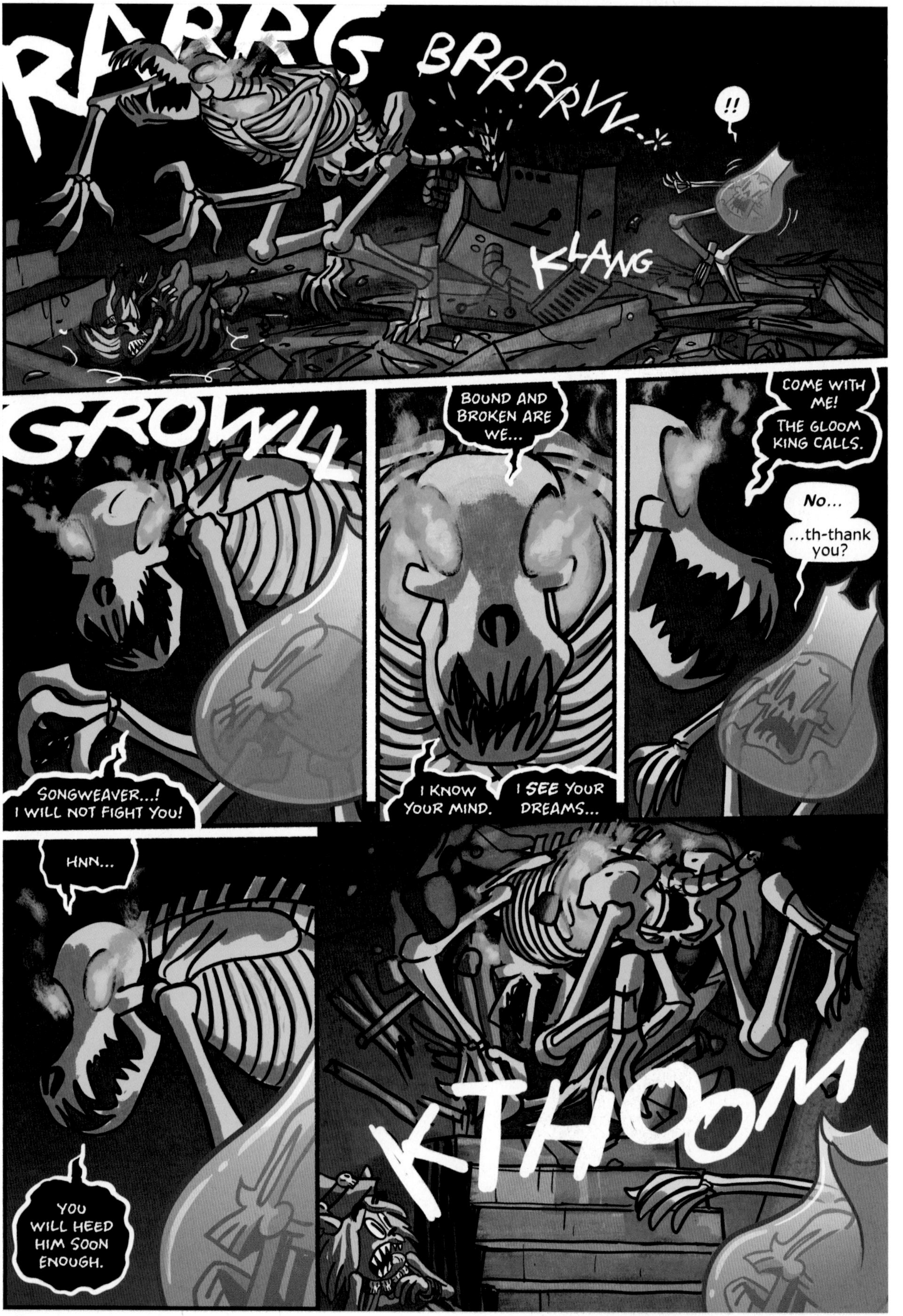
RARRG
BRRRRRVV...
!!
KLANG
GROWLL
SONGWEAVER...! I WILL NOT FIGHT YOU!
BOUND AND BROKEN ARE WE...
I KNOW YOUR MIND.
I SEE YOUR DREAMS...
COME WITH ME!
THE GLOOM KING CALLS.
No...
...th-thank you?
HNN...
YOU WILL HEED HIM SOON ENOUGH.
KTHOOM

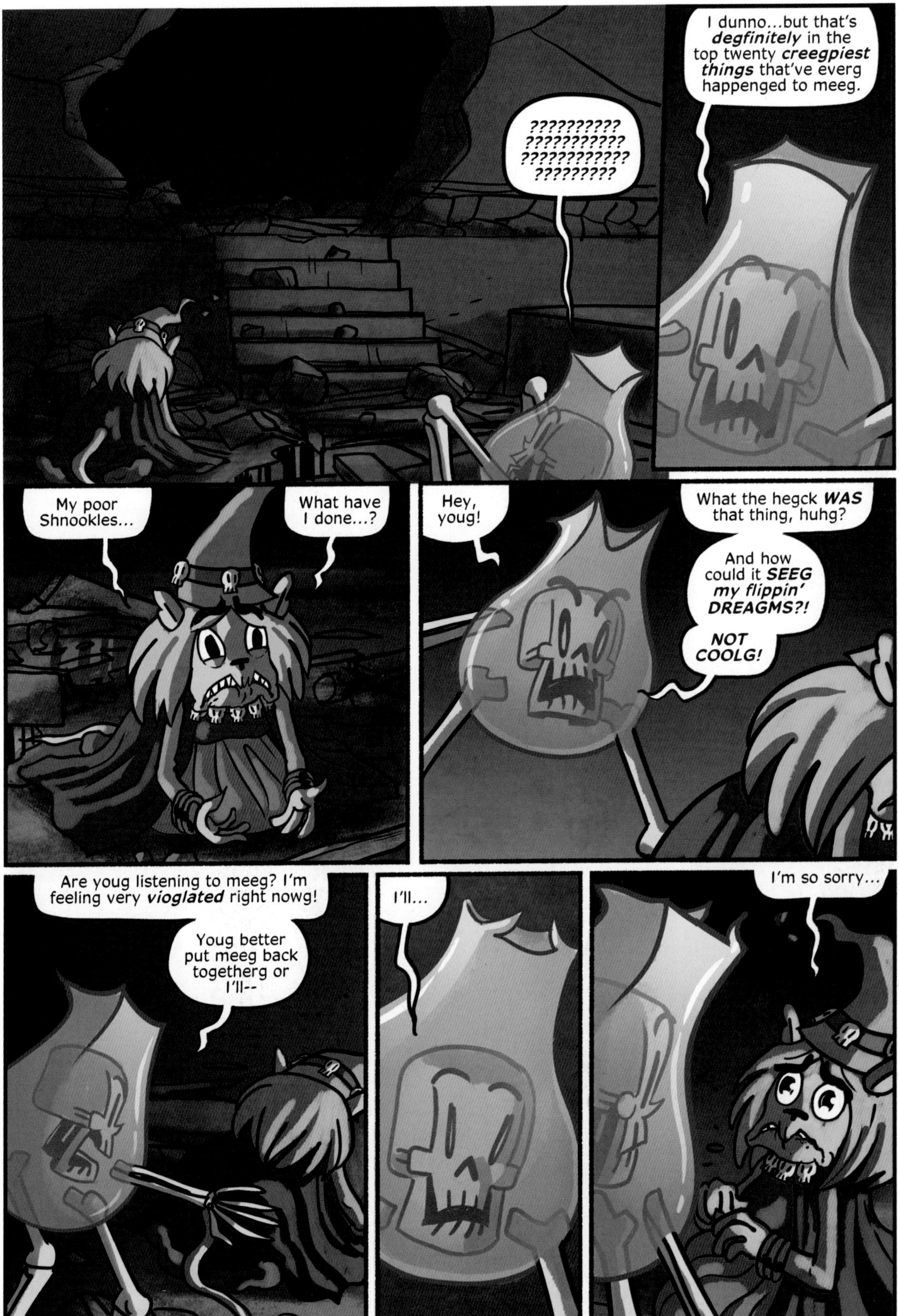
??????????
???????????
?????????????
?????????
I dunno...but that's *degfinitely* in the top twenty *creegpiest things* that've everg happenged to meeg.
My poor Shnookles...
What have I done...?
Hey, youg!
What the hegck *WAS* that thing, huhg?
And how could it *SEEG my flippin' DREAGMS?!*
NOT COOLG!
Are youg listening to meeg? I'm feeling very *vioglated* right nowg!
Youg better put meeg back togetherg or I'll--
I'll...
I'm so sorry...

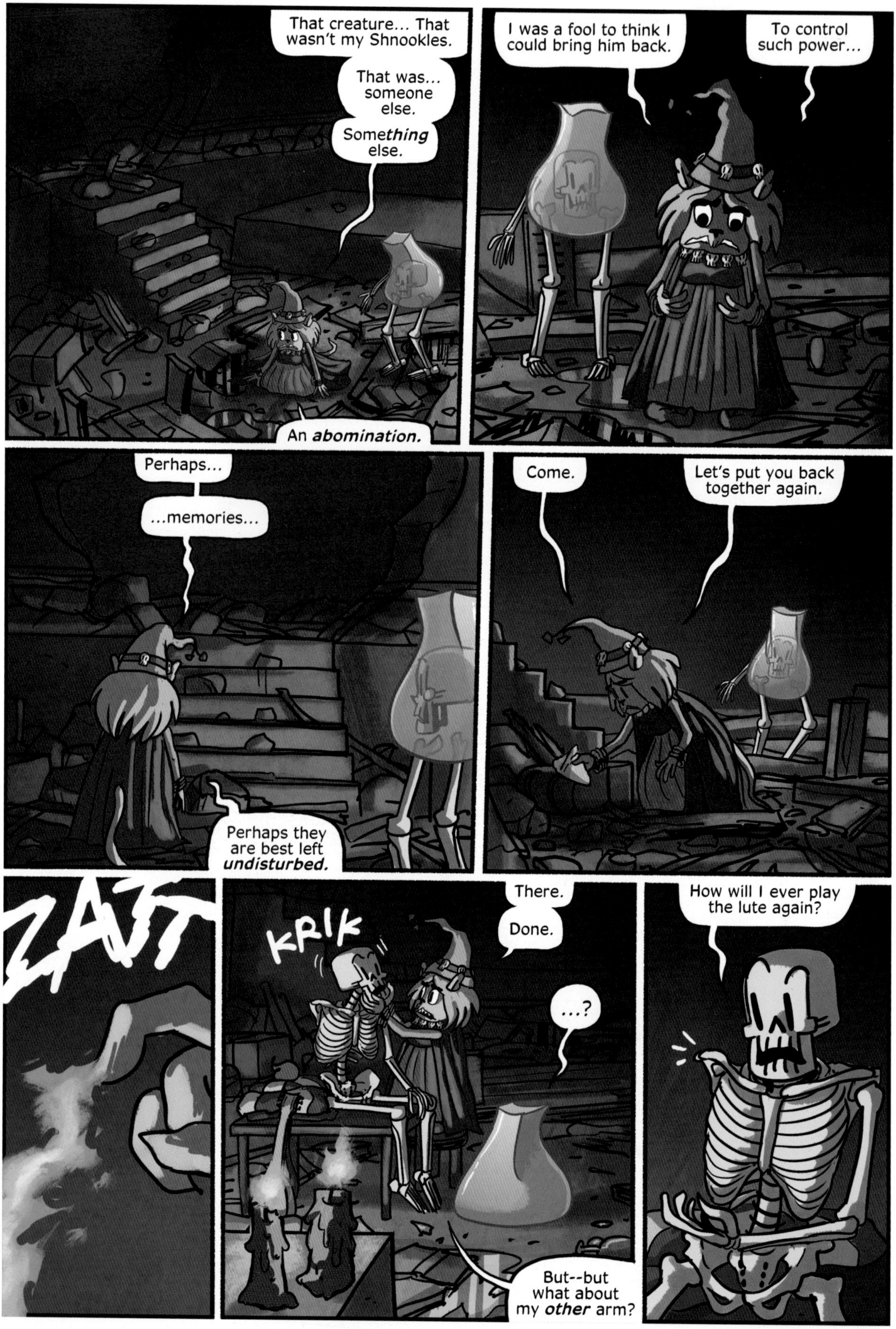
That creature... That wasn't my Shnookles.
That was... someone else.
Something else.
An *abomination.*
I was a fool to think I could bring him back.
To control such power...
Perhaps...
...memories...
Perhaps they are best left *undisturbed.*
Come.
Let's put you back together again.
ZAT
KRIK
There.
Done.
...?
But--but what about my *other* arm?
How will I ever play the lute again?

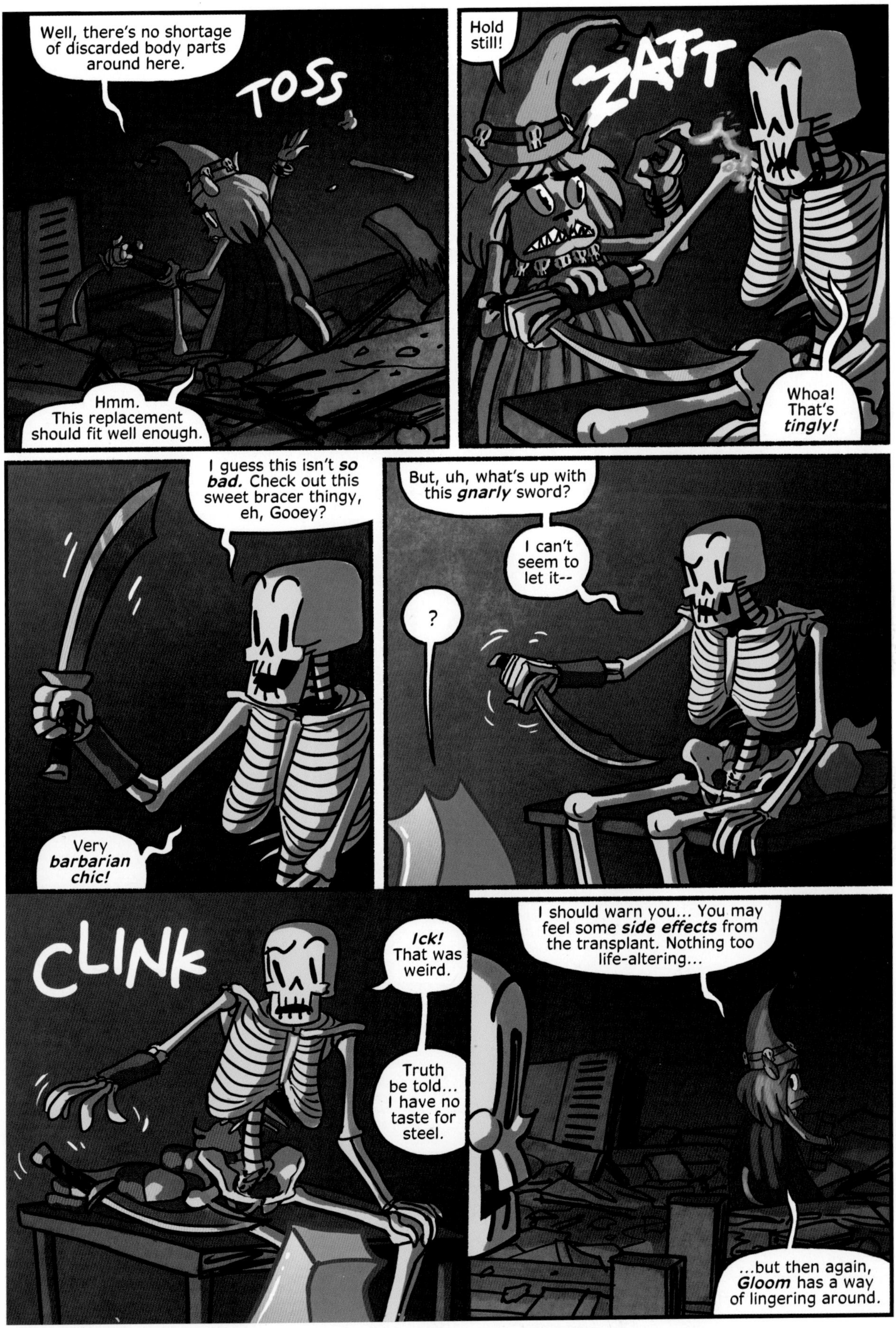
Well, there's no shortage of discarded body parts around here.
TOSS
Hmm. This replacement should fit well enough.
Hold still!
ZATT
Whoa! That's *tingly!*
I guess this isn't ***so bad.*** Check out this sweet bracer thingy, eh, Gooey?
Very ***barbarian chic!***
But, uh, what's up with this ***gnarly*** sword?
I can't seem to let it--
?
CLINK
Ick! That was weird.
Truth be told... I have no taste for steel.
I should warn you... You may feel some ***side effects*** from the transplant. Nothing too life-altering...
...but then again, ***Gloom*** has a way of lingering around.

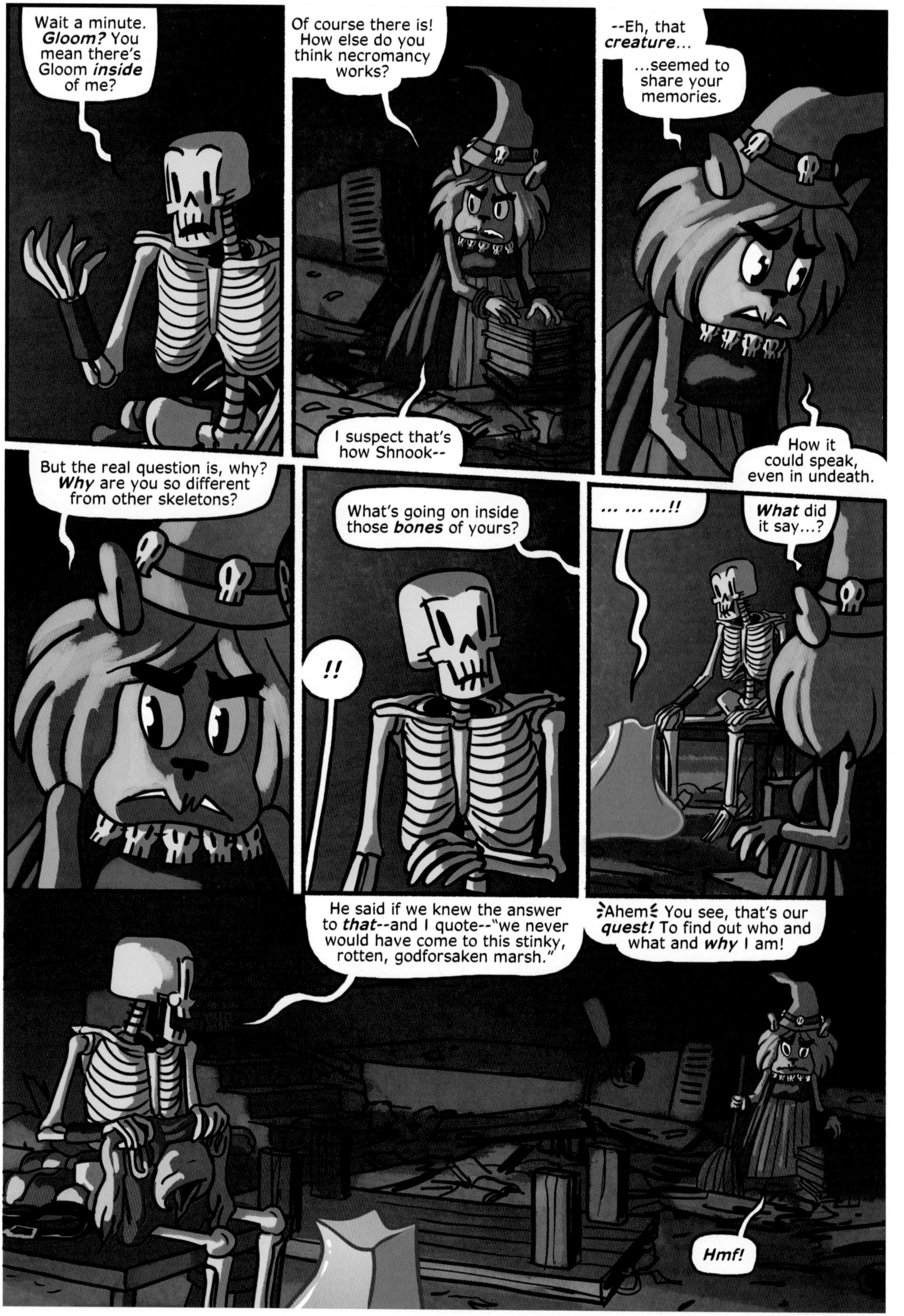
Wait a minute. Gloom? You mean there's Gloom inside of me?
Of course there is! How else do you think necromancy works?
I suspect that's how Shnook--
--Eh, that creature...
...seemed to share your memories.
How it could speak, even in undeath.
But the real question is, why? Why are you so different from other skeletons?
What's going on inside those bones of yours?
!!
... ...!!
What did it say...?
He said if we knew the answer to that--and I quote--"we never would have come to this stinky, rotten, godforsaken marsh."
Ahem You see, that's our quest! To find out who and what and why I am!
Hmf!

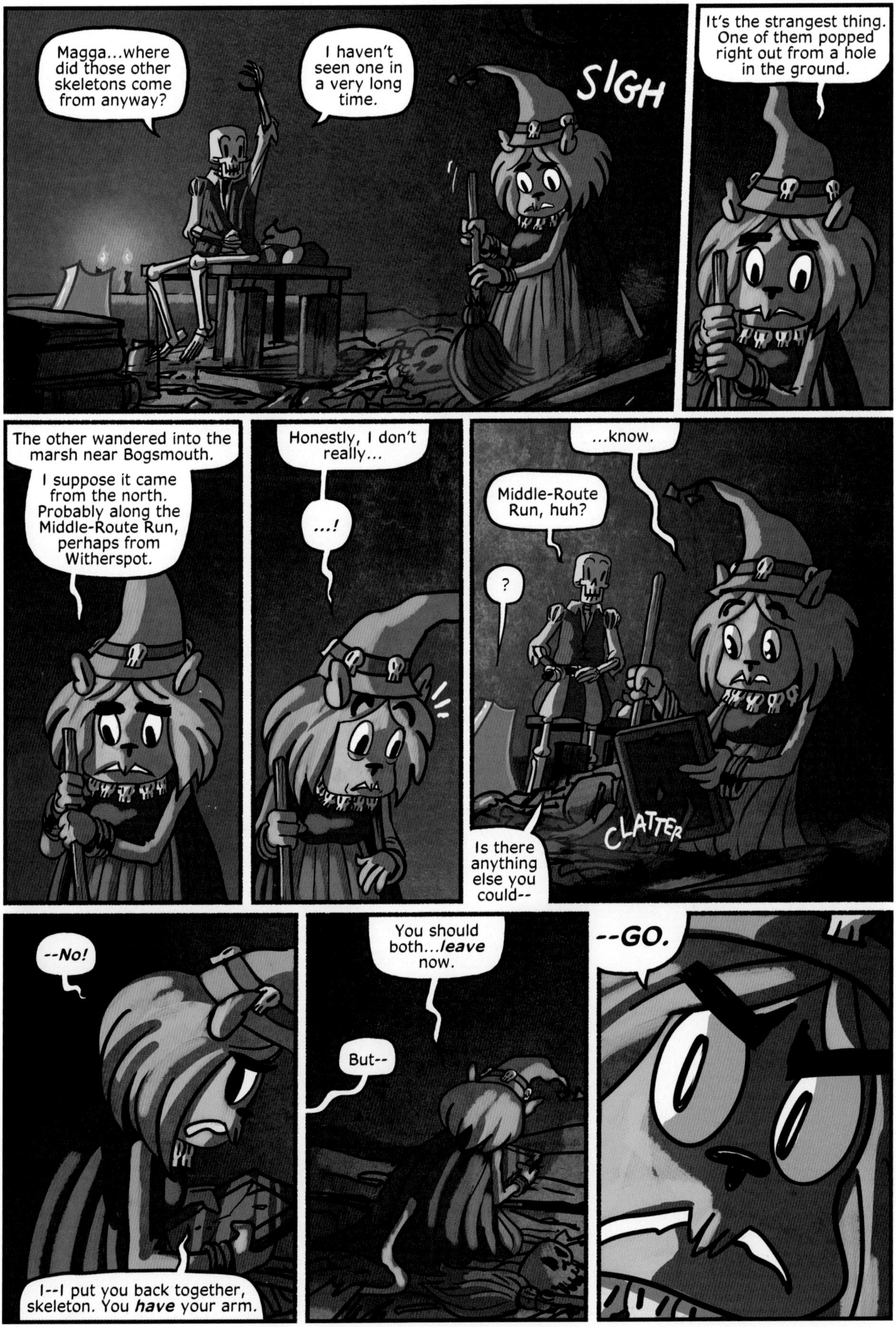

Magga...where did those other skeletons come from anyway?
I haven't seen one in a very long time.
SIGH
It's the strangest thing. One of them popped right out from a hole in the ground.
The other wandered into the marsh near Bogsmouth.
I suppose it came from the north. Probably along the Middle-Route Run, perhaps from Witherspot.
Honestly, I don't really...
...!
...know.
Middle-Route Run, huh?
?
CLATTER
Is there anything else you could--
--No!
I--I put you back together, skeleton. You *have* your arm.
You should both...*leave* now.
But--
--GO.

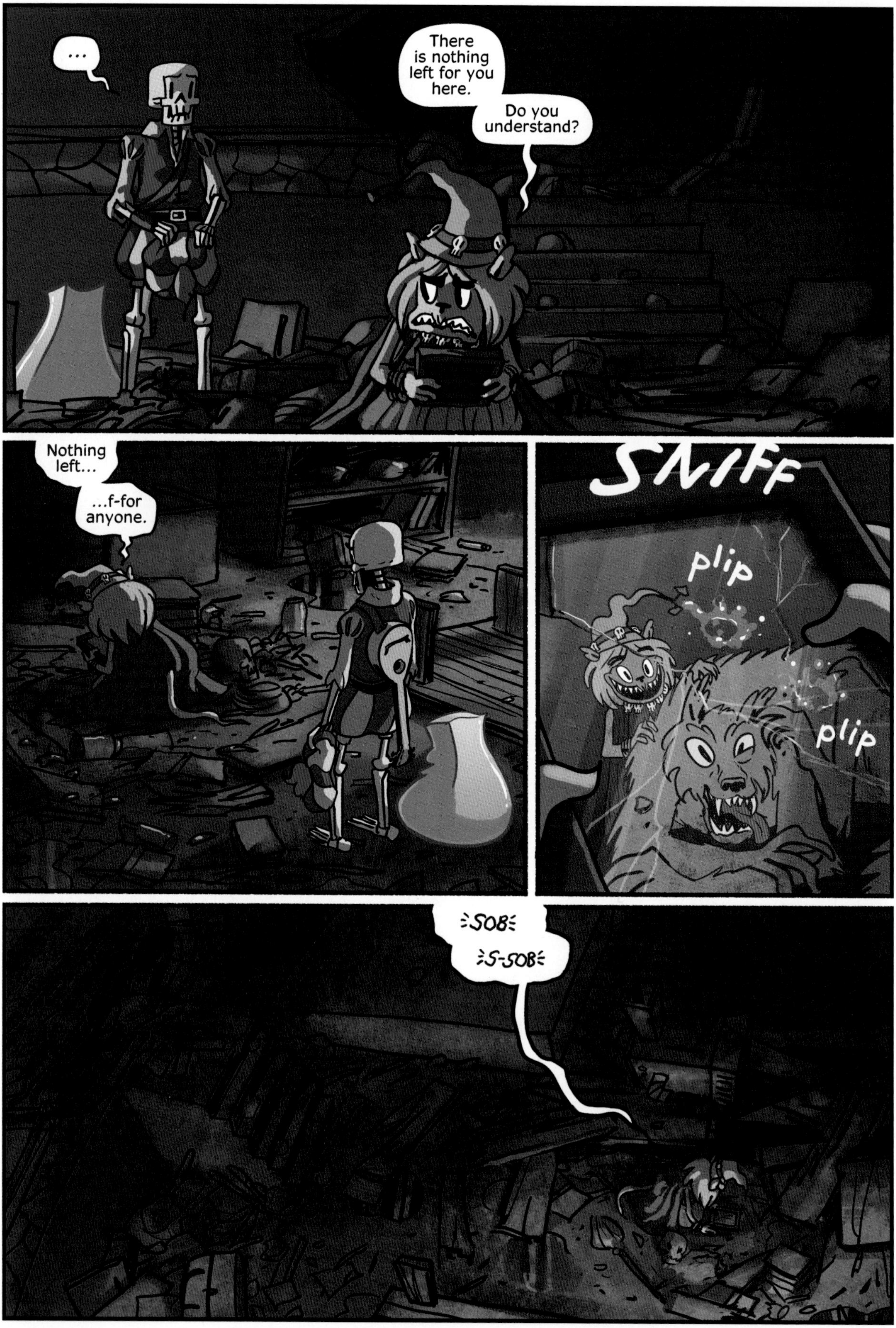
...
There is nothing left for you here.
Do you understand?
Nothing left...
...f-for anyone.
SNIFF
plip
plip
SOB
S-SOB

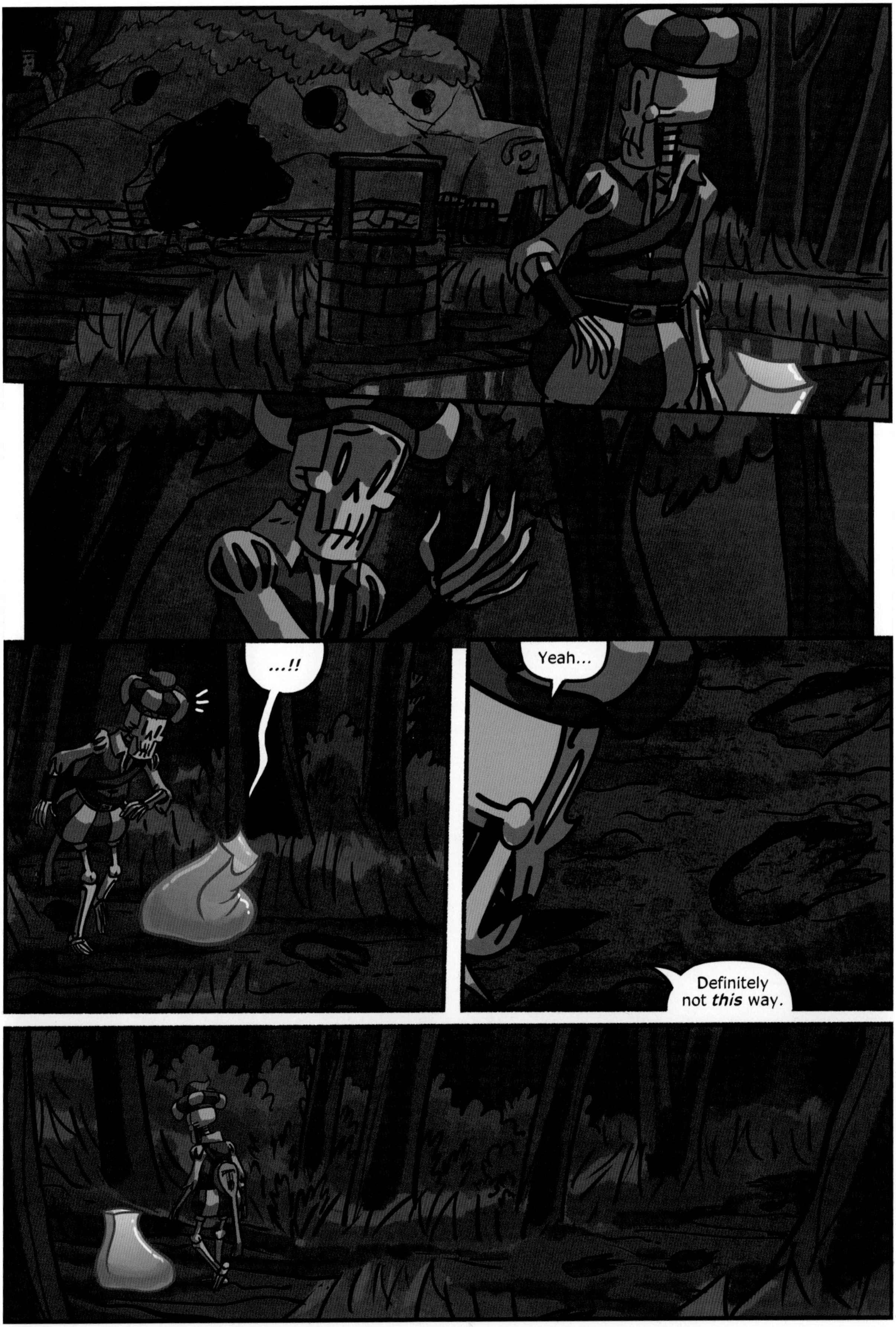
...!!
Yeah...
Definitely not *this* way.

Chapter 3
The Dig

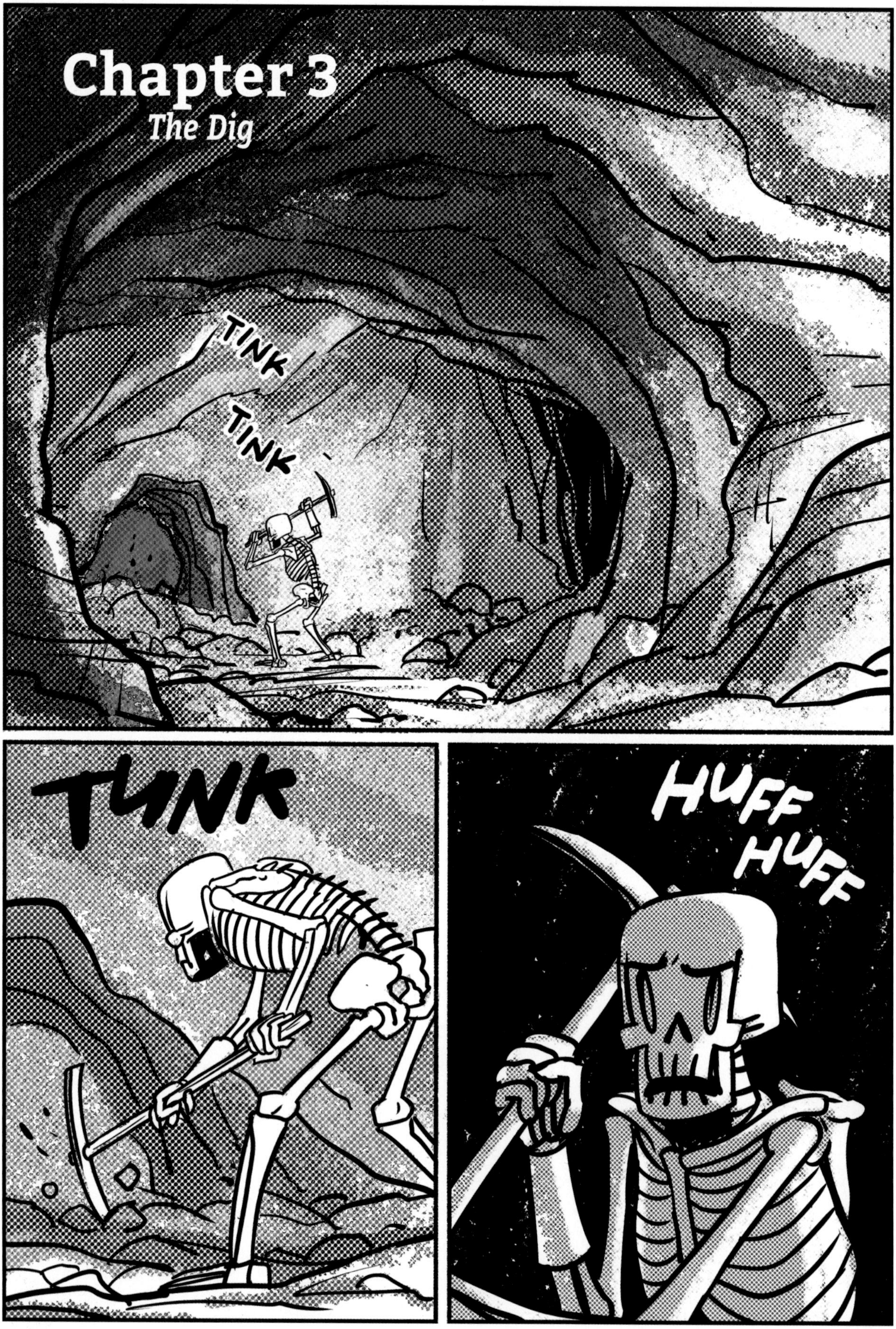
TINK
TINK
TUNK
HUFF HUFF

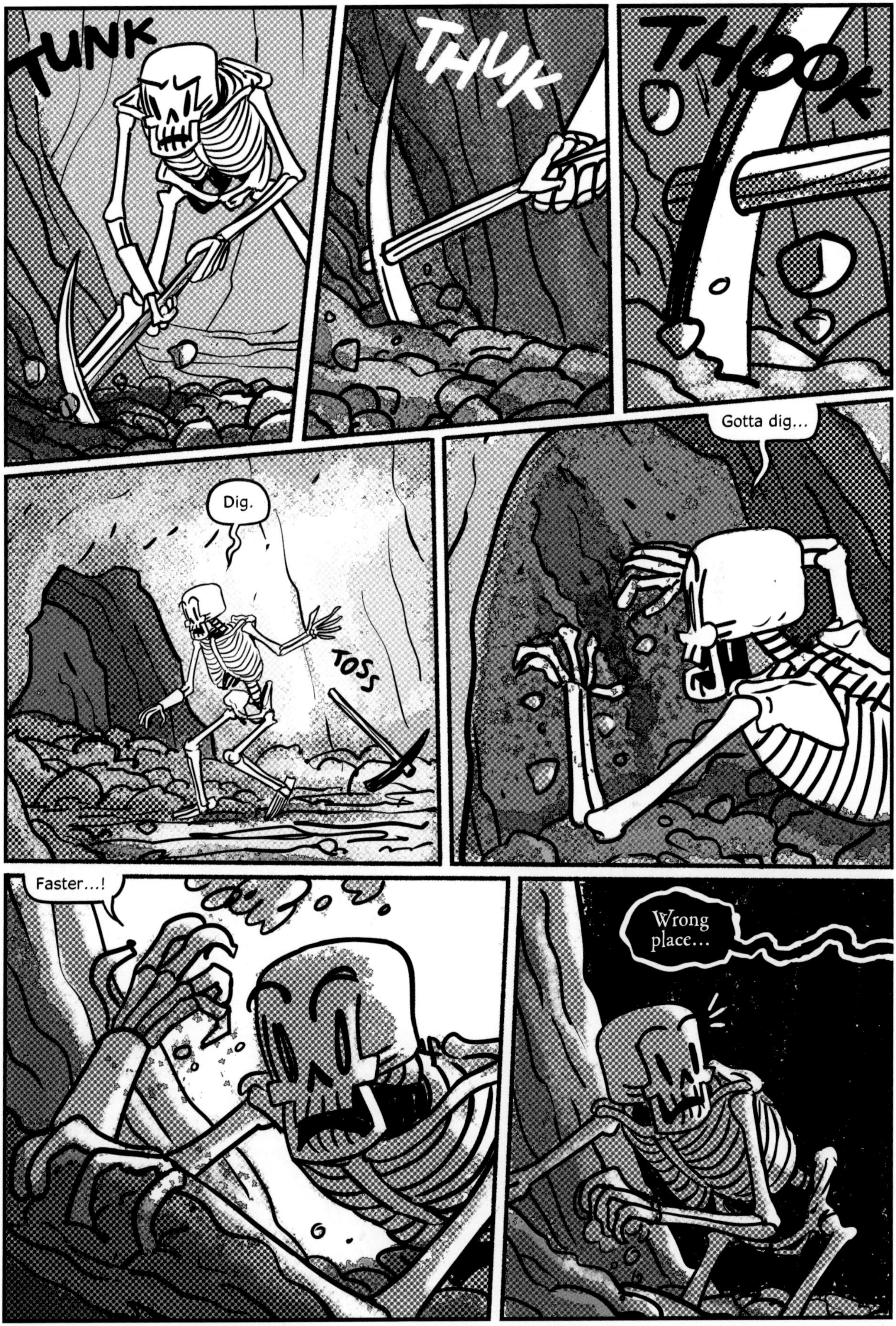

TUNK
THUK
THOOK
Dig.
TOSS
Gotta dig...
Faster...!
Wrong place...

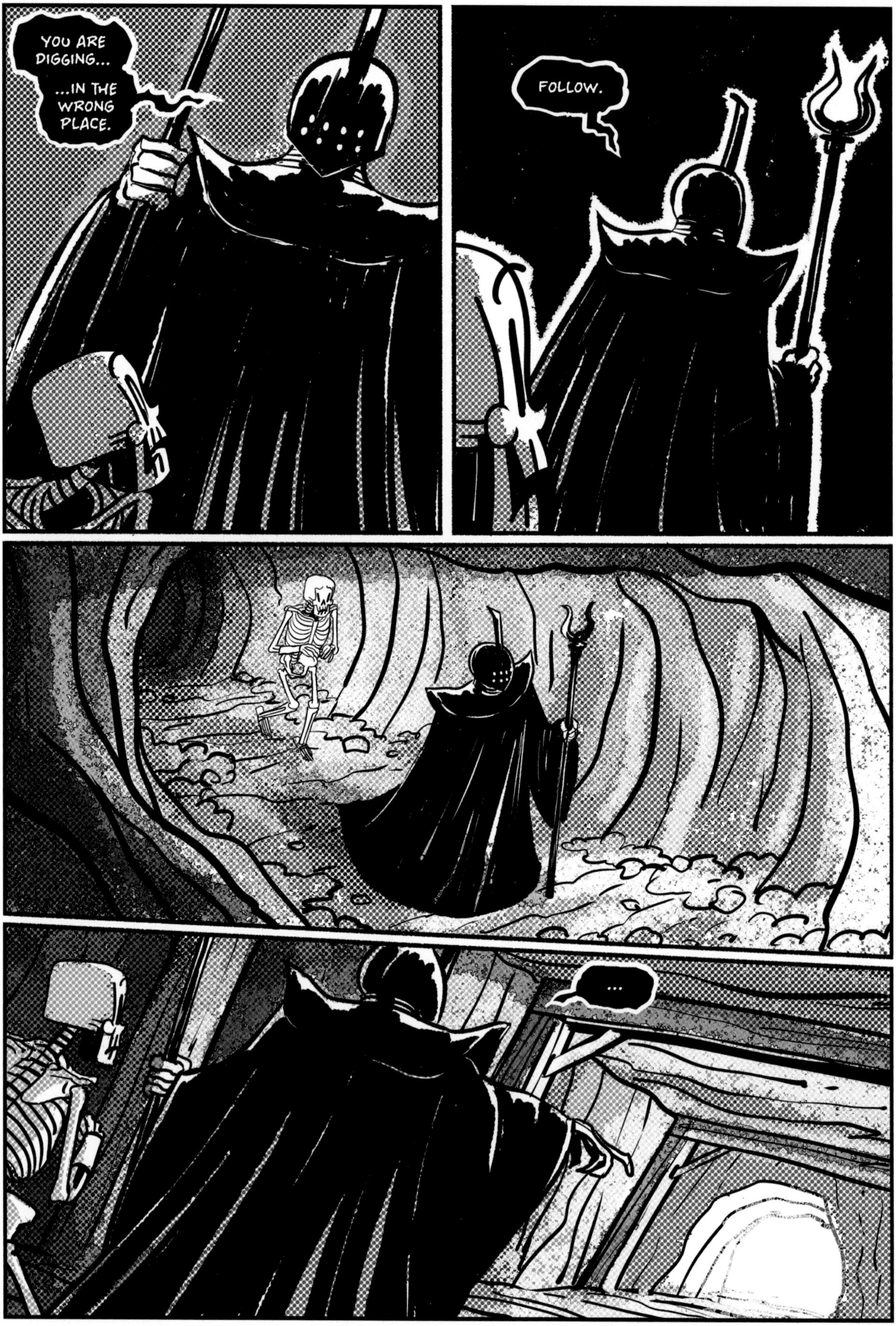
YOU ARE DIGGING...
...IN THE WRONG PLACE.
FOLLOW.
...

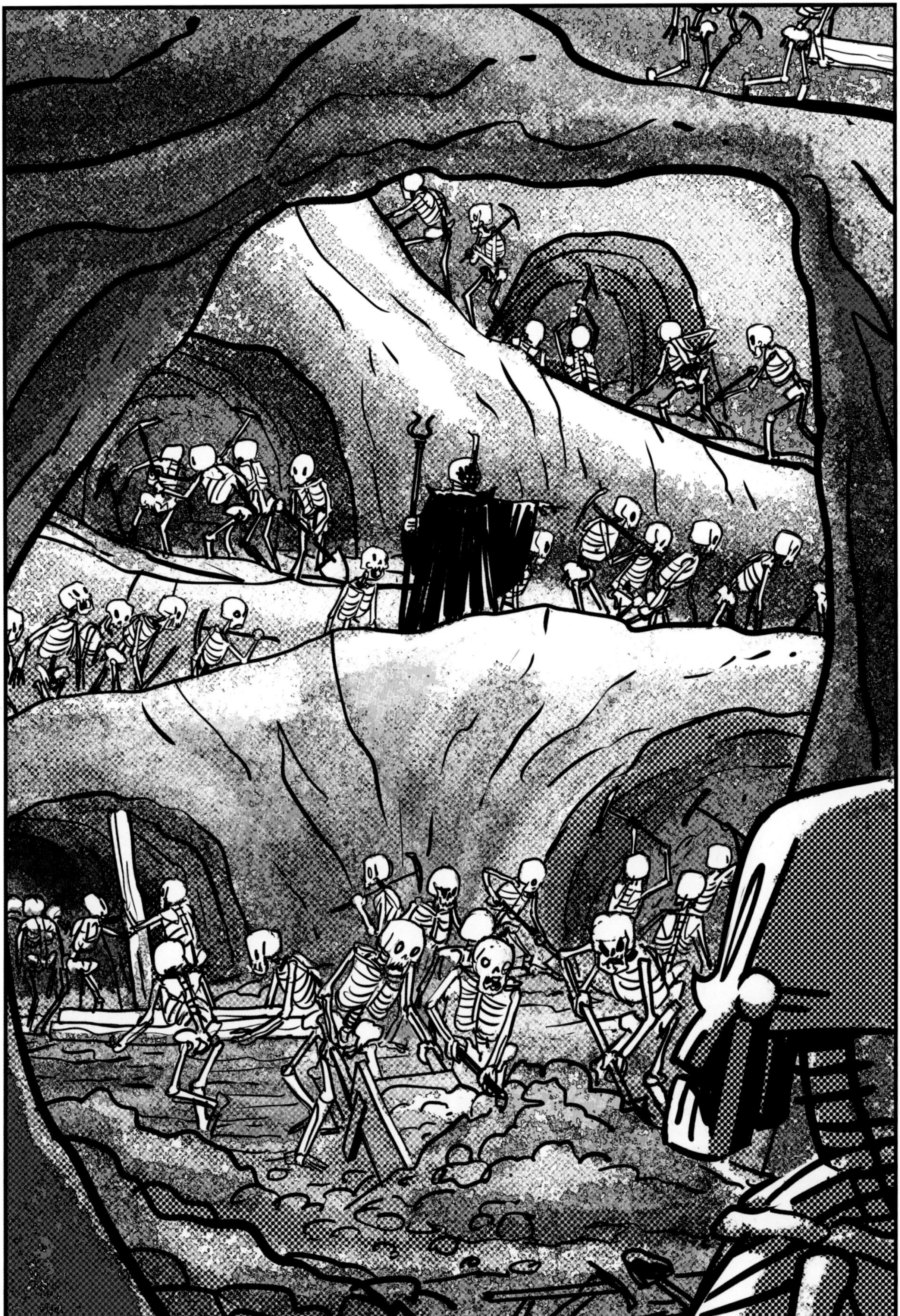

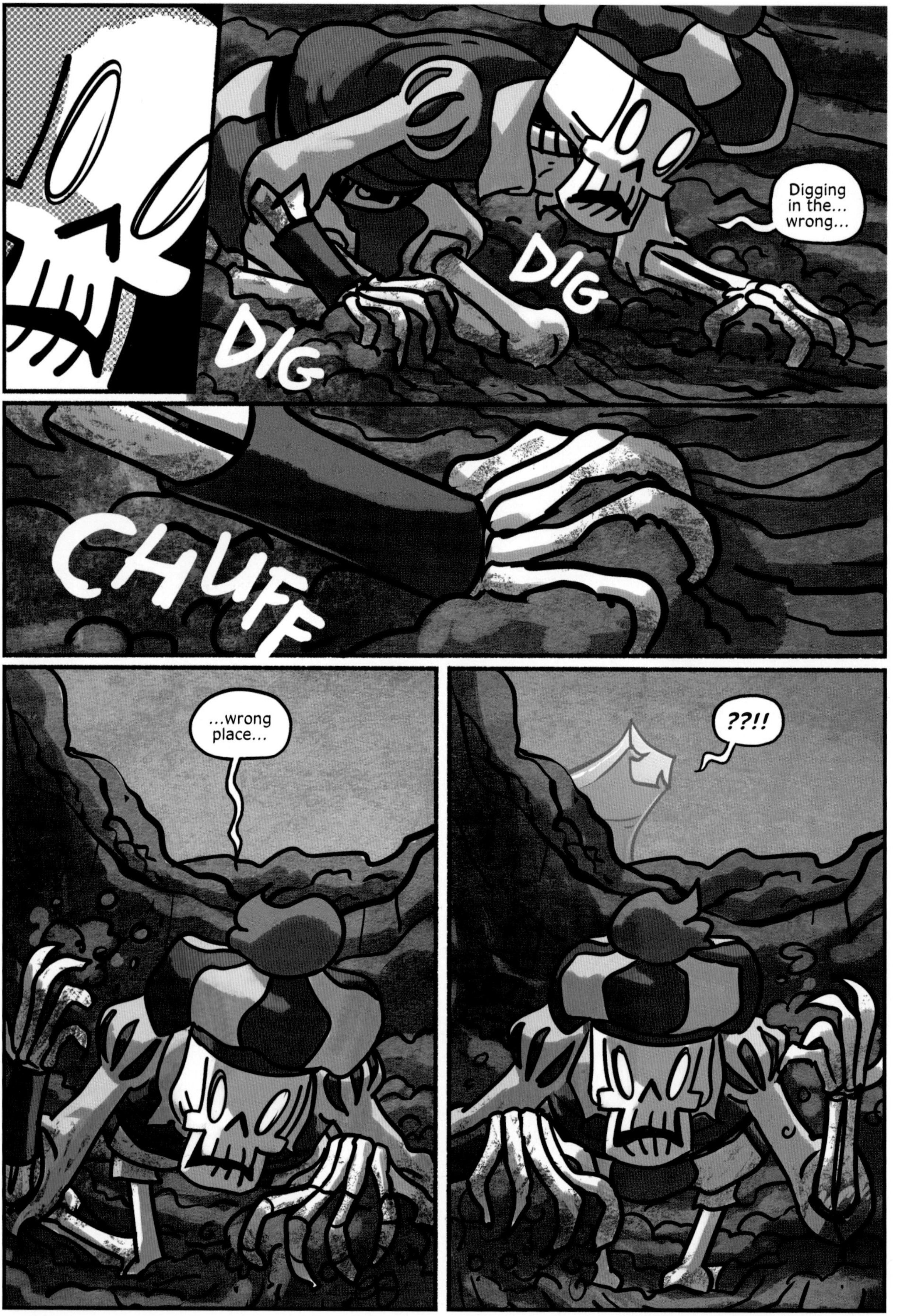
Digging in the... wrong...
DIG
DIG
CHUFF
...wrong place...
??!!

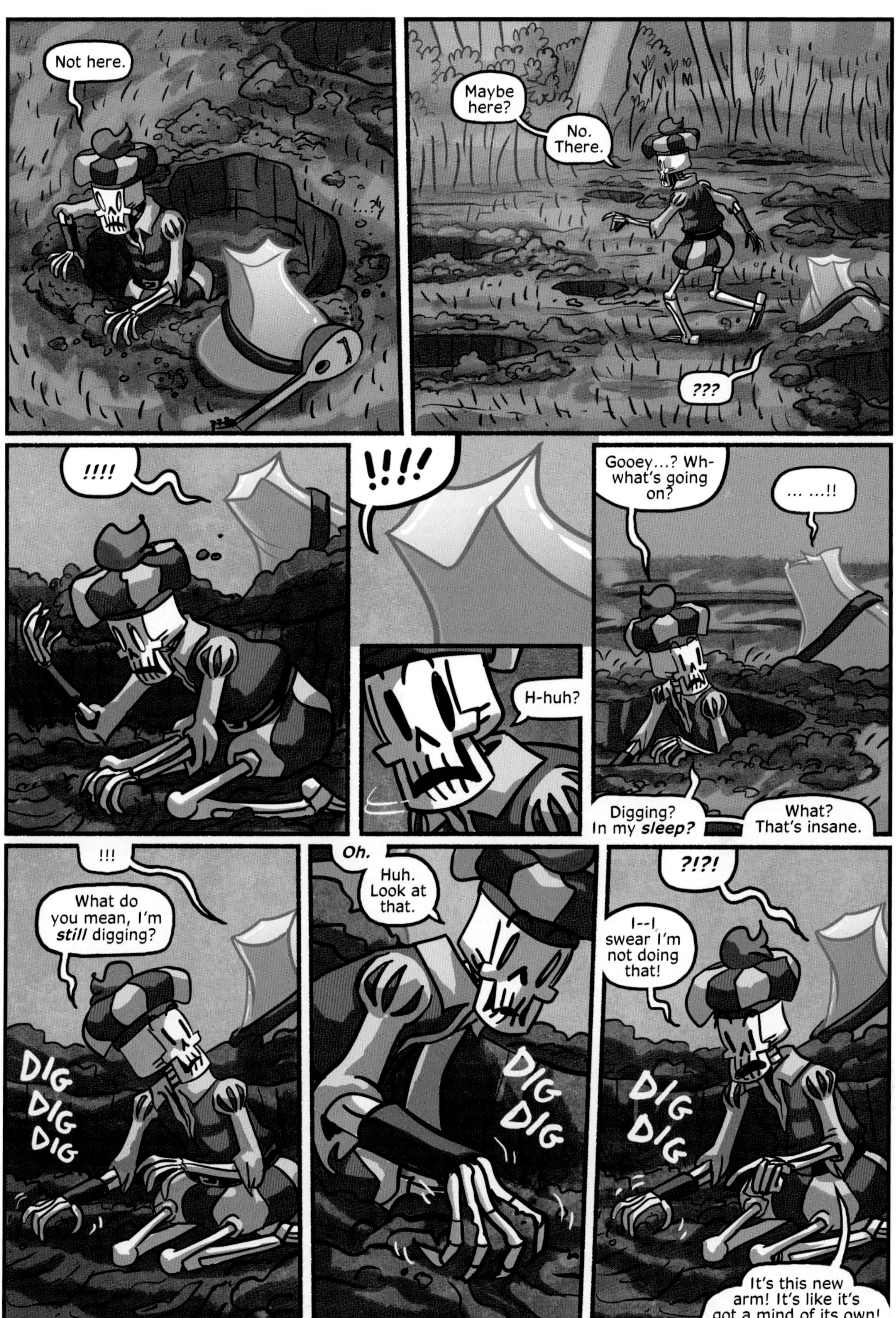
Not here.
Maybe here?
No. There.
???
!!!!
!!!!
H-huh?
Gooey...? Wh- what's going on?
... ...!!
Digging? In my *sleep?*
What? That's insane.
!!!
What do you mean, I'm *still* digging?
DIG DIG DIG
Oh.
Huh. Look at that.
DIG DIG
?!?!
I--I swear I'm not doing that!
DIG DIG
It's this new arm! It's like it's got a mind of its own!

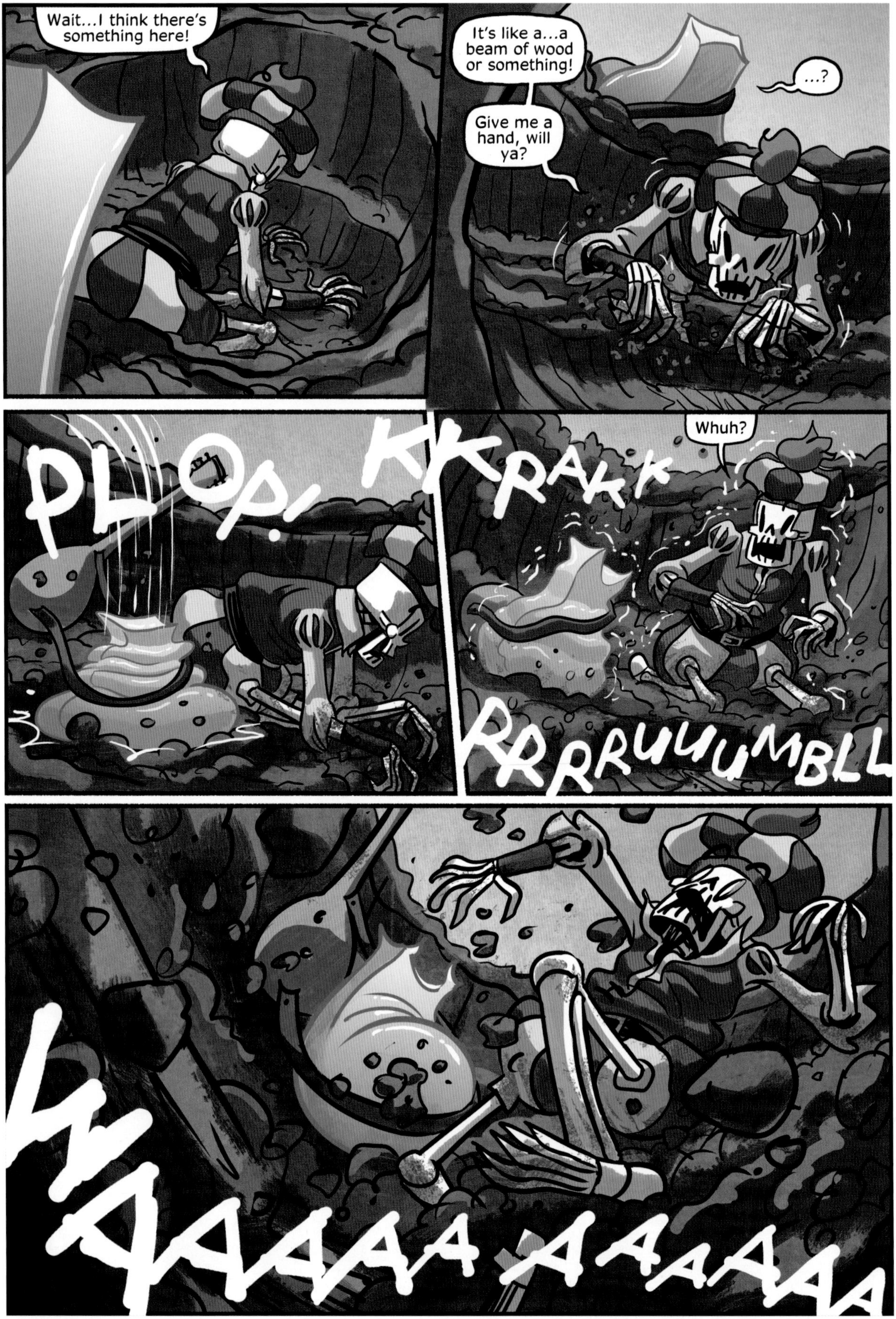
Wait...I think there's something here!
It's like a...a beam of wood or something!
Give me a hand, will ya?
...?
PLOP!
KKRAKK
Whuh?
RRRRUUUMBLL
WAAAAAAAAAAAA

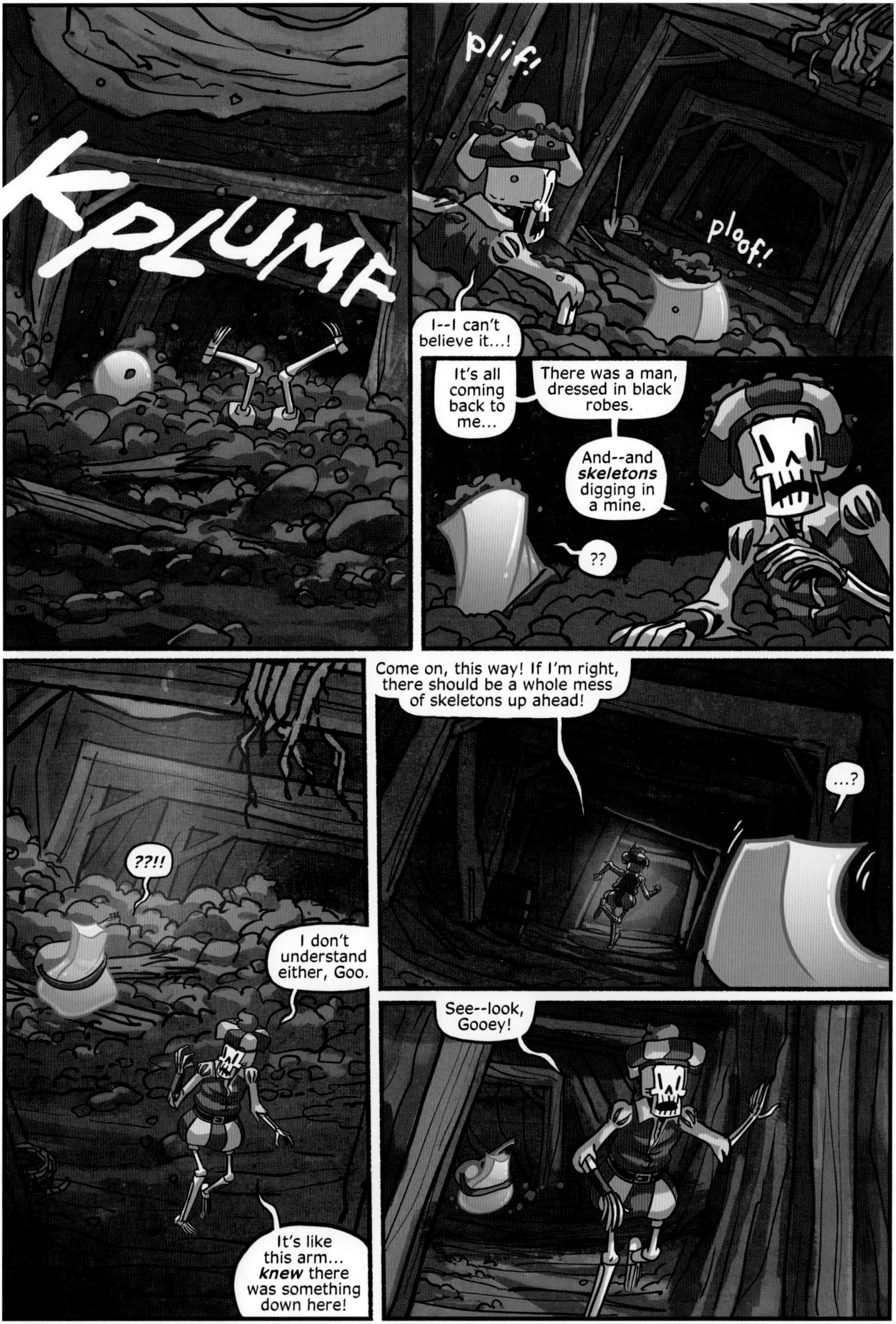
KPLUMF
plif!
ploof!
I--I can't believe it...!
It's all coming back to me...
There was a man, dressed in black robes.
And--and *skeletons* digging in a mine.
??
??!!
I don't understand either, Goo.
It's like this arm... *knew* there was something down here!
Come on, this way! If I'm right, there should be a whole mess of skeletons up ahead!
...?
See--look, Gooey!

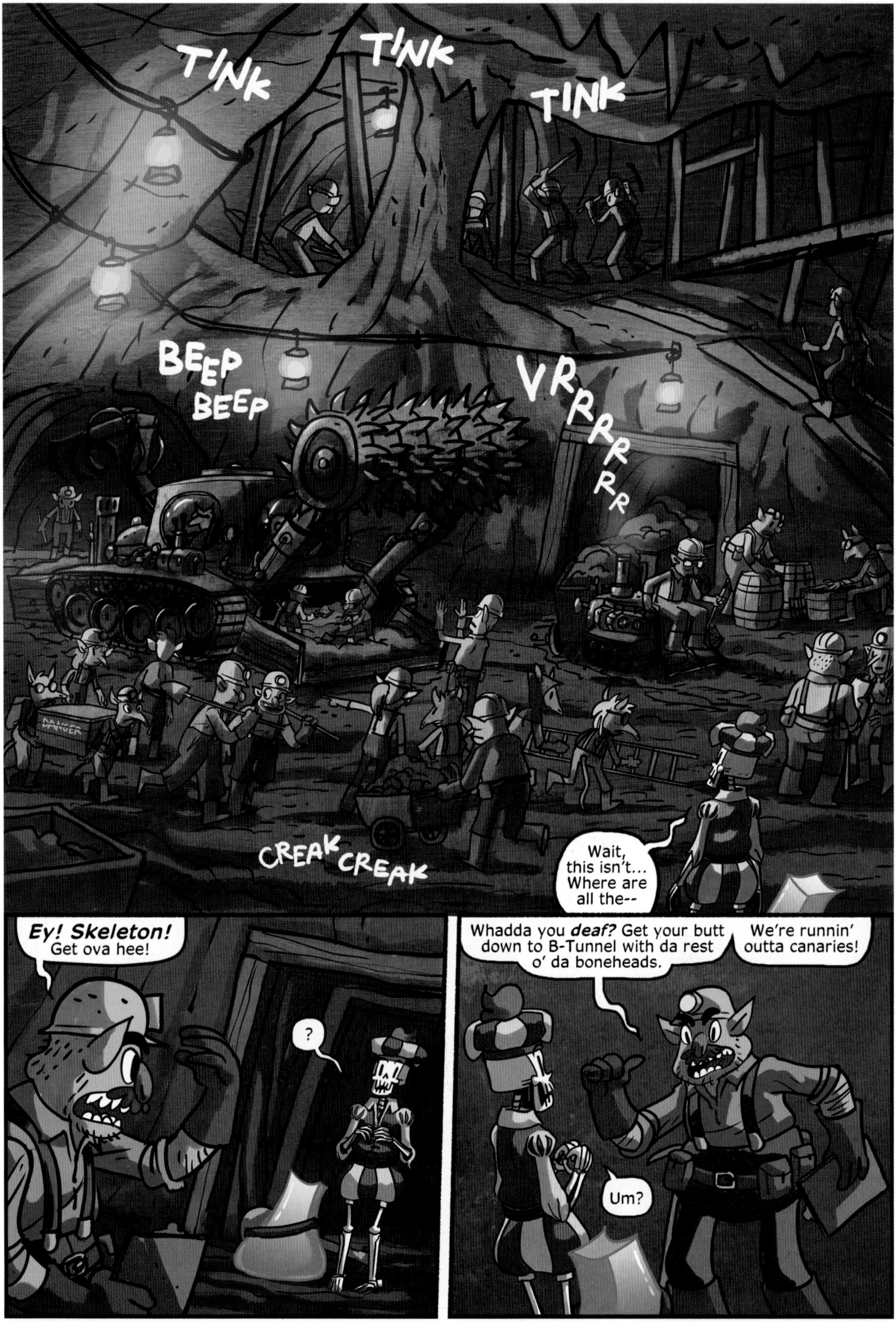
TINK
TINK
TINK
BEEP BEEP
VRRRRRR
DANGER
CREAK CREAK
Wait, this isn't... Where are all the--
Ey! Skeleton! Get ova hee!
?
Whadda you *deaf?* Get your butt down to B-Tunnel with da rest o' da boneheads.
We're runnin' outta canaries!
Um?

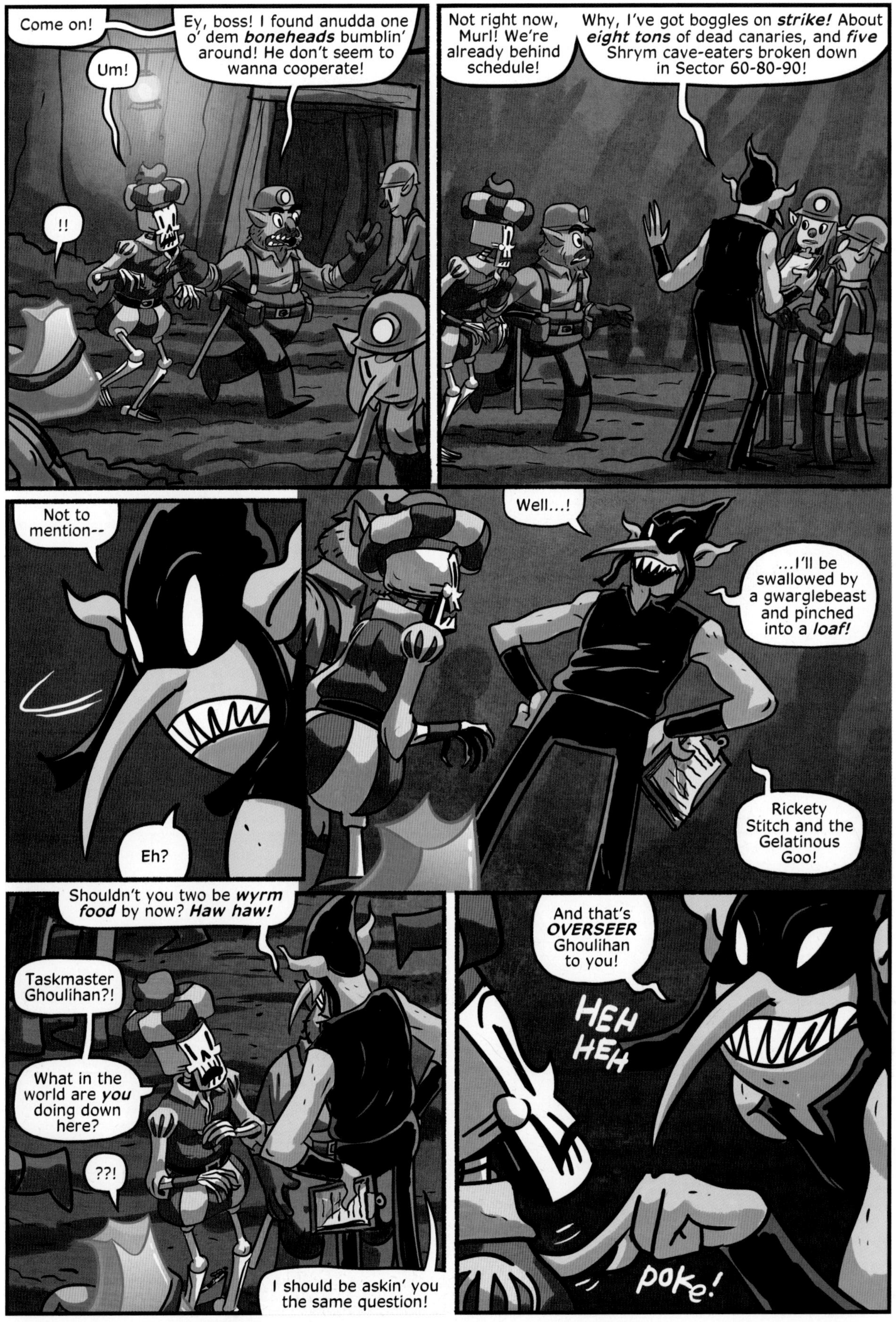

Come on!
Ey, boss! I found anudda one o' dem **boneheads** bumblin' around! He don't seem to wanna cooperate!
Um!
!!
Not right now, Murl! We're already behind schedule!
Why, I've got boggles on **strike!** About **eight tons** of dead canaries, and **five** Shrym cave-eaters broken down in Sector 60-80-90!
Not to mention--
Eh?
Well...!
...I'll be swallowed by a gwarglebeast and pinched into a **loaf!**
Rickety Stitch and the Gelatinous Goo!
Shouldn't you two be **wyrm food** by now? **Haw haw!**
Taskmaster Ghoulihan?!
What in the world are **you** doing down here?
??!
I should be askin' you the same question!
And that's **OVERSEER** Ghoulihan to you!
HEH HEH
poke!

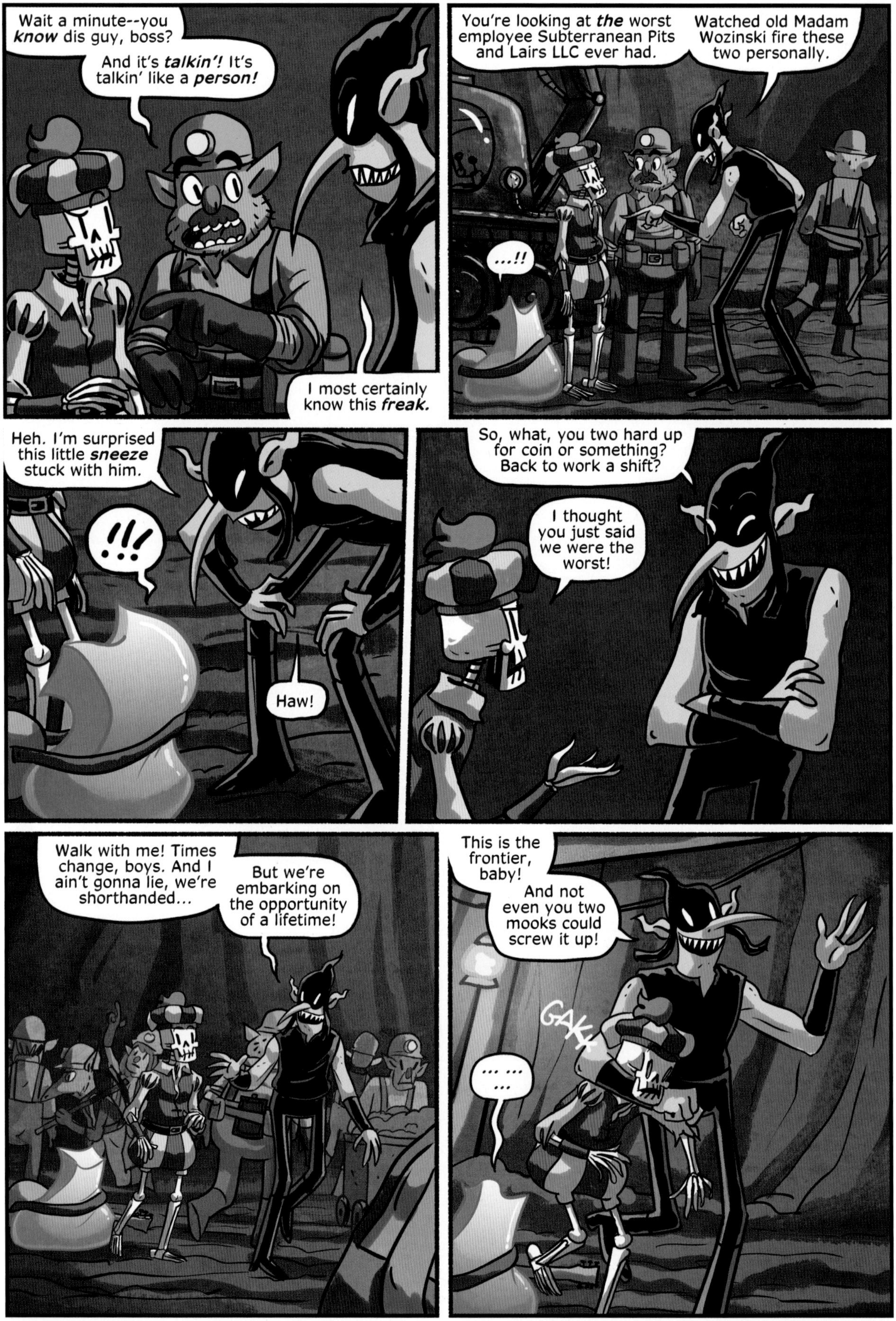
Wait a minute--you *know* dis guy, boss?
And it's *talkin'!* It's talkin' like a *person!*
I most certainly know this *freak.*
You're looking at *the* worst employee Subterranean Pits and Lairs LLC ever had.
Watched old Madam Wozinski fire these two personally.
...!!
Heh. I'm surprised this little *sneeze* stuck with him.
!!!
Haw!
So, what, you two hard up for coin or something? Back to work a shift?
I thought you just said we were the worst!
Walk with me! Times change, boys. And I ain't gonna lie, we're shorthanded...
But we're embarking on the opportunity of a lifetime!
This is the frontier, baby!
And not even you two mooks could screw it up!
GAKK
... ...

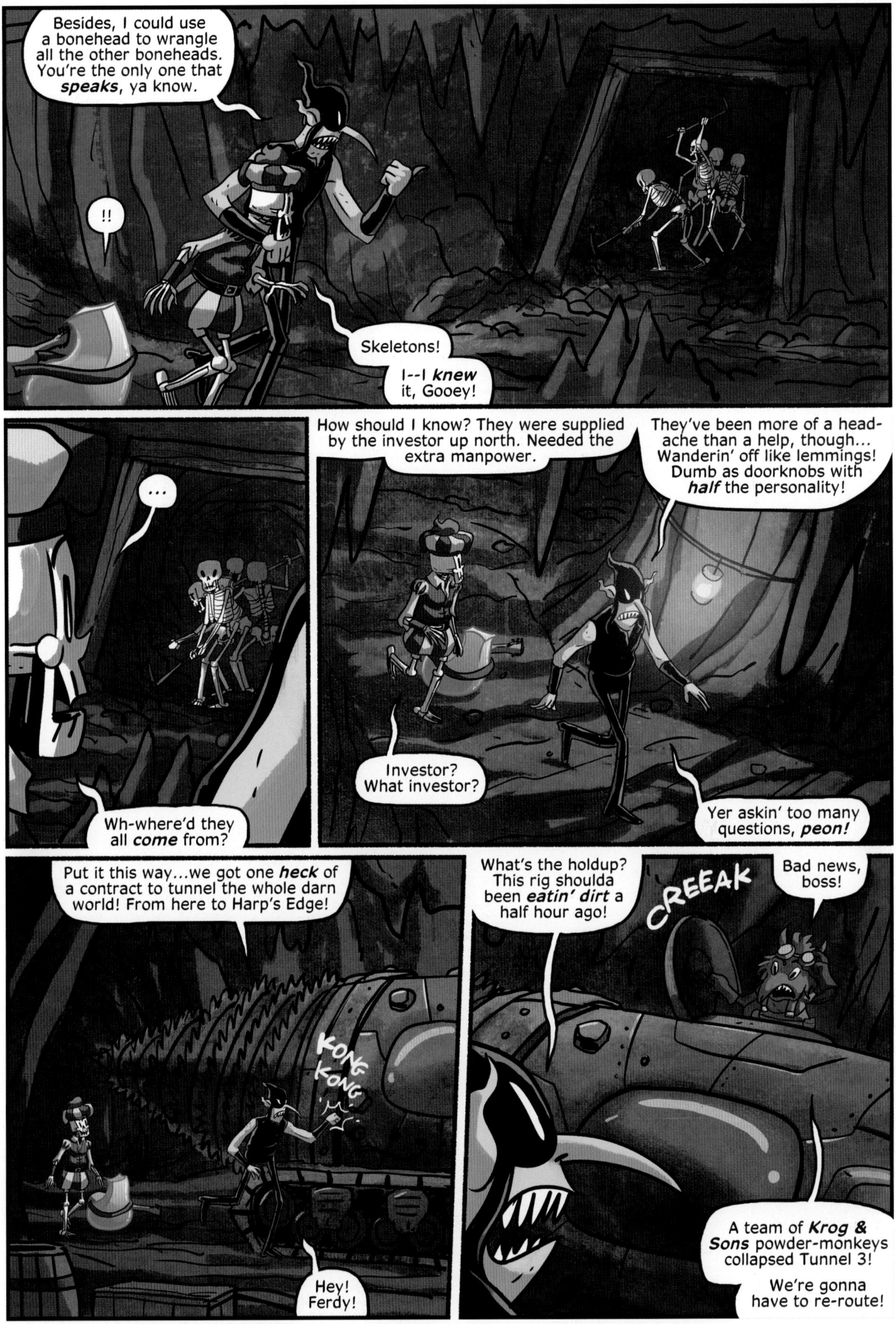

Besides, I could use a bonehead to wrangle all the other boneheads. You're the only one that ***speaks***, ya know.
!!
Skeletons!
I--I ***knew*** it, Gooey!
...
Wh-where'd they all ***come*** from?
How should I know? They were supplied by the investor up north. Needed the extra manpower.
They've been more of a head-ache than a help, though... Wanderin' off like lemmings! Dumb as doorknobs with ***half*** the personality!
Investor? What investor?
Yer askin' too many questions, ***peon!***
Put it this way...we got one ***heck*** of a contract to tunnel the whole darn world! From here to Harp's Edge!
KONG KONG
Hey! Ferdy!
What's the holdup? This rig shoulda been ***eatin' dirt*** a half hour ago!
CREEAK
Bad news, boss!
A team of ***Krog & Sons*** powder-monkeys collapsed Tunnel 3!
We're gonna have to re-route!

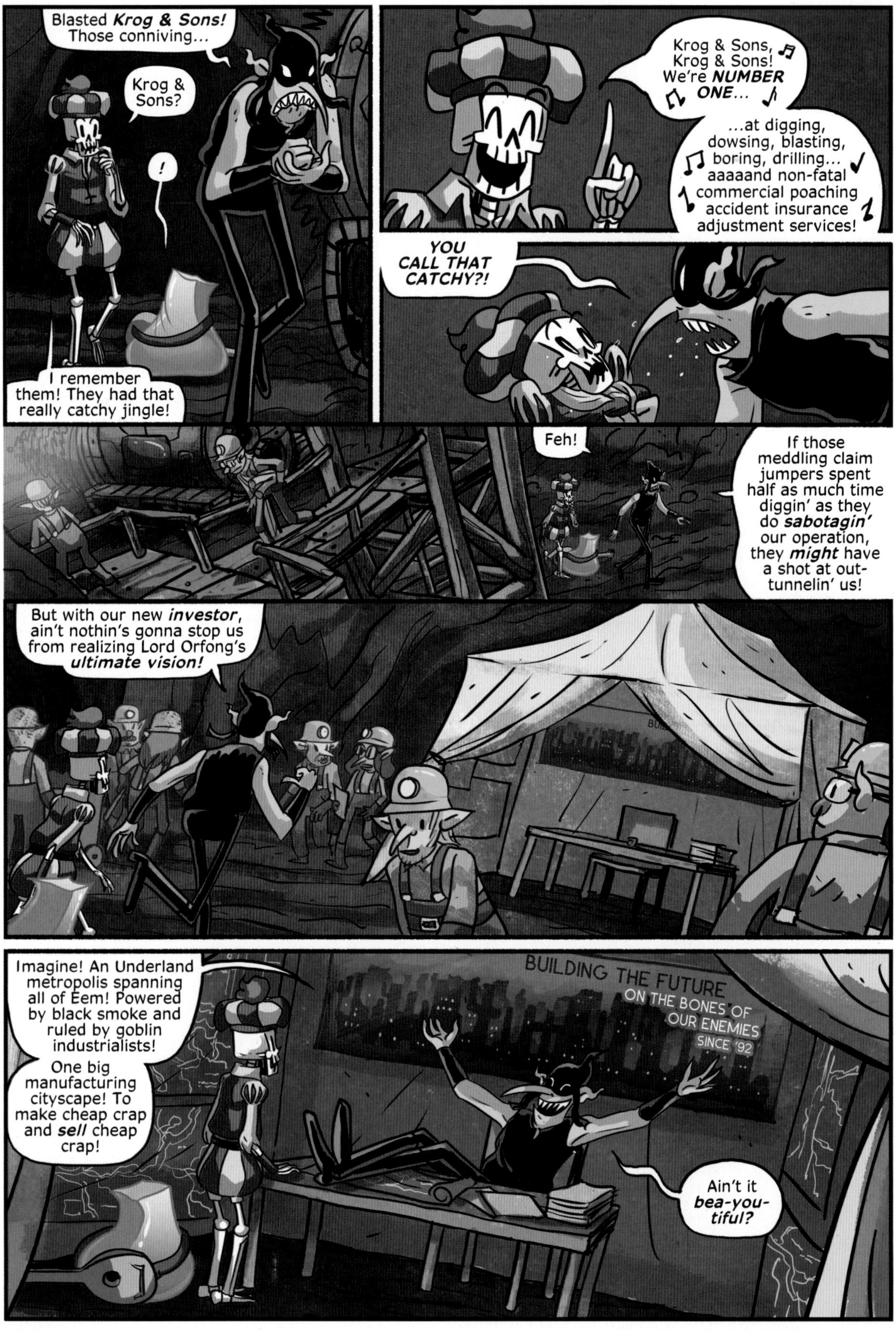

Blasted Krog & Sons! Those conniving...
Krog & Sons?
!
I remember them! They had that really catchy jingle!
Krog & Sons, Krog & Sons! We're NUMBER ONE...
...at digging, dowsing, blasting, boring, drilling... aaaaand non-fatal commercial poaching accident insurance adjustment services!
YOU CALL THAT CATCHY?!
Feh!
If those meddling claim jumpers spent half as much time diggin' as they do sabotagin' our operation, they might have a shot at out-tunnelin' us!
But with our new investor, ain't nothin's gonna stop us from realizing Lord Orfong's ultimate vision!
Imagine! An Underland metropolis spanning all of Eem! Powered by black smoke and ruled by goblin industrialists!
One big manufacturing cityscape! To make cheap crap and sell cheap crap!
BUILDING THE FUTURE
ON THE BONES OF OUR ENEMIES
SINCE '92
Ain't it bea-you-tiful?

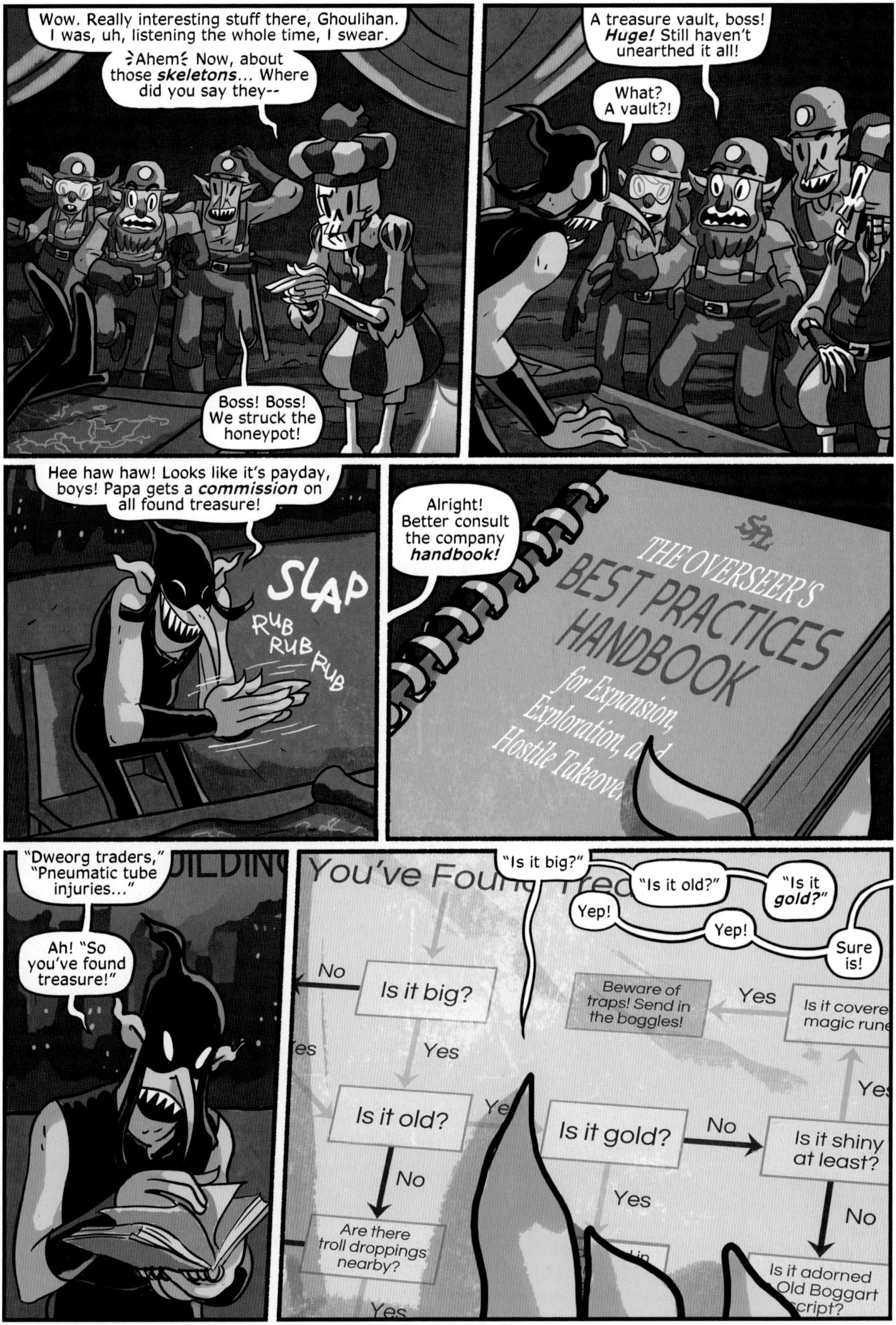

Wow. Really interesting stuff there, Ghoulihan. I was, uh, listening the whole time, I swear.
Ahem Now, about those *skeletons*... Where did you say they--
Boss! Boss! We struck the honeypot!
A treasure vault, boss! *Huge!* Still haven't unearthed it all!
What? A vault?!
Hee haw haw! Looks like it's payday, boys! Papa gets a *commission* on all found treasure!
SLAP
RUB RUB RUB
Alright! Better consult the company *handbook!*
THE OVERSEER'S BEST PRACTICES HANDBOOK for Expansion, Exploration, and Hostile Takeover
"Dweorg traders," "Pneumatic tube injuries..."
Ah! "So you've found treasure!"
"Is it big?"
Yep!
"Is it old?"
Yep!
"Is it *gold?*"
Sure is!
Is it big?
No
Yes
Yes
Is it old?
No
Are there troll droppings nearby?
Is it gold?
No
Yes
Is it shiny at least?
No
Is it adorned
Old Boggart
Beware of traps! Send in the boggles!
Yes

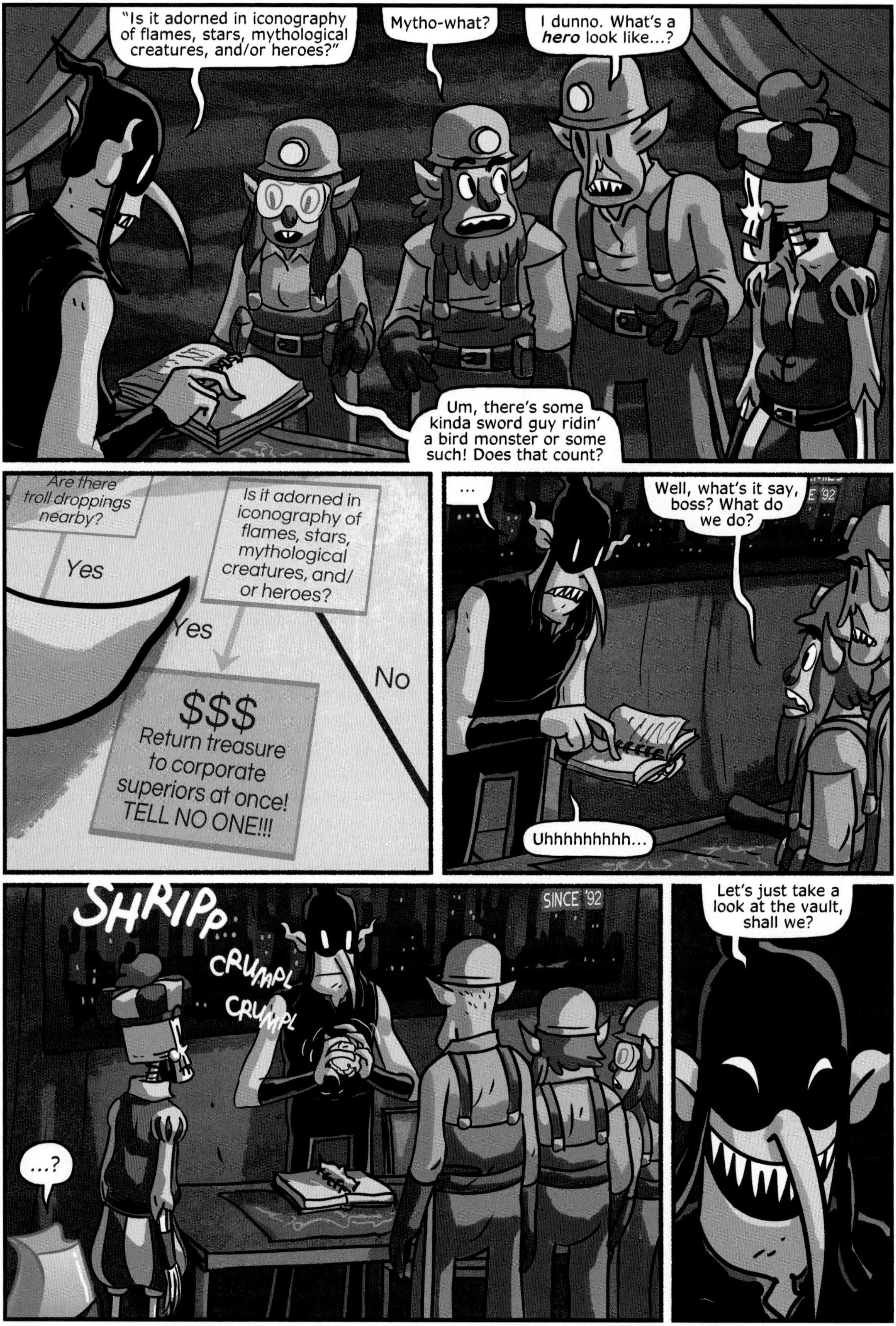

"Is it adorned in iconography of flames, stars, mythological creatures, and/or heroes?"
Mytho-what?
I dunno. What's a ***hero*** look like...?
Um, there's some kinda sword guy ridin' a bird monster or some such! Does that count?
Are there troll droppings nearby?
Yes
Is it adorned in iconography of flames, stars, mythological creatures, and/or heroes?
Yes
No
$$$ Return treasure to corporate superiors at once! TELL NO ONE!!!
...
Well, what's it say, boss? What do we do?
Uhhhhhhhhh...
SHRIPP...
CRUMPL
CRUMPL
SINCE '92
...?
Let's just take a look at the vault, shall we?

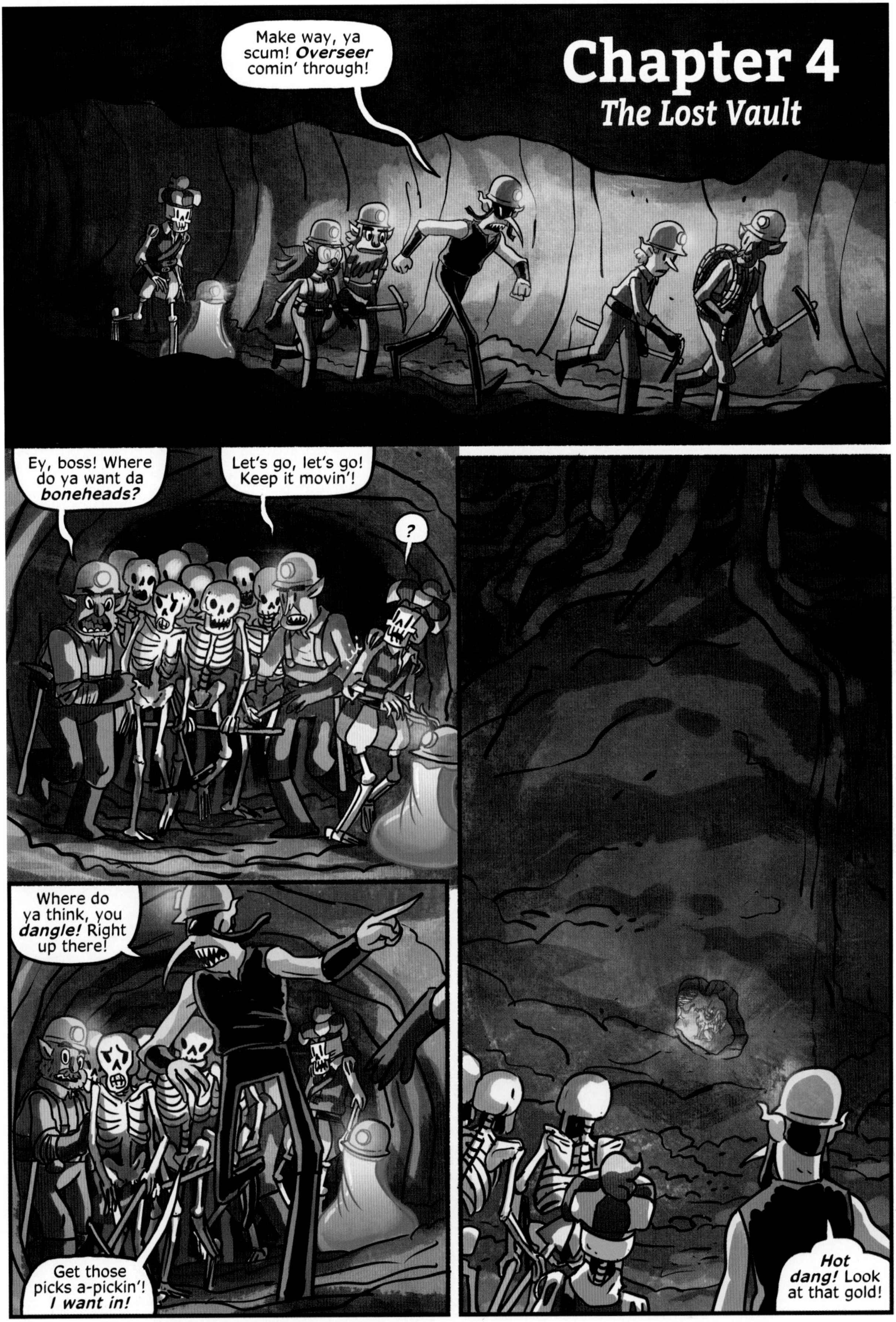

Chapter 4
The Lost Vault
Make way, ya scum! *Overseer* comin' through!
Ey, boss! Where do ya want da ***boneheads?***
Let's go, let's go! Keep it movin'!
?
Where do ya think, you ***dangle!*** Right up there!
Get those picks a-pickin'! ***I want in!***
Hot dang! Look at that gold!

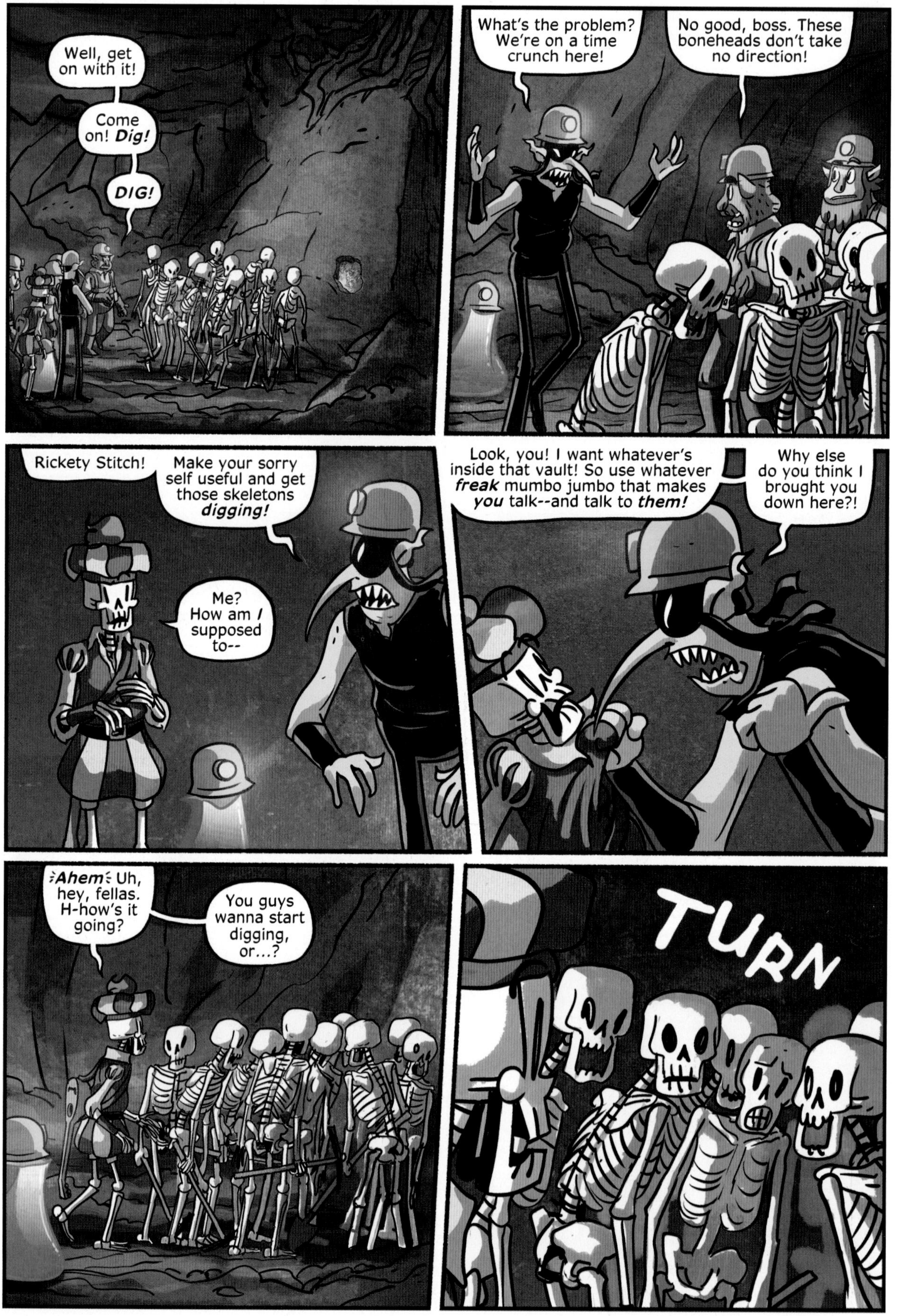
Well, get on with it!
Come on! *Dig!*
DIG!
What's the problem? We're on a time crunch here!
No good, boss. These boneheads don't take no direction!
Rickety Stitch!
Make your sorry self useful and get those skeletons ***digging!***
Me? How am *I* supposed to--
Look, you! I want whatever's inside that vault! So use whatever ***freak*** mumbo jumbo that makes ***you*** talk--and talk to ***them!***
Why else do you think I brought you down here?!
Ahem Uh, hey, fellas. H-how's it going?
You guys wanna start digging, or...?
TURN

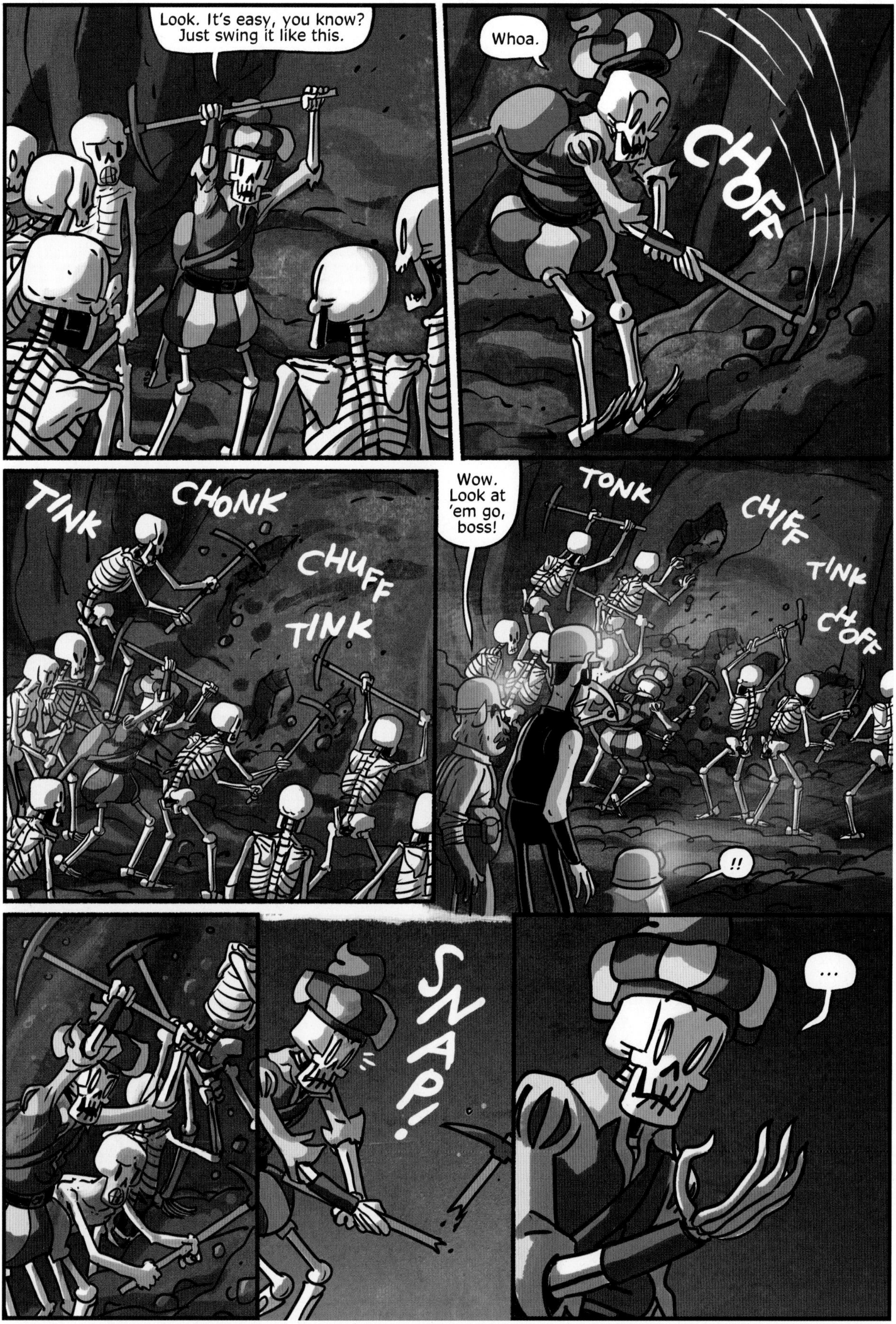
Look. It's easy, you know? Just swing it like this.
Whoa.
CHOFF
TINK
CHONK
CHUFF
TINK
Wow. Look at 'em go, boss!
TONK
CHIFF
TINK
CHOFF
!!
SNAP!
...

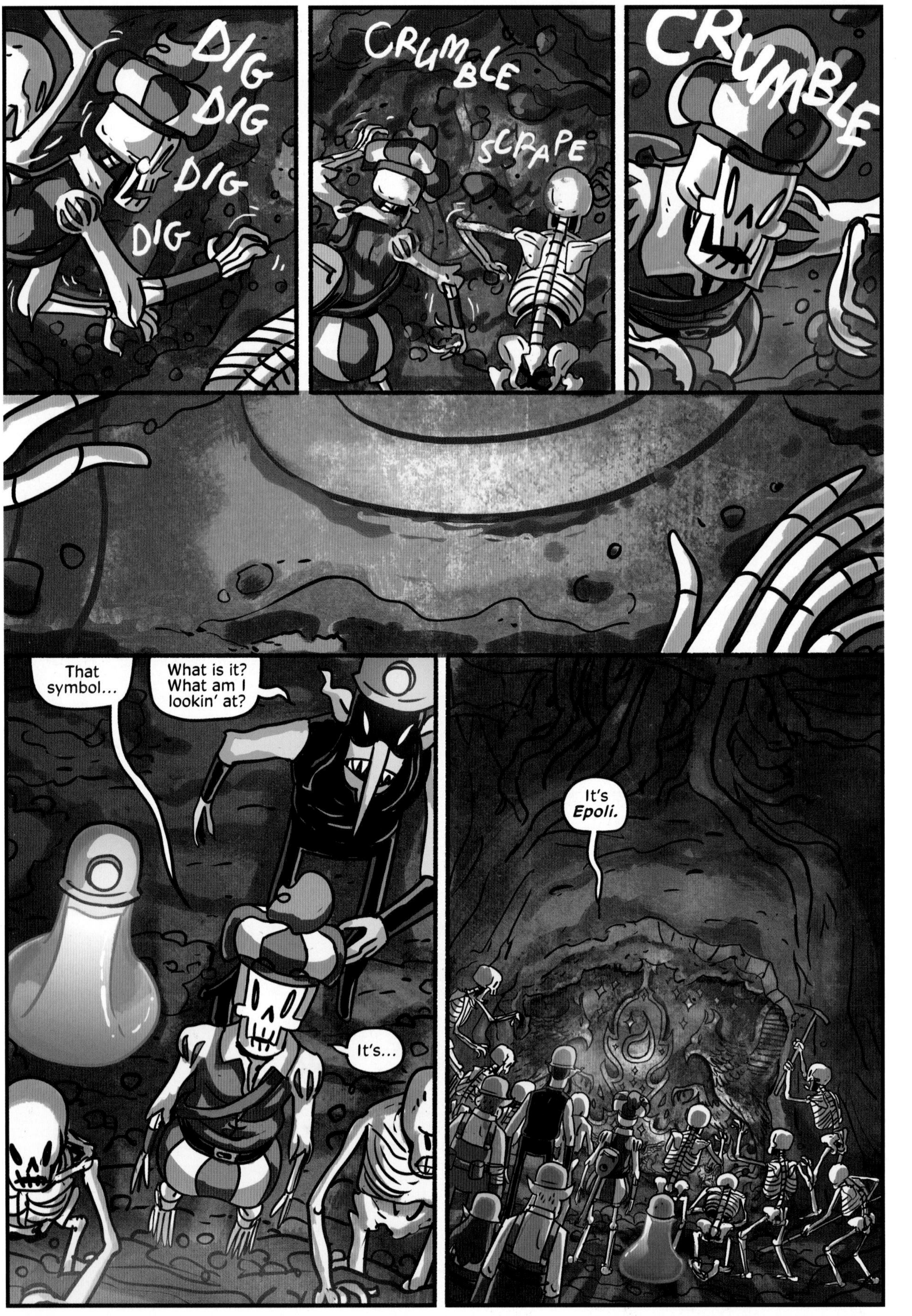
DIG
DIG
DIG
DIG
CRUMBLE
SCRAPE
CRUMBLE
That symbol...
What is it? What am I lookin' at?
It's...
It's *Epoli.*

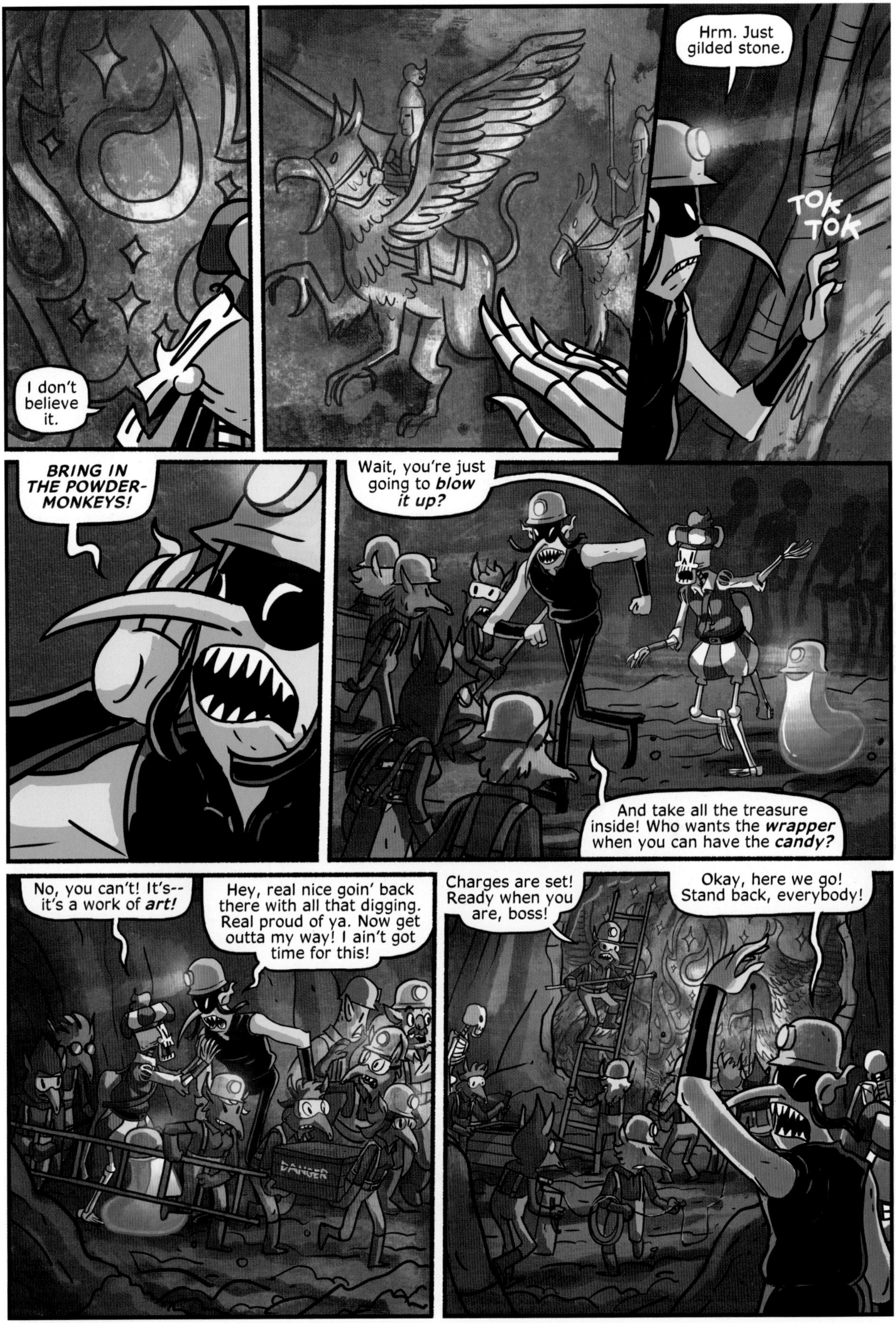
I don't believe it.
Hrm. Just gilded stone.
TOK TOK
BRING IN THE POWDER-MONKEYS!
Wait, you're just going to *blow it up?*
And take all the treasure inside! Who wants the *wrapper* when you can have the *candy?*
No, you can't! It's--it's a work of *art!*
Hey, real nice goin' back there with all that digging. Real proud of ya. Now get outta my way! I ain't got time for this!
DANGER
Charges are set! Ready when you are, boss!
Okay, here we go! Stand back, everybody!

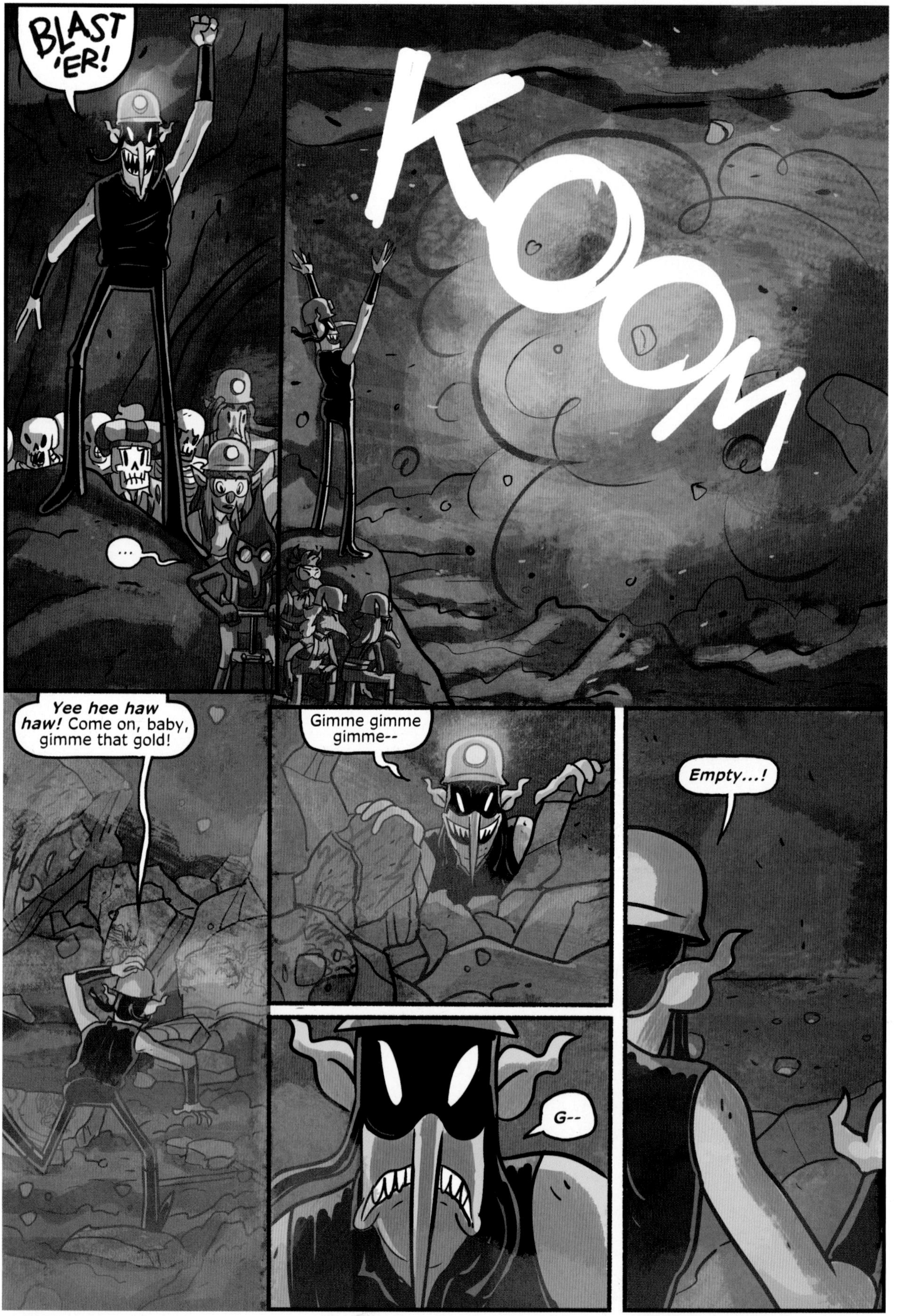
BLAST 'ER!
KOOOM
...
Yee hee haw haw! Come on, baby, gimme that gold!
Gimme gimme gimme--
Empty...!
G--

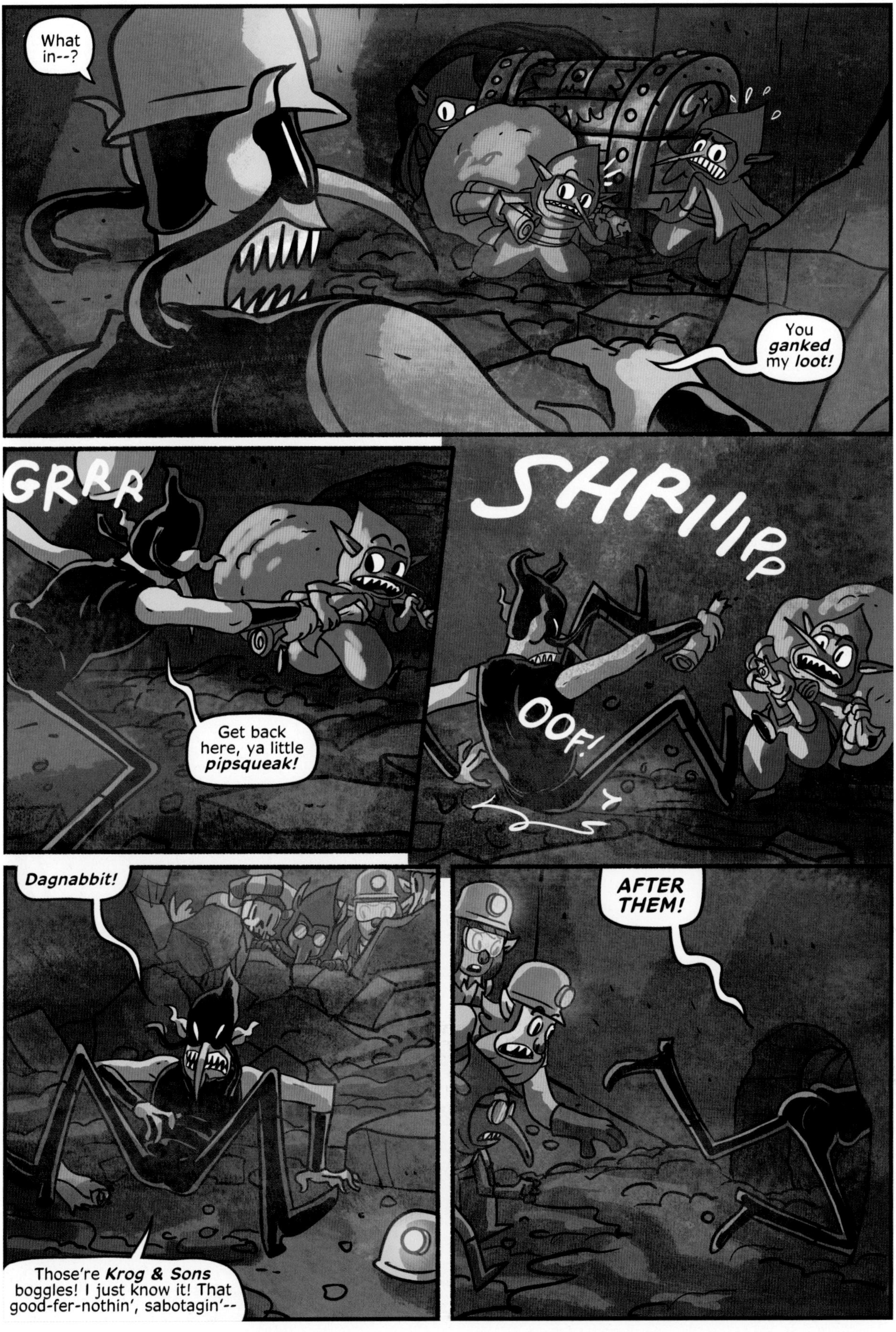
What in--?
You ganked my loot!
GRRR
Get back here, ya little pipsqueak!
SHRIIIPP
OOF!
Dagnabbit!
Those're Krog & Sons boggles! I just know it! That good-fer-nothin', sabotagin'--
AFTER THEM!

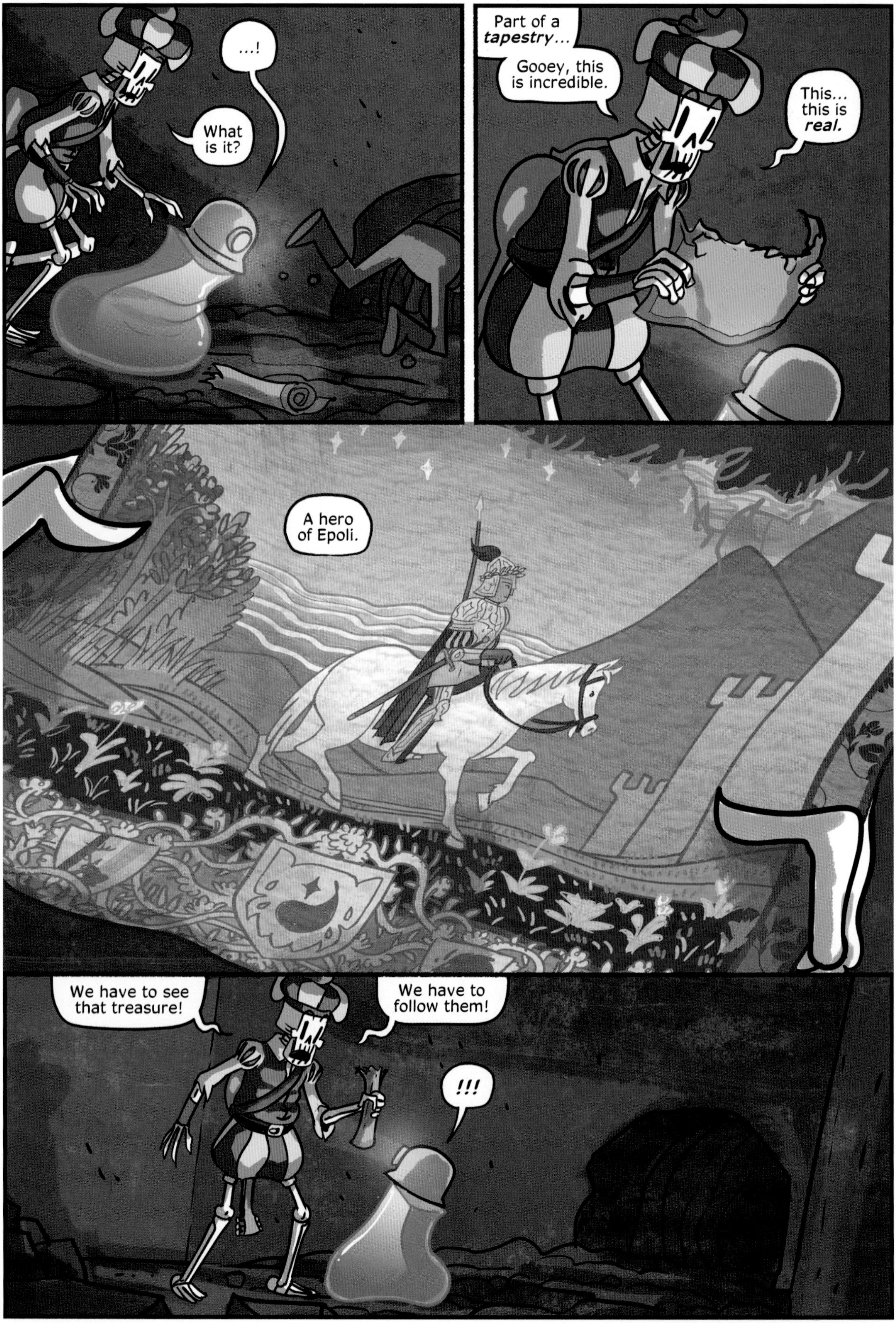
...!
What is it?
Part of a *tapestry*...
Gooey, this is incredible.
This... this is *real.*
A hero of Epoli.
We have to see that treasure!
We have to follow them!
!!!

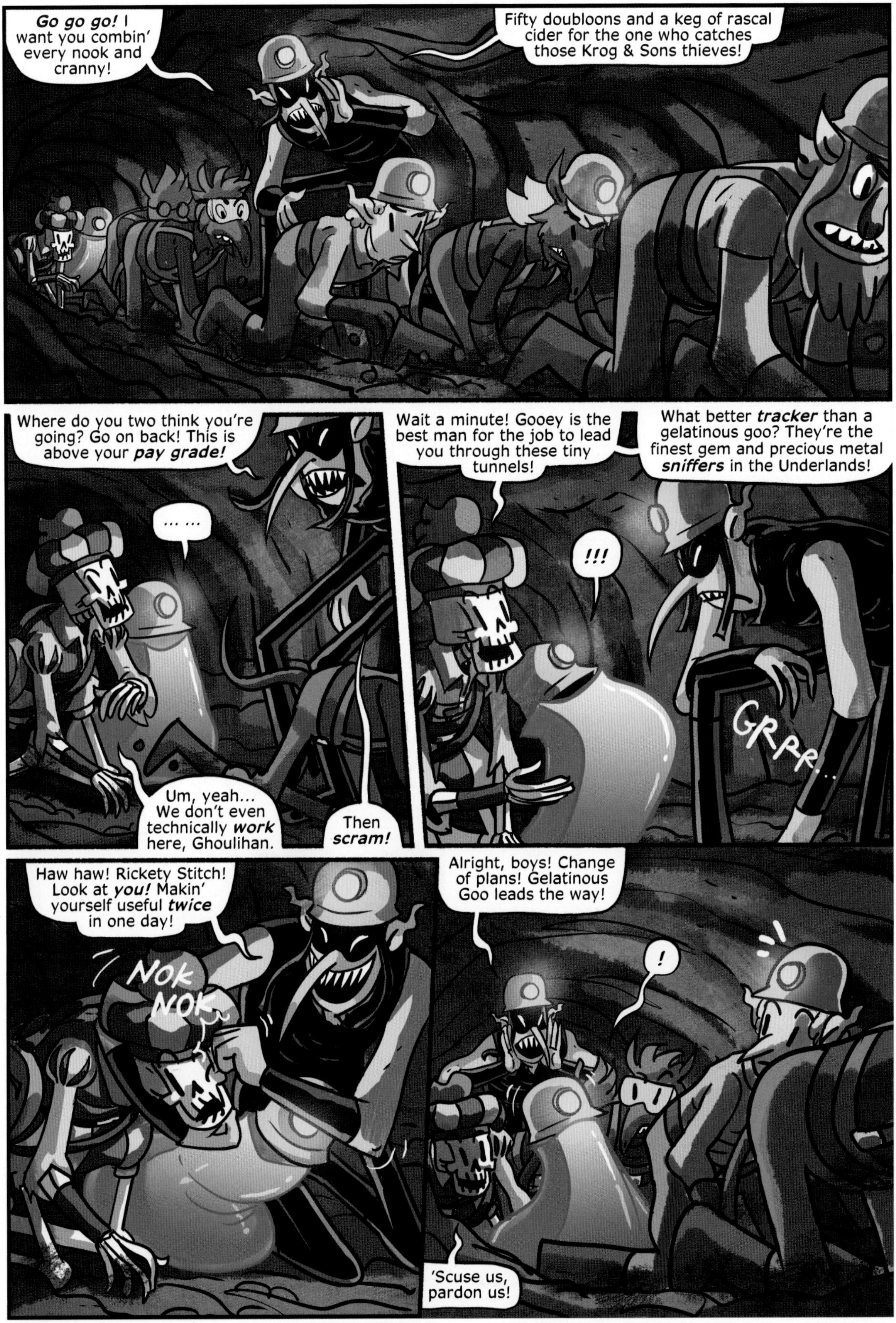

Go go go! I want you combin' every nook and cranny!
Fifty doubloons and a keg of rascal cider for the one who catches those Krog & Sons thieves!
Where do you two think you're going? Go on back! This is above your *pay grade!*
... ...
Um, yeah... We don't even technically *work* here, Ghoulihan.
Then *scram!*
Wait a minute! Gooey is the best man for the job to lead you through these tiny tunnels!
What better *tracker* than a gelatinous goo? They're the finest gem and precious metal *sniffers* in the Underlands!
!!!
GRRR...
Haw haw! Rickety Stitch! Look at *you!* Makin' yourself useful *twice* in one day!
NOK NOK
Alright, boys! Change of plans! Gelatinous Goo leads the way!
!
'Scuse us, pardon us!

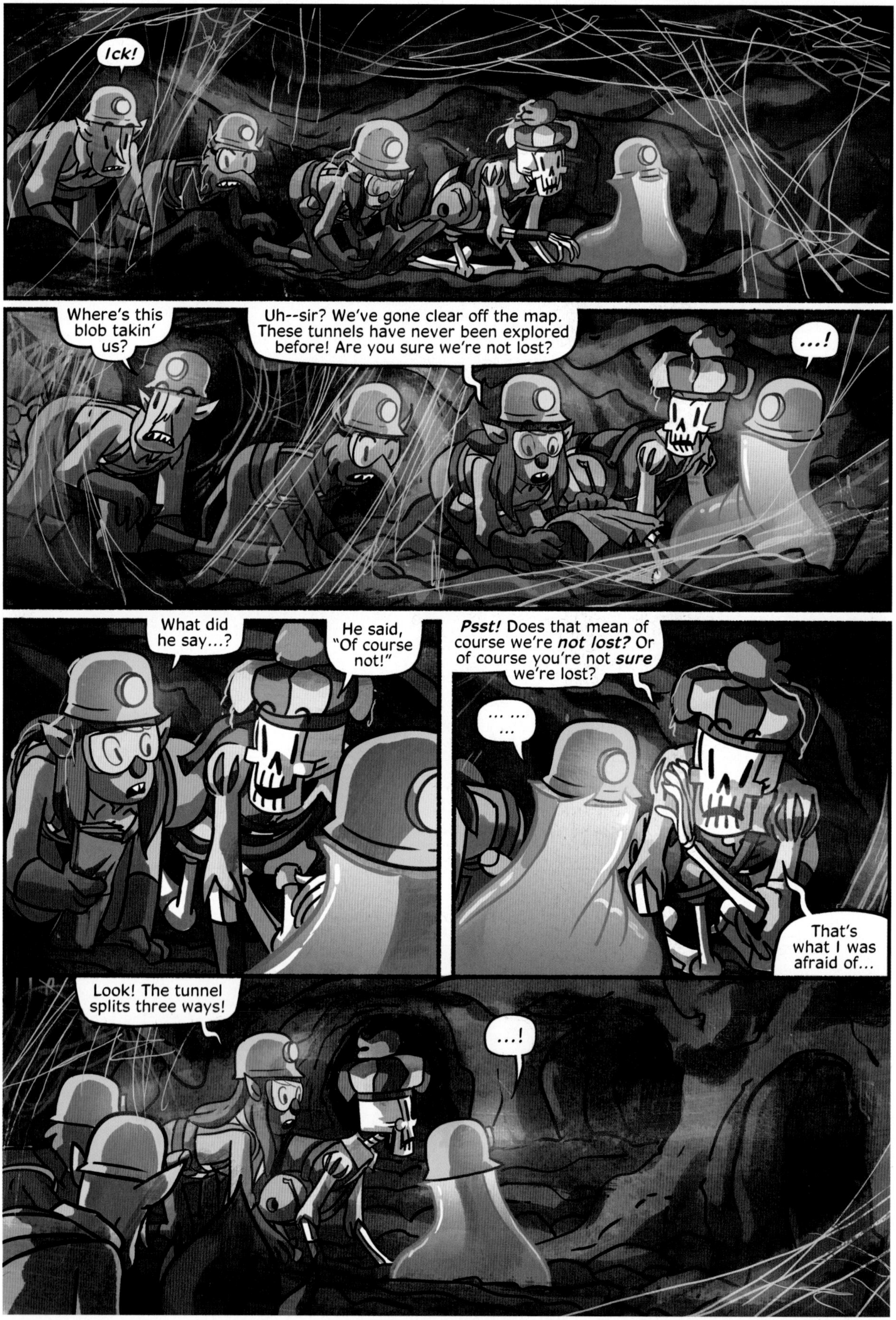
Ick!
Where's this blob takin' us?
Uh--sir? We've gone clear off the map. These tunnels have never been explored before! Are you sure we're not lost?
...!
What did he say...?
He said, "Of course not!"
Psst! Does that mean of course we're not lost? Or of course you're not sure we're lost?
... ...
That's what I was afraid of...
Look! The tunnel splits three ways!
...!

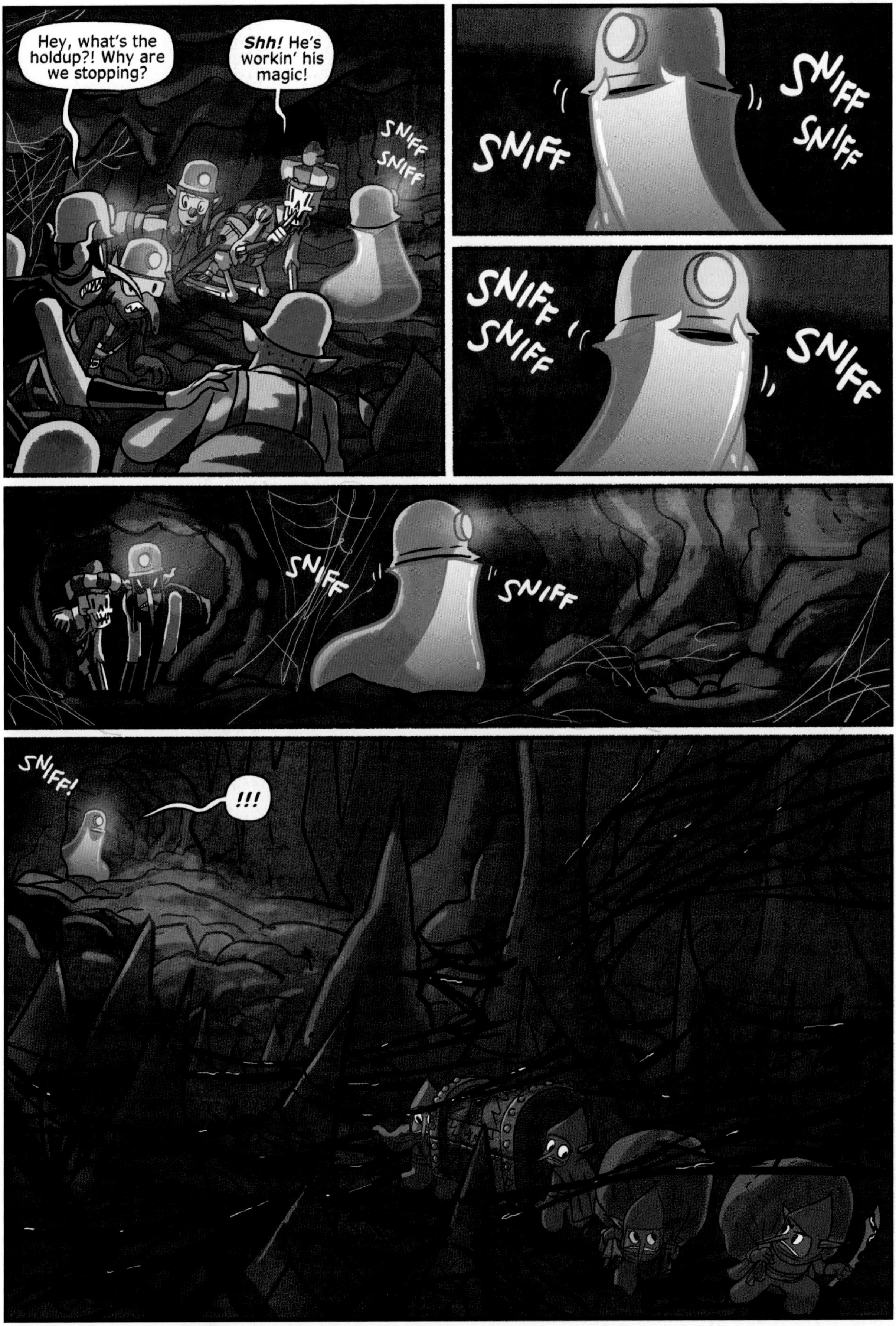
Hey, what's the holdup?! Why are we stopping?
Shh! He's workin' his magic!
SNIFF SNIFF
SNIFF
SNIFF SNIFF
SNIFF SNIFF
SNIFF
SNIFF
SNIFF
SNIFF!
!!!

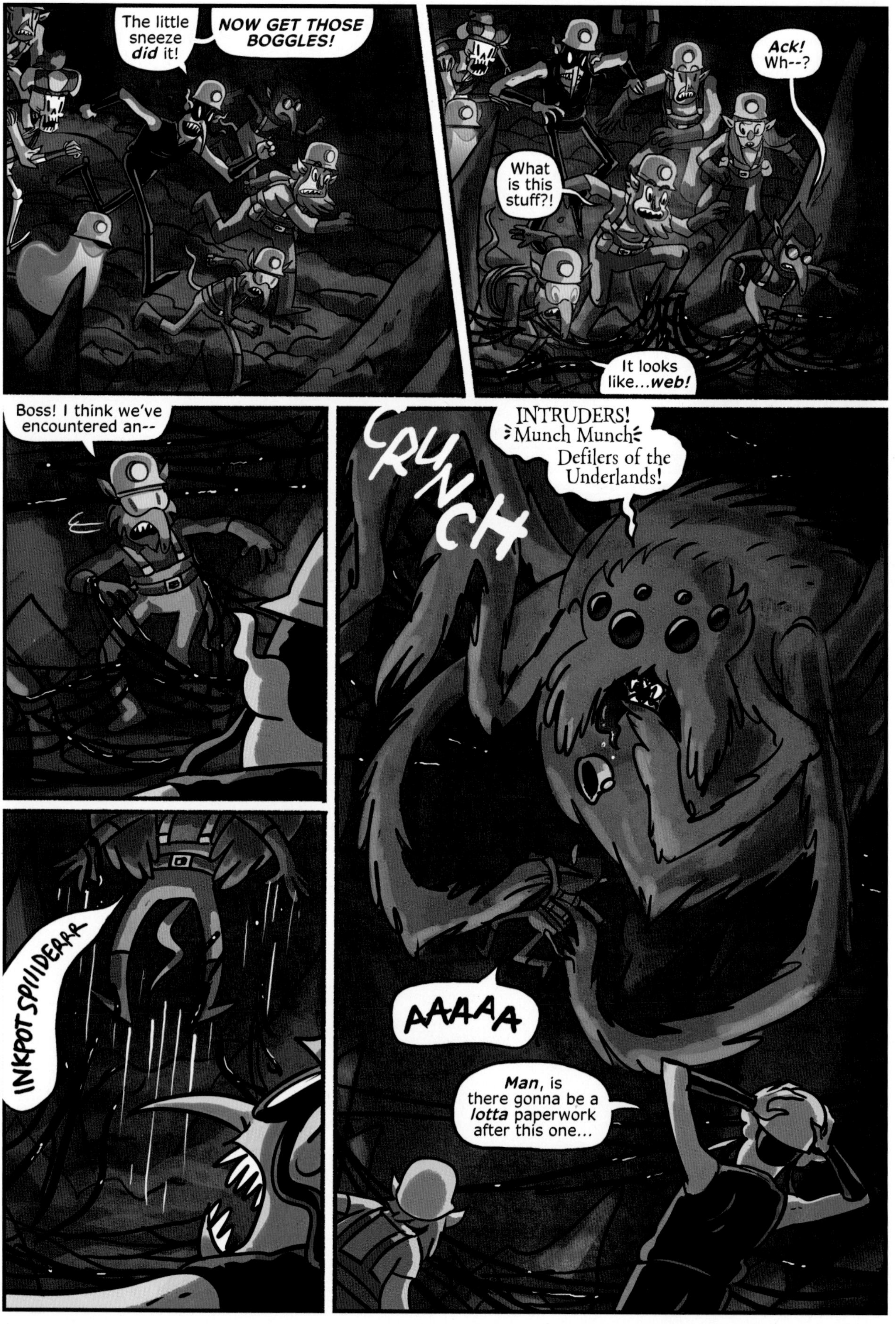
The little sneeze *did* it!
NOW GET THOSE BOGGLES!
Ack! Wh--?
What is this stuff?!
It looks like...***web!***
Boss! I think we've encountered an--
CRUNCH
INTRUDERS!
Munch Munch
Defilers of the Underlands!
INKPOT SPIIIDERRR
AAAAA
Man, is there gonna be a ***lotta*** paperwork after this one...

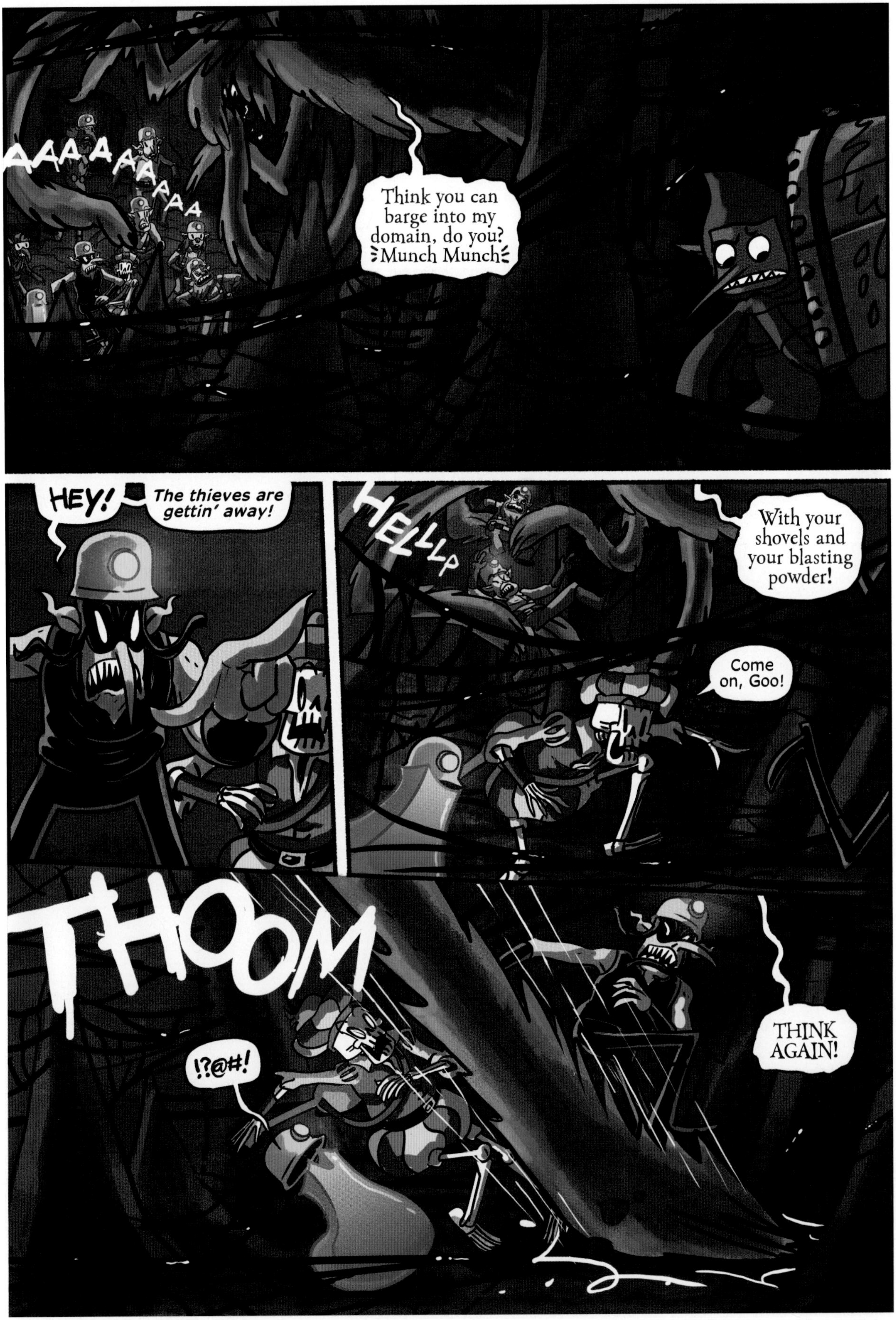
AAAAAAAAAAA
Think you can barge into my domain, do you? Munch Munch
HEY!
The thieves are gettin' away!
HELLLP
With your shovels and your blasting powder!
Come on, Goo!
THOOM
!?@#!
THINK AGAIN!

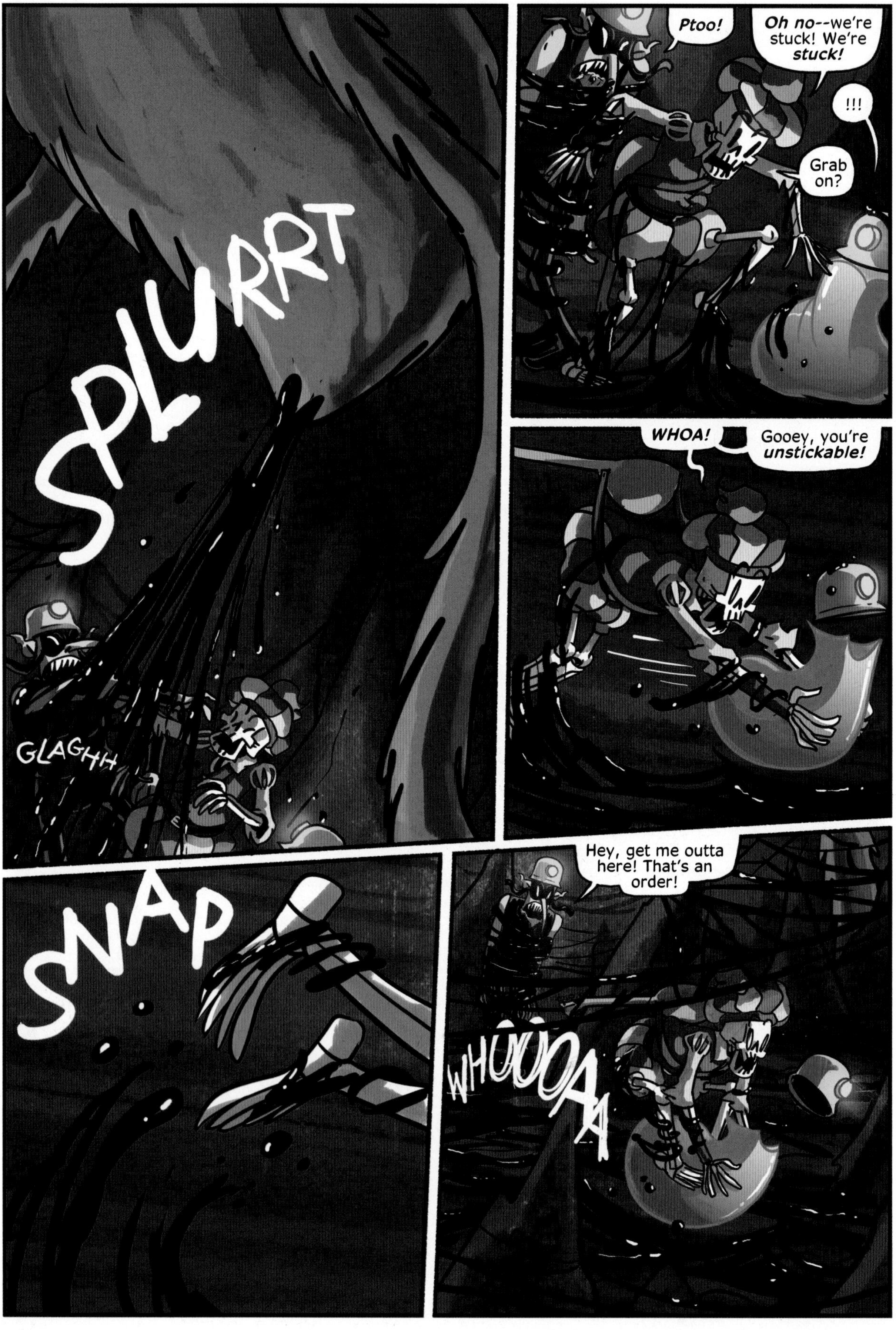
SPLURRT
GLAGHH
Ptoo!
Oh no--we're stuck! We're stuck!
!!!
Grab on?
WHOA!
Gooey, you're unstickable!
SNAP
Hey, get me outta here! That's an order!
WHUUUOAA

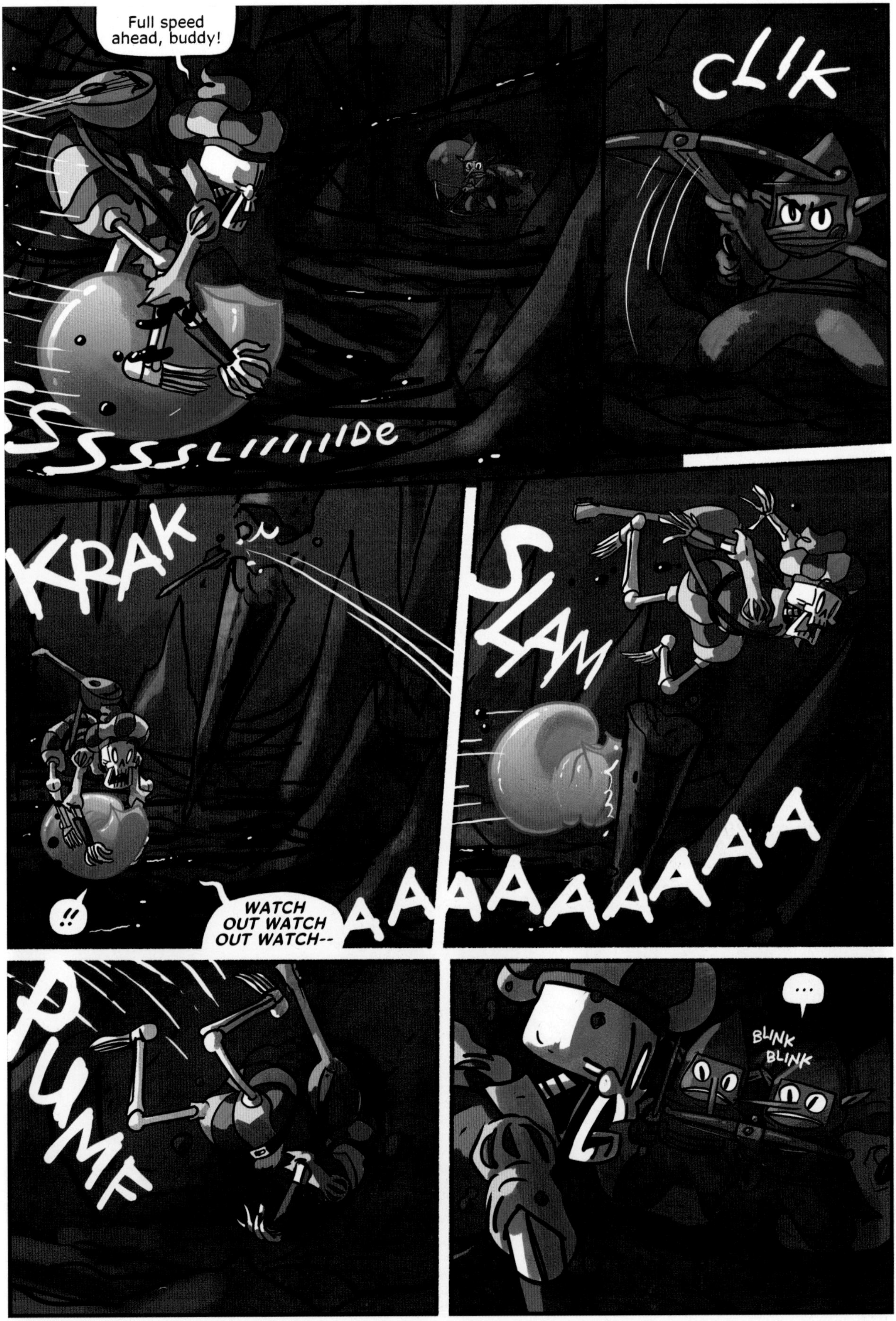
Full speed ahead, buddy!
SSSSSLIIIIIIDE
CLIK
KRAK
!!
WATCH OUT WATCH OUT WATCH--
SLAM
AAAAAAAAAA
PUMF
...
BLINK BLINK

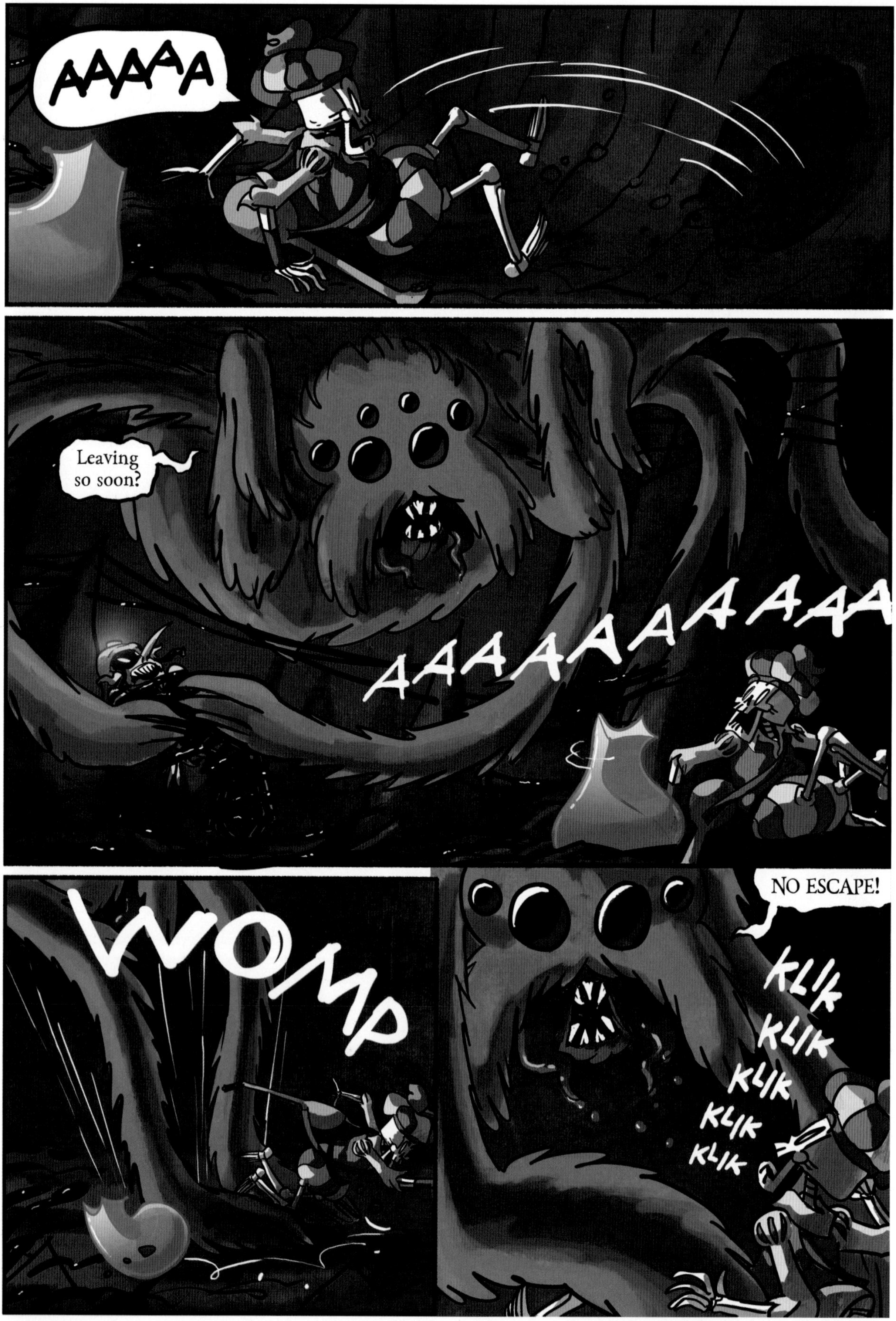
AAAAA
Leaving so soon?
AAAAAAAAAAAA
WOMP
NO ESCAPE!
KLIK
KLIK
KLIK
KLIK
KLIK

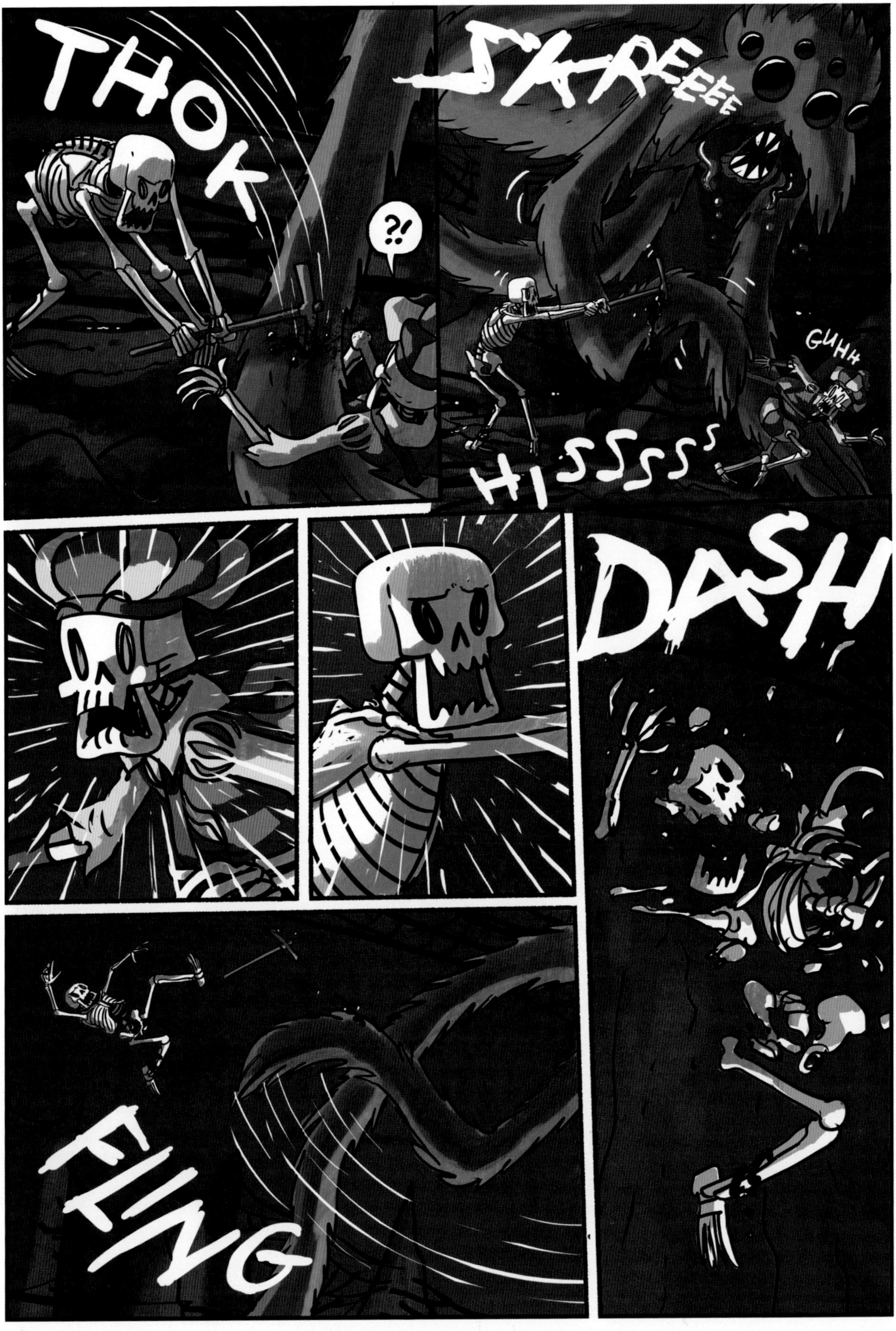
THOK
?!
SKREEEE
GUHH
HISSSSS
DASH
FLING

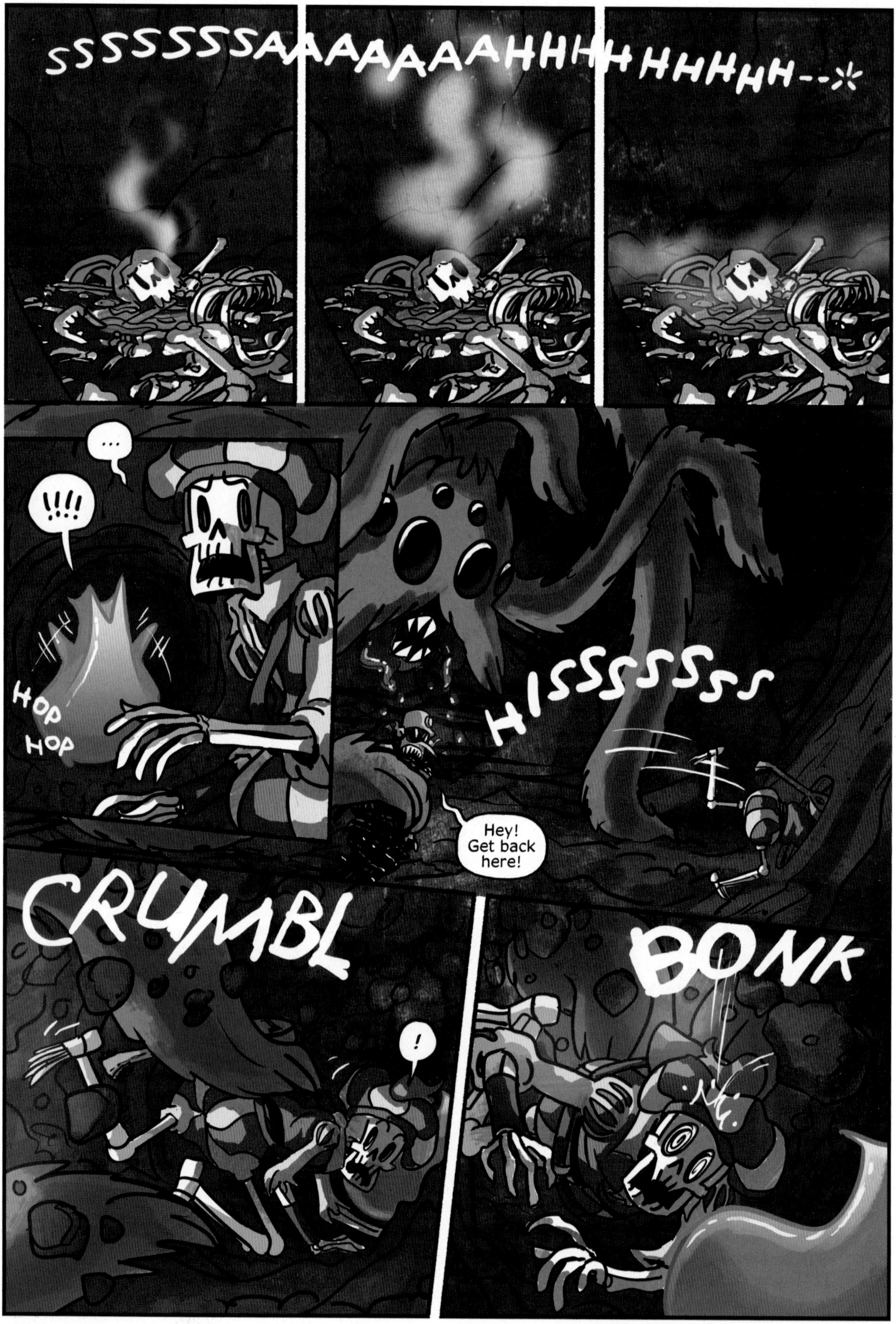
SSSSSSSAAAAAAAAHHHHHHHHH--*
...
!!!!
HOP HOP
HISSSSSSS
Hey! Get back here!
CRUMBL
!
BONK

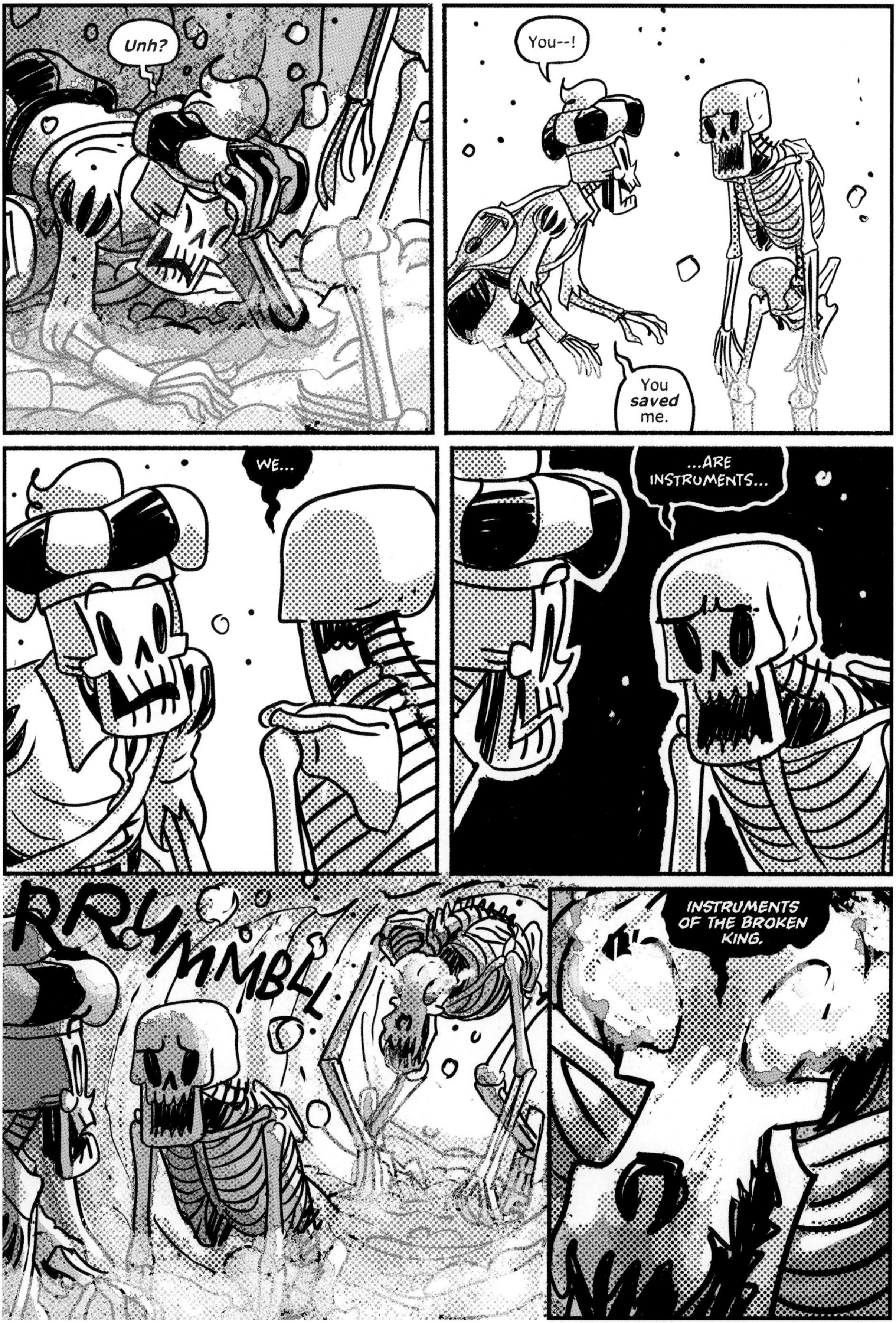
Unh?
You--!
You *saved* me.
WE...
...ARE INSTRUMENTS...
RRUMMBLL
INSTRUMENTS OF THE BROKEN KING.

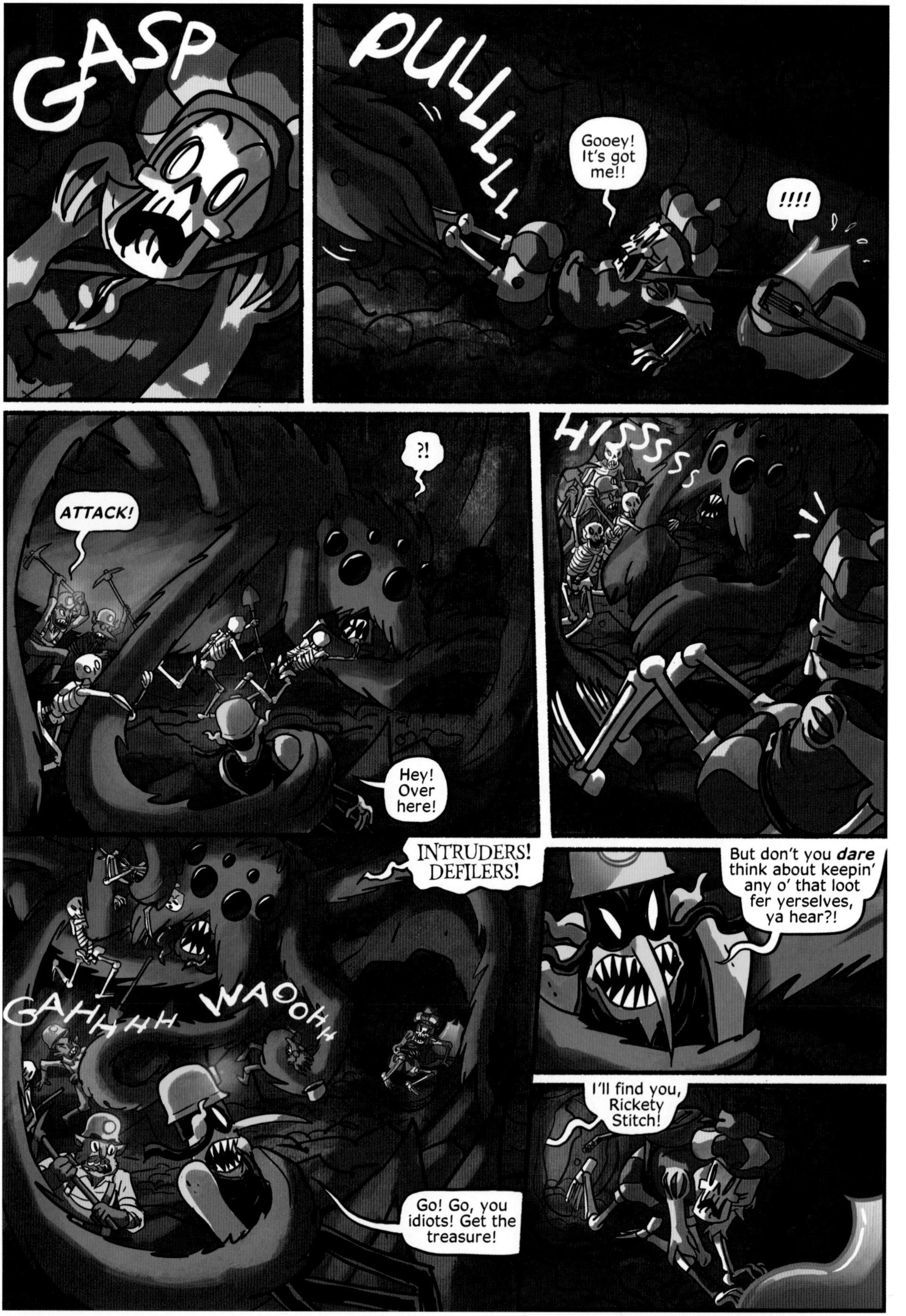
GASP
PULLLLL
Gooey! It's got me!!
!!!!
ATTACK!
?!
Hey! Over here!
HISSSSS
INTRUDERS! DEFILERS!
GAHHHH
WAOOHH
Go! Go, you idiots! Get the treasure!
But don't you ***dare*** think about keepin' any o' that loot fer yerselves, ya hear?!
I'll find you, Rickety Stitch!

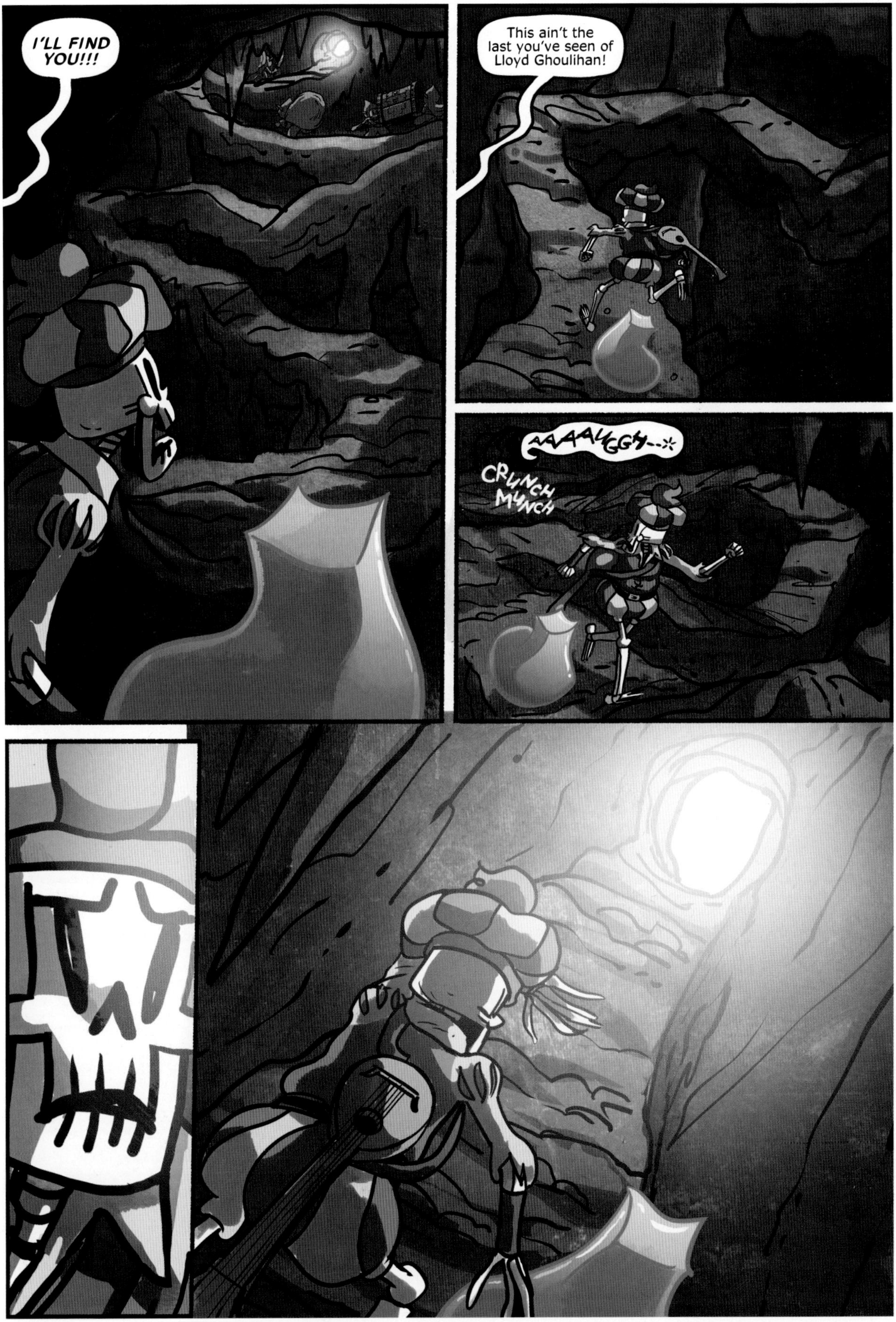
I'LL FIND YOU!!!
This ain't the last you've seen of Lloyd Ghoulihan!
AAAAAUGGH--
CRUNCH MUNCH

Chapter 5
Slogtown

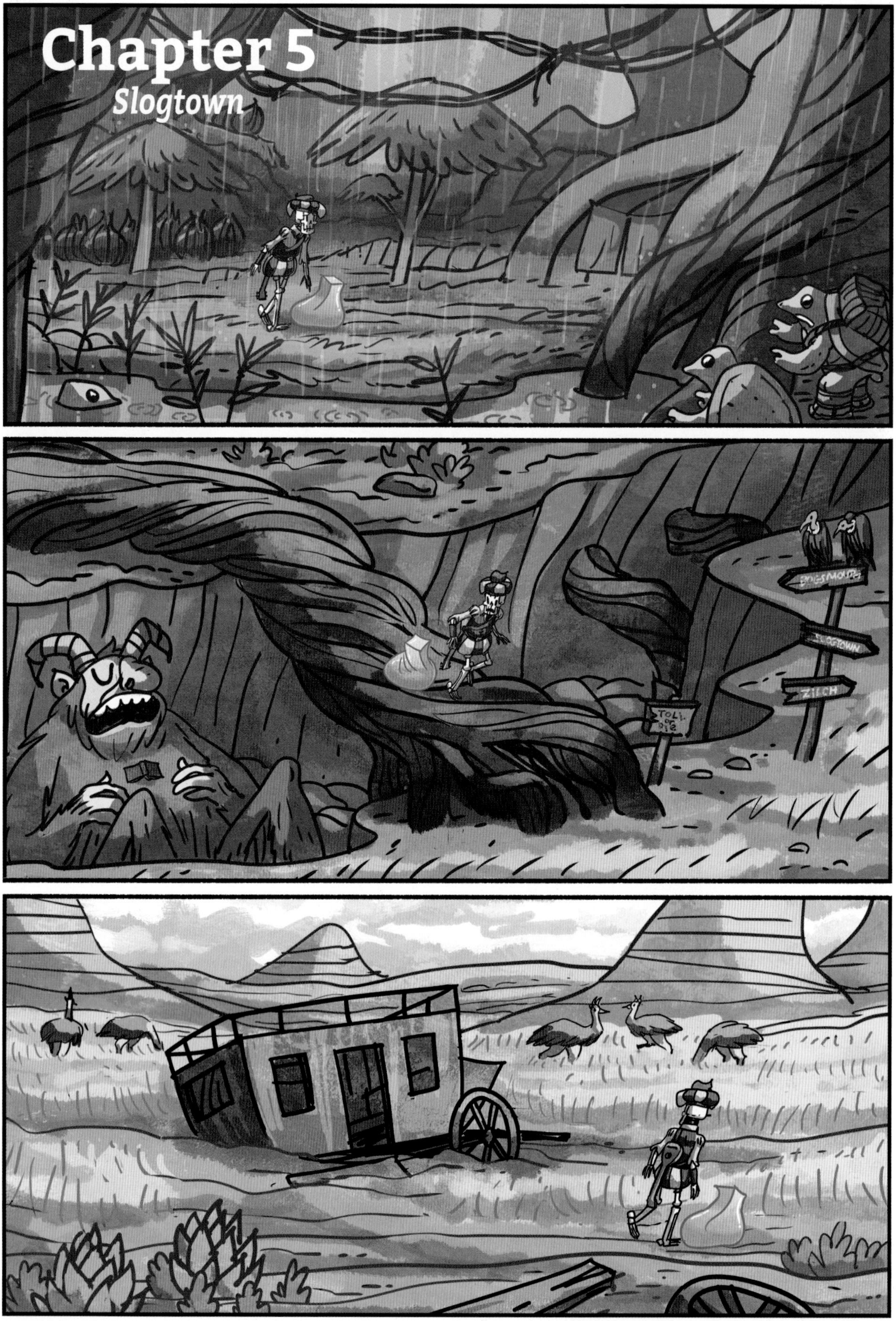
BOGSMOUTH
SLOGTOWN
ZILCH
TOLL or DIE

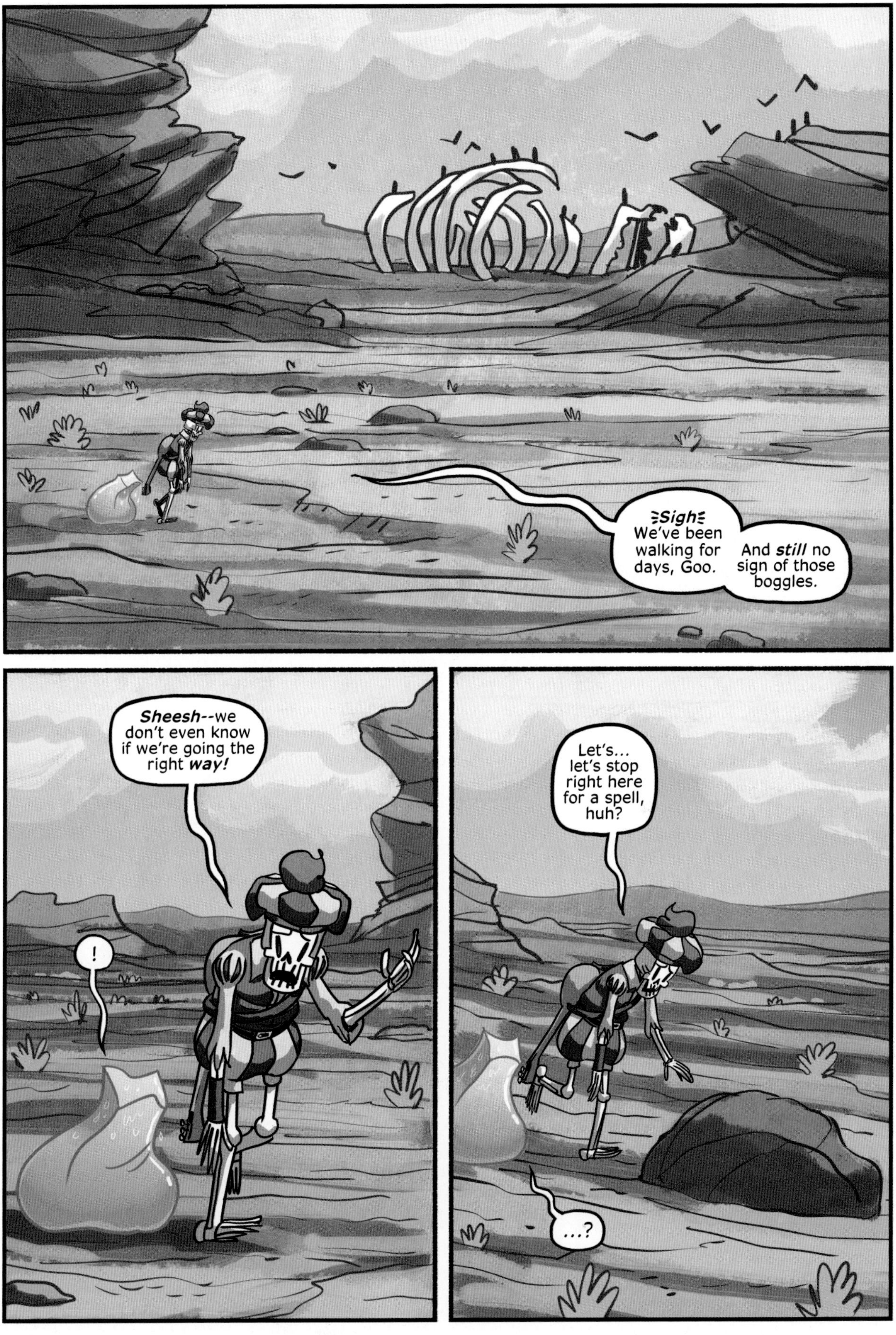

Sigh We've been walking for days, Goo.
And *still* no sign of those boggles.
Sheesh--we don't even know if we're going the right *way!*
!
Let's... let's stop right here for a spell, huh?
...?

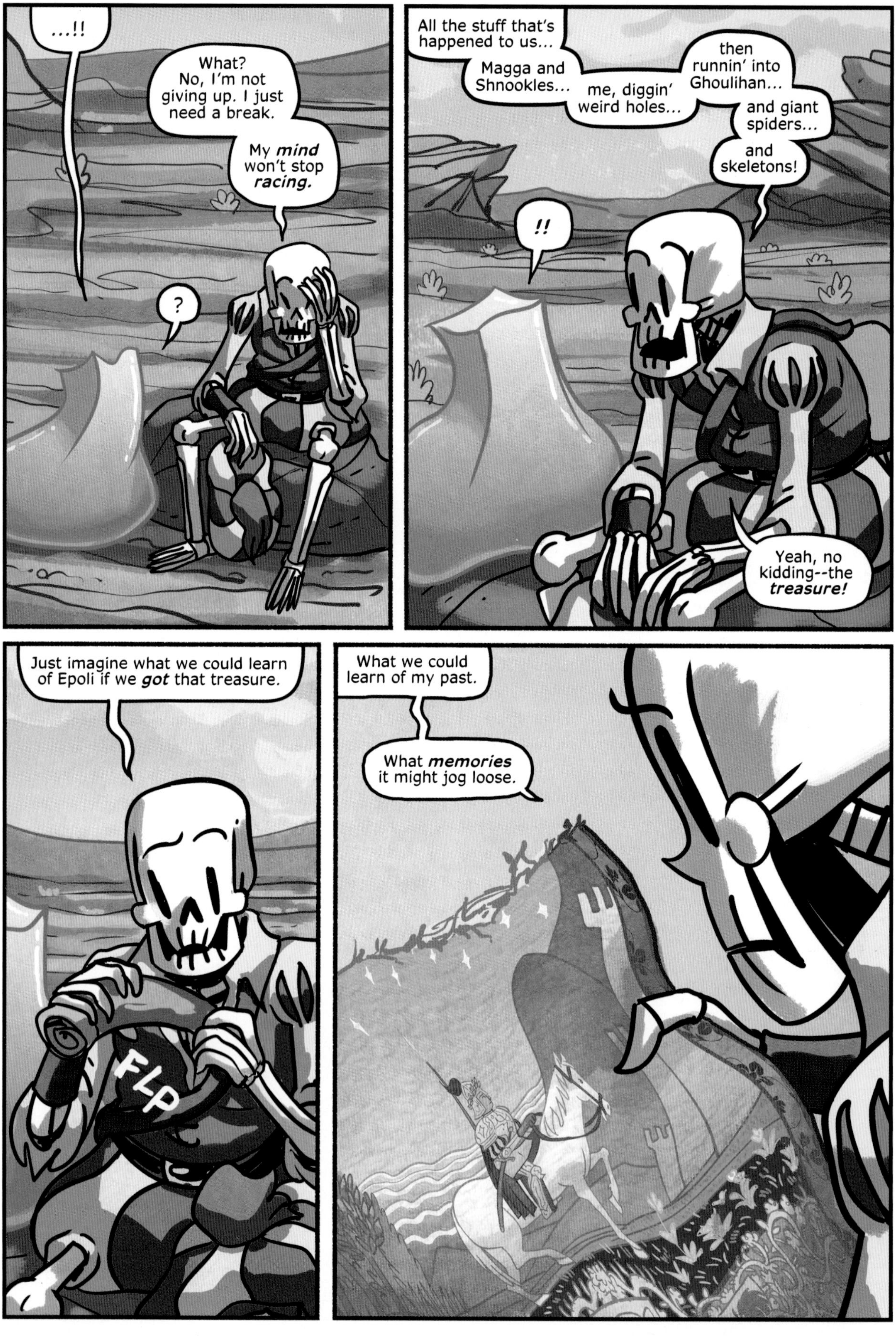

...!!
What? No, I'm not giving up. I just need a break.
My *mind* won't stop *racing.*
?
All the stuff that's happened to us...
Magga and Shnookles...
me, diggin' weird holes...
then runnin' into Ghoulihan...
and giant spiders...
and skeletons!
!!
Yeah, no kidding--the *treasure!*
Just imagine what we could learn of Epoli if we *got* that treasure.
FLP
What we could learn of my past.
What *memories* it might jog loose.

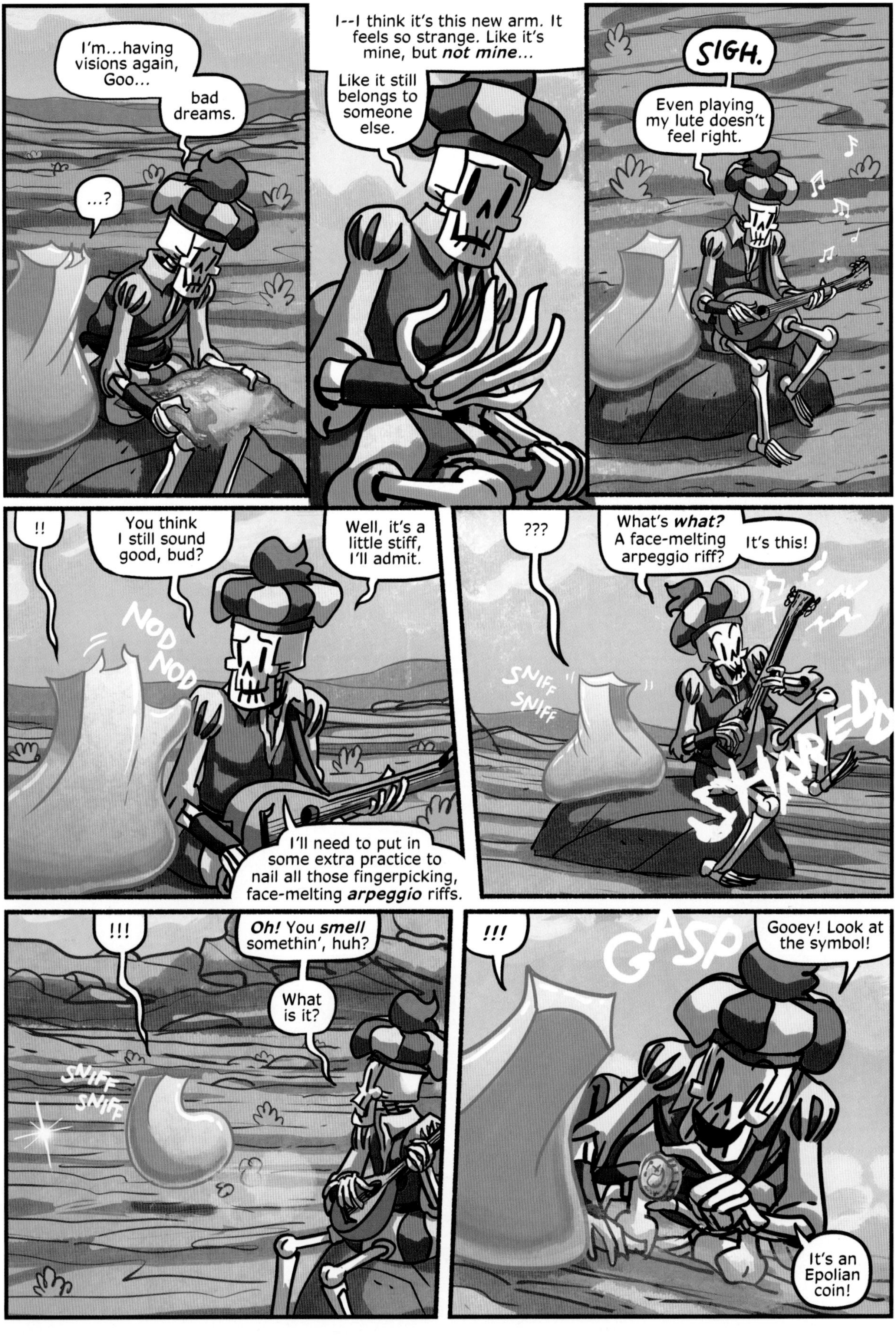
I'm...having visions again, Goo...
bad dreams.
...?
I--I think it's this new arm. It feels so strange. Like it's mine, but *not mine*...
Like it still belongs to someone else.
SIGH.
Even playing my lute doesn't feel right.
!!
You think I still sound good, bud?
Well, it's a little stiff, I'll admit.
NOD NOD
I'll need to put in some extra practice to nail all those fingerpicking, face-melting *arpeggio* riffs.
???
What's *what?* A face-melting arpeggio riff?
It's this!
SNIFF SNIFF
SHREDD
!!!
Oh! You *smell* somethin', huh?
What is it?
SNIFF SNIFF
!!!
GASP
Gooey! Look at the symbol!
It's an Epolian coin!

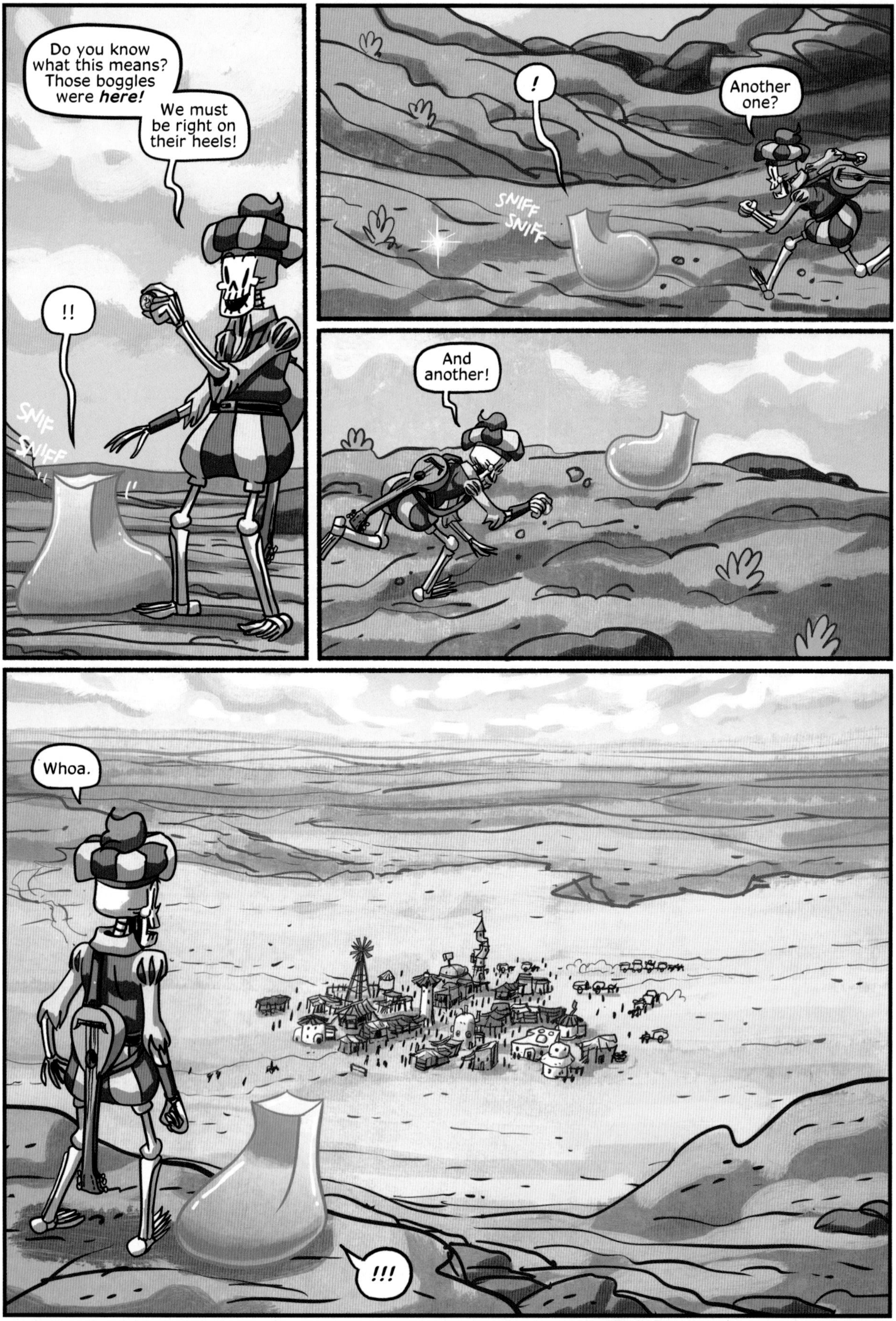
Do you know what this means? Those boggles were *here!*
We must be right on their heels!
!!
SNIF SNIFF
!
Another one?
SNIFF SNIFF
And another!
Whoa.
!!!

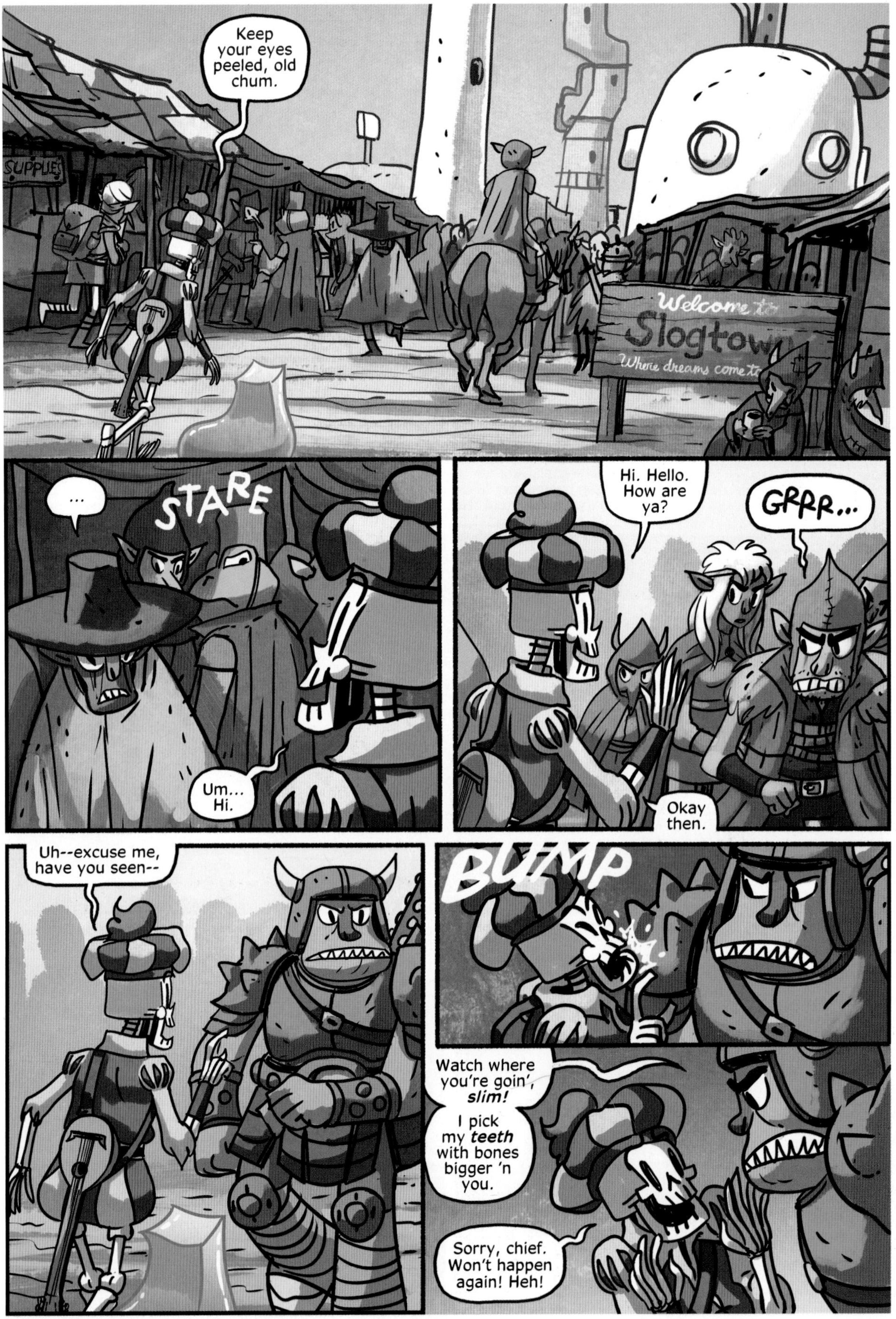
Keep your eyes peeled, old chum.
SUPPLIES
Welcome to Slogtown
Where dreams come to
...
STARE
Um... Hi.
Hi. Hello. How are ya?
GRRR...
Okay then.
Uh--excuse me, have you seen--
BUMP
Watch where you're goin', ***slim!***
I pick my ***teeth*** with bones bigger 'n you.
Sorry, chief. Won't happen again! Heh!

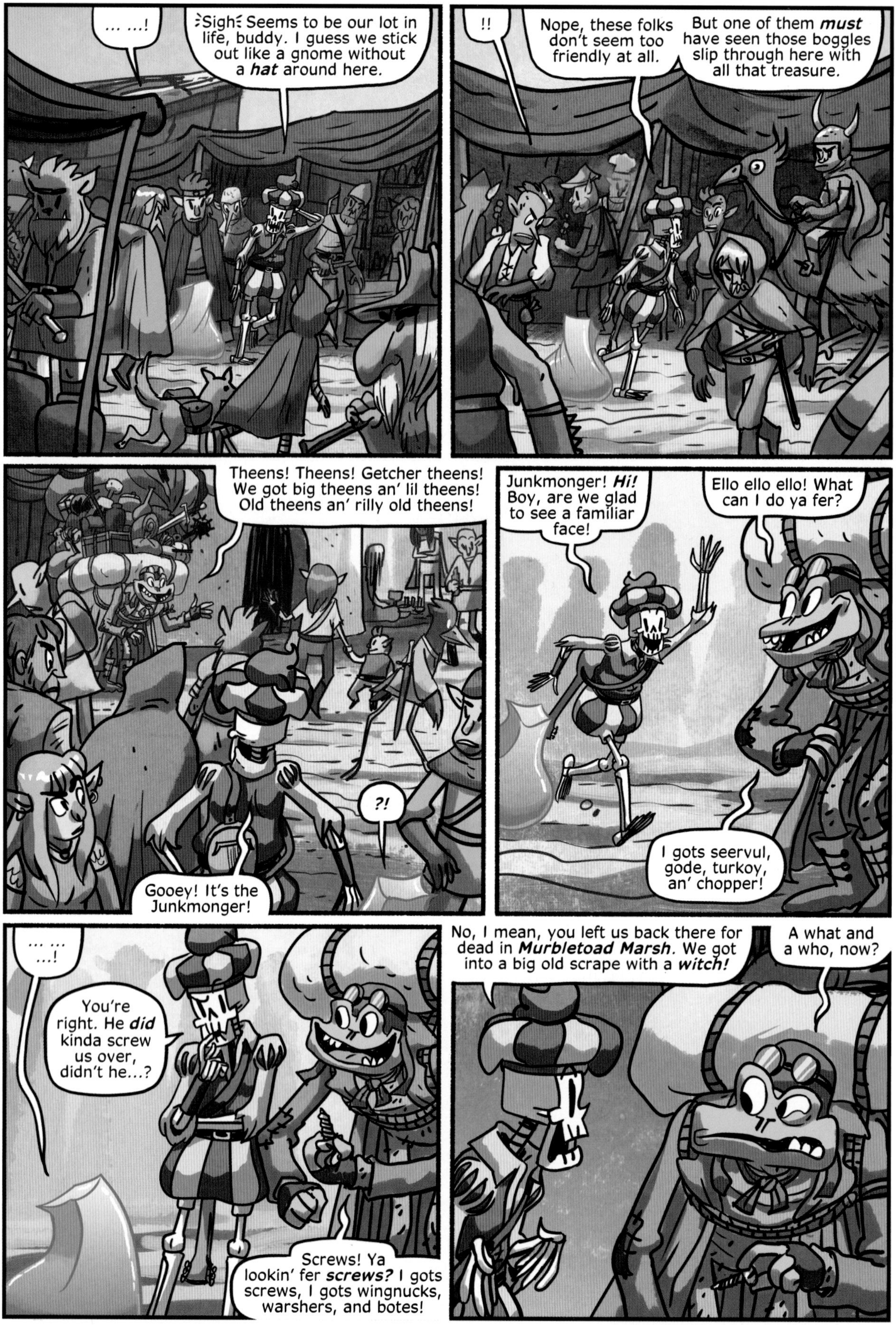
... ...!
⋛Sigh⋚ Seems to be our lot in life, buddy. I guess we stick out like a gnome without a *hat* around here.
!!
Nope, these folks don't seem too friendly at all.
But one of them *must* have seen those boggles slip through here with all that treasure.
Theens! Theens! Getcher theens! We got big theens an' lil theens! Old theens an' rilly old theens!
?!
Gooey! It's the Junkmonger!
Junkmonger! *Hi!* Boy, are we glad to see a familiar face!
Ello ello ello! What can I do ya fer?
I gots seervul, gode, turkoy, an' chopper!
... ...!
You're right. He *did* kinda screw us over, didn't he...?
Screws! Ya lookin' fer *screws?* I gots screws, I gots wingnucks, warshers, and botes!
No, I mean, you left us back there for dead in *Murbletoad Marsh*. We got into a big old scrape with a *witch!*
A what and a who, now?

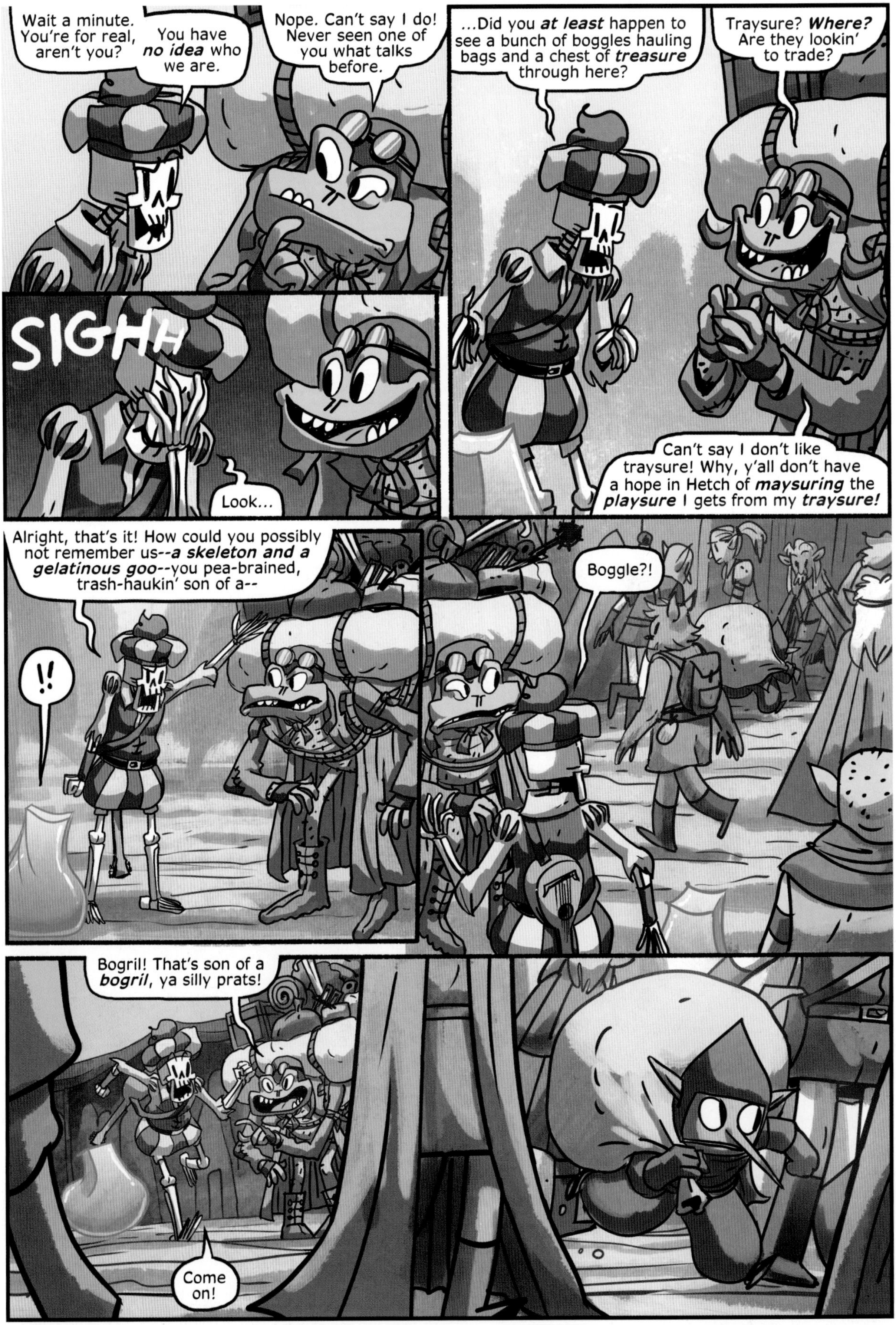
Wait a minute. You're for real, aren't you?
You have *no idea* who we are.
Nope. Can't say I do! Never seen one of you what talks before.
...Did you *at least* happen to see a bunch of boggles hauling bags and a chest of *treasure* through here?
Traysure? *Where?* Are they lookin' to trade?
SIGHH
Look...
Can't say I don't like traysure! Why, y'all don't have a hope in Hetch of *maysuring* the *playsure* I gets from my *traysure!*
Alright, that's it! How could you possibly not remember us--*a skeleton and a gelatinous goo*--you pea-brained, trash-haukin' son of a--
!!
Boggle?!
Bogril! That's son of a *bogril*, ya silly prats!
Come on!

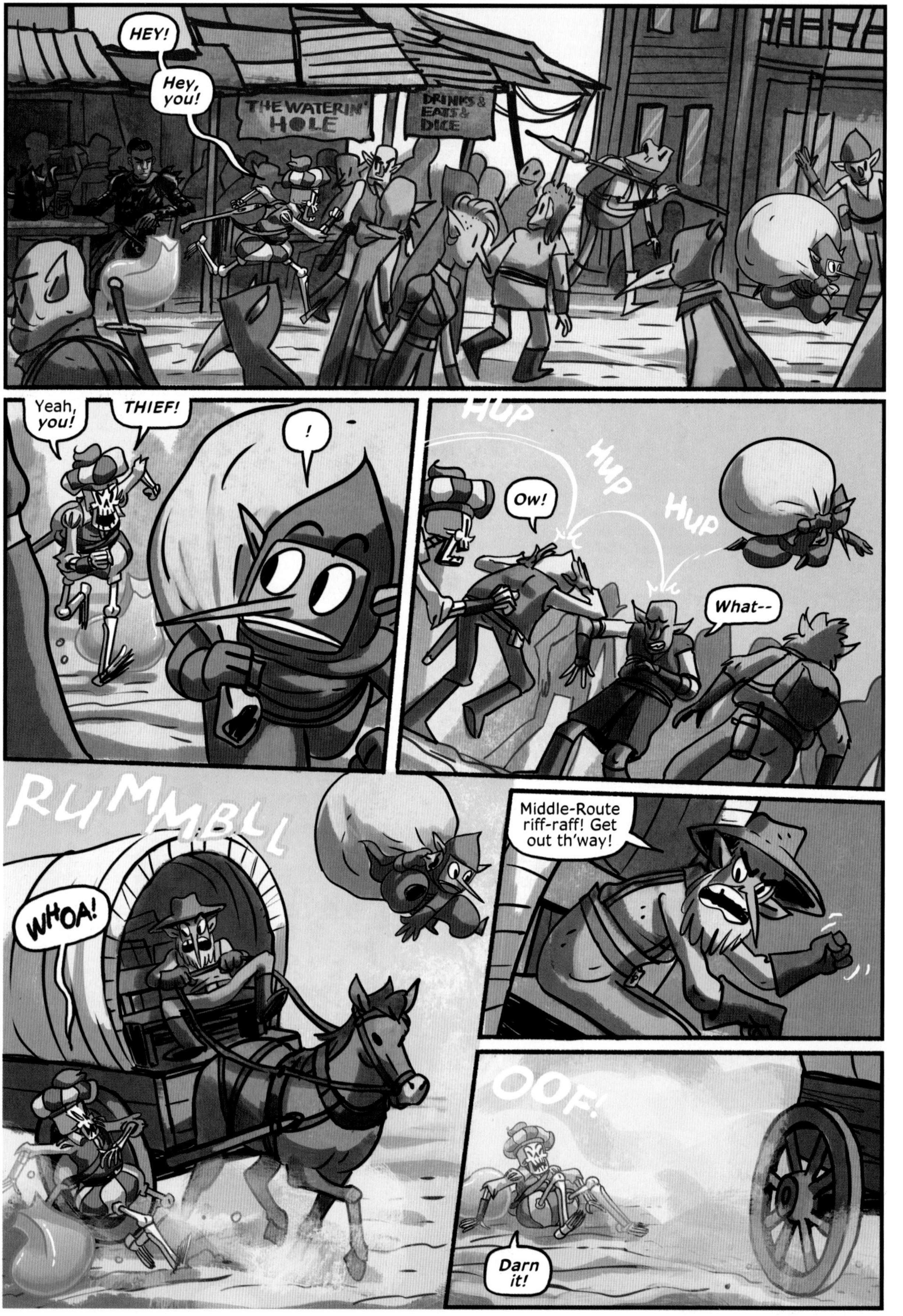
HEY!
Hey, you!
THE WATERIN' HOLE
DRINKS & EATS & DICE
Yeah, you!
THIEF!
!
HUP
HUP
HUP
Ow!
What--
RUMMMBLL
WHOA!
Middle-Route riff-raff! Get out th'way!
OOF!
Darn it!

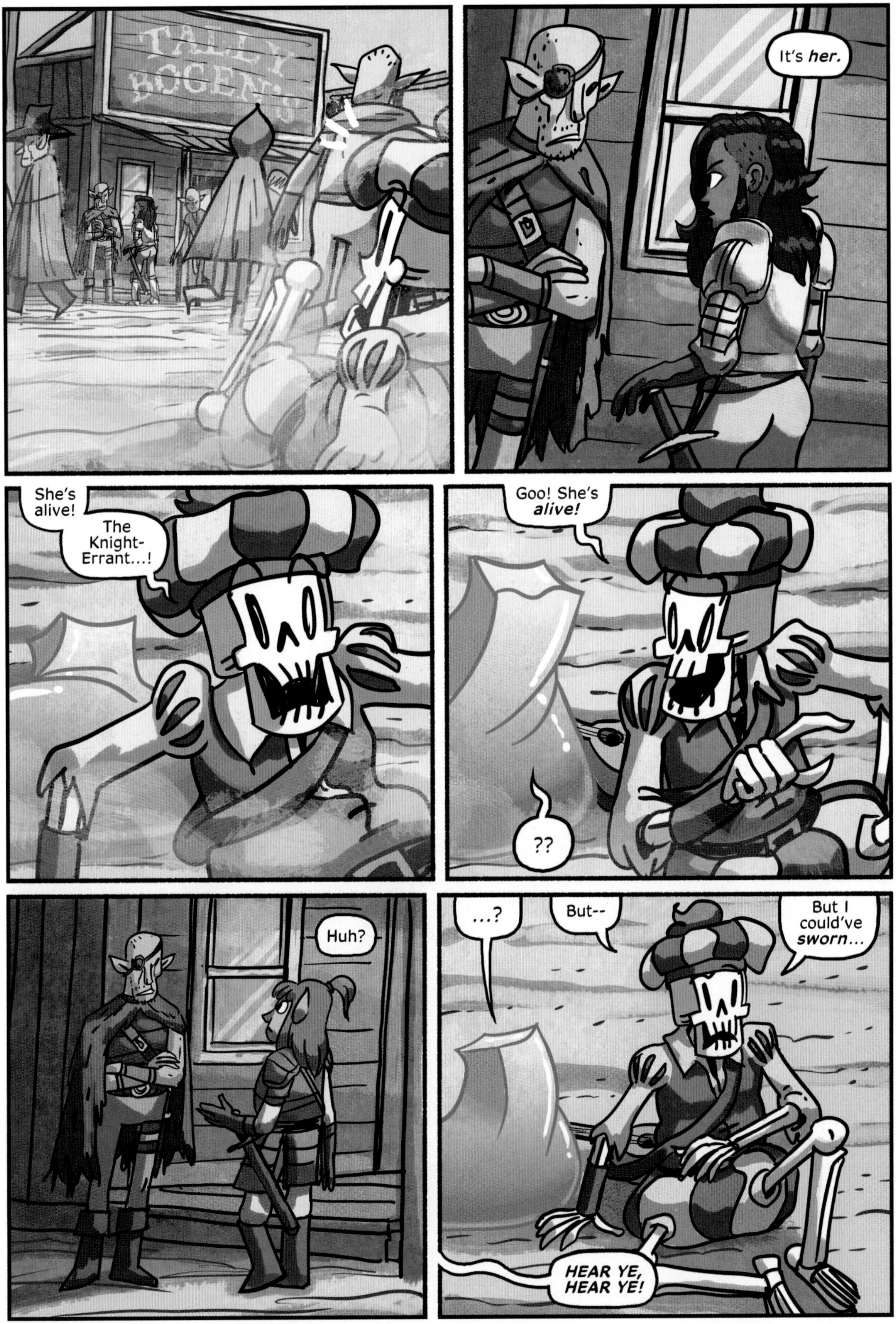
TALLY BOGEN'S
It's her.
She's alive!
The Knight-Errant...!
Goo! She's alive!
??
Huh?
...?
But--
But I could've sworn...
HEAR YE, HEAR YE!

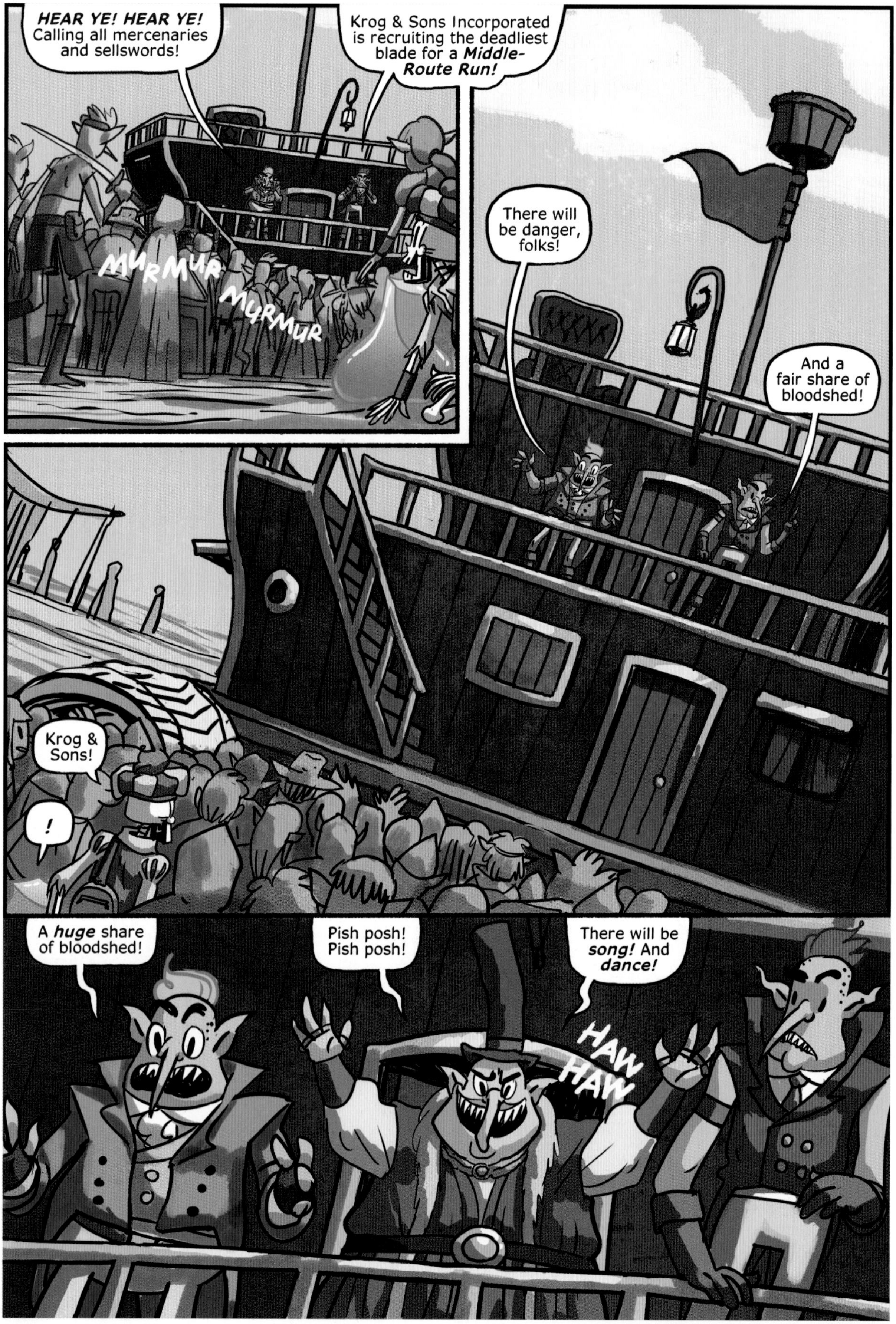
HEAR YE! HEAR YE! Calling all mercenaries and sellswords!
Krog & Sons Incorporated is recruiting the deadliest blade for a Middle-Route Run!
MURMUR MURMUR
There will be danger, folks!
And a fair share of bloodshed!
Krog & Sons!
!
A huge share of bloodshed!
Pish posh! Pish posh!
There will be song! And dance!
HAW HAW

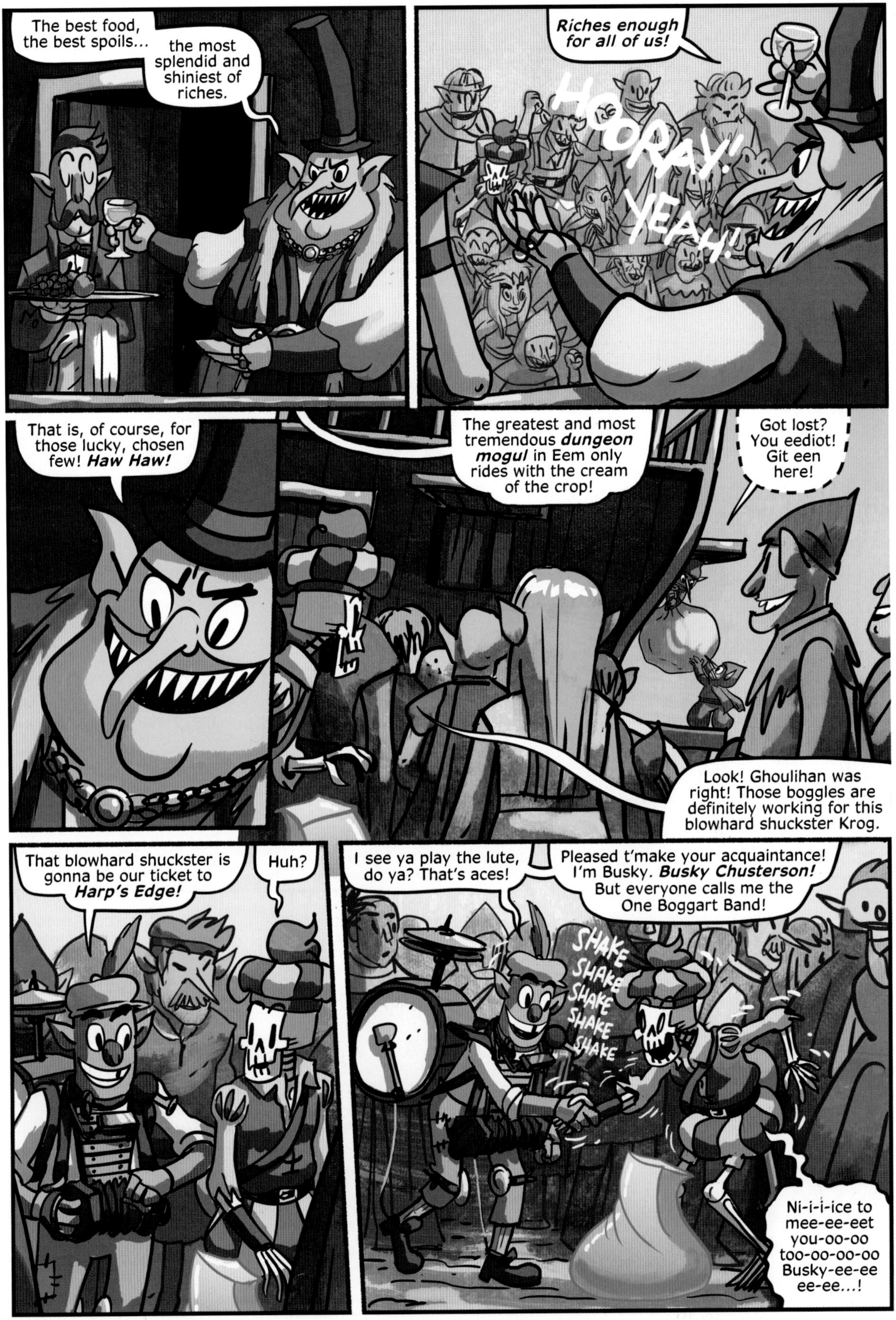

The best food, the best spoils...
the most splendid and shiniest of riches.
Riches enough for all of us!
HOORAY! YEAH! YEAH!
That is, of course, for those lucky, chosen few! Haw Haw!
The greatest and most tremendous dungeon mogul in Eem only rides with the cream of the crop!
Got lost? You eediot! Git een here!
Look! Ghoulihan was right! Those boggles are definitely working for this blowhard shuckster Krog.
That blowhard shuckster is gonna be our ticket to Harp's Edge!
Huh?
I see ya play the lute, do ya? That's aces!
Pleased t'make your acquaintance! I'm Busky. Busky Chusterson! But everyone calls me the One Boggart Band!
SHAKE SHAKE SHAKE SHAKE SHAKE
Ni-i-i-ice to mee-ee-eet you-oo-oo too-oo-oo-oo Busky-ee-ee ee-ee...!

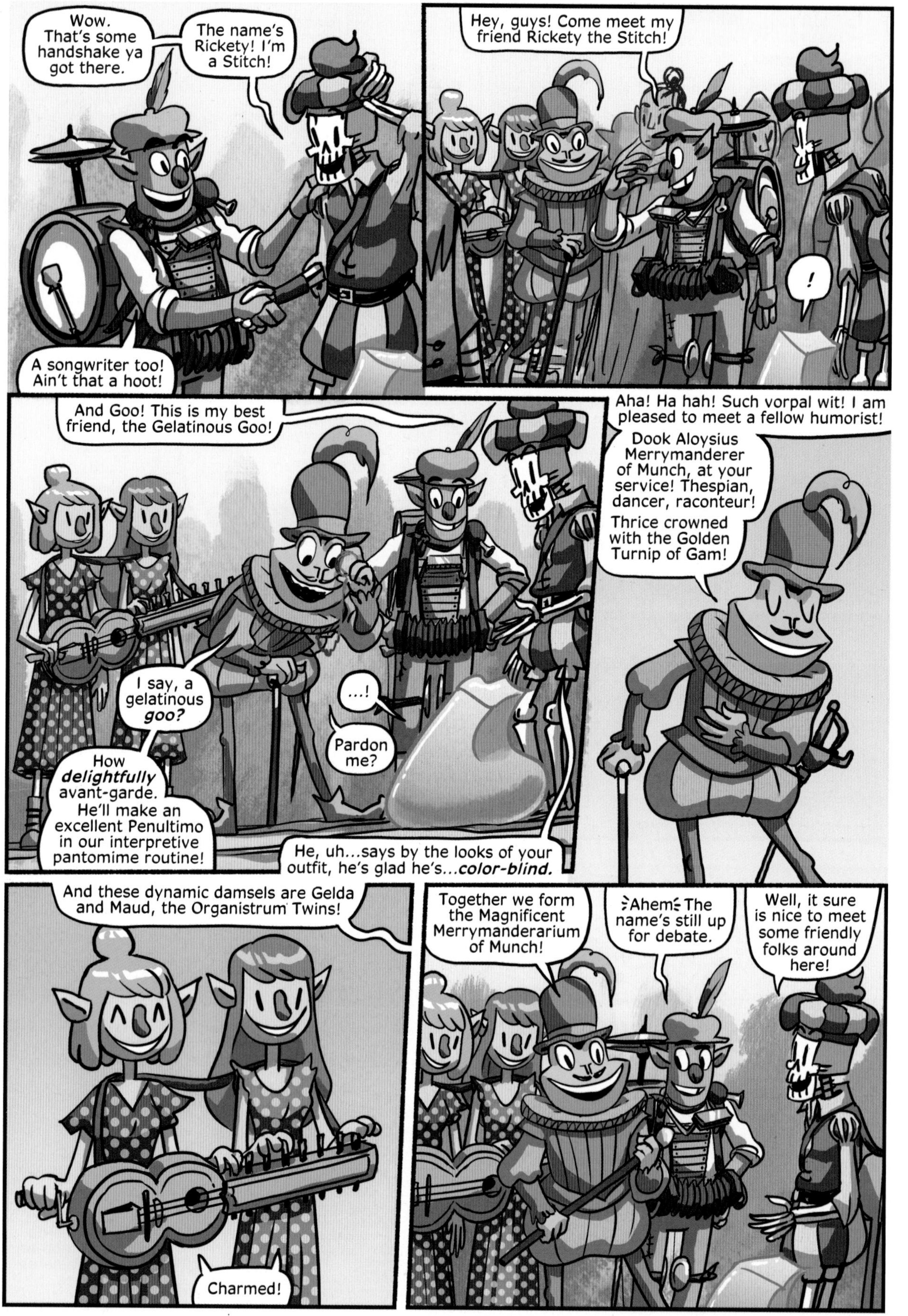

Wow. That's some handshake ya got there.
The name's Rickety! I'm a Stitch!
A songwriter too! Ain't that a hoot!
Hey, guys! Come meet my friend Rickety the Stitch!
!
And Goo! This is my best friend, the Gelatinous Goo!
I say, a gelatinous *goo?*
How *delightfully* avant-garde.
He'll make an excellent Penultimo in our interpretive pantomime routine!
...!
Pardon me?
He, uh...says by the looks of your outfit, he's glad he's...*color-blind.*
Aha! Ha hah! Such vorpal wit! I am pleased to meet a fellow humorist!
Dook Aloysius Merrymanderer of Munch, at your service! Thespian, dancer, raconteur!
Thrice crowned with the Golden Turnip of Gam!
And these dynamic damsels are Gelda and Maud, the Organistrum Twins!
Charmed!
Together we form the Magnificent Merrymanderarium of Munch!
Ahem The name's still up for debate.
Well, it sure is nice to meet some friendly folks around here!

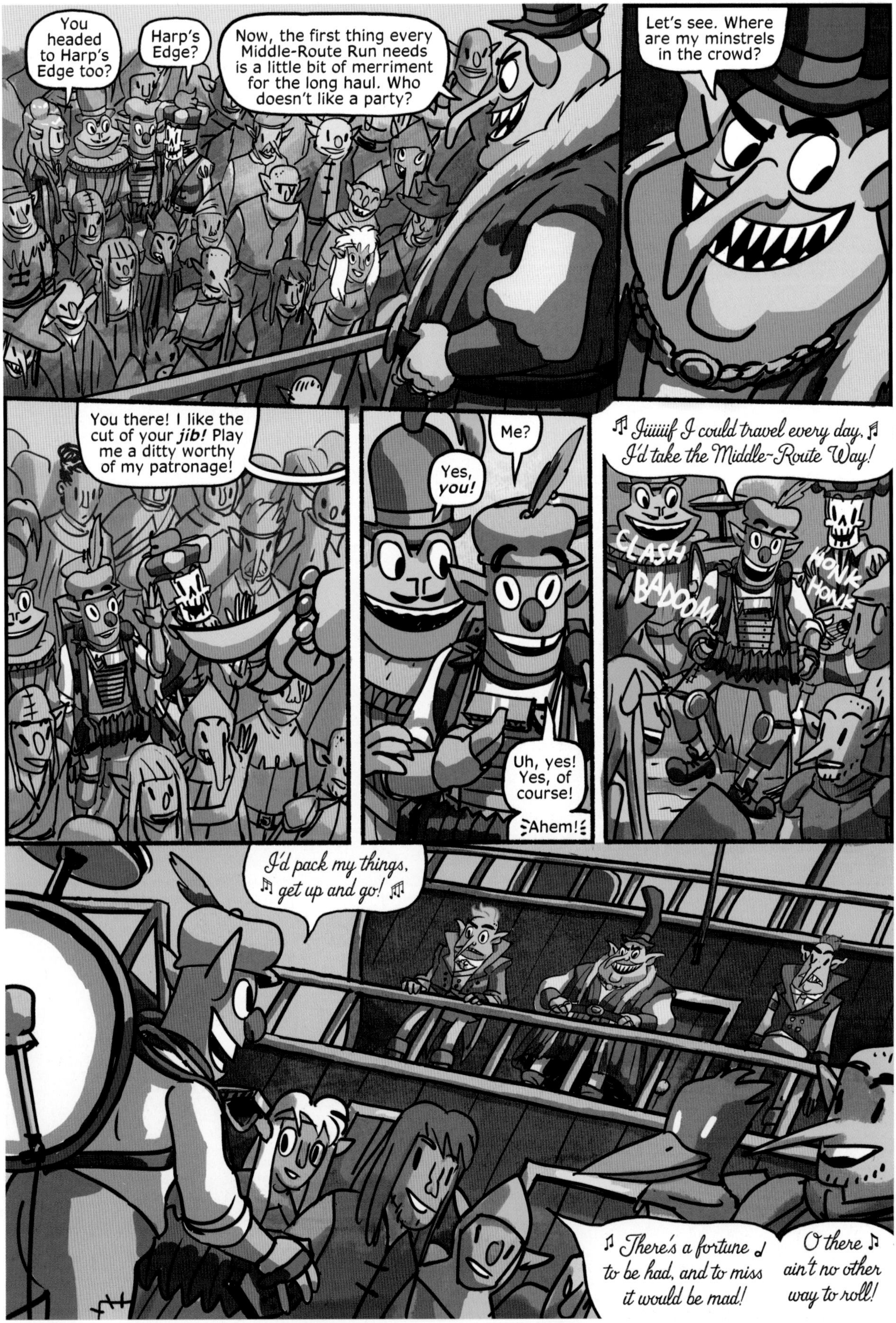
You headed to Harp's Edge too?
Harp's Edge?
Now, the first thing every Middle-Route Run needs is a little bit of merriment for the long haul. Who doesn't like a party?
Let's see. Where are my minstrels in the crowd?
You there! I like the cut of your *jib!* Play me a ditty worthy of my patronage!
Me?
Yes, *you!*
Uh, yes! Yes, of course!
Ahem!
♫ Iiiiiif I could travel every day, ♫ I'd take the Middle-Route Way!
CLASH
BADOOM
HONK HONK
I'd pack my things, ♫ get up and go! ♫
♪ There's a fortune ♩ to be had, and to miss it would be mad!
O there ♪ ain't no other way to roll!

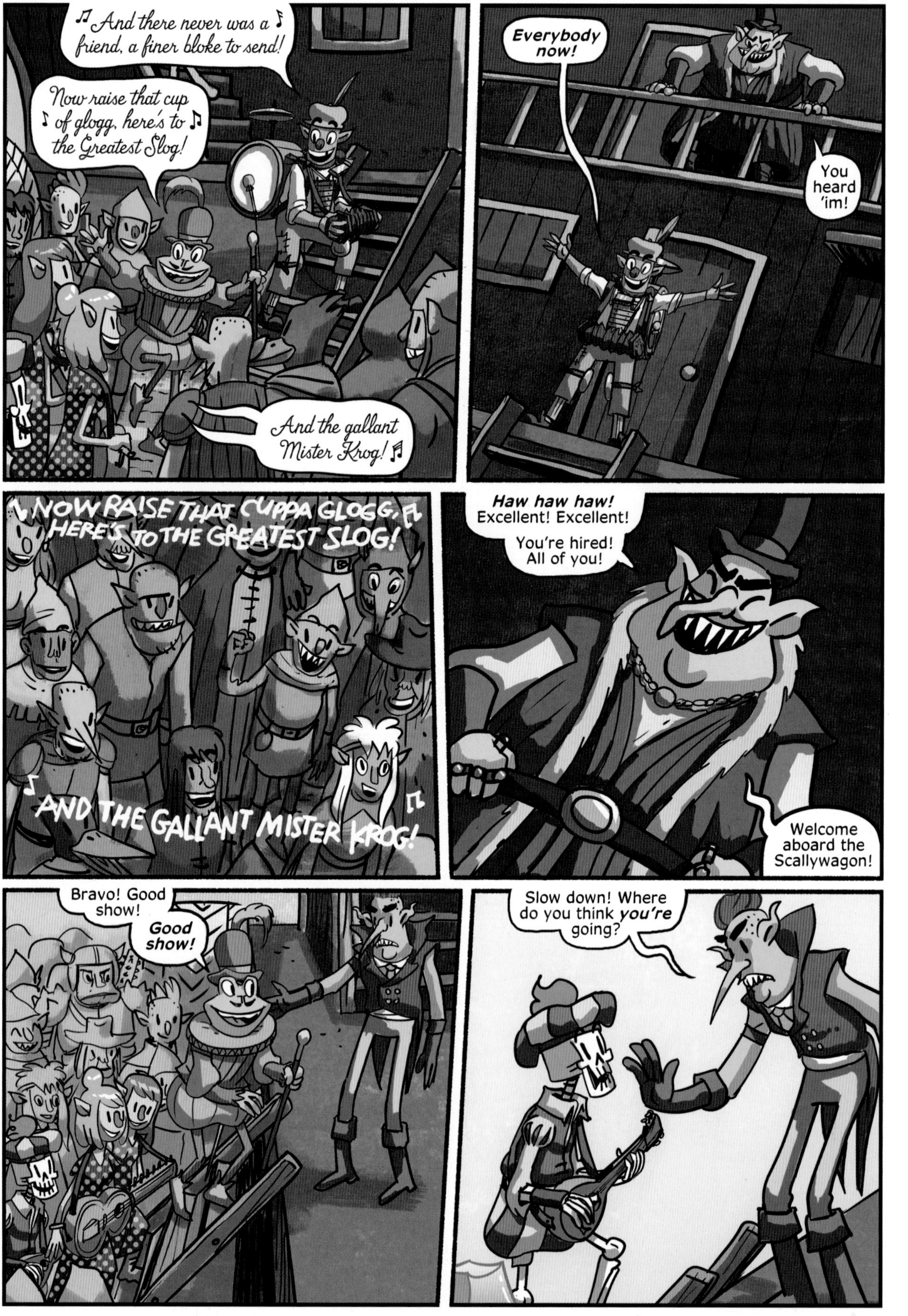

♫ And there never was a ♪ friend, a finer bloke to send!
Now raise that cup ♪ of glogg, here's to ♫ the Greatest Slog!
And the gallant Mister Krog! ♬
Everybody now!
You heard 'im!
NOW RAISE THAT CUPPA GLOGG, HERE'S TO THE GREATEST SLOG!
AND THE GALLANT MISTER KROG!
Haw haw haw! Excellent! Excellent!
You're hired! All of you!
Welcome aboard the Scallywagon!
Bravo! Good show!
Good show!
Slow down! Where do you think you're going?

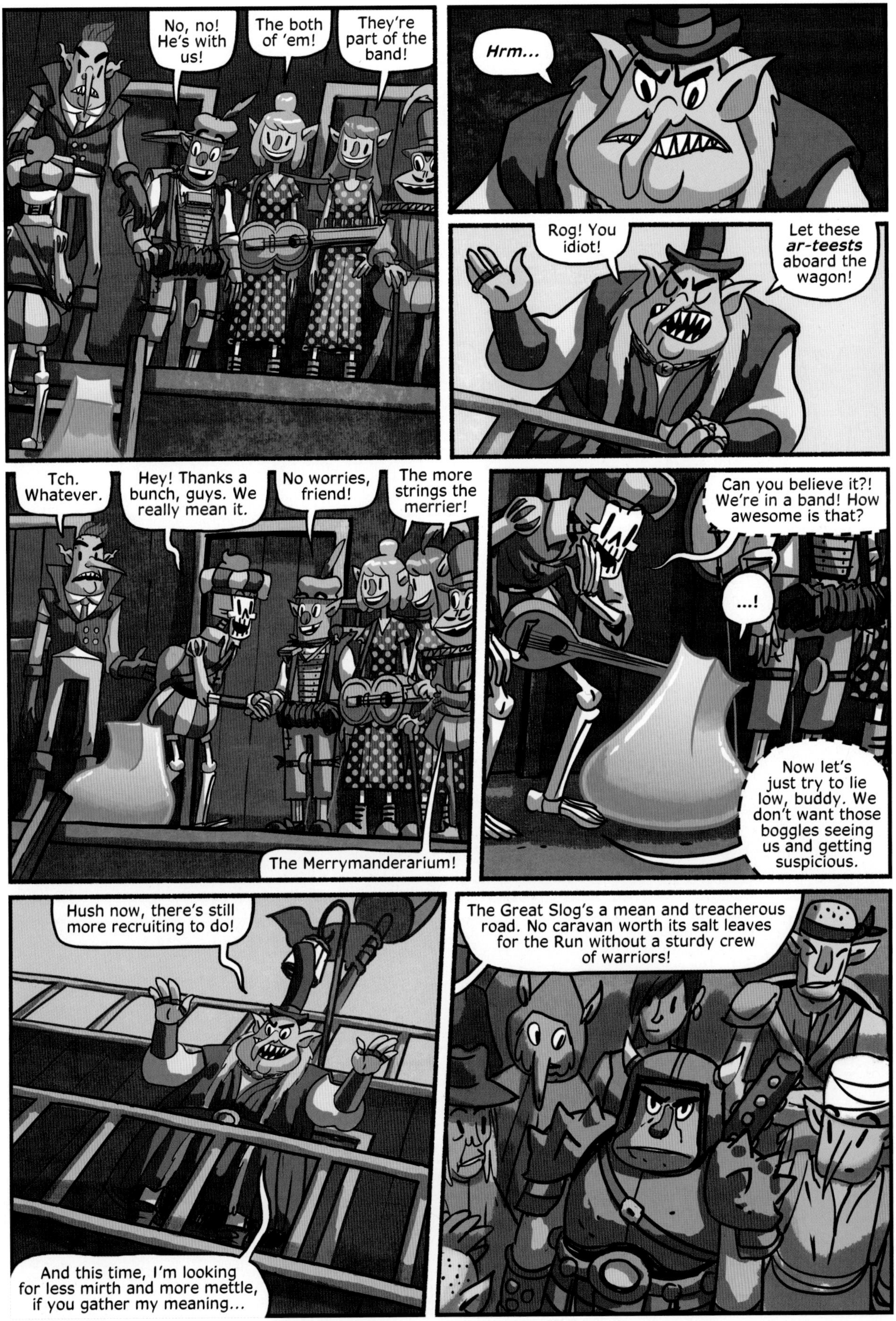

No, no! He's with us!
The both of 'em!
They're part of the band!
Hrm...
Rog! You idiot!
Let these ***ar-teests*** aboard the wagon!
Tch. Whatever.
Hey! Thanks a bunch, guys. We really mean it.
No worries, friend!
The more strings the merrier!
The Merrymanderarium!
Can you believe it?! We're in a band! How awesome is that?
...!
Now let's just try to lie low, buddy. We don't want those boggles seeing us and getting suspicious.
Hush now, there's still more recruiting to do!
And this time, I'm looking for less mirth and more mettle, if you gather my meaning...
The Great Slog's a mean and treacherous road. No caravan worth its salt leaves for the Run without a sturdy crew of warriors!

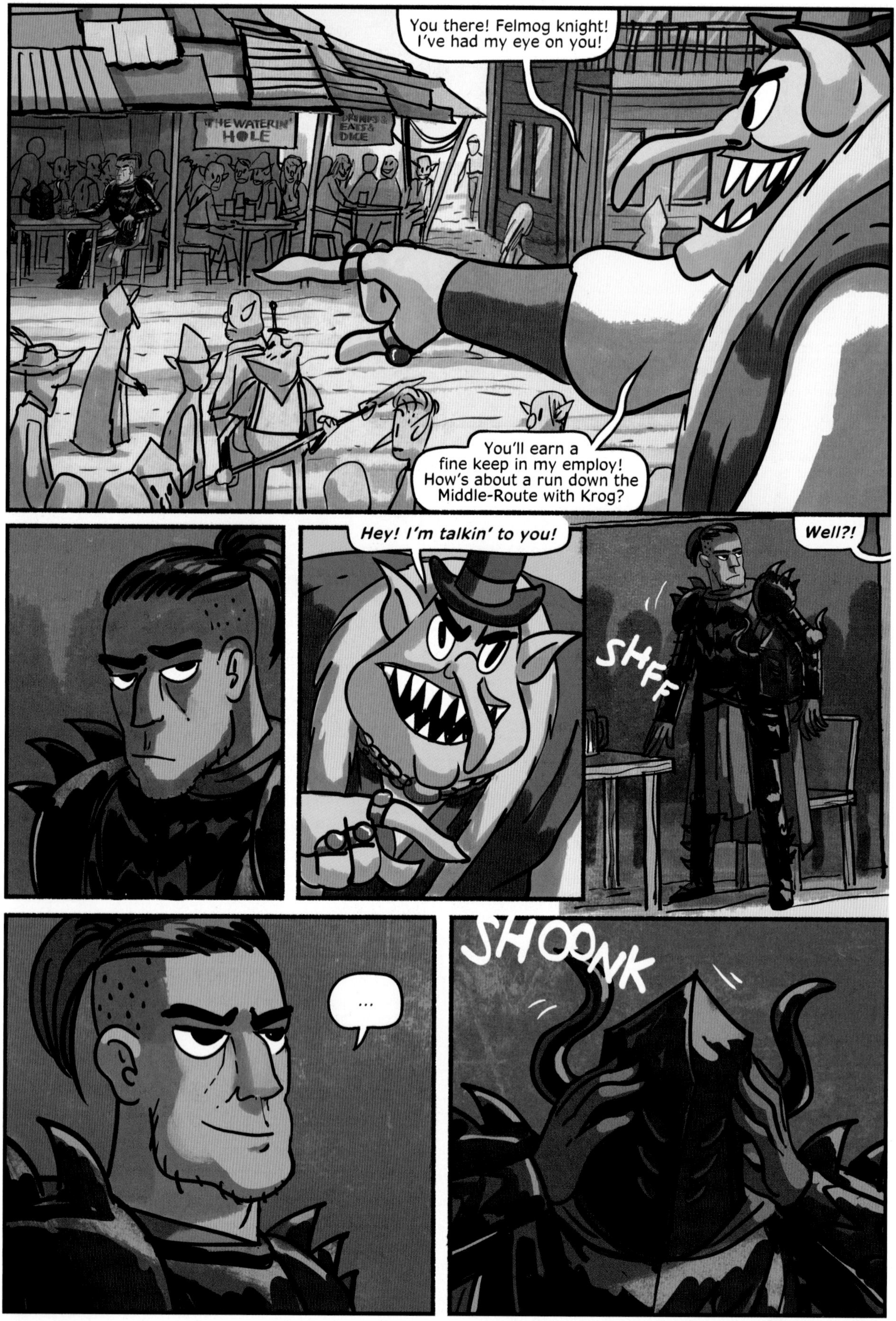
THE WATERIN' HOLE
DRINKS & EATS & DICE
You there! Felmog knight! I've had my eye on you!
You'll earn a fine keep in my employ! How's about a run down the Middle-Route with Krog?
Hey! I'm talkin' to you!
Well?!
SHFF
...
SHOONK

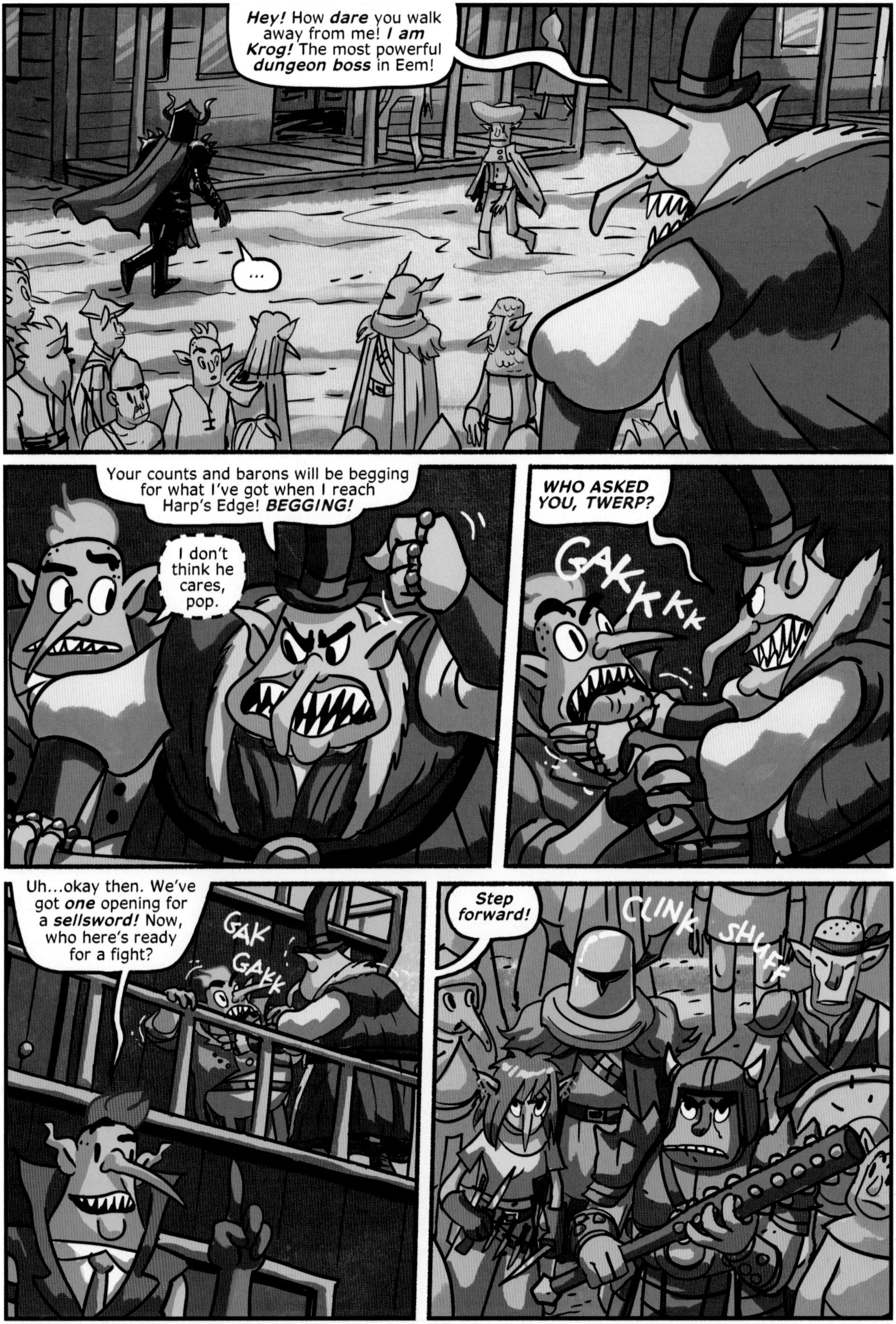
Hey! How dare you walk away from me! I am Krog! The most powerful dungeon boss in Eem!
...
Your counts and barons will be begging for what I've got when I reach Harp's Edge! BEGGING!
I don't think he cares, pop.
WHO ASKED YOU, TWERP?
GAKKKKK
Uh...okay then. We've got one opening for a sellsword! Now, who here's ready for a fight?
GAK GAKK
Step forward!
CLINK SHUFF

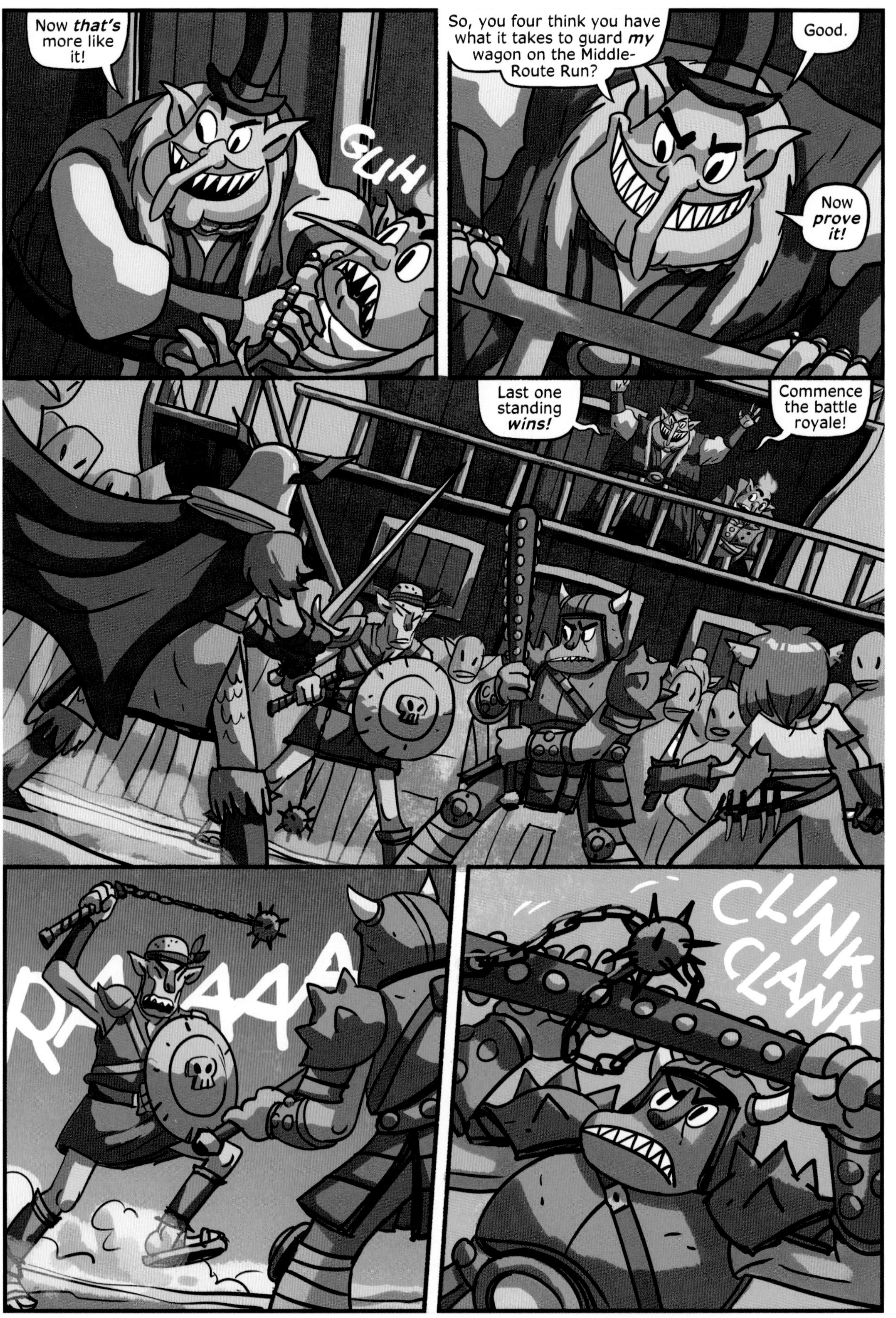
Now *that's* more like it!
GUH
So, you four think you have what it takes to guard *my* wagon on the Middle-Route Run?
Good.
Now *prove it!*
Last one standing *wins!*
Commence the battle royale!
CLINK CLANK

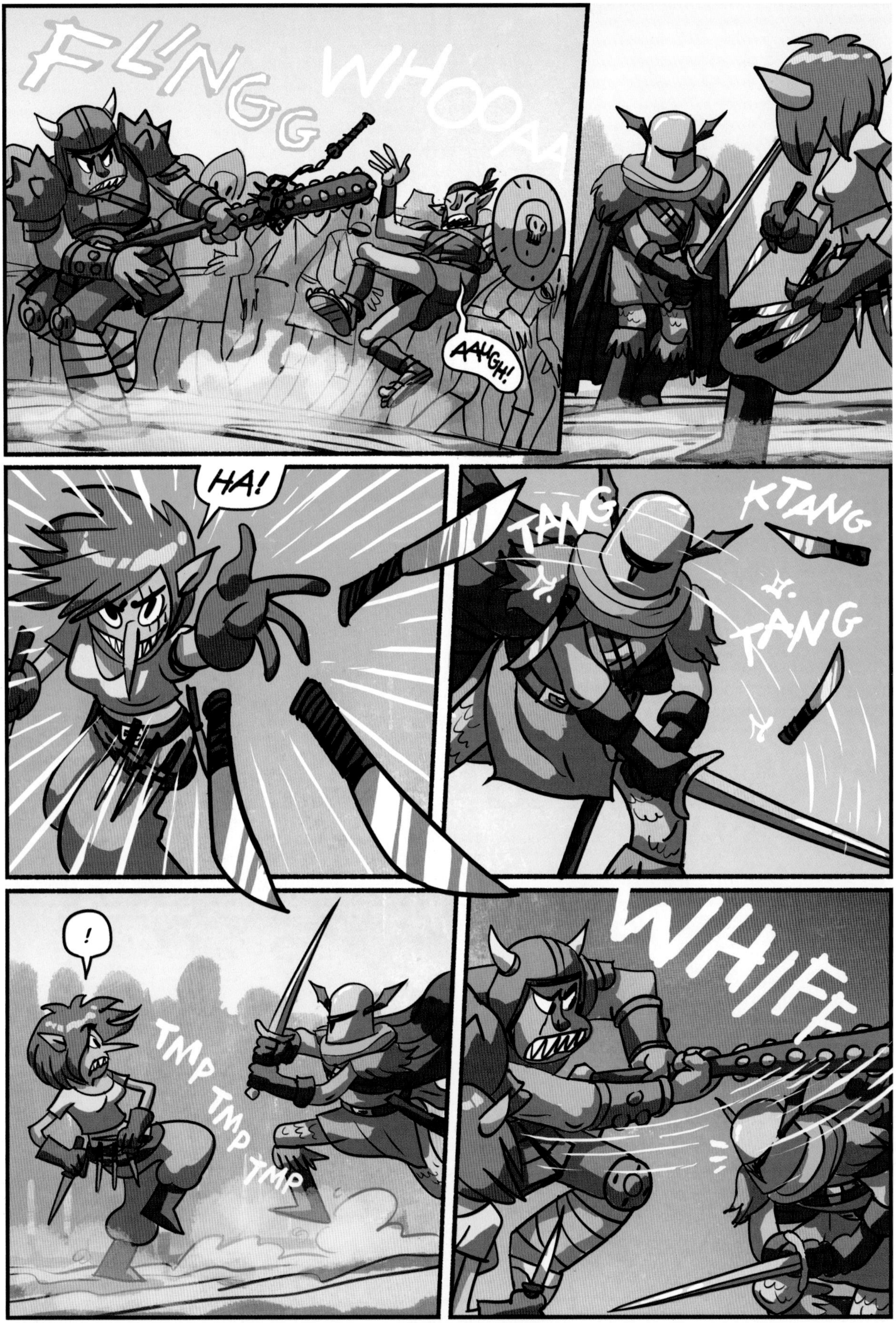

FLINGG
WHOOAA
AAUGH!
HA!
TANG
KTANG
TANG
!
TMP TMP TMP TMP
WHIFF

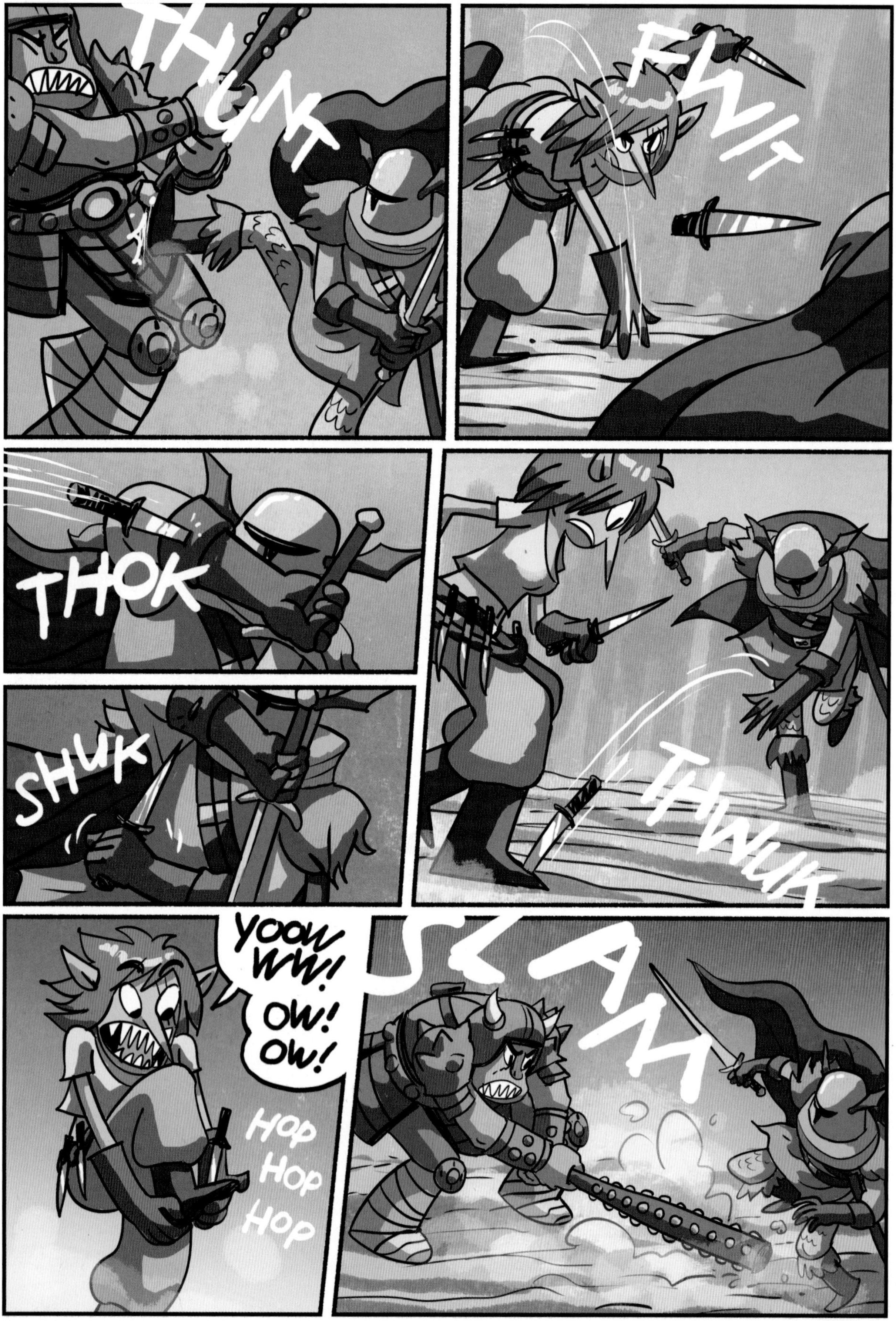
THUNK
FWIT
THOK
SHUK
THWUK
YOOWWW! OW! OW!
HOP
HOP
HOP
SKAM

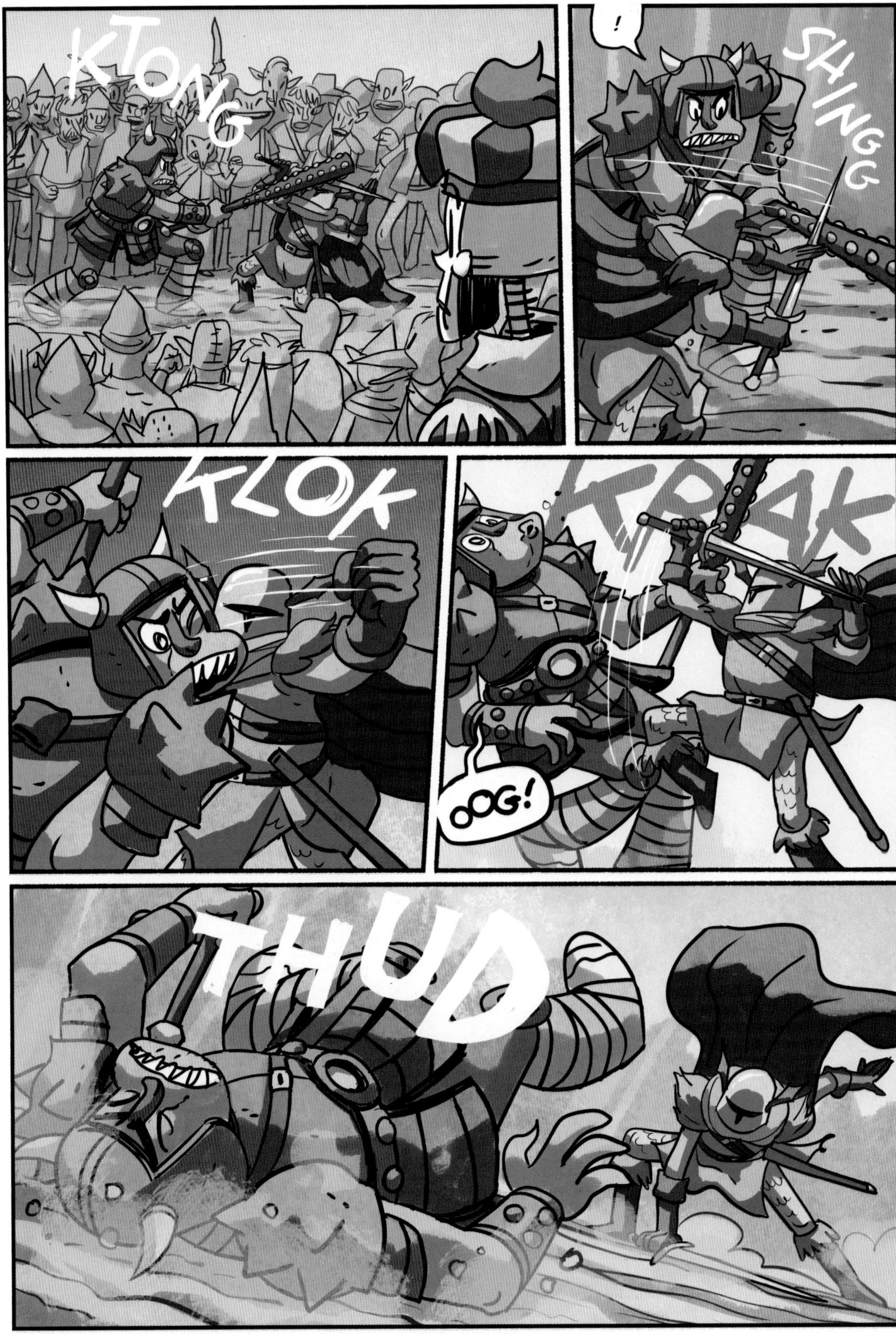
KTONG
!
SHINGG
KLOK
KRAK
OOG!
THUD

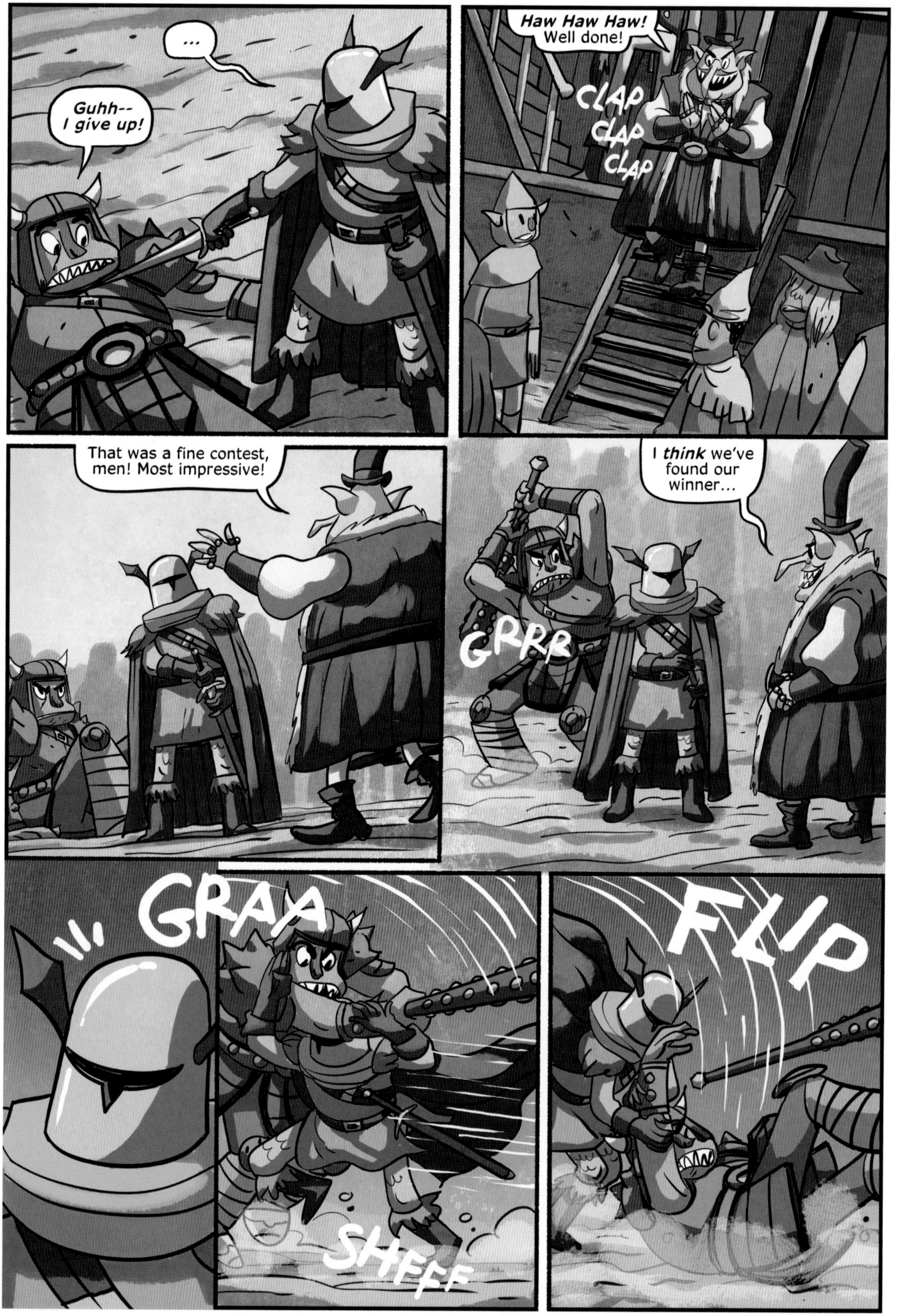
Guhh--
I give up!
...
Haw Haw Haw!
Well done!
CLAP
CLAP
CLAP
That was a fine contest, men! Most impressive!
I *think* we've found our winner...
GRRR
GRAA
SHFFF
FLIP

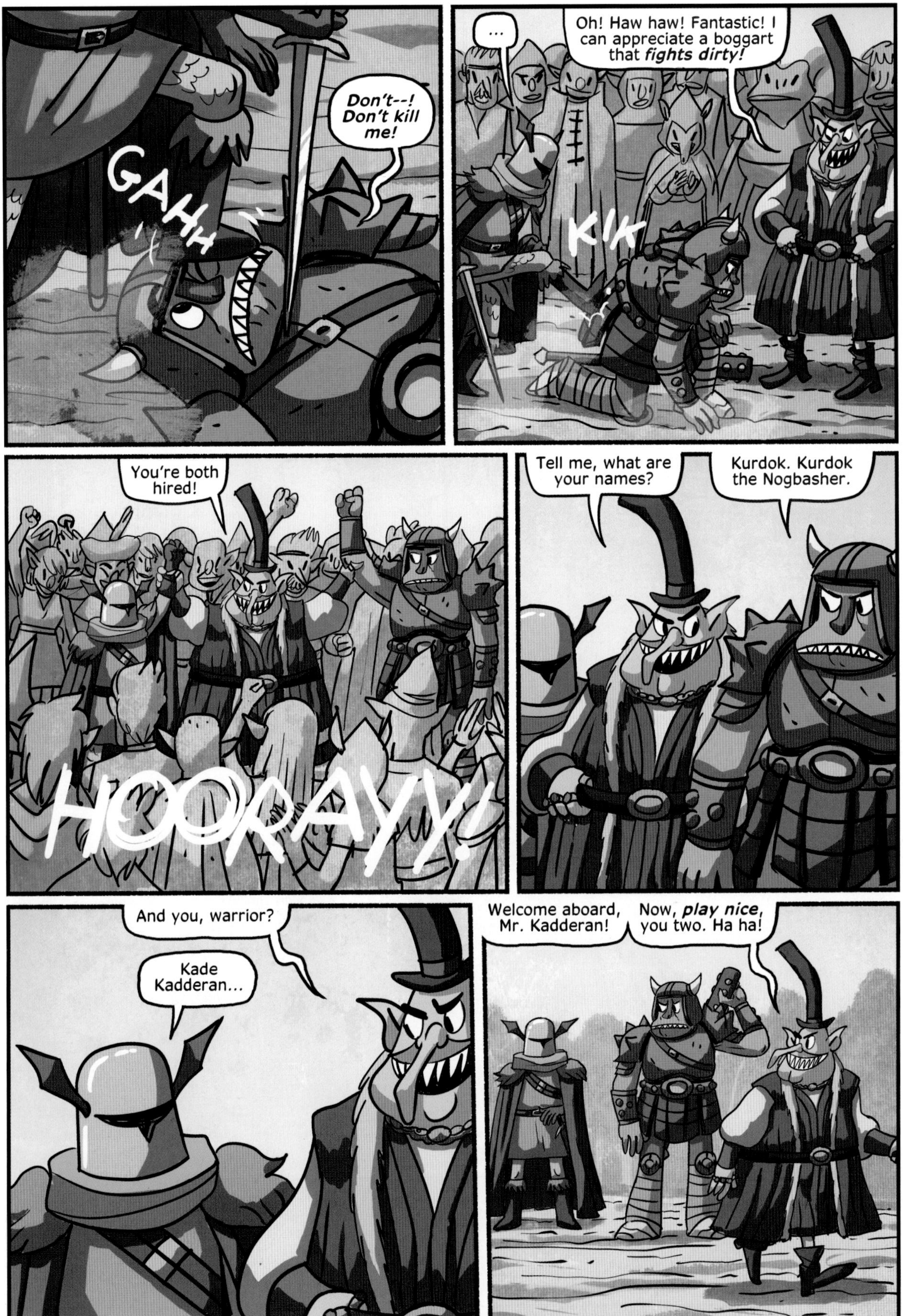
GAHH
Don't--! Don't kill me!
...
Oh! Haw haw! Fantastic! I can appreciate a boggart that *fights dirty!*
KIK
You're both hired!
HOORAYY!
Tell me, what are your names?
Kurdok. Kurdok the Nogbasher.
And you, warrior?
Kade Kadderan...
Welcome aboard, Mr. Kadderan!
Now, *play nice*, you two. Ha ha!

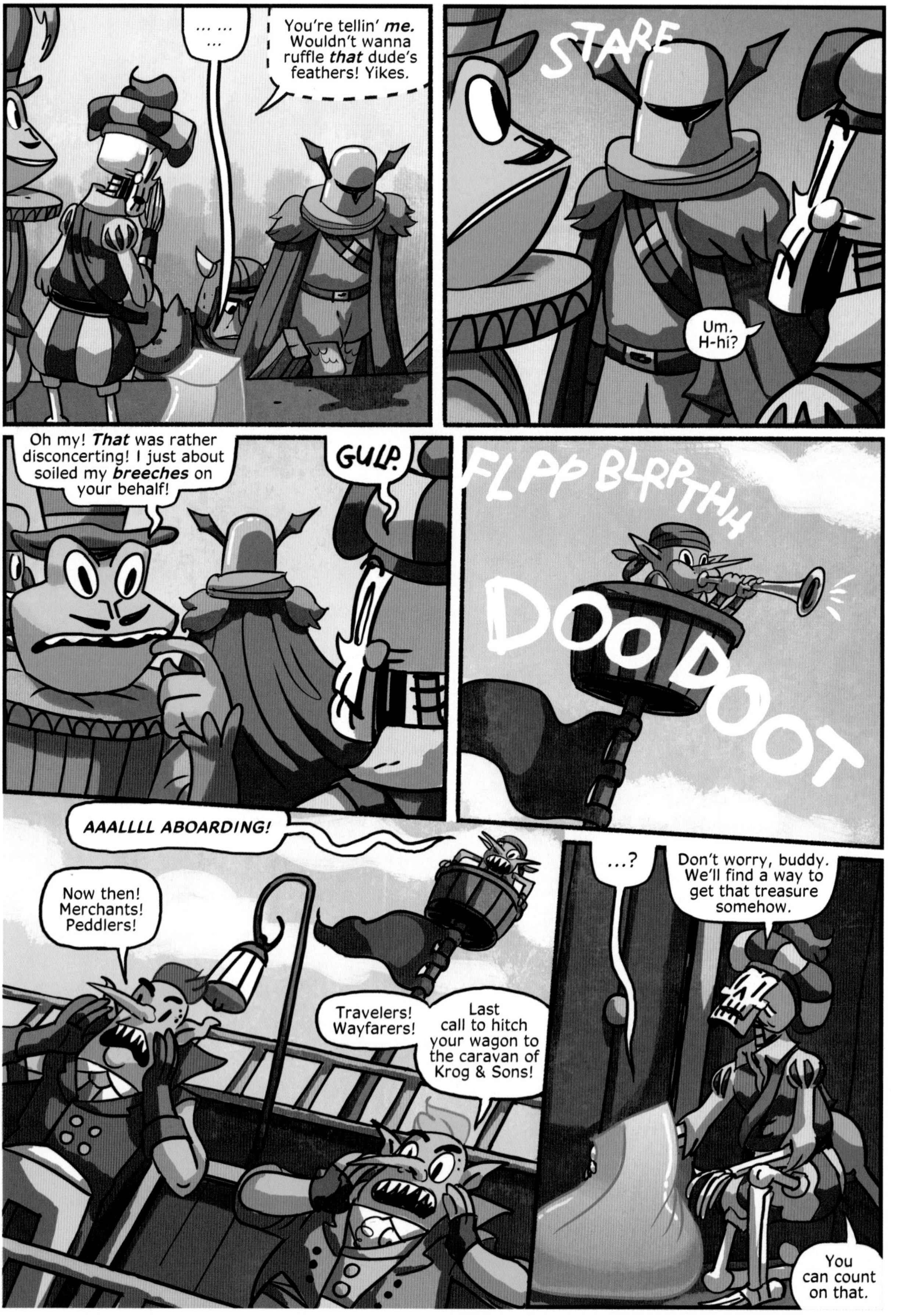

... ...
You're tellin' *me.* Wouldn't wanna ruffle *that* dude's feathers! Yikes.
STARE
Um. H-hi?
Oh my! *That* was rather disconcerting! I just about soiled my *breeches* on your behalf!
GULP.
FLPP BLRPTHH
DOO DOOT
AAALLLL ABOARDING!
Now then! Merchants! Peddlers!
Travelers! Wayfarers!
Last call to hitch your wagon to the caravan of Krog & Sons!
...?
Don't worry, buddy. We'll find a way to get that treasure somehow.
You can count on that.

Chapter 6
Rollin' Down the Road

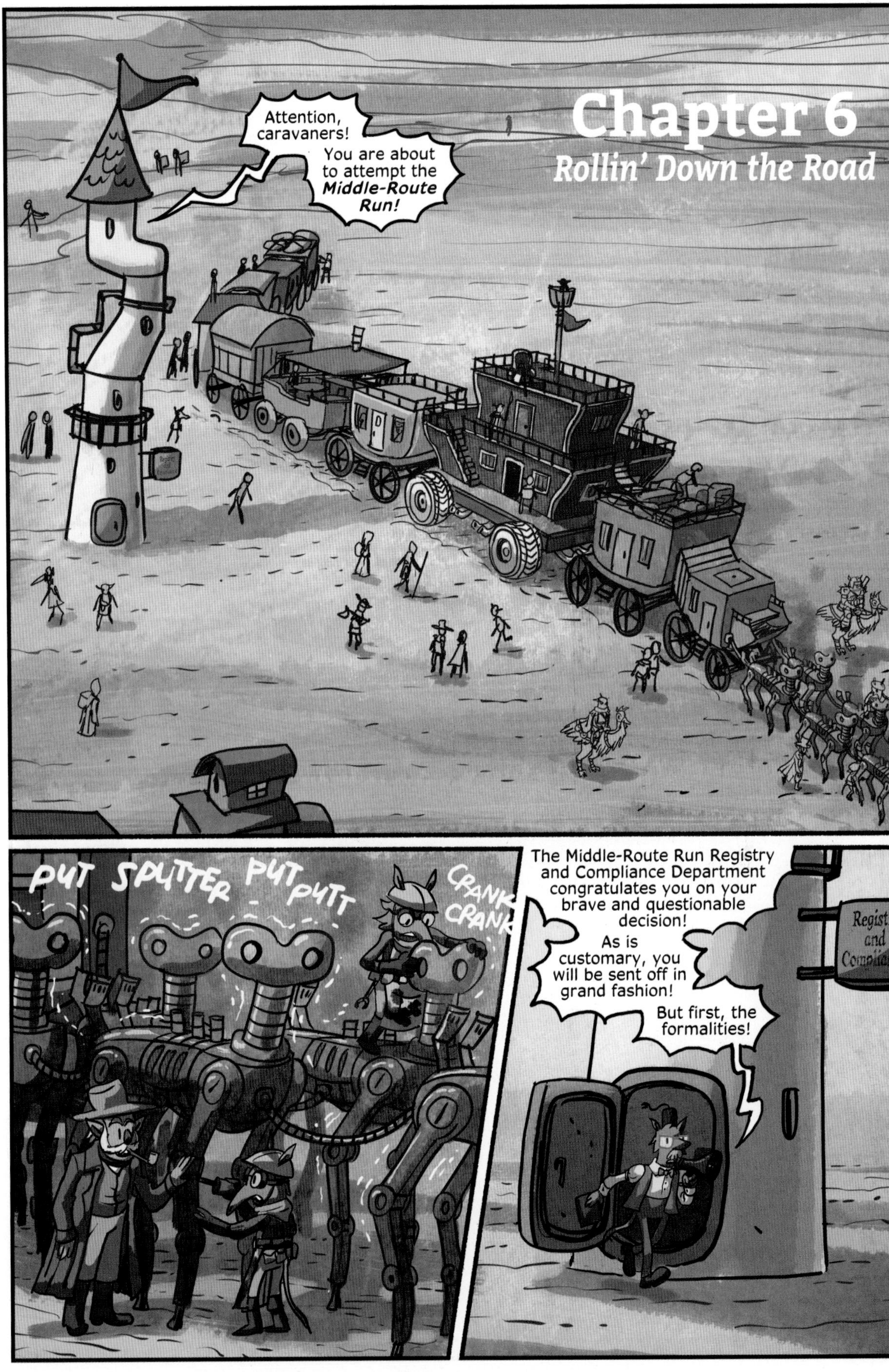
Attention, caravaners!
You are about to attempt the *Middle-Route Run!*
PUT SPLUTTER PUT PUTT
CRANK CRANK
The Middle-Route Run Registry and Compliance Department congratulates you on your brave and questionable decision!
As is customary, you will be sent off in grand fashion!
But first, the formalities!
Registry and Compliance

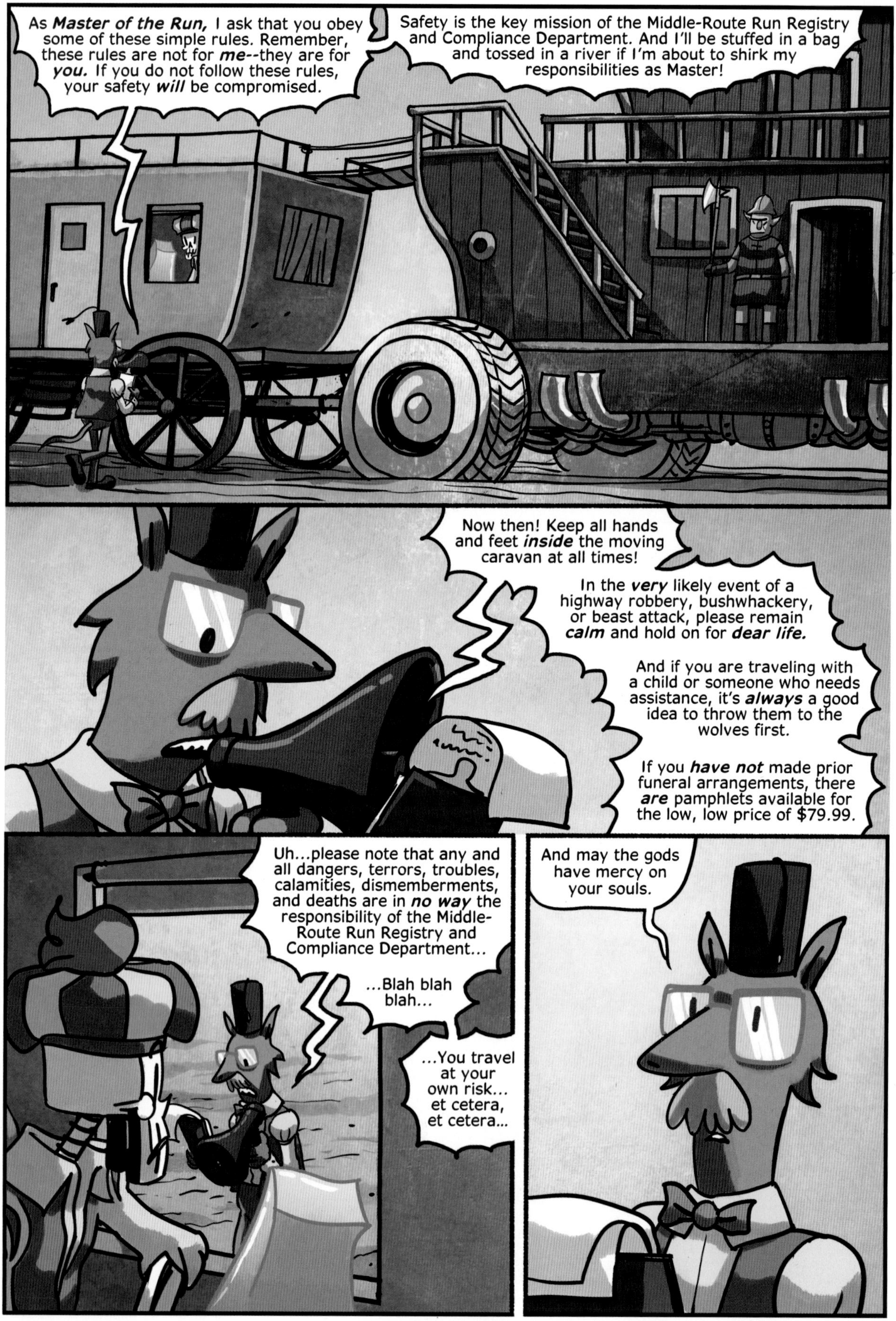

As *Master of the Run,* I ask that you obey some of these simple rules. Remember, these rules are not for *me*--they are for *you.* If you do not follow these rules, your safety *will* be compromised.
Safety is the key mission of the Middle-Route Run Registry and Compliance Department. And I'll be stuffed in a bag and tossed in a river if I'm about to shirk my responsibilities as Master!
Now then! Keep all hands and feet *inside* the moving caravan at all times!
In the *very* likely event of a highway robbery, bushwhackery, or beast attack, please remain *calm* and hold on for *dear life.*
And if you are traveling with a child or someone who needs assistance, it's *always* a good idea to throw them to the wolves first.
If you *have not* made prior funeral arrangements, there *are* pamphlets available for the low, low price of $79.99.
Uh...please note that any and all dangers, terrors, troubles, calamities, dismemberments, and deaths are in *no way* the responsibility of the Middle-Route Run Registry and Compliance Department...
...Blah blah blah...
...You travel at your own risk... et cetera, et cetera...
And may the gods have mercy on your souls.

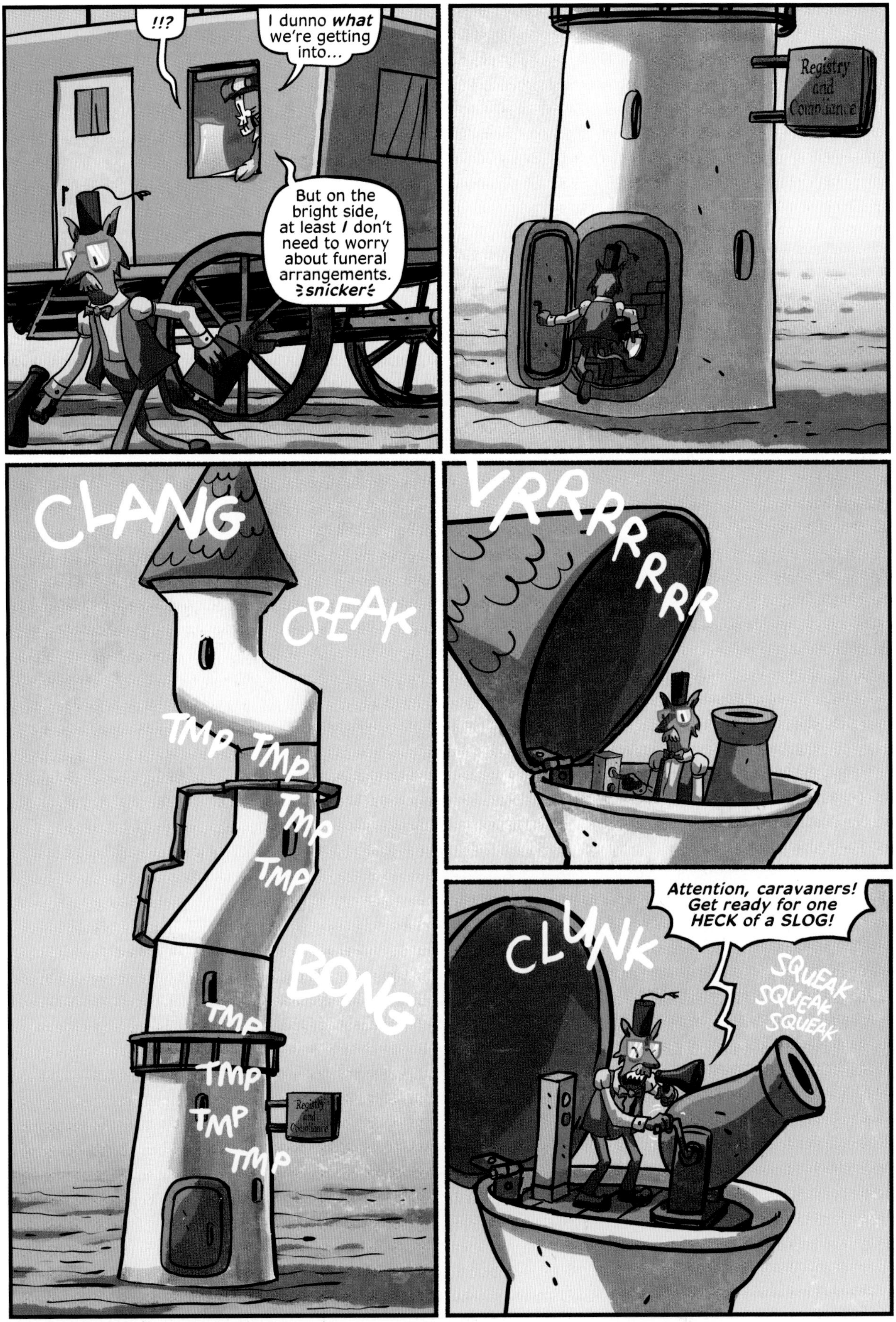
!!?
I dunno *what* we're getting into...
But on the bright side, at least *I* don't need to worry about funeral arrangements. *snicker*
Registry and Compliance
CLANG
CREAK
TMP TMP TMP TMP
BONG
TMP TMP TMP TMP
Registry and Compliance
VRRRRRRRR
CLUNK
Attention, caravaners! Get ready for one HECK of a SLOG!
SQUEAK SQUEAK SQUEAK

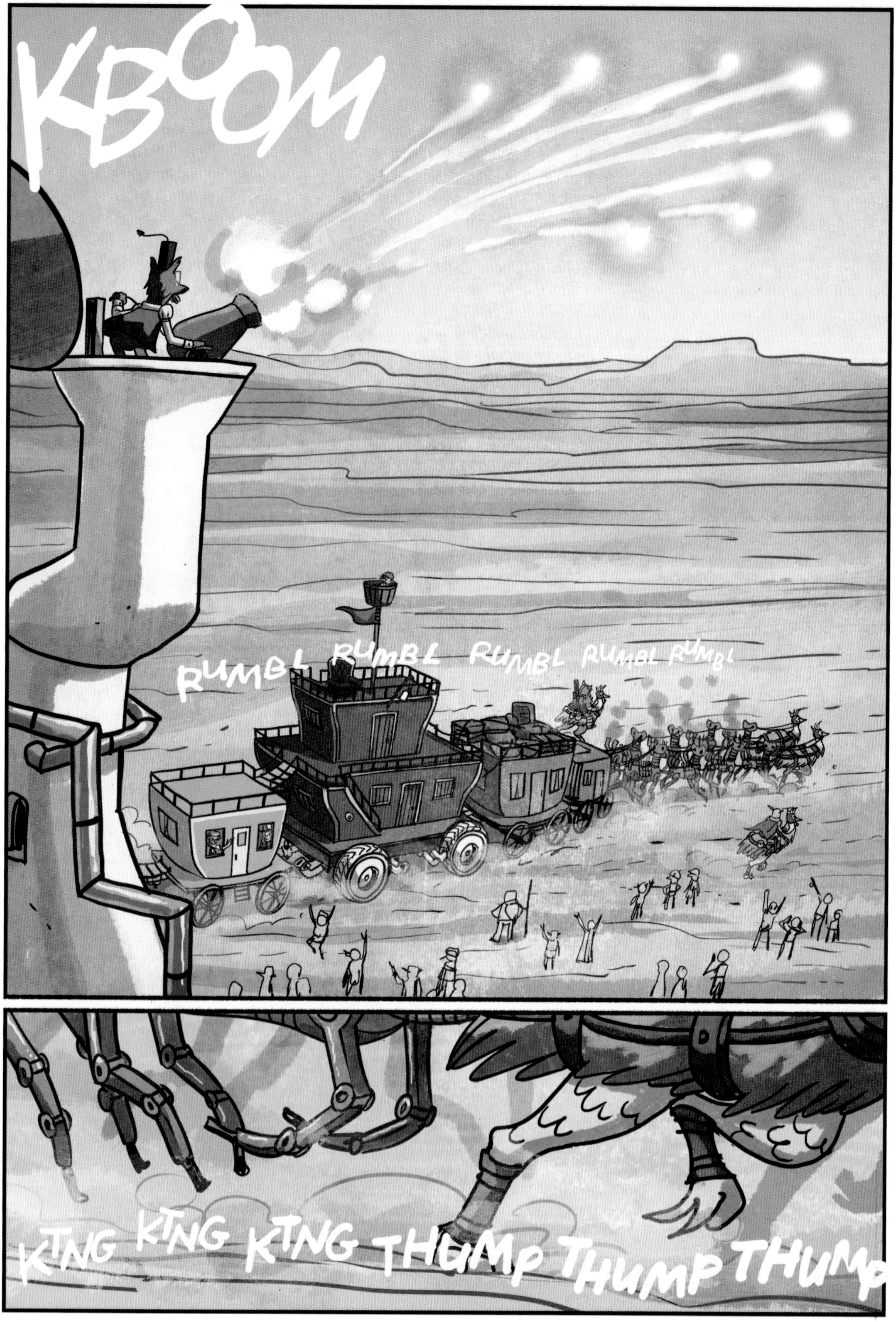
KBOOOM
RUMBL RUMBL RUMBL RUMBL RUMBL
KTNG KTNG KTNG THUMP THUMP THUMP

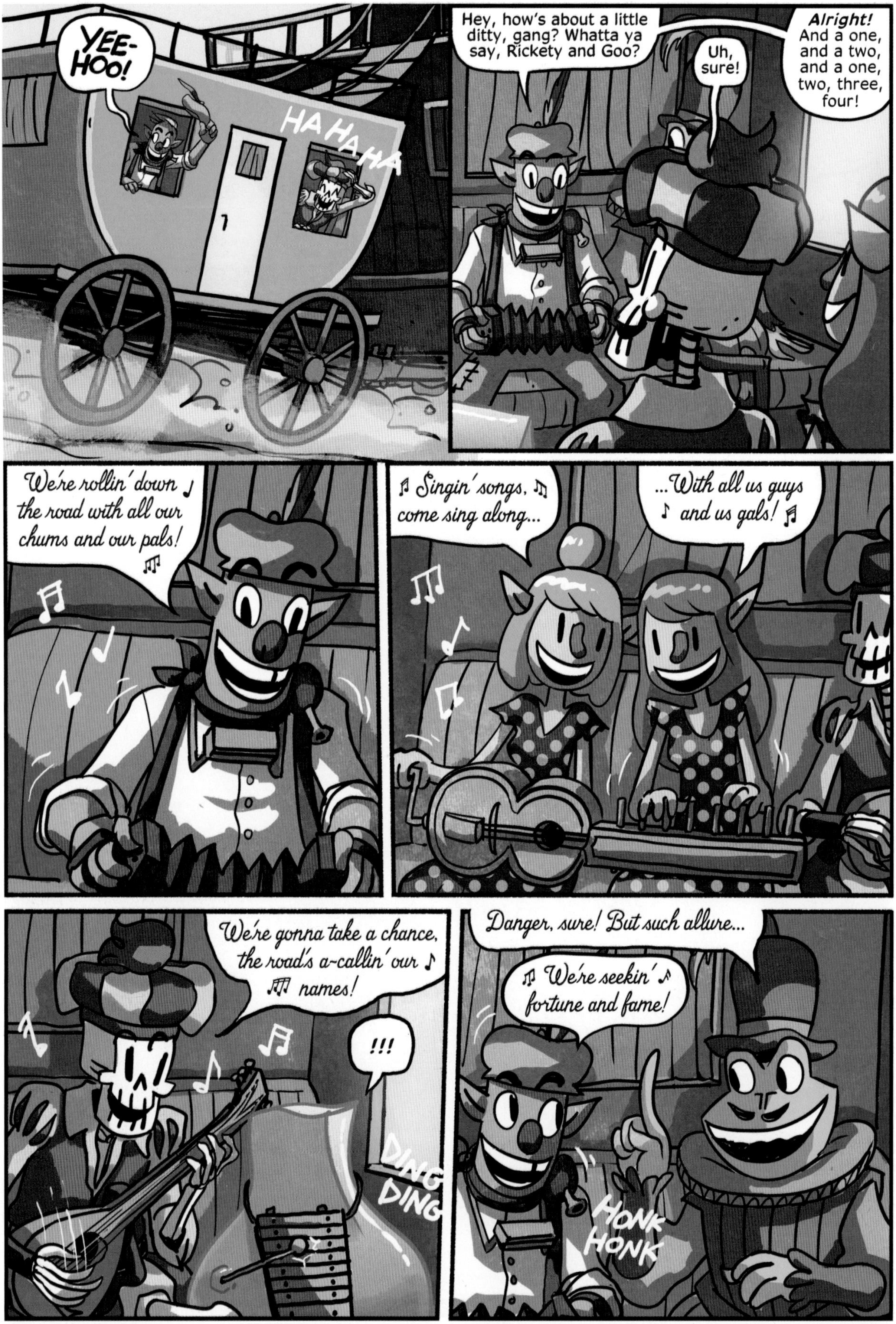
YEE-HOO!
HA HA HA HA
Hey, how's about a little ditty, gang? Whatta ya say, Rickety and Goo?
Uh, sure!
Alright! And a one, and a two, and a one, two, three, four!
We're rollin' down the road with all our chums and our pals!
Singin' songs, come sing along...
...With all us guys and us gals!
We're gonna take a chance, the road's a-callin' our names!
!!!
DING DING
Danger, sure! But such allure...
We're seekin' fortune and fame!
HONK HONK

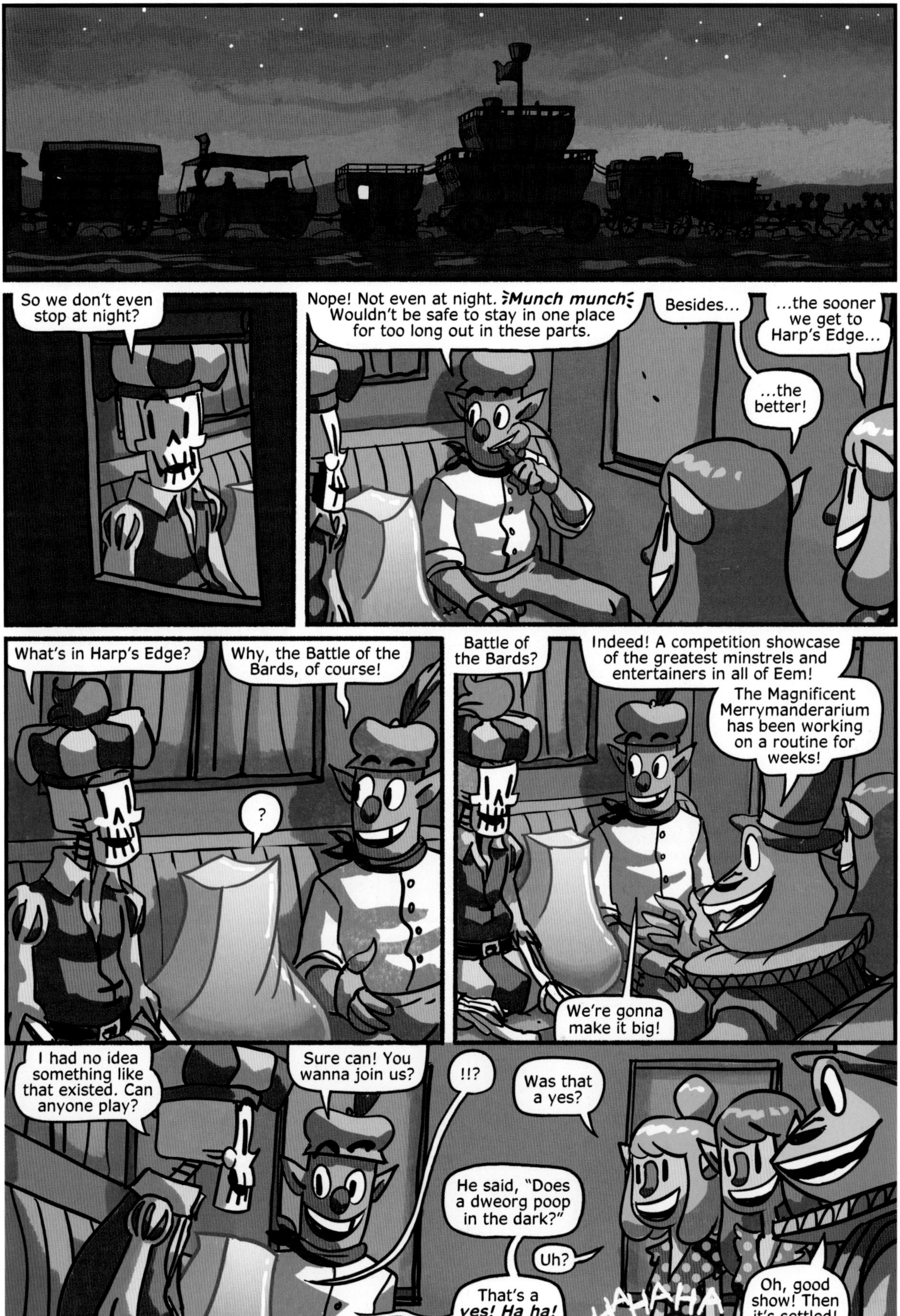
So we don't even stop at night?
Nope! Not even at night. *Munch munch* Wouldn't be safe to stay in one place for too long out in these parts.
Besides...
...the sooner we get to Harp's Edge...
...the better!
What's in Harp's Edge?
Why, the Battle of the Bards, of course!
?
Battle of the Bards?
Indeed! A competition showcase of the greatest minstrels and entertainers in all of Eem!
The Magnificent Merrymanderarium has been working on a routine for weeks!
We're gonna make it big!
I had no idea something like that existed. Can anyone play?
Sure can! You wanna join us?
!!?
Was that a yes?
He said, "Does a dweorg poop in the dark?"
Uh?
That's a *yes! Ha ha!*
HAHAHA
Oh, good show! Then it's settled!

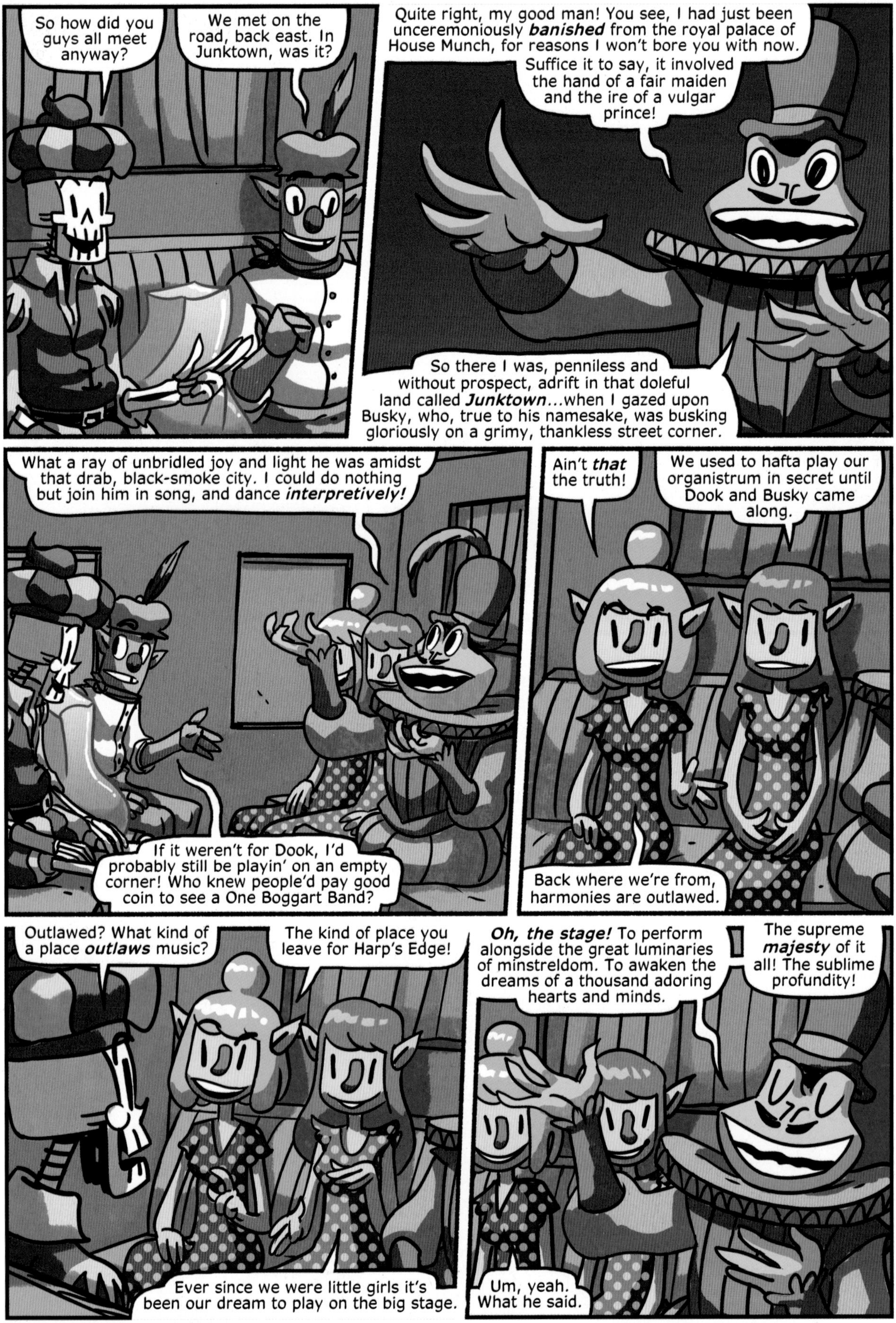
So how did you guys all meet anyway?
We met on the road, back east. In Junktown, was it?
Quite right, my good man! You see, I had just been unceremoniously ***banished*** from the royal palace of House Munch, for reasons I won't bore you with now.
Suffice it to say, it involved the hand of a fair maiden and the ire of a vulgar prince!
So there I was, penniless and without prospect, adrift in that doleful land called ***Junktown***...when I gazed upon Busky, who, true to his namesake, was busking gloriously on a grimy, thankless street corner.
What a ray of unbridled joy and light he was amidst that drab, black-smoke city. I could do nothing but join him in song, and dance ***interpretively!***
If it weren't for Dook, I'd probably still be playin' on an empty corner! Who knew people'd pay good coin to see a One Boggart Band?
Ain't ***that*** the truth!
We used to hafta play our organistrum in secret until Dook and Busky came along.
Back where we're from, harmonies are outlawed.
Outlawed? What kind of a place ***outlaws*** music?
The kind of place you leave for Harp's Edge!
Ever since we were little girls it's been our dream to play on the big stage.
Oh, the stage! To perform alongside the great luminaries of minstreldom. To awaken the dreams of a thousand adoring hearts and minds.
The supreme ***majesty*** of it all! The sublime profundity!
Um, yeah. What he said.

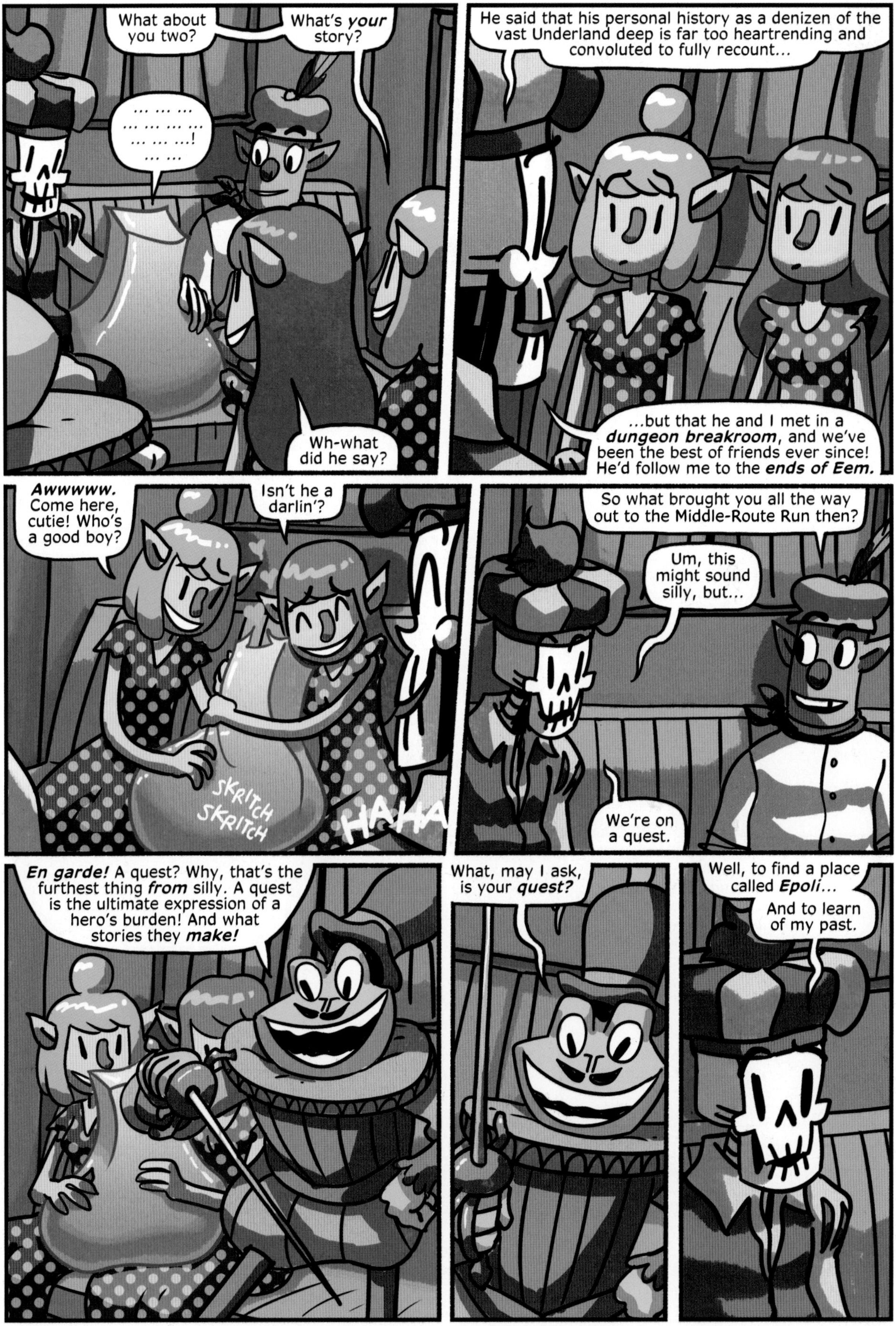
What about you two?
What's *your* story?
... ...! ... ...
Wh-what did he say?
He said that his personal history as a denizen of the vast Underland deep is far too heartrending and convoluted to fully recount...
...but that he and I met in a ***dungeon breakroom***, and we've been the best of friends ever since! He'd follow me to the ***ends of Eem.***
Awwwww. Come here, cutie! Who's a good boy?
Isn't he a darlin'?
SKRITCH SKRITCH
HAHA
So what brought you all the way out to the Middle-Route Run then?
Um, this might sound silly, but...
We're on a quest.
En garde! A quest? Why, that's the furthest thing ***from*** silly. A quest is the ultimate expression of a hero's burden! And what stories they ***make!***
What, may I ask, is your ***quest?***
Well, to find a place called ***Epoli***...
And to learn of my past.

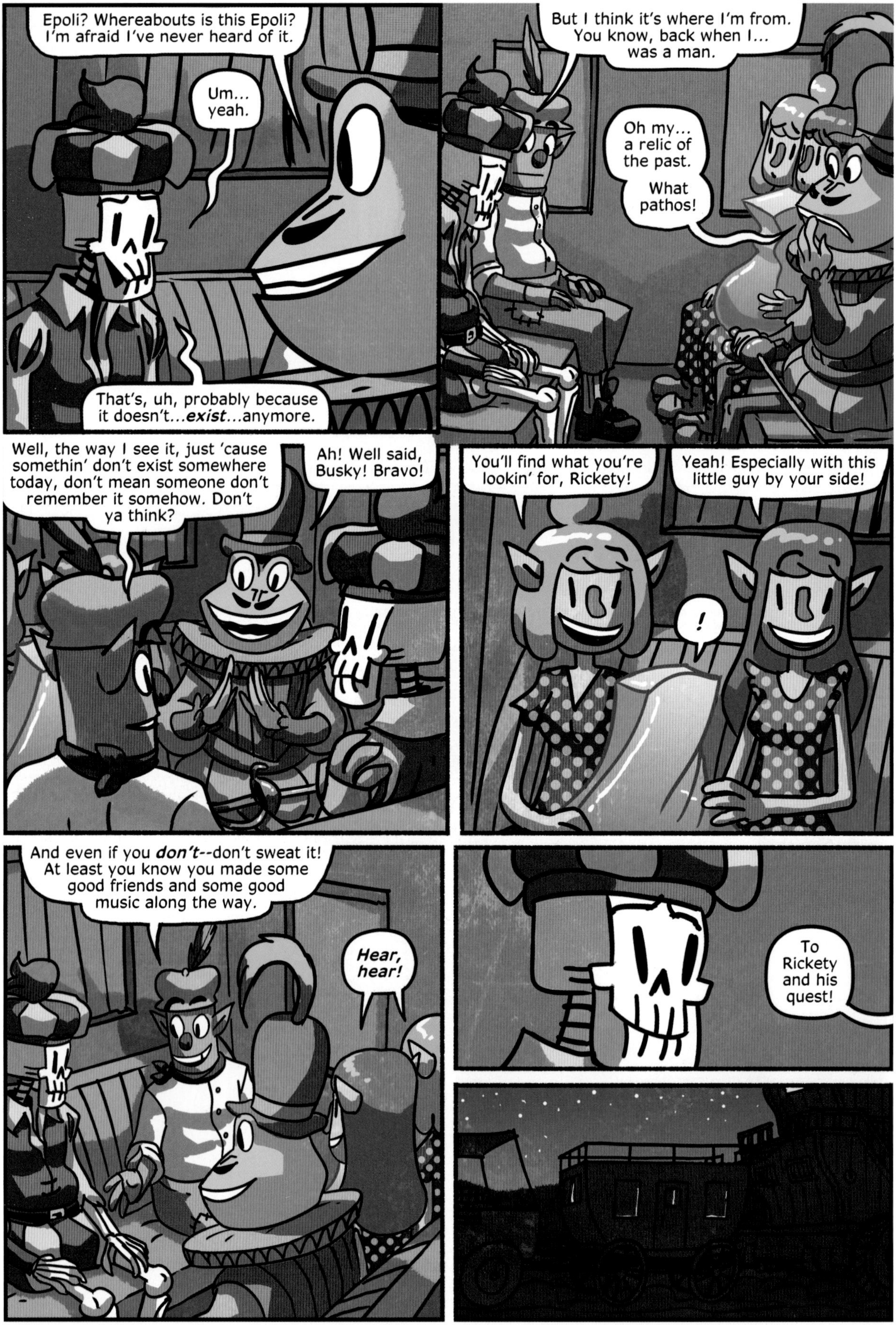
Epoli? Whereabouts is this Epoli? I'm afraid I've never heard of it.
Um... yeah.
That's, uh, probably because it doesn't...*exist*...anymore.
But I think it's where I'm from. You know, back when I... was a man.
Oh my... a relic of the past.
What pathos!
Well, the way I see it, just 'cause somethin' don't exist somewhere today, don't mean someone don't remember it somehow. Don't ya think?
Ah! Well said, Busky! Bravo!
You'll find what you're lookin' for, Rickety!
Yeah! Especially with this little guy by your side!
!
And even if you *don't*--don't sweat it! At least you know you made some good friends and some good music along the way.
Hear, hear!
To Rickety and his quest!

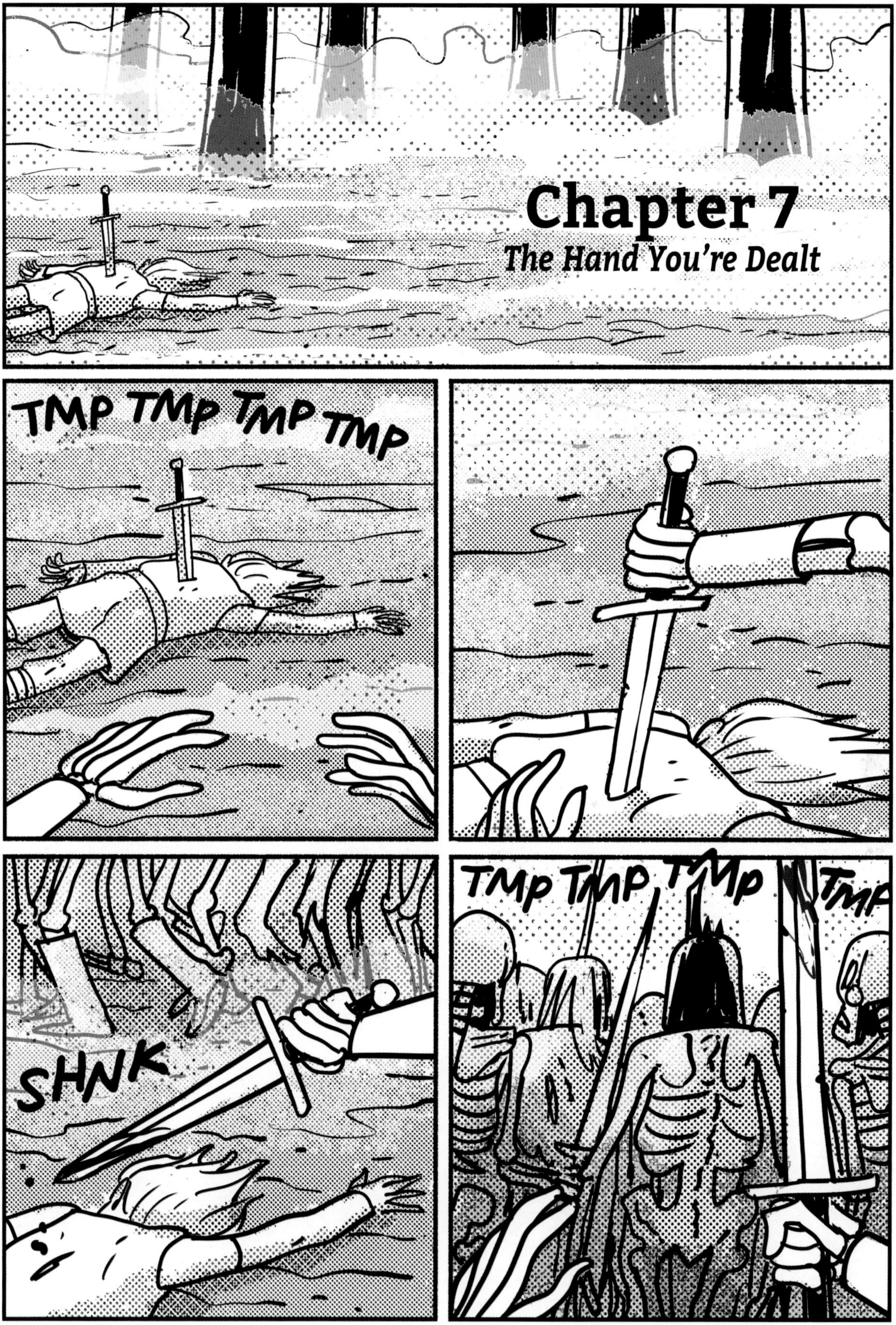
Chapter 7
The Hand You're Dealt
TMP TMP TMP TMP
SHNK
TMP TMP TMP

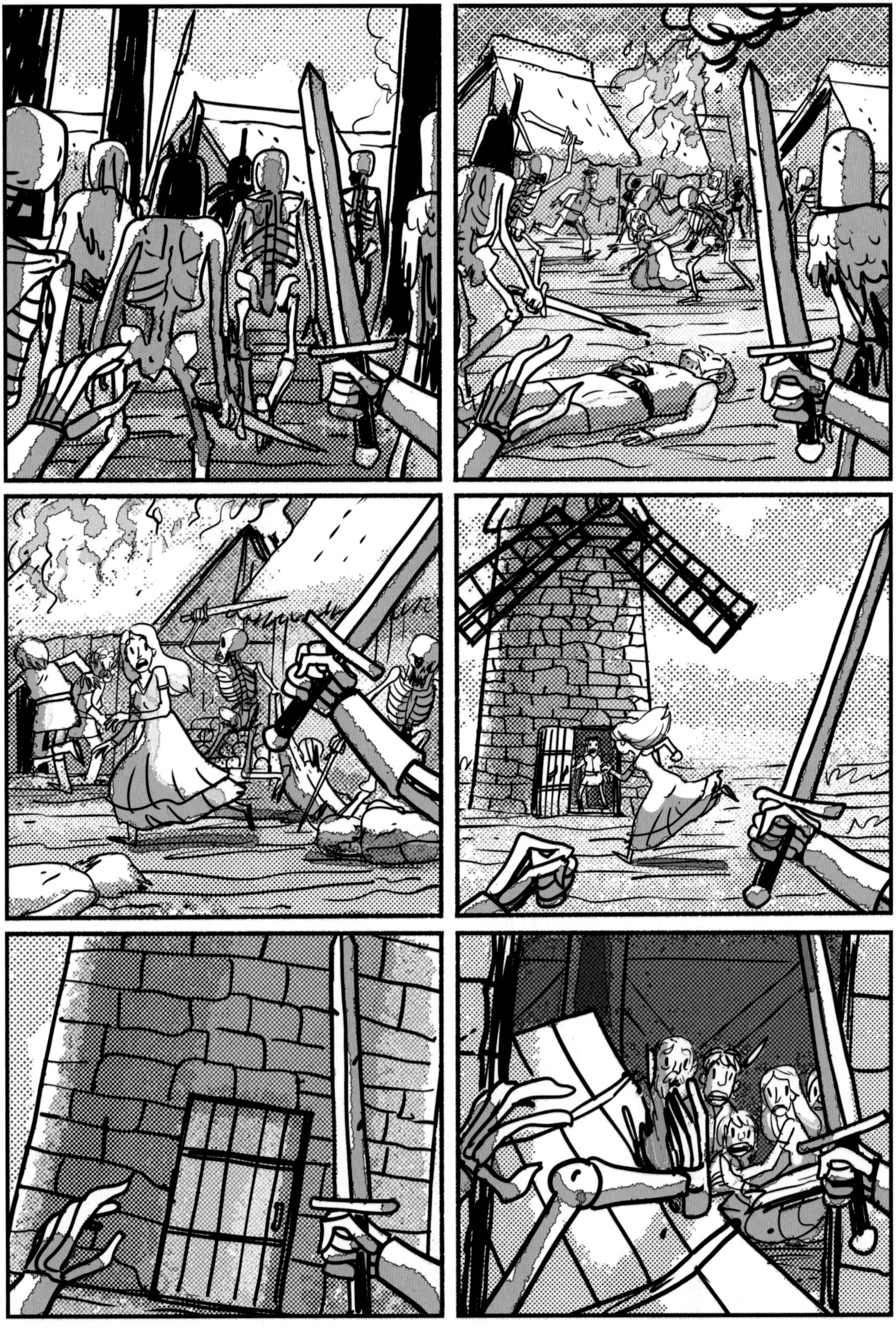

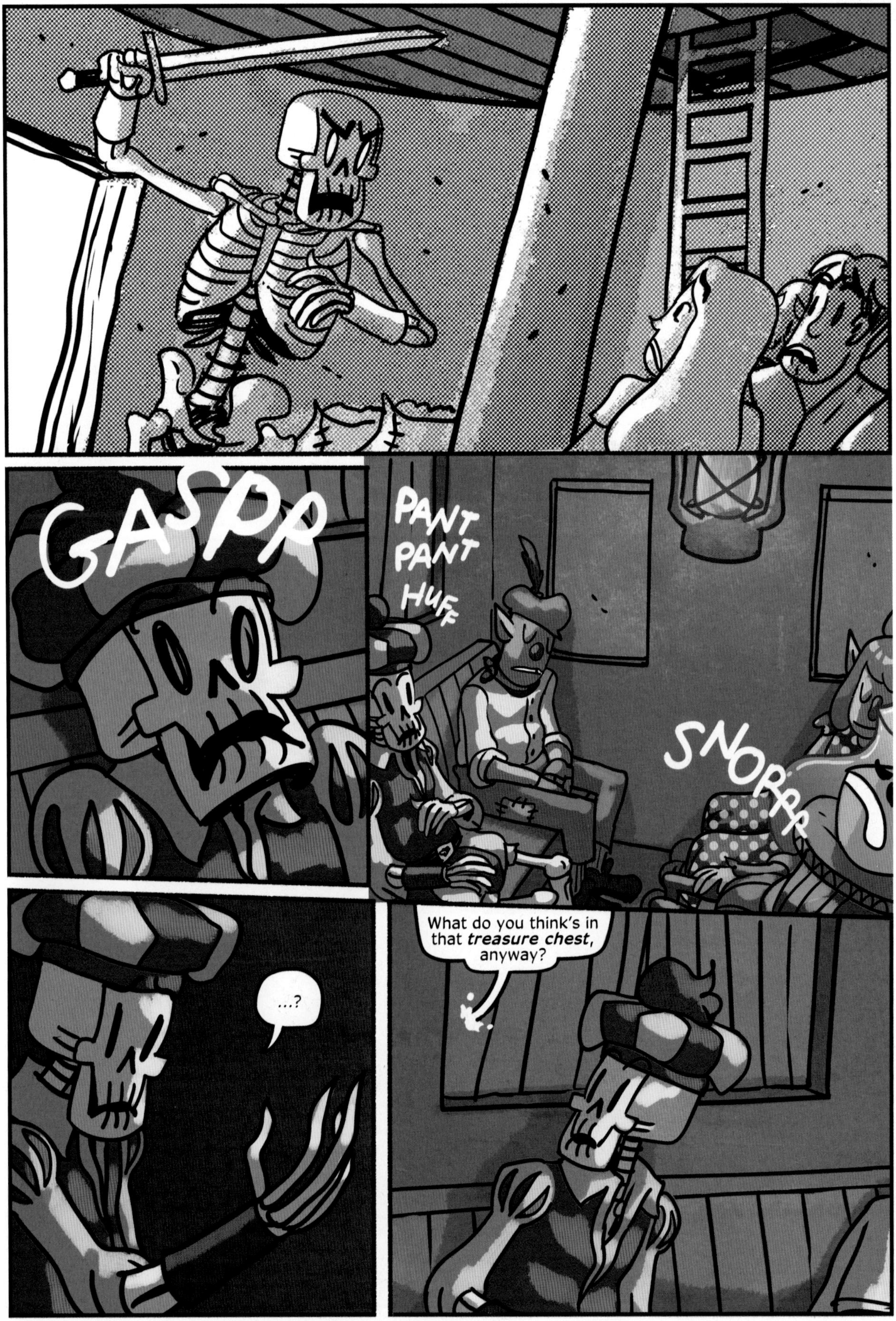
GASPP
PANT PANT HUFF
SNORRR
...?
What do you think's in that ***treasure chest***, anyway?

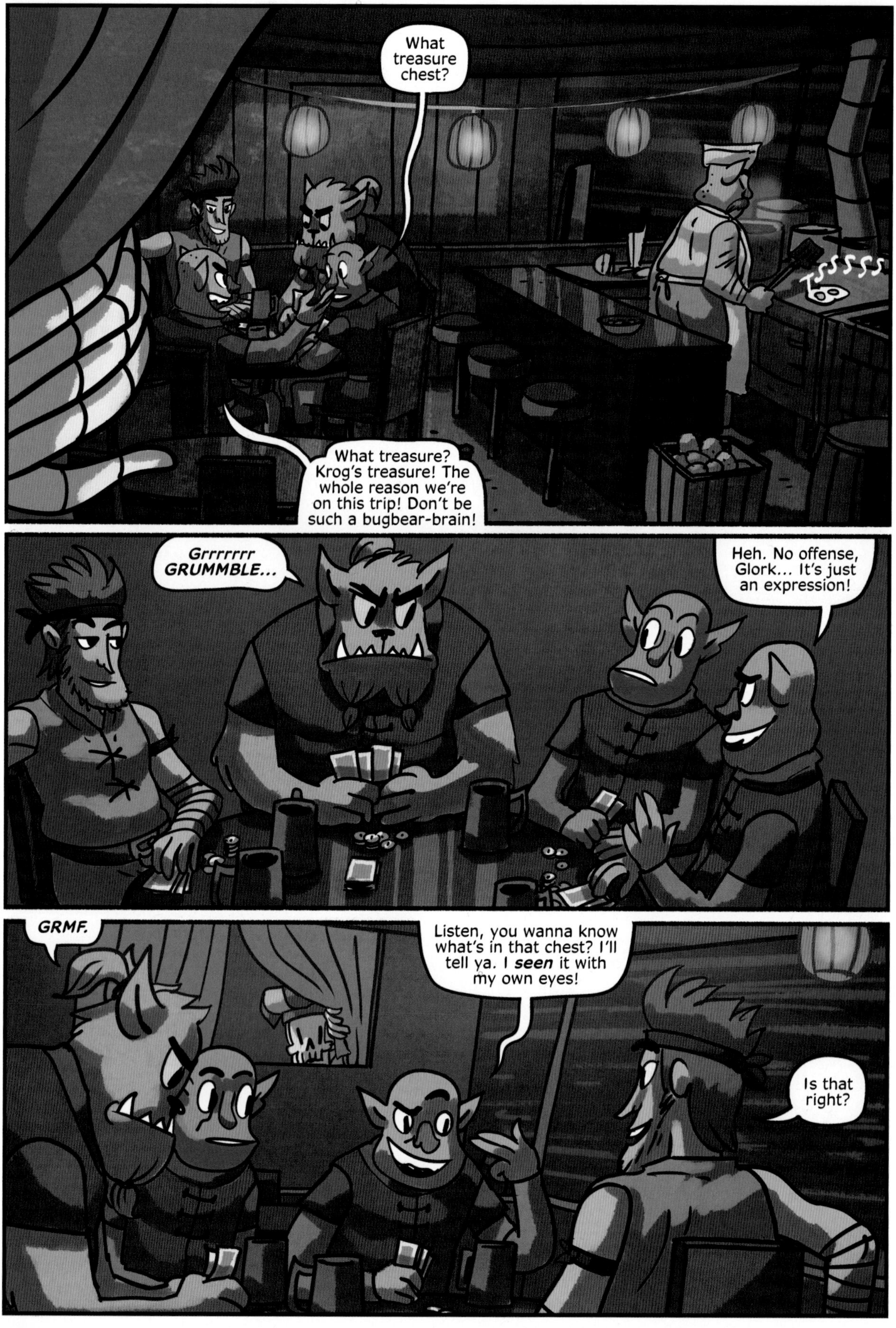
What treasure chest?
TSSSSS
What treasure? Krog's treasure! The whole reason we're on this trip! Don't be such a bugbear-brain!
Grrrrrrr GRUMMBLE...
Heh. No offense, Glork... It's just an expression!
GRMF.
Listen, you wanna know what's in that chest? I'll tell ya. I *seen* it with my own eyes!
Is that right?

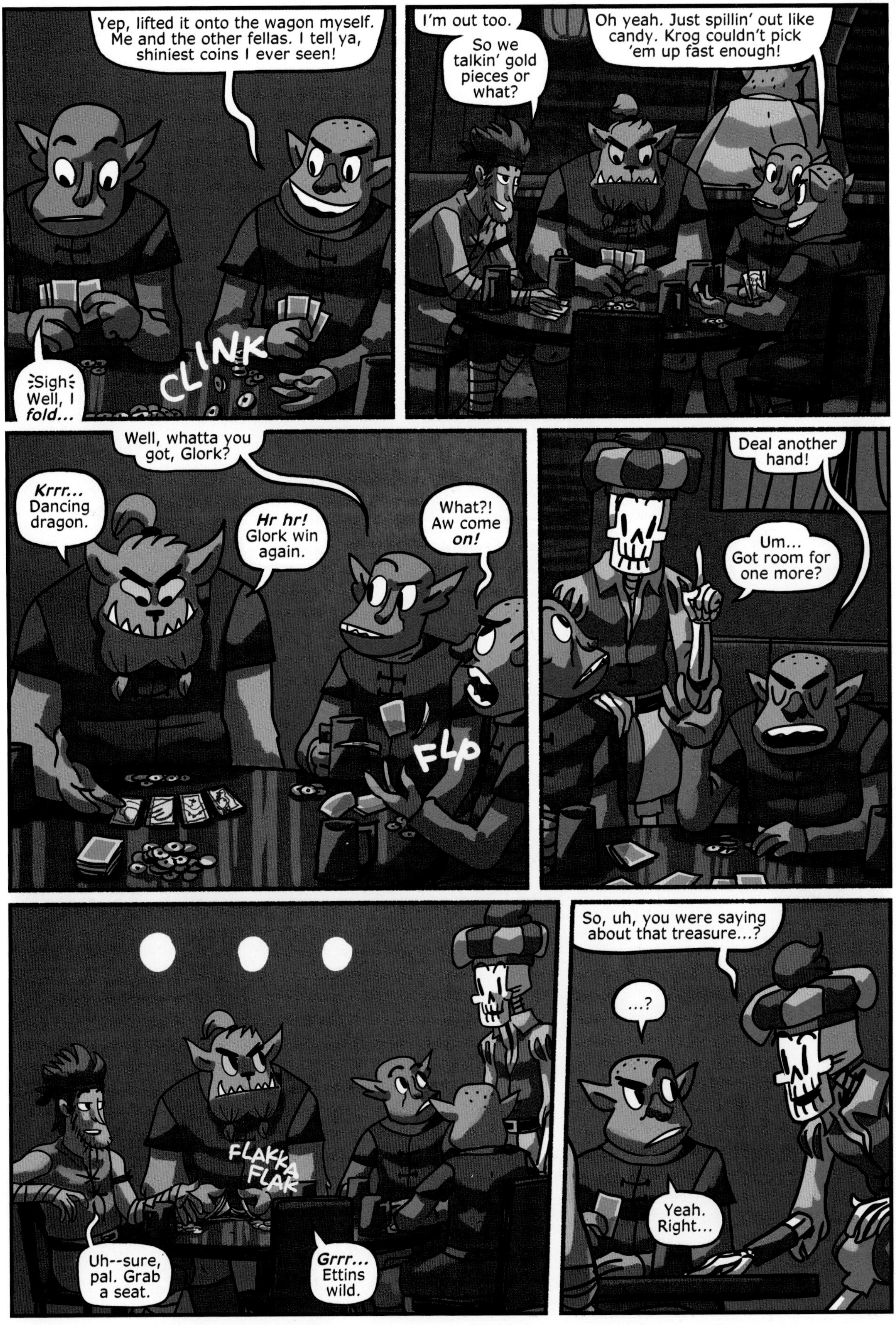

Yep, lifted it onto the wagon myself. Me and the other fellas. I tell ya, shiniest coins I ever seen!
Sigh Well, I *fold...*
CLINK
I'm out too.
So we talkin' gold pieces or what?
Oh yeah. Just spillin' out like candy. Krog couldn't pick 'em up fast enough!
Well, whatta you got, Glork?
Krrr... Dancing dragon.
Hr hr! Glork win again.
What?! Aw come *on!*
FLIP
Deal another hand!
Um... Got room for one more?
• • •
FLAKKA FLAK
Uh--sure, pal. Grab a seat.
Grrr... Ettins wild.
So, uh, you were saying about that treasure...?
...?
Yeah. Right...

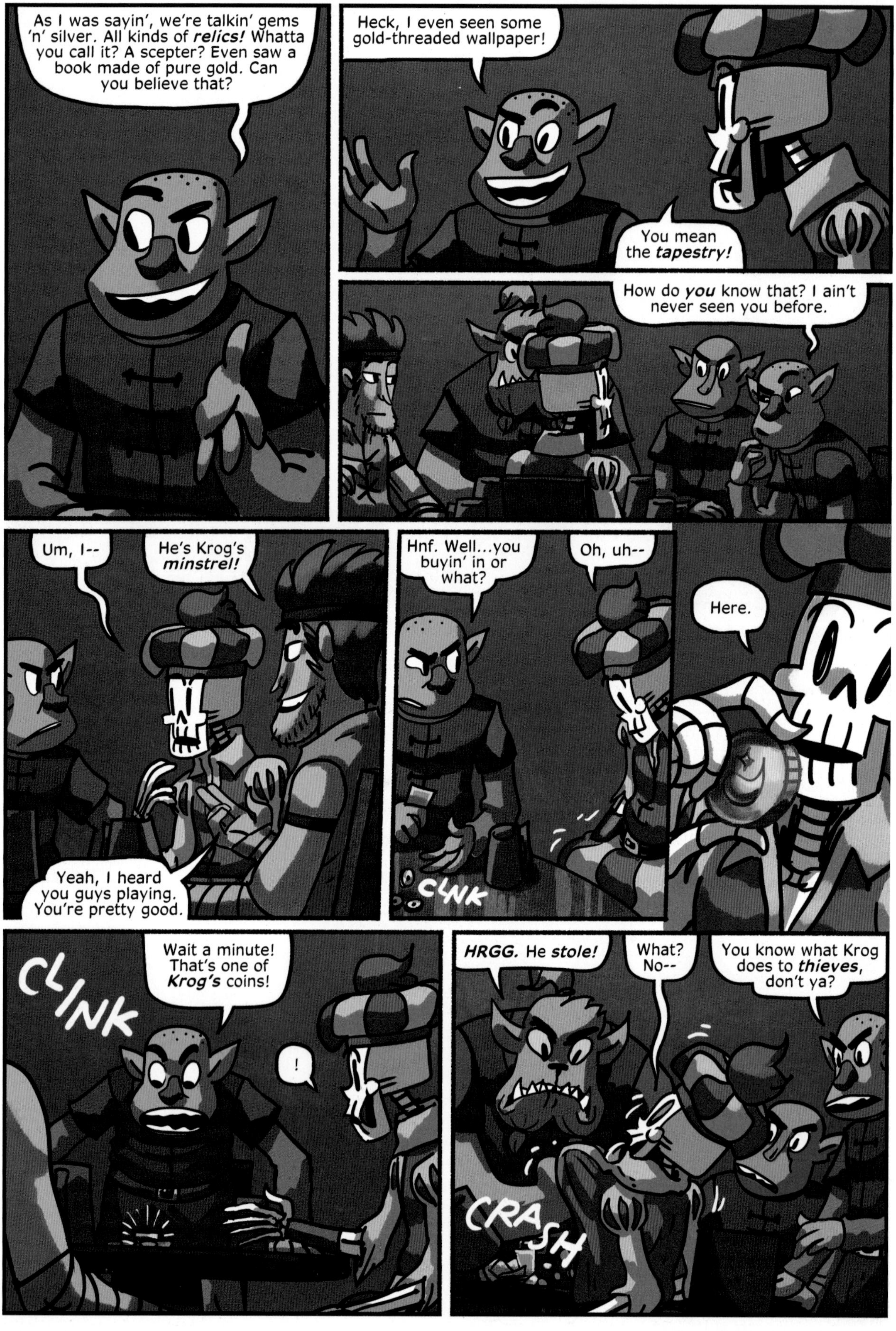
As I was sayin', we're talkin' gems 'n' silver. All kinds of ***relics!*** Whatta you call it? A scepter? Even saw a book made of pure gold. Can you believe that?
Heck, I even seen some gold-threaded wallpaper!
You mean the ***tapestry!***
How do ***you*** know that? I ain't never seen you before.
Um, I--
He's Krog's ***minstrel!***
Yeah, I heard you guys playing. You're pretty good.
Hnf. Well...you buyin' in or what?
Oh, uh--
CLINK
Here.
CLINK
Wait a minute! That's one of ***Krog's*** coins!
!
HRGG. He ***stole!***
What? No--
You know what Krog does to ***thieves***, don't ya?
CRASH

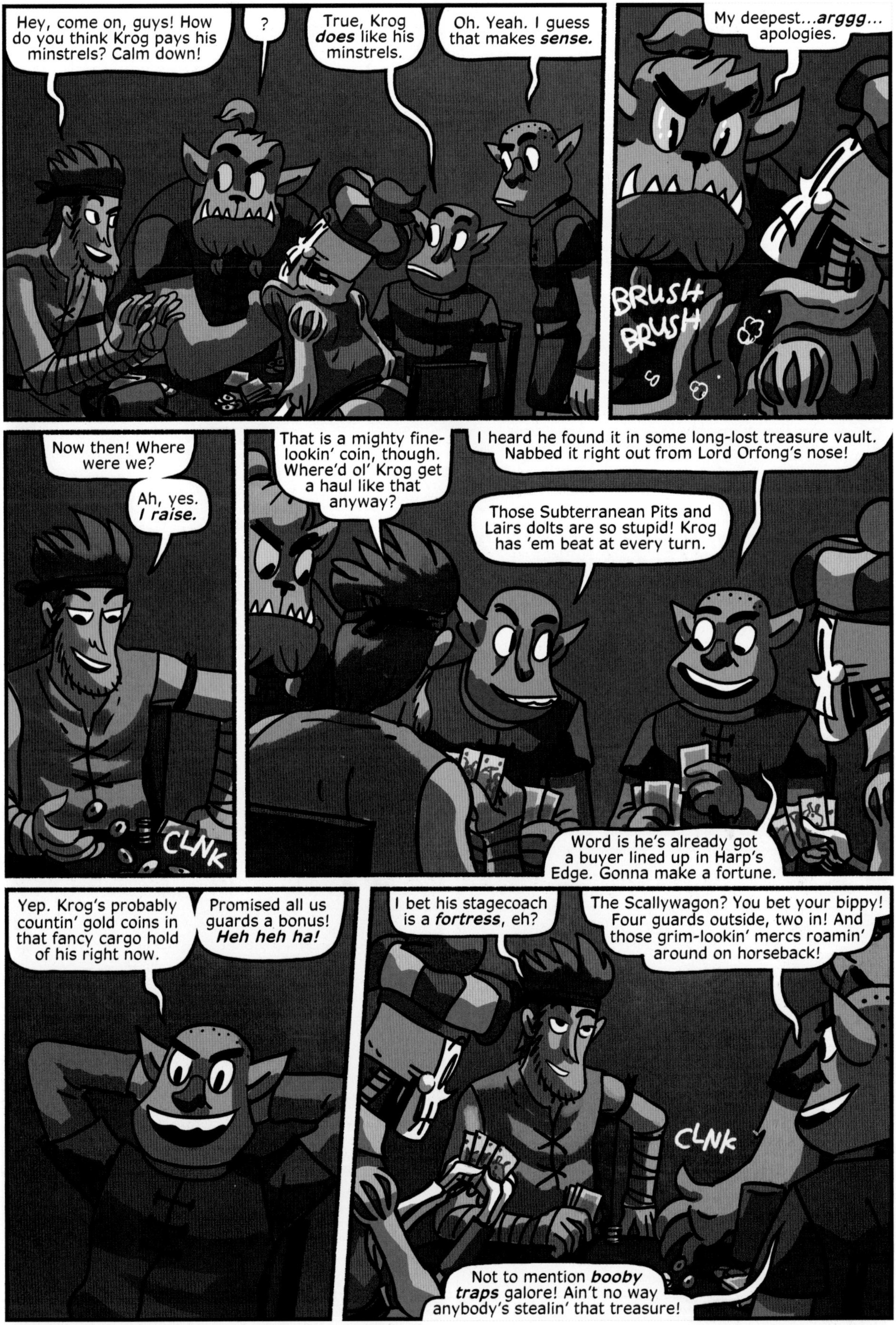
Hey, come on, guys! How do you think Krog pays his minstrels? Calm down!
?
True, Krog *does* like his minstrels.
Oh. Yeah. I guess that makes *sense.*
My deepest...*arggg*... apologies.
BRUSH BRUSH
Now then! Where were we?
Ah, yes. *I raise.*
CLNK
That is a mighty fine-lookin' coin, though. Where'd ol' Krog get a haul like that anyway?
I heard he found it in some long-lost treasure vault. Nabbed it right out from Lord Orfong's nose!
Those Subterranean Pits and Lairs dolts are so stupid! Krog has 'em beat at every turn.
Word is he's already got a buyer lined up in Harp's Edge. Gonna make a fortune.
Yep. Krog's probably countin' gold coins in that fancy cargo hold of his right now.
Promised all us guards a bonus! *Heh heh ha!*
I bet his stagecoach is a *fortress*, eh?
The Scallywagon? You bet your bippy! Four guards outside, two in! And those grim-lookin' mercs roamin' around on horseback!
CLNK
Not to mention *booby traps* galore! Ain't no way anybody's stealin' that treasure!

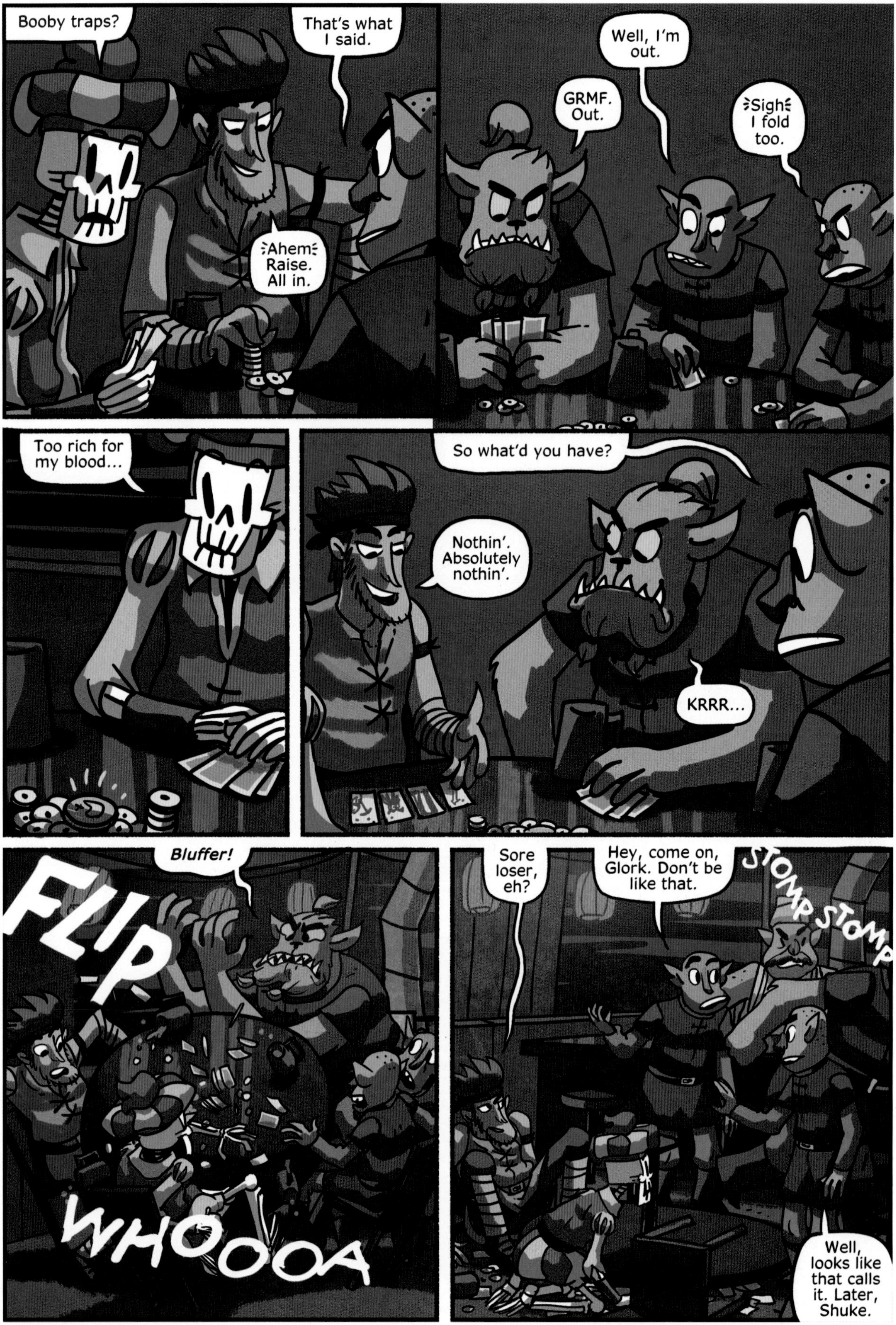
Booby traps?
That's what I said.
GRMF. Out.
Well, I'm out.
Sigh I fold too.
Ahem Raise. All in.
Too rich for my blood...
So what'd you have?
Nothin'. Absolutely nothin'.
KRRR...
Bluffer!
FLIP
WHOOOA
Sore loser, eh?
Hey, come on, Glork. Don't be like that.
STOMP STOMP STOMP
Well, looks like that calls it. Later, Shuke.

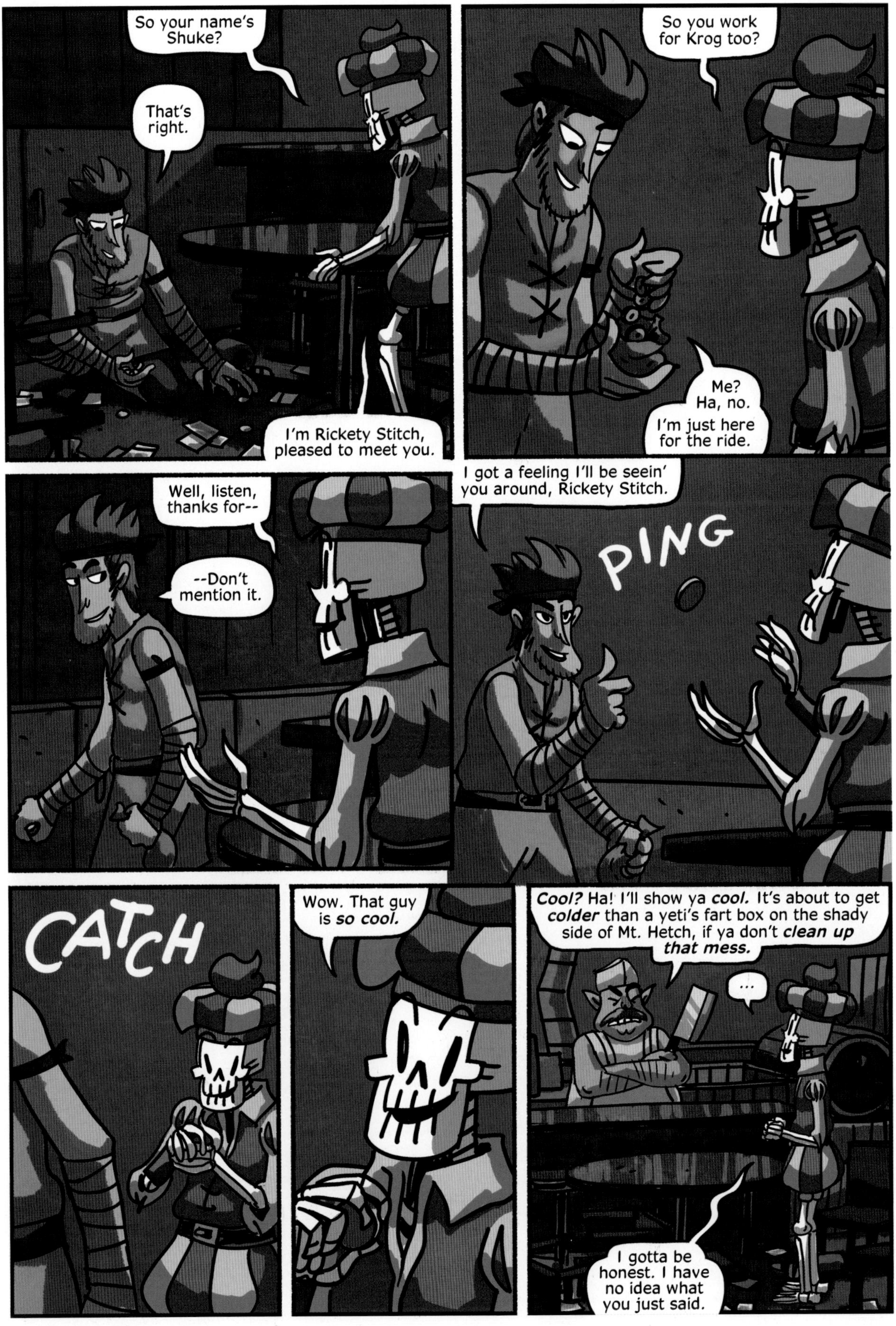
So your name's Shuke?
That's right.
I'm Rickety Stitch, pleased to meet you.
So you work for Krog too?
Me? Ha, no.
I'm just here for the ride.
Well, listen, thanks for--
--Don't mention it.
I got a feeling I'll be seein' you around, Rickety Stitch.
PING
CATCH
Wow. That guy is *so cool.*
Cool? Ha! I'll show ya *cool.* It's about to get *colder* than a yeti's fart box on the shady side of Mt. Hetch, if ya don't *clean up that mess.*
...
I gotta be honest. I have no idea what you just said.

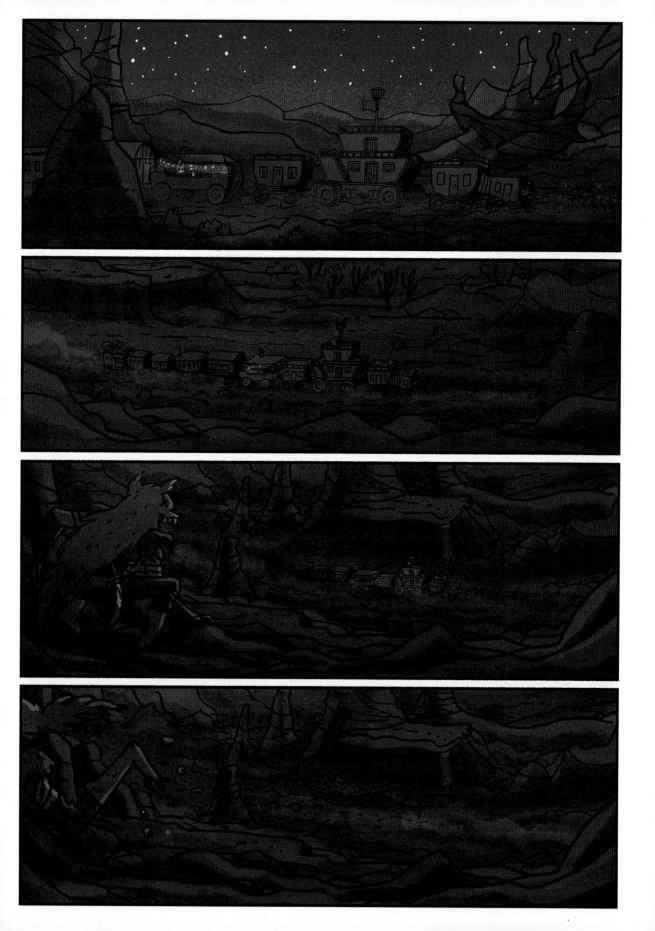

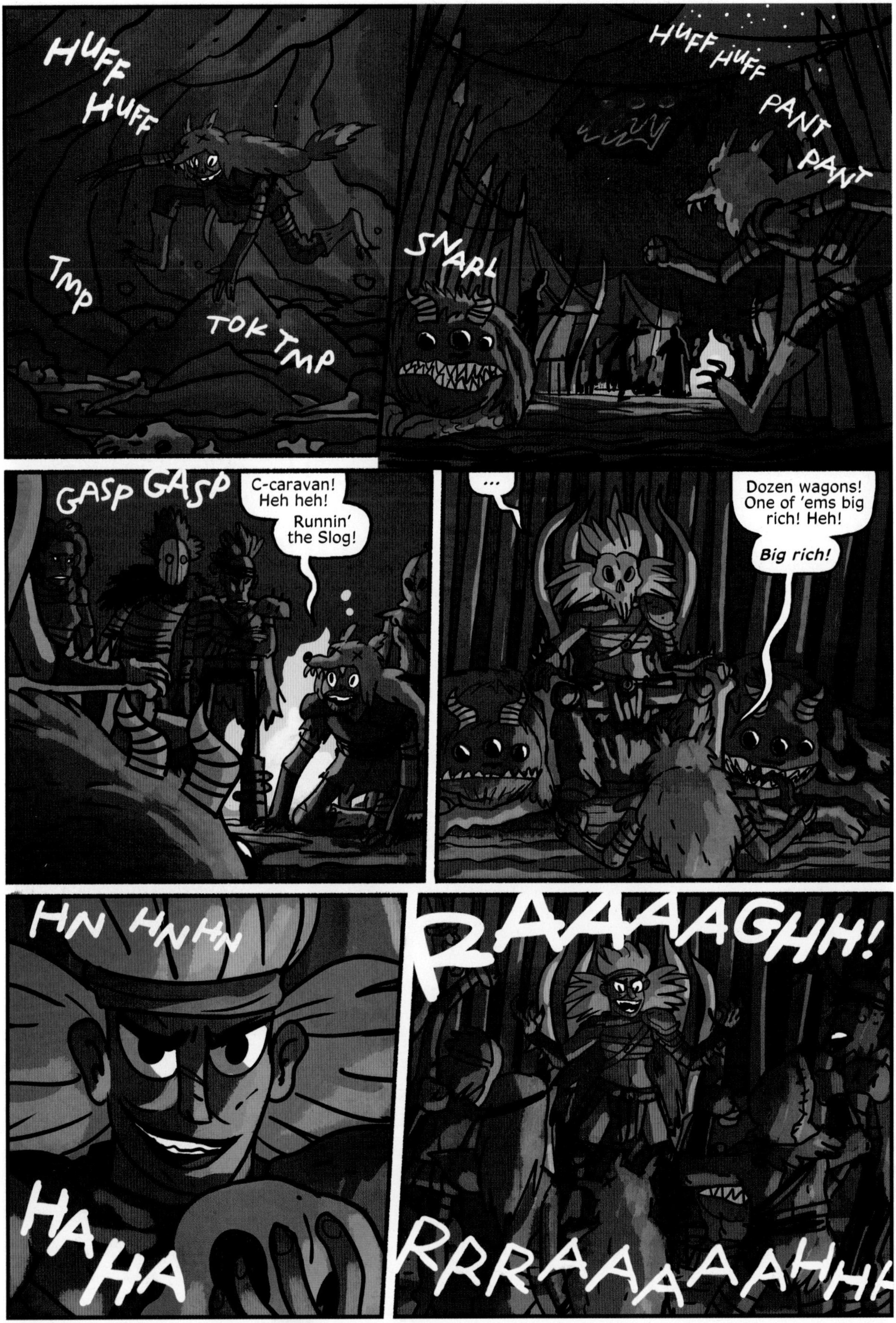
HUFF HUFF
TMP
TOK TMP
HUFF HUFF
PANT PANT
SNARL
GASP GASP
C-caravan! Heh heh!
Runnin' the Slog!
...
Dozen wagons! One of 'ems big rich! Heh!
Big rich!
HN HNHN
HA HA HA
RAAAAAGHH!
RRRAAAAAAHHH

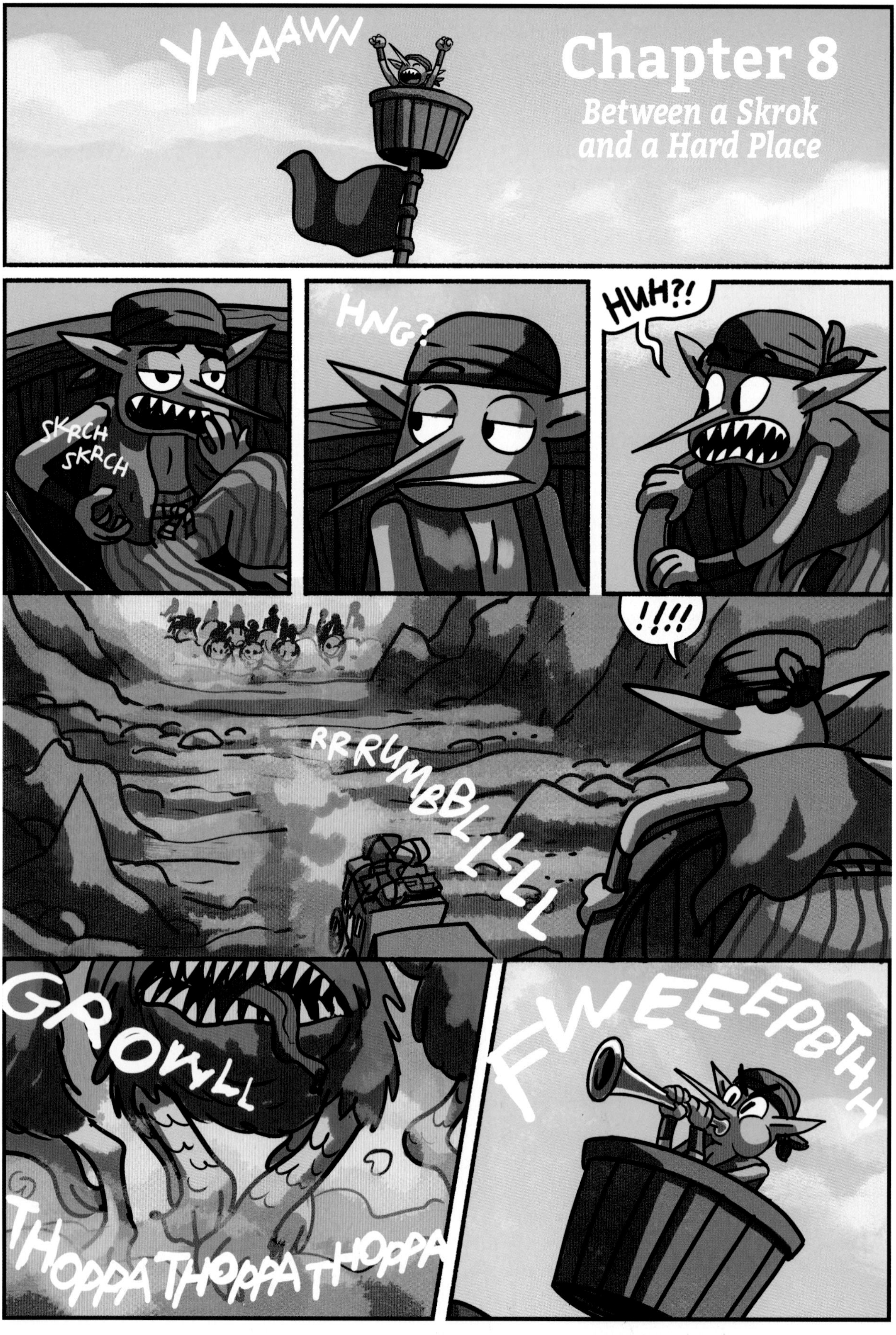
YAAAWN
Chapter 8
Between a Skrok and a Hard Place
SKRCH SKRCH
HNG?
HUH?!
!!!!
RRRUMBBLLLLL
GROWLL
THOPPA THOPPA THOPPA
FWEEEPBTHH

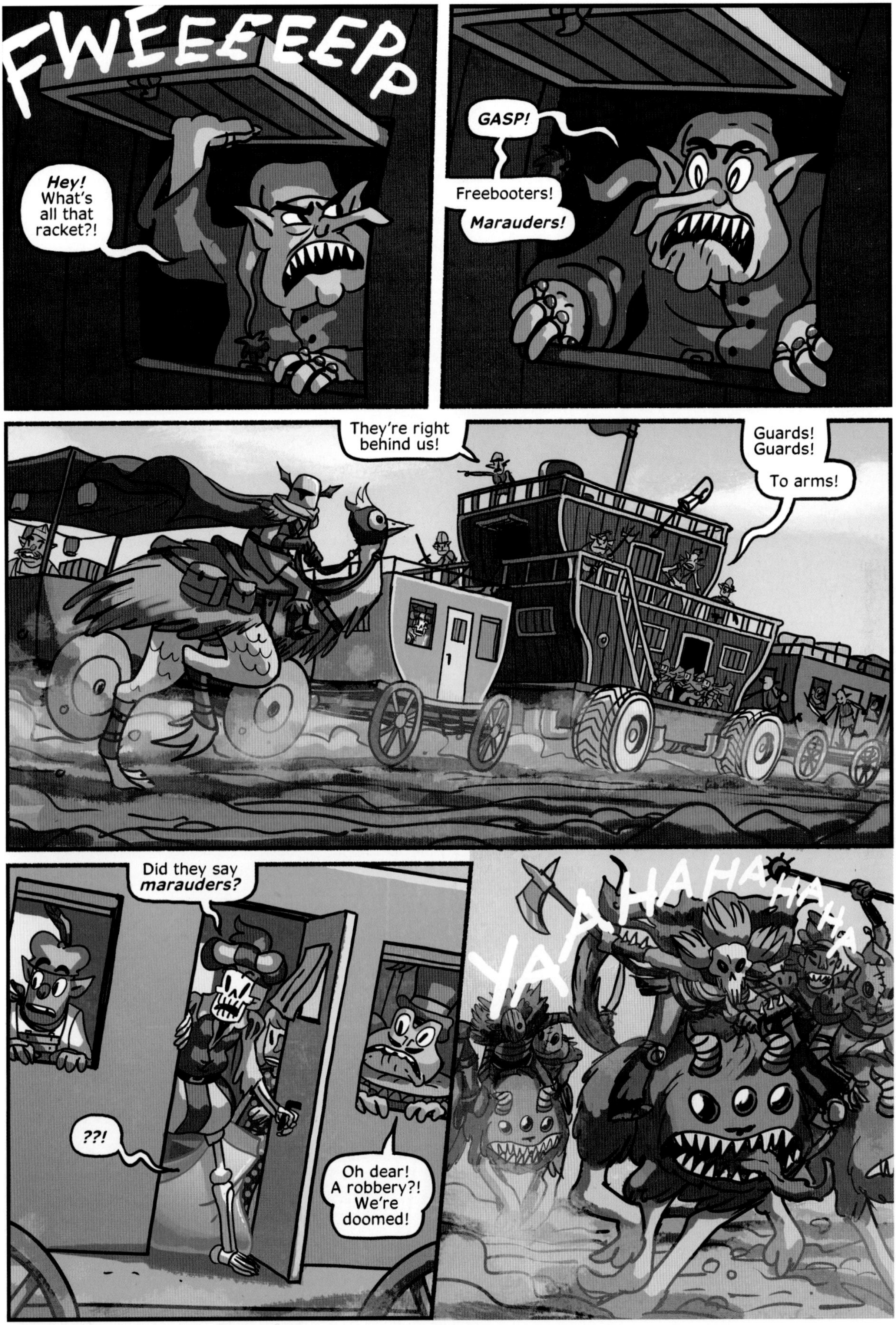
FWEEEEEPP
Hey! What's all that racket?!
GASP!
Freebooters!
Marauders!
They're right behind us!
Guards! Guards!
To arms!
Did they say marauders?
??!
Oh dear! A robbery?! We're doomed!
YAAHAHAHAHAHA

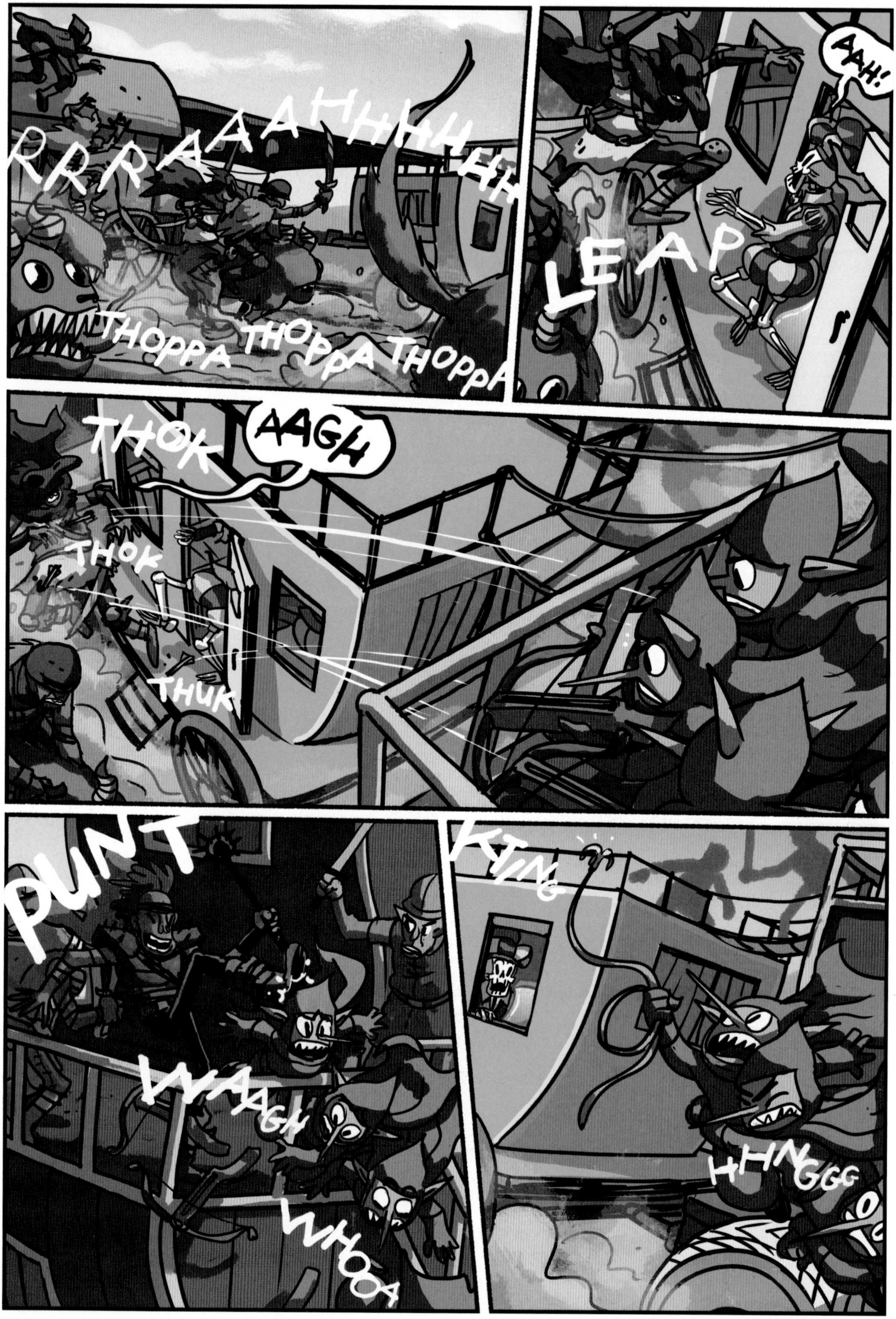
RRRAAAHHHHHH
THOPPA THOPPA THOPPA
AAH!
LEAP
THOK
AAGH
THOK
THUK
PUNT
WAAAGH
WHOOA
KTING
HHNGGG

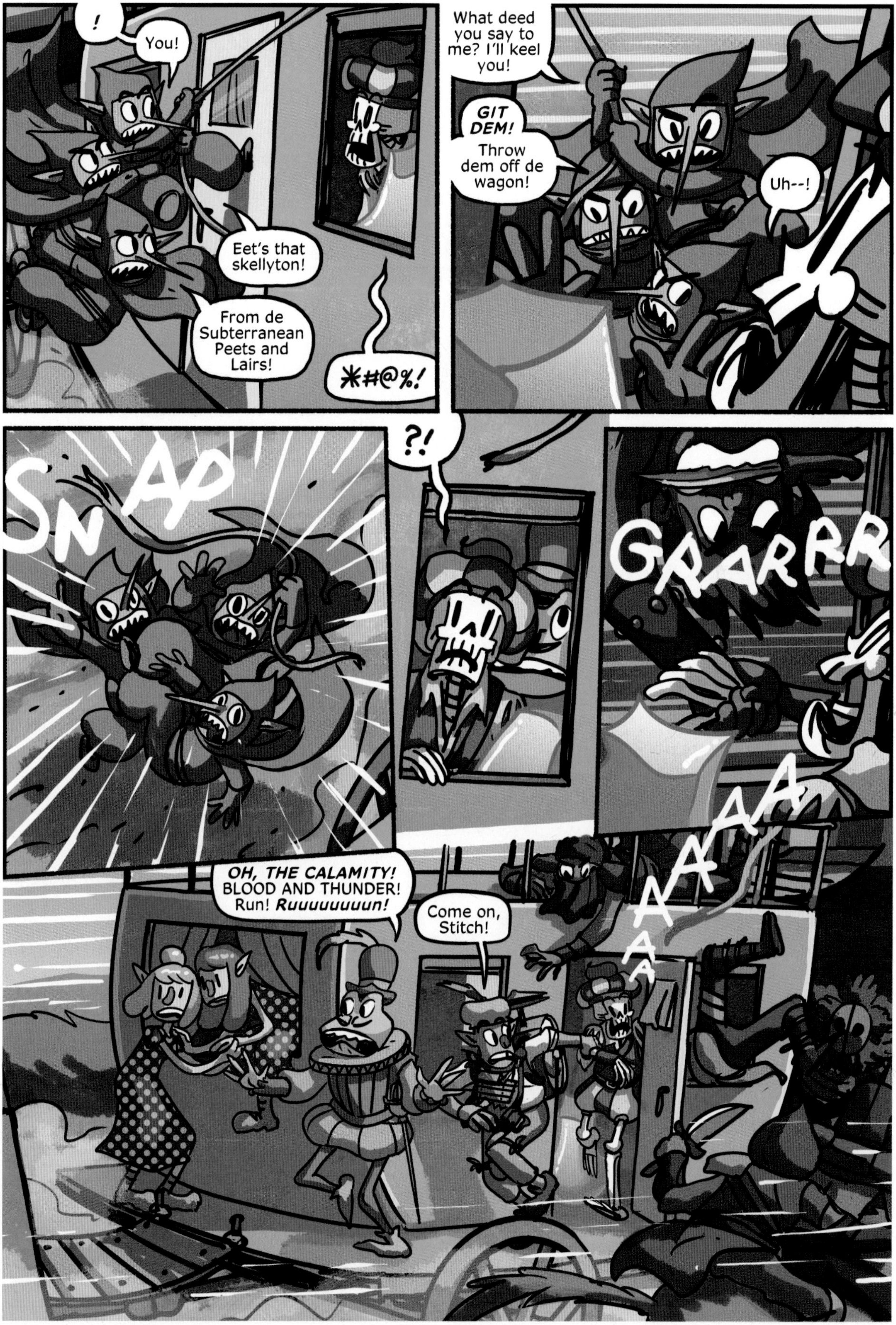
!
You!
Eet's that skellyton!
From de Subterranean Peets and Lairs!
*#@%!
What deed you say to me? I'll keel you!
GIT DEM!
Throw dem off de wagon!
Uh--!
SNAP
?!
GRARRR
OH, THE CALAMITY! BLOOD AND THUNDER! Run! Ruuuuuuuun!
Come on, Stitch!
AAAAAAAAA

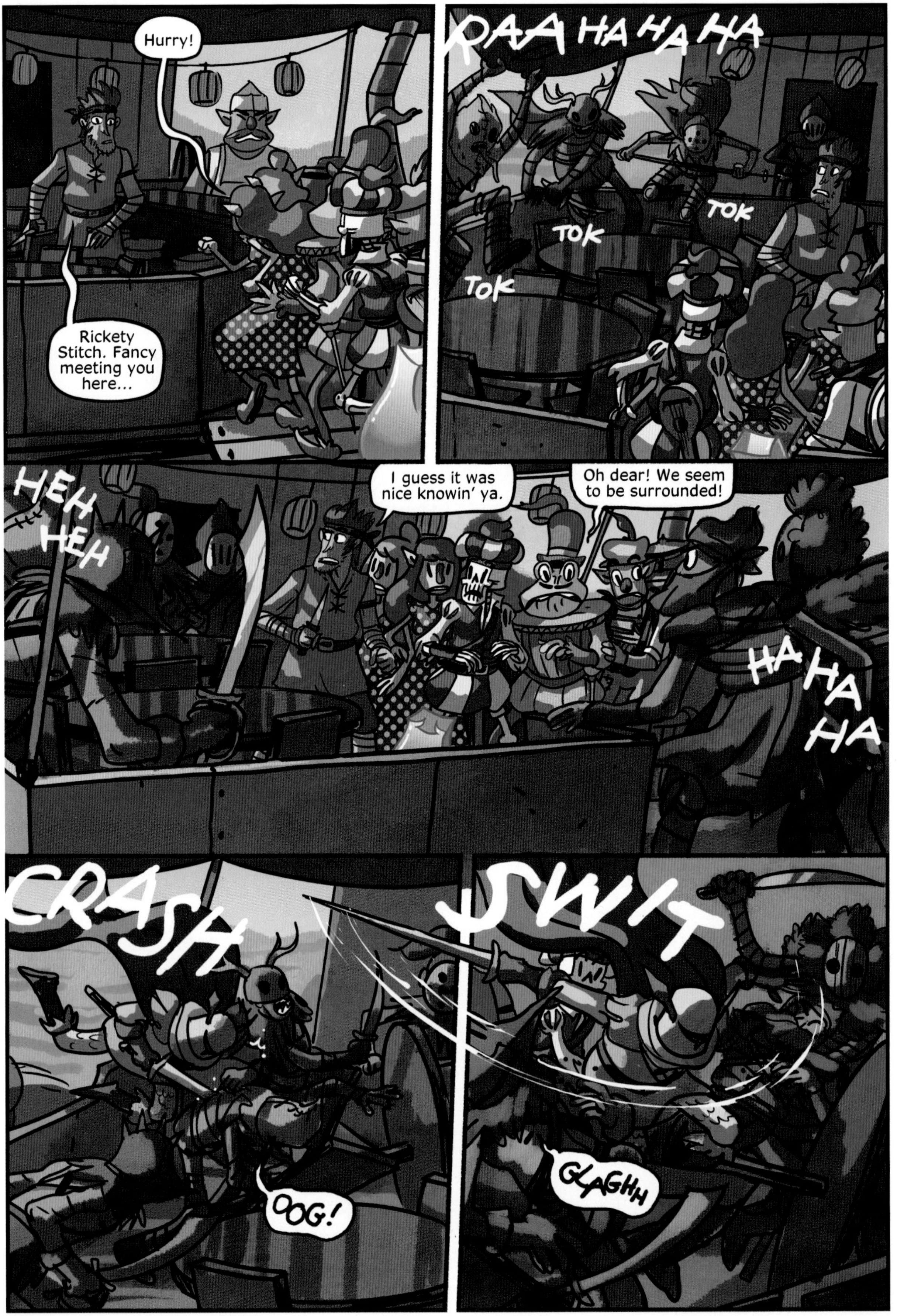
Hurry!
Rickety Stitch. Fancy meeting you here...
RAA HA HA HA HA
TOK
TOK
TOK
HEH HEH
I guess it was nice knowin' ya.
Oh dear! We seem to be surrounded!
HA HA HA
CRASH
OOG!
SWIT
GLAGHH

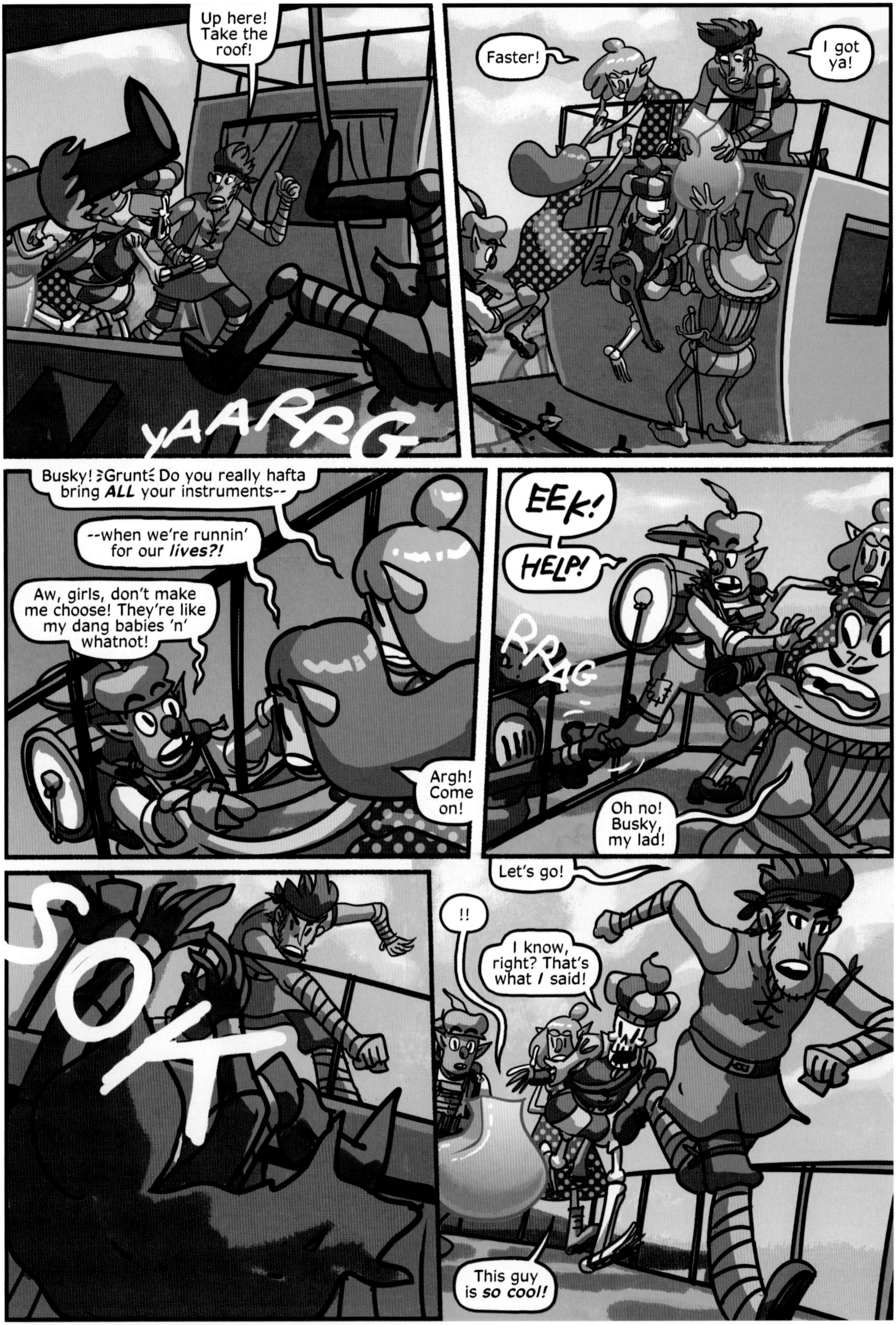
Up here! Take the roof!
YAARRG
Faster!
I got ya!
Busky! ⁝Grunt⁝ Do you really hafta bring ALL your instruments--
--when we're runnin' for our lives?!
Aw, girls, don't make me choose! They're like my dang babies 'n' whatnot!
Argh! Come on!
EEK!
HELP!
RRAG
Oh no! Busky, my lad!
SOK
Let's go!
!!
I know, right? That's what I said!
This guy is so cool!

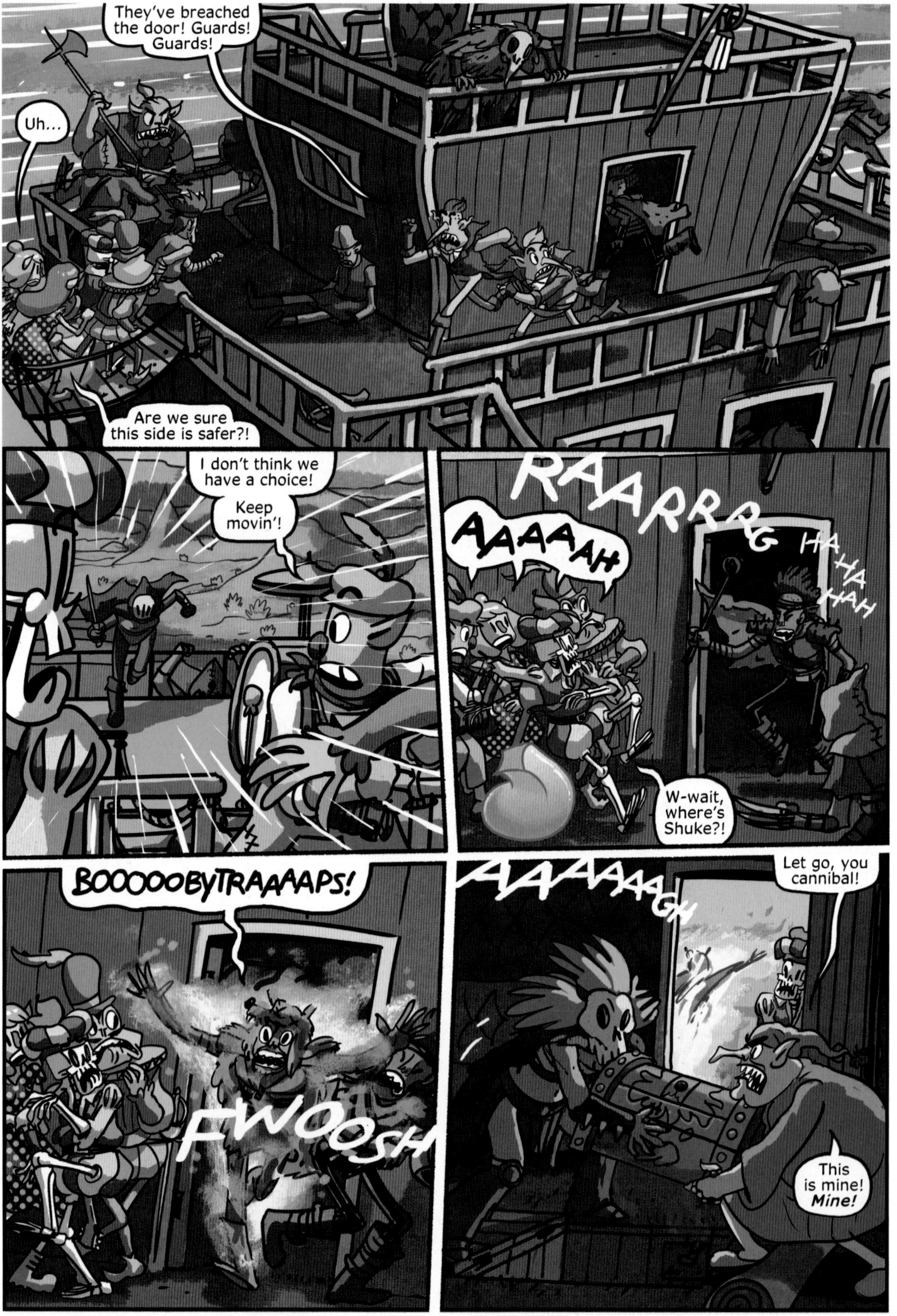
They've breached the door! Guards! Guards!
Uh...
Are we sure this side is safer?!
I don't think we have a choice!
Keep movin'!
RAARRRG
AAAAAH
HA HA HA HAH
W-wait, where's Shuke?!
BOOOOOBYTRAAAAPS!
FWOOSH
AAAAAAAGH
Let go, you cannibal!
This is mine! *Mine!*

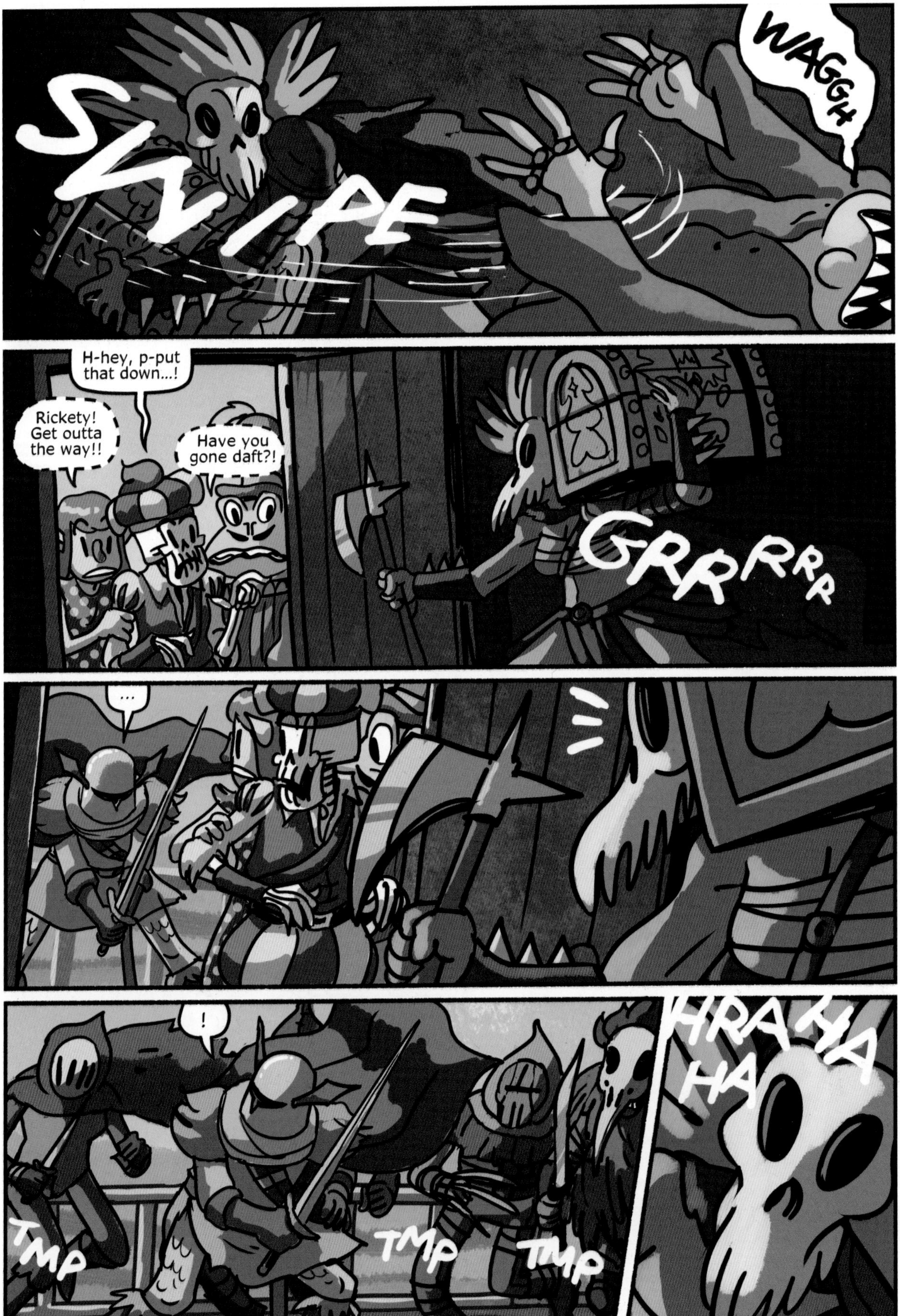
SWIPE
WAGGH
H-hey, p-put that down...!
Rickety! Get outta the way!!
Have you gone daft?!
GRRRRR
...
!
TMP
TMP
TMP
HRA HA HA

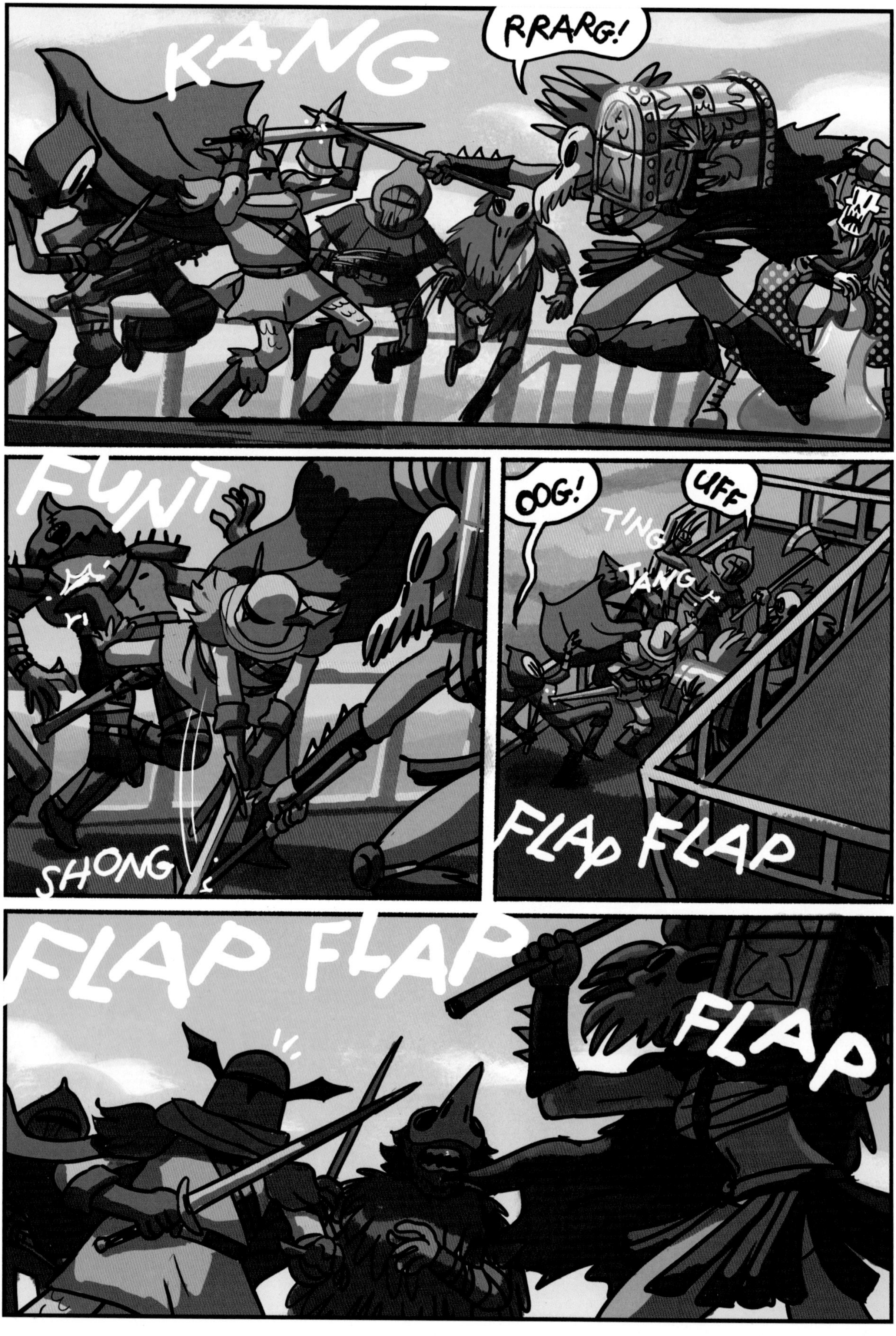
KANG
RRARG!
FUNT
SHONG
OOG!
UFF
TING
TANG
FLAP FLAP
FLAP FLAP
FLAP

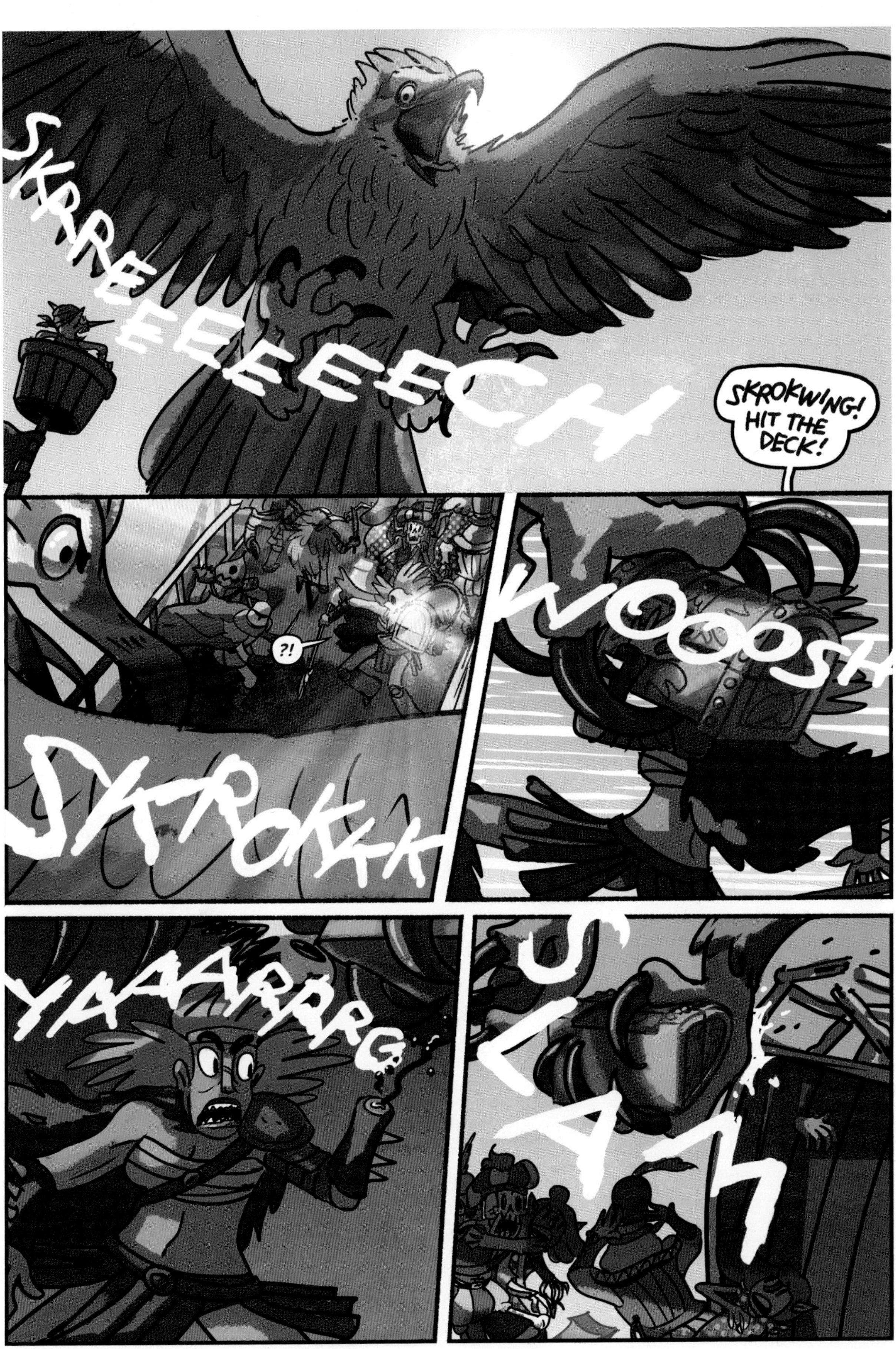
SKREEEEEEECH
SKROKWING! HIT THE DECK!
?!
SKROKKK
WOOOSH
YAAARRRG
SLAM

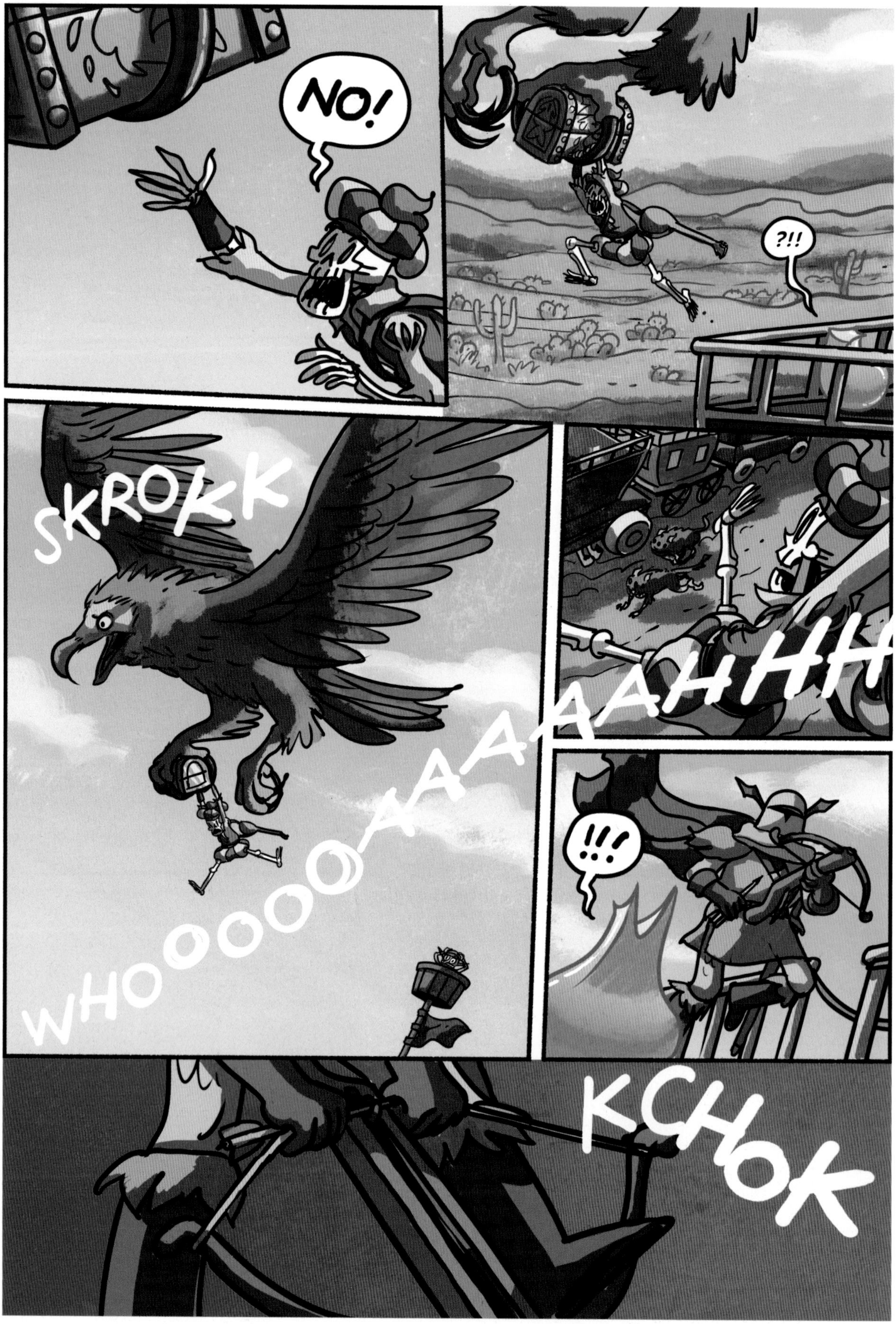
NO!
?!!
SKROKK
WHOOOOOOAAAAAAAHHH
!!!
KCHOK

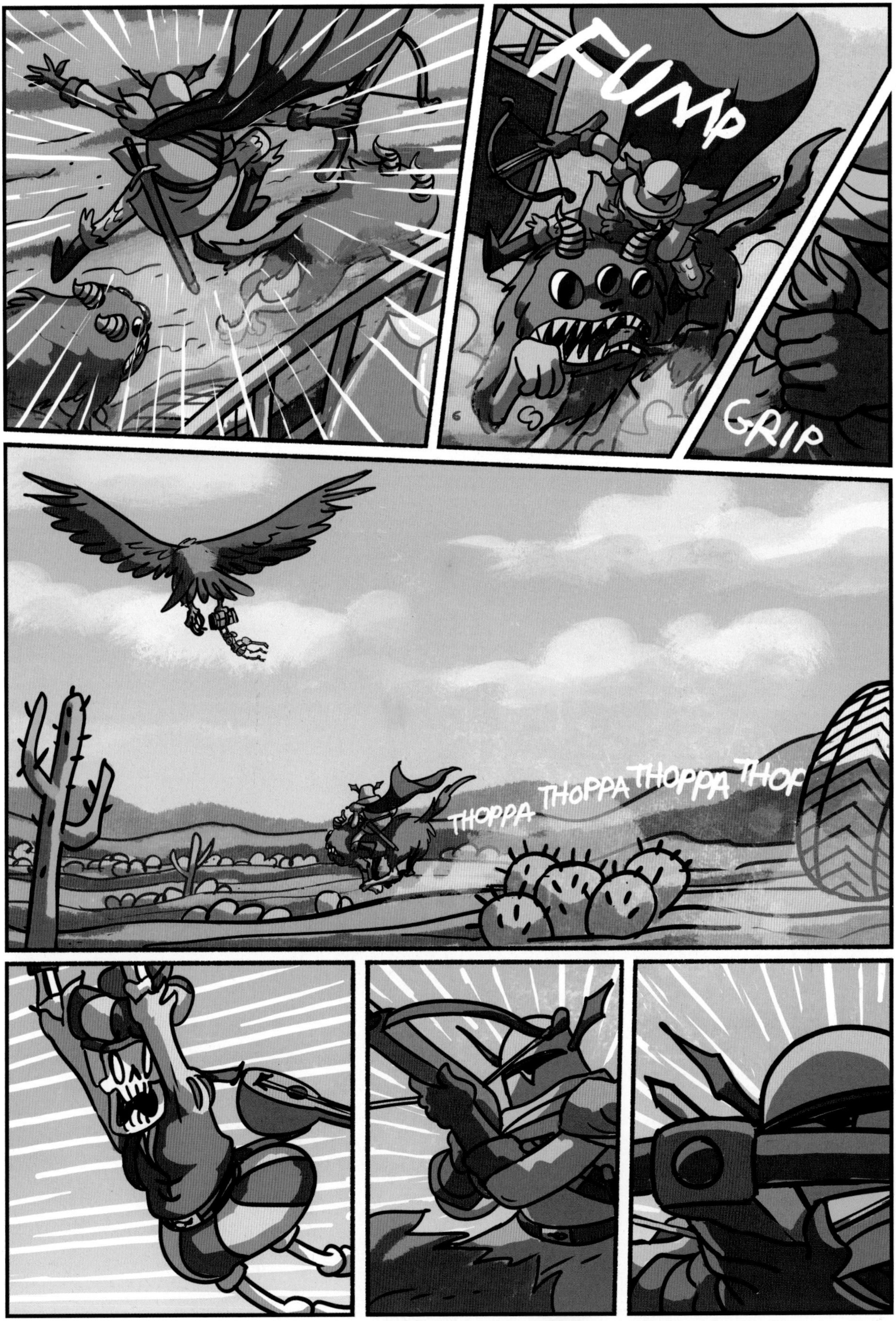
FUMP
GRIP
THOPPA THOPPA THOPPA THOP

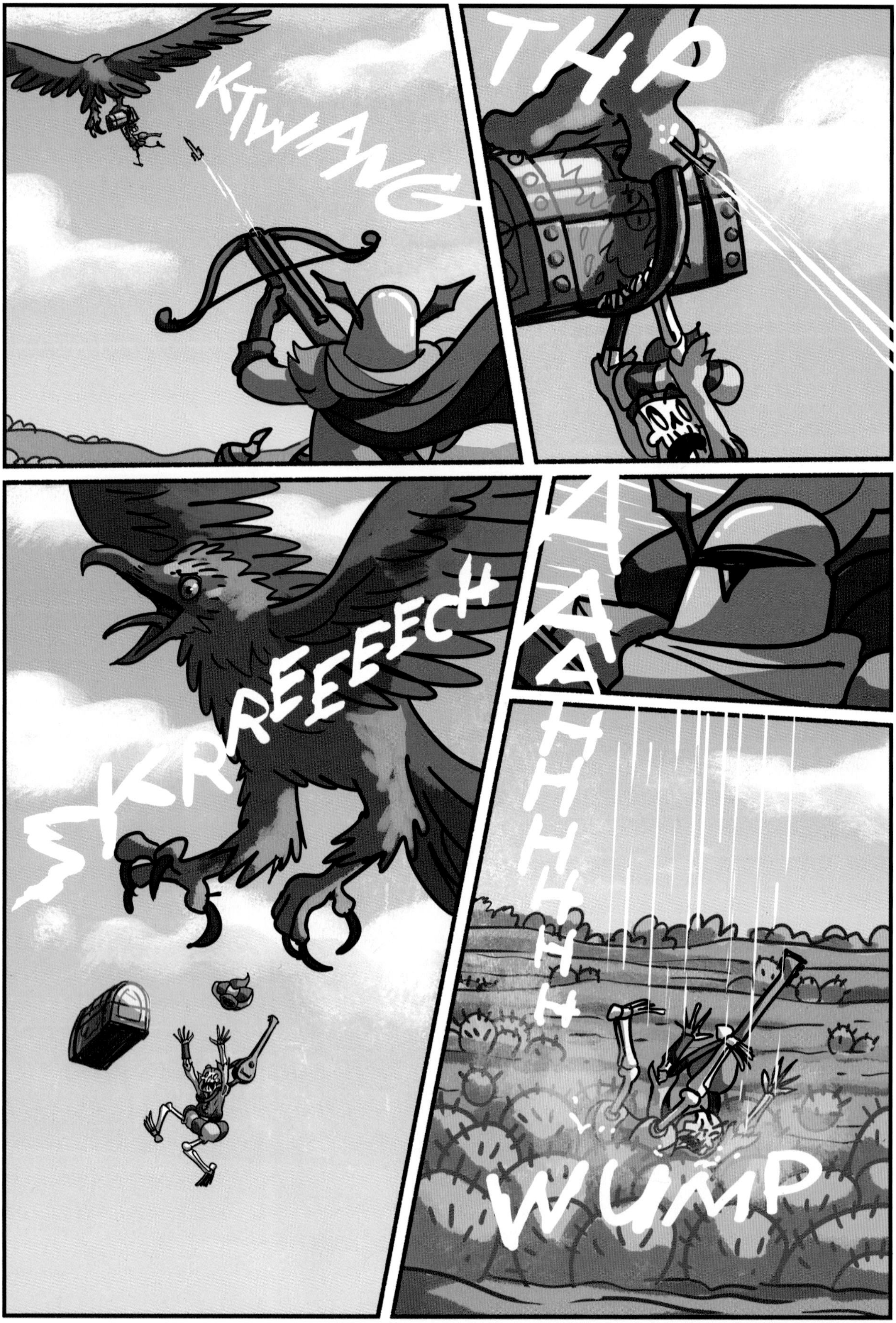
KTWANG
THP
SKRREEEEECH
AAAAHHHHHHH
WUMP

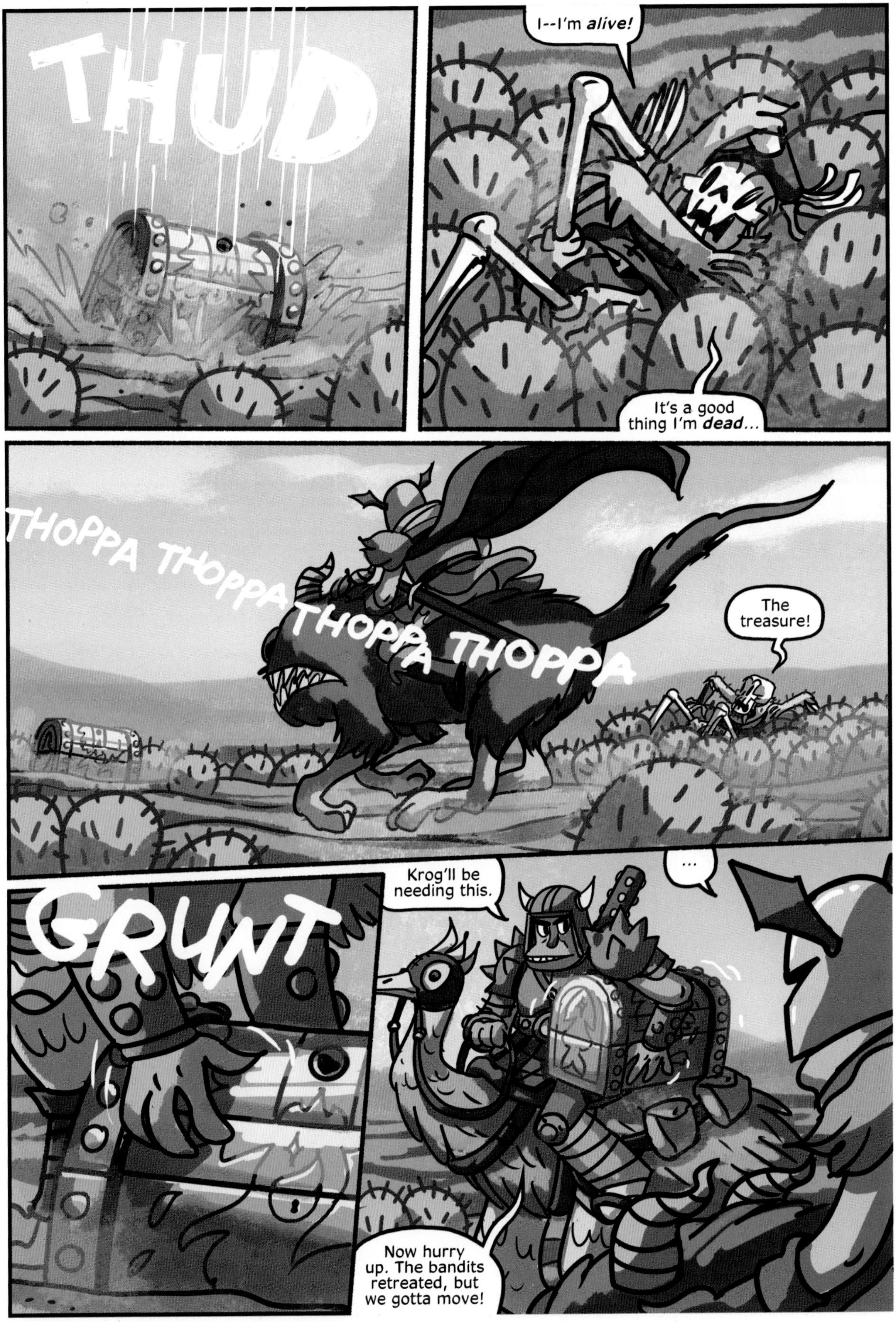
THUD
I--I'm *alive!*
It's a good thing I'm ***dead***...
THOPPA THOPPA THOPPA THOPPA THOPPA
The treasure!
GRUNT
Krog'll be needing this.
...
Now hurry up. The bandits retreated, but we gotta move!

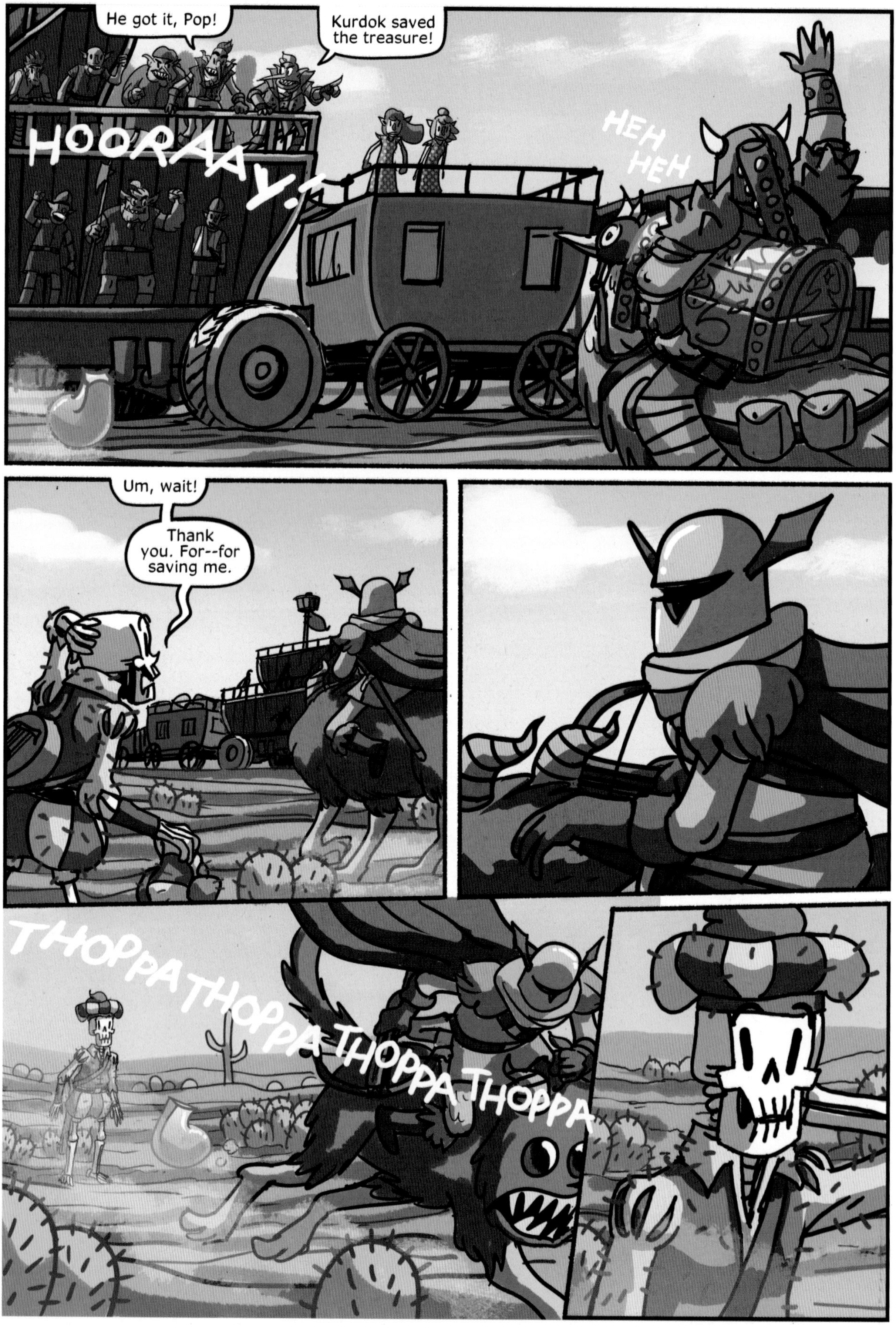
He got it, Pop!
Kurdok saved the treasure!
HOORAAY!!
HEH HEH
Um, wait!
Thank you. For--for saving me.
THOPPATHOPPATHOPPATHOPPA

Chapter 9
A Hero in Name Only

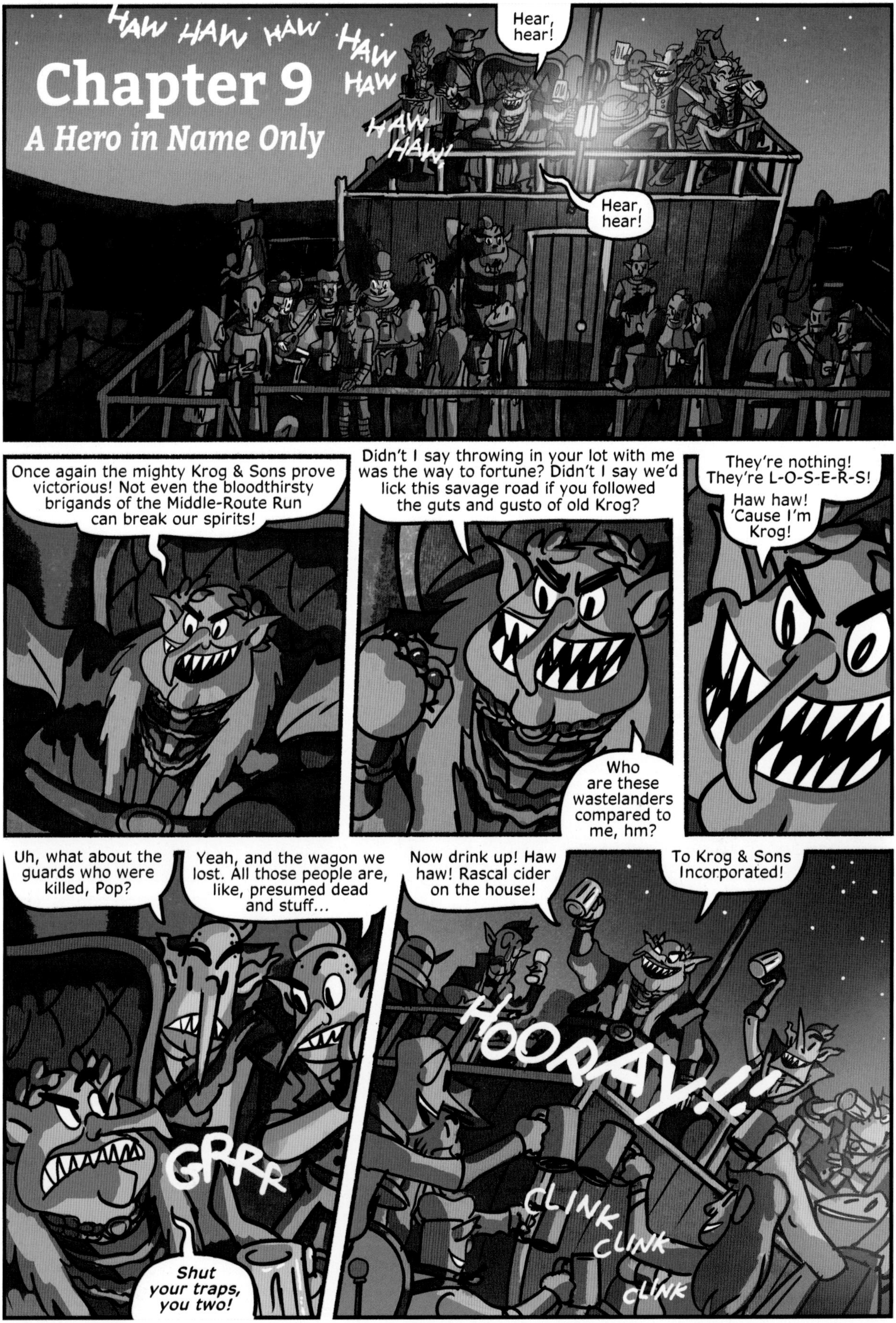
HAW HAW HAW HAW HAW HAW HAW HAW!
Hear, hear!
Hear, hear!
Once again the mighty Krog & Sons prove victorious! Not even the bloodthirsty brigands of the Middle-Route Run can break our spirits!
Didn't I say throwing in your lot with me was the way to fortune? Didn't I say we'd lick this savage road if you followed the guts and gusto of old Krog?
Who are these wastelanders compared to me, hm?
They're nothing! They're L-O-S-E-R-S!
Haw haw! 'Cause I'm Krog!
Uh, what about the guards who were killed, Pop?
Yeah, and the wagon we lost. All those people are, like, presumed dead and stuff...
GRRR
Shut your traps, you two!
Now drink up! Haw haw! Rascal cider on the house!
To Krog & Sons Incorporated!
HOORAY!!!
CLINK
CLINK
CLINK

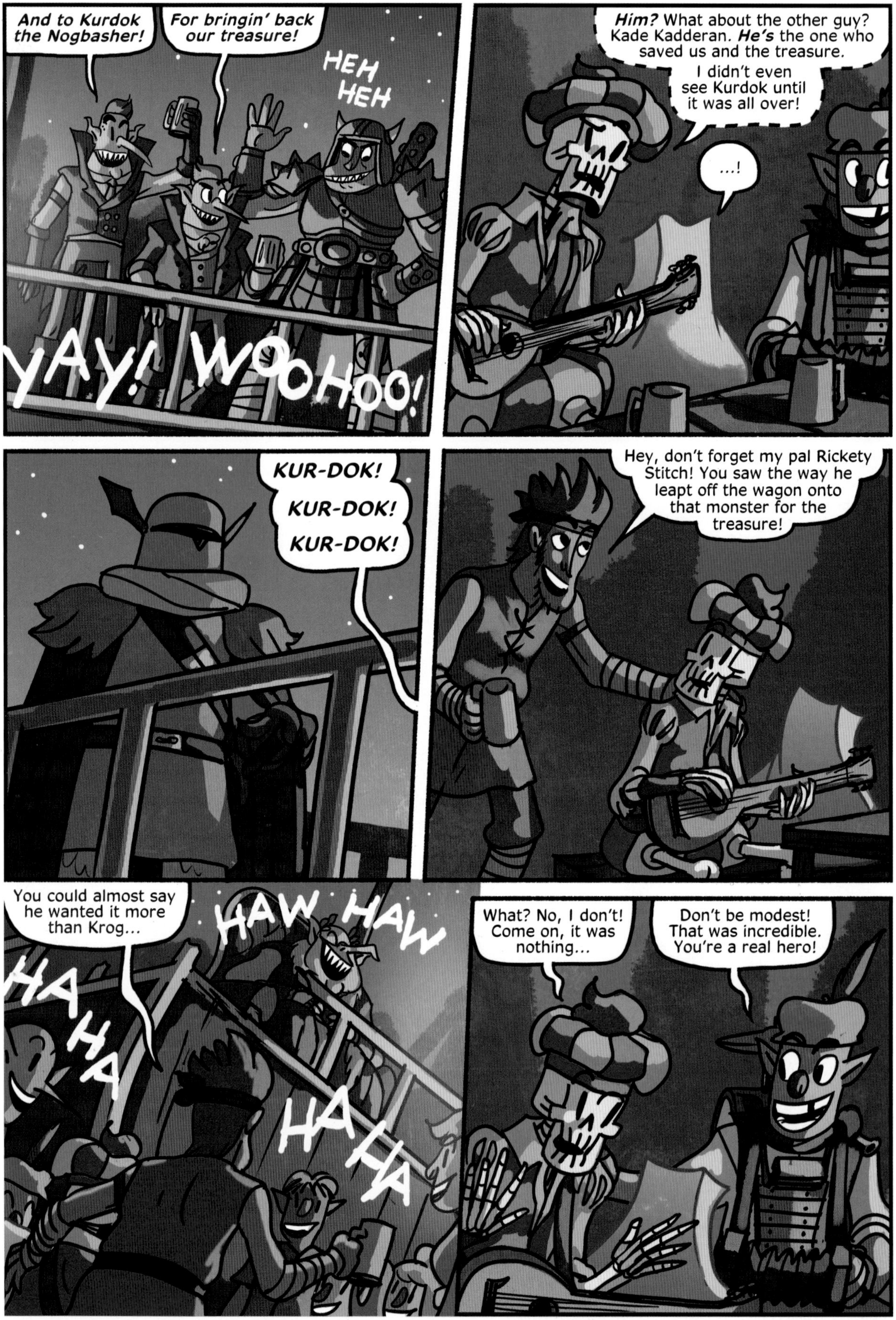
And to Kurdok the Nogbasher!
For bringin' back our treasure!
HEH HEH
YAY! WOOHOO!
Him? What about the other guy? Kade Kadderan. He's the one who saved us and the treasure.
I didn't even see Kurdok until it was all over!
...!
KUR-DOK!
KUR-DOK!
KUR-DOK!
Hey, don't forget my pal Rickety Stitch! You saw the way he leapt off the wagon onto that monster for the treasure!
You could almost say he wanted it more than Krog...
HAW HAW
HAHAHA
HAHA
What? No, I don't! Come on, it was nothing...
Don't be modest! That was incredible. You're a real hero!

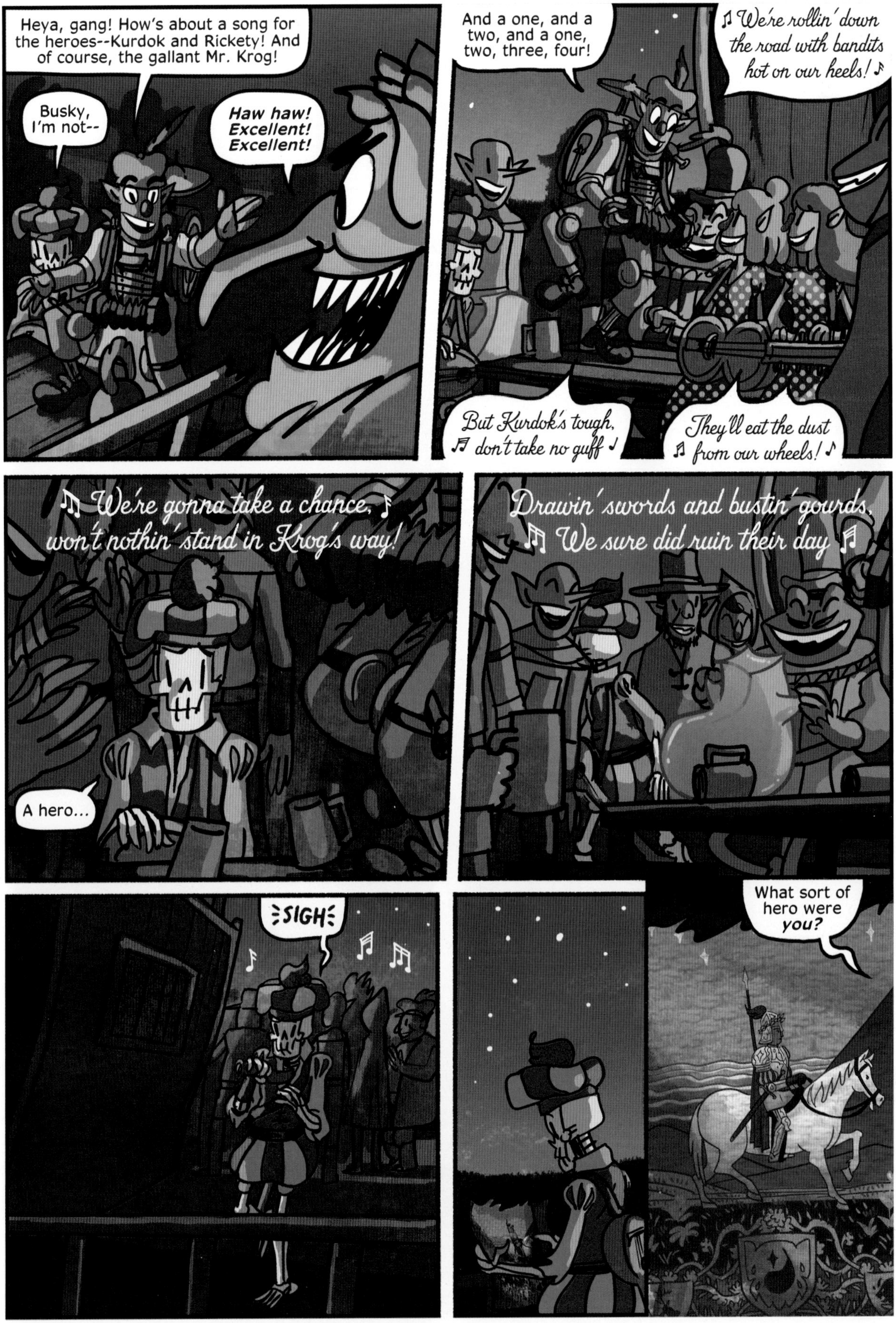
Heya, gang! How's about a song for the heroes--Kurdok and Rickety! And of course, the gallant Mr. Krog!
Busky, I'm not--
Haw haw! Excellent! Excellent!
And a one, and a two, and a one, two, three, four!
♫ We're rollin' down the road with bandits hot on our heels! ♪
But Kurdok's tough, ♫ don't take no guff ♩
They'll eat the dust ♫ from our wheels! ♪
♫ We're gonna take a chance, ♪ won't nothin' stand in Krog's way!
A hero...
Drawin' swords and bustin' gourds, ♫ We sure did ruin their day ♫
SIGH
What sort of hero were you?

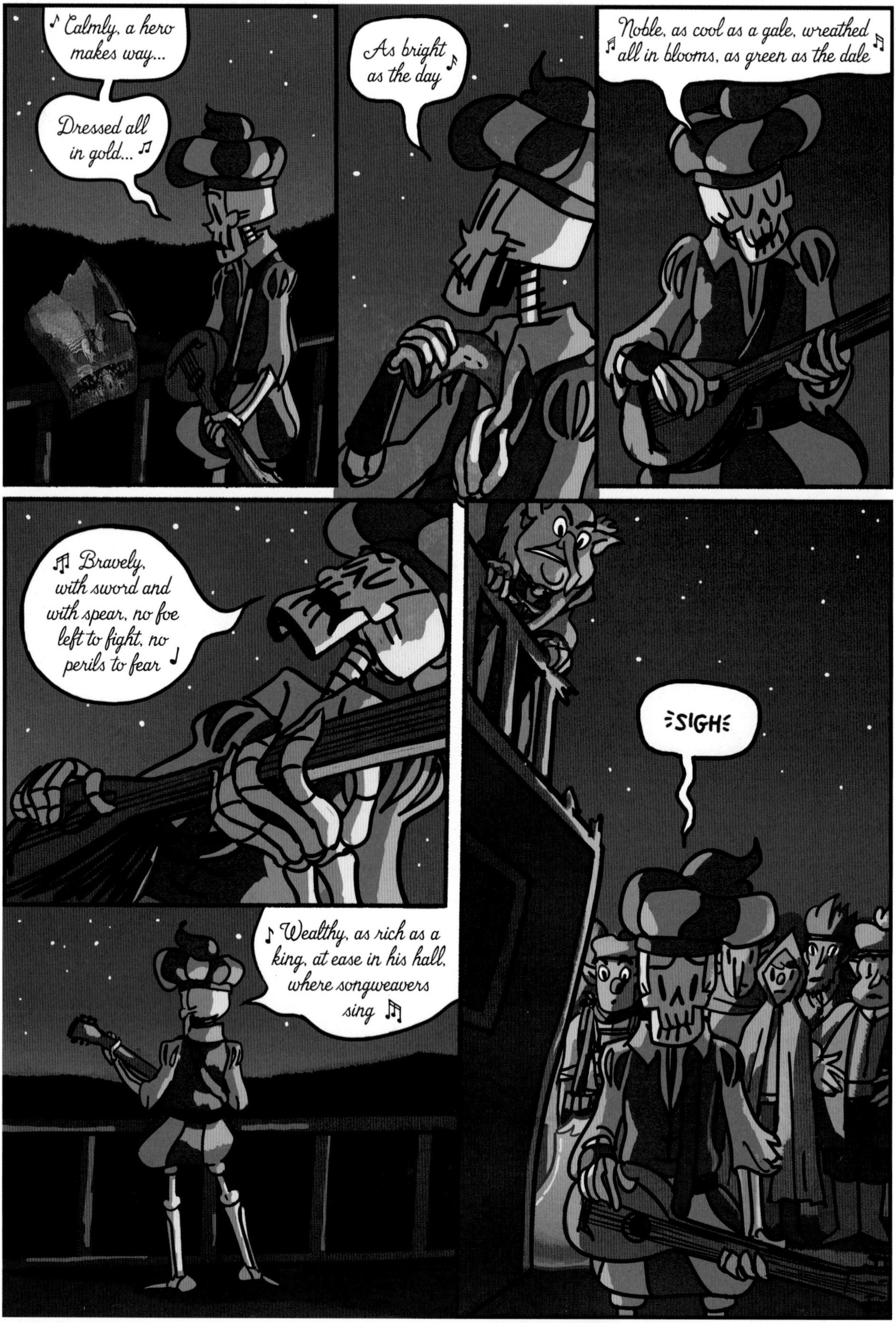
Calmly, a hero makes way...
Dressed all in gold...
As bright as the day
Noble, as cool as a gale, wreathed all in blooms, as green as the dale
Bravely, with sword and with spear, no foe left to fight, no perils to fear
Wealthy, as rich as a king, at ease in his hall, where songweavers sing
SIGH

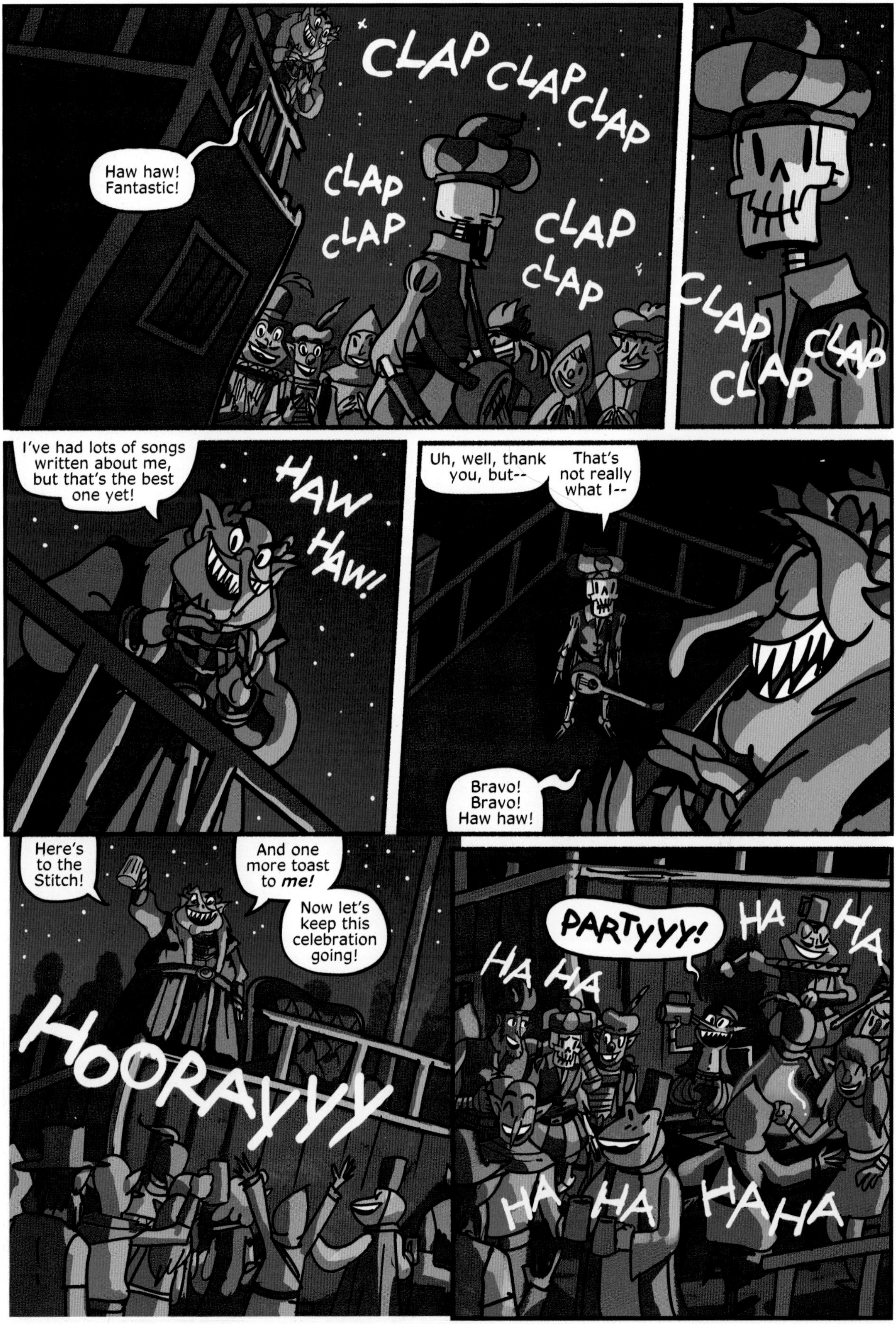
CLAP CLAP CLAP
Haw haw! Fantastic!
CLAP CLAP
CLAP CLAP
CLAP CLAP CLAP
I've had lots of songs written about me, but that's the best one yet!
HAW HAW!
Uh, well, thank you, but--
That's not really what I--
Bravo! Bravo! Haw haw!
Here's to the Stitch!
And one more toast to *me!*
Now let's keep this celebration going!
HOORAYYY
PARTYYY!
HA HA
HA HA
HA HA HAHA

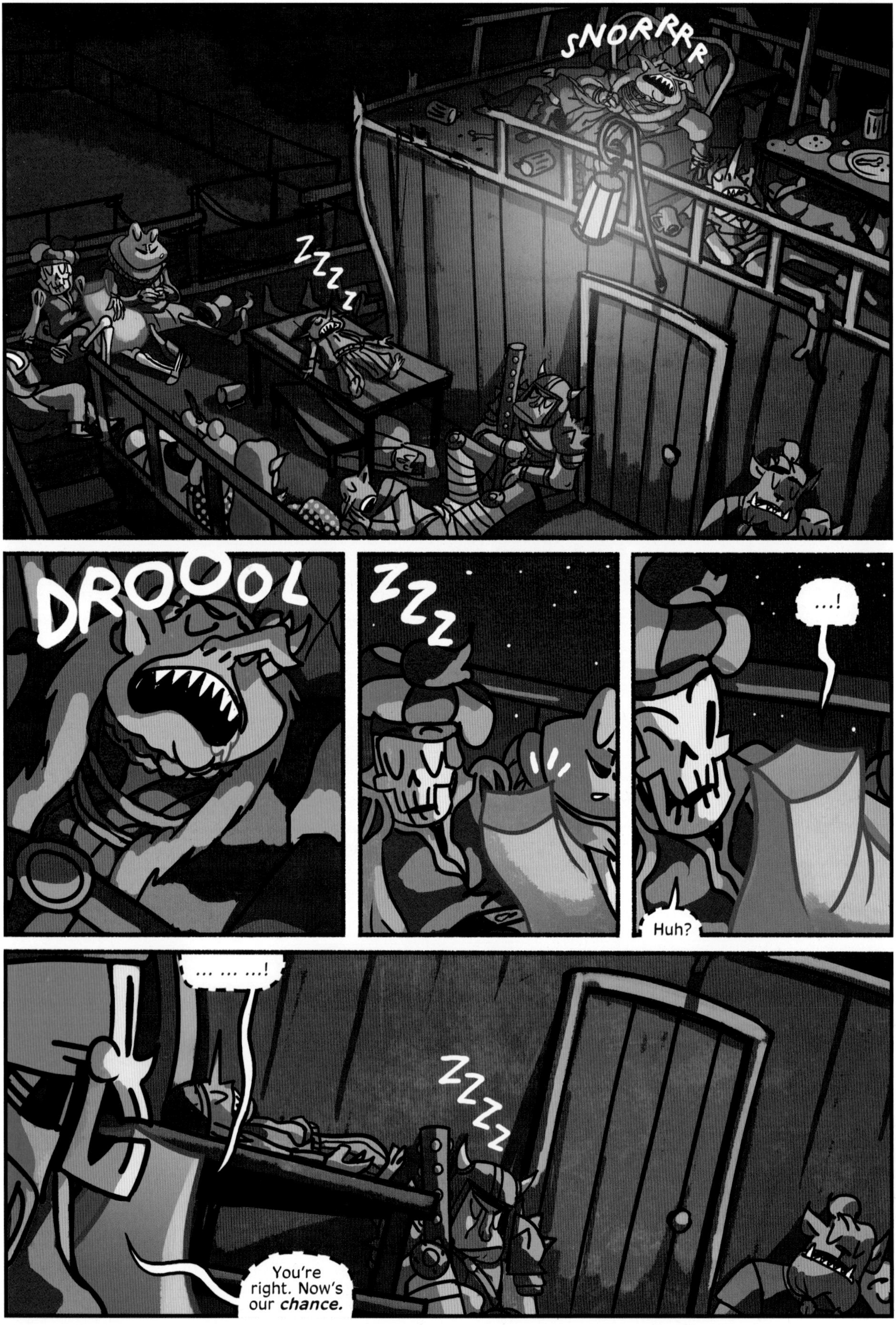
SNORRRR
ZZZZ
DROOOL
ZZZ
...!
Huh?
... ...!
ZZZZ
You're right. Now's our *chance.*

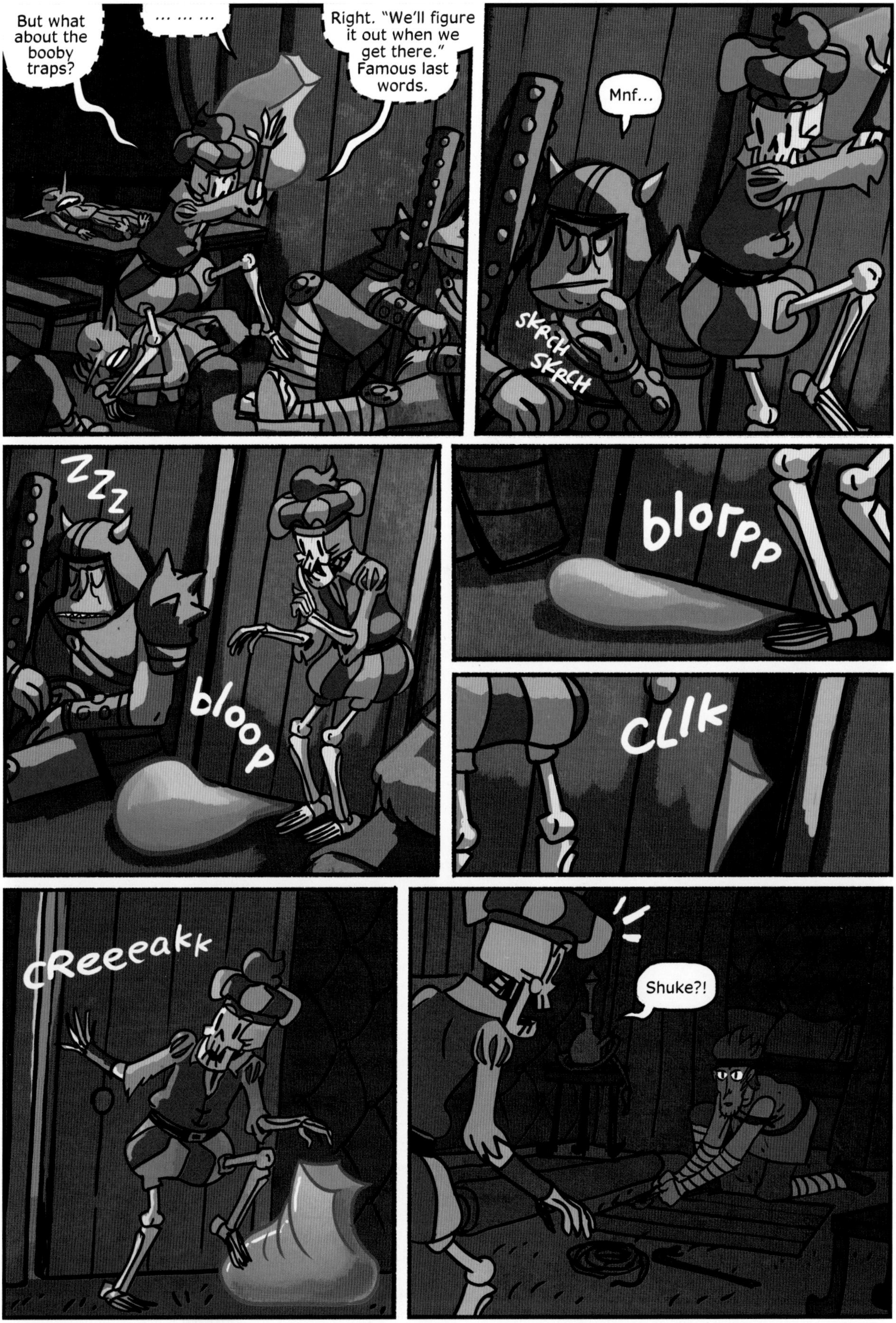
But what about the booby traps?
... ...
Right. "We'll figure it out when we get there." Famous last words.
Mnf...
SKRCH SKRCH
ZZZ
bloop
blorpp
CLIK
CReeeakk
Shuke?!

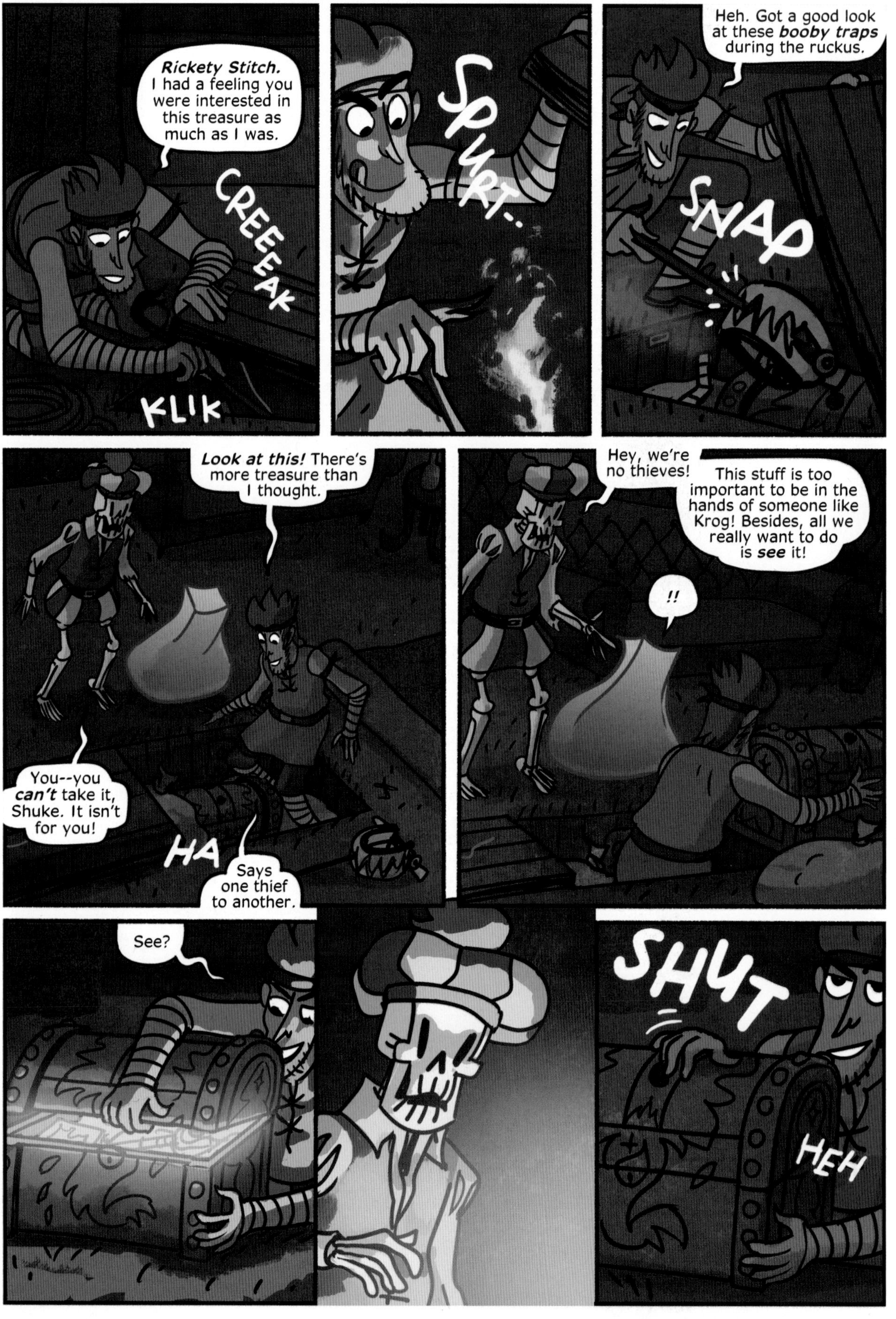
Rickety Stitch. I had a feeling you were interested in this treasure as much as I was.
CREEEAK
KLIK
SPURT--
Heh. Got a good look at these booby traps during the ruckus.
SNAP
Look at this! There's more treasure than I thought.
You--you can't take it, Shuke. It isn't for you!
HA
Says one thief to another.
Hey, we're no thieves!
This stuff is too important to be in the hands of someone like Krog! Besides, all we really want to do is see it!
!!
See?
SHUT
HEH

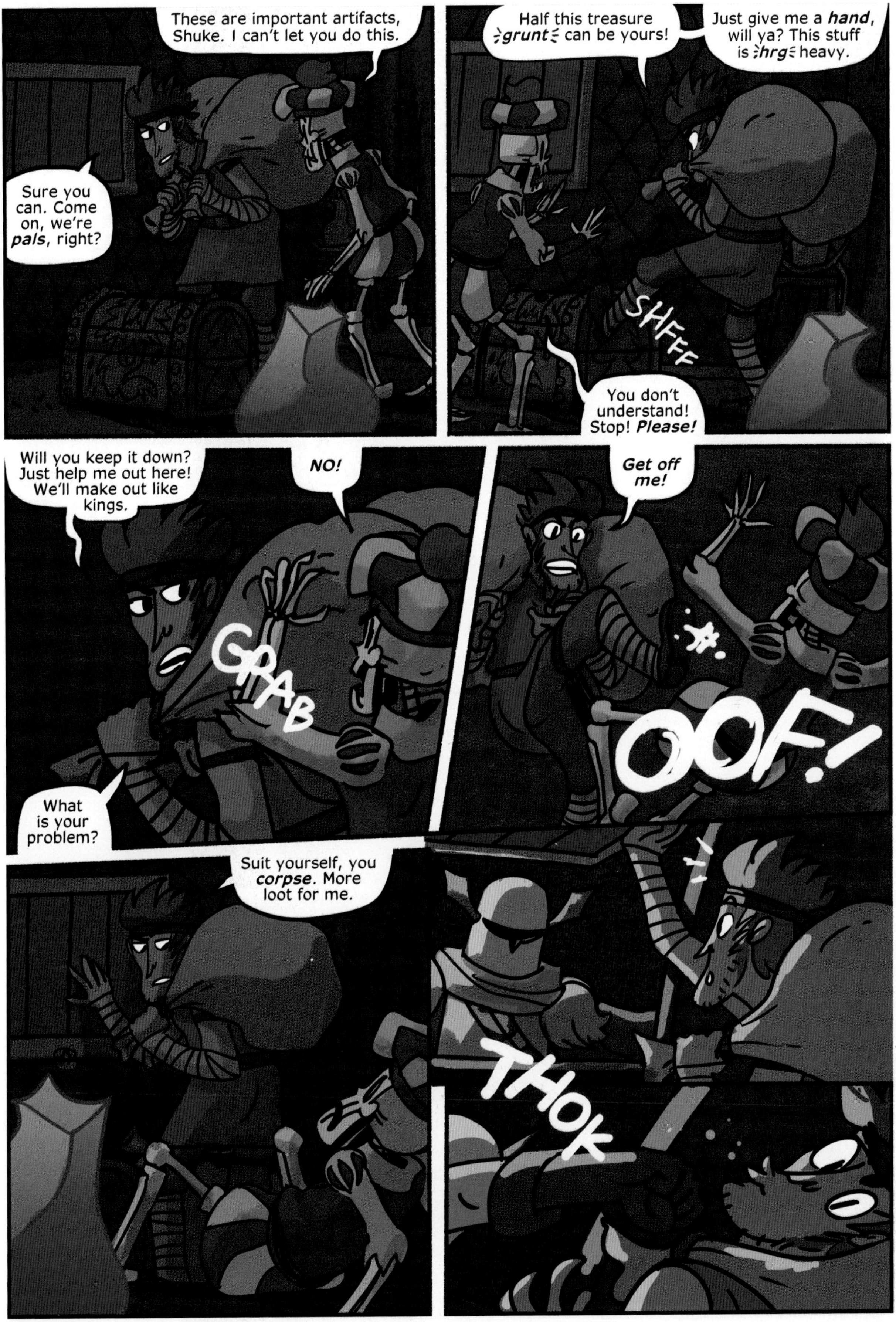
These are important artifacts, Shuke. I can't let you do this.
Sure you can. Come on, we're *pals*, right?
Half this treasure *grunt* can be yours!
Just give me a *hand*, will ya? This stuff is *hrg* heavy.
SHFFF
You don't understand! Stop! *Please!*
Will you keep it down? Just help me out here! We'll make out like kings.
NO!
GRAB
What is your problem?
Get off me!
OOF!
Suit yourself, you *corpse*. More loot for me.
THOK

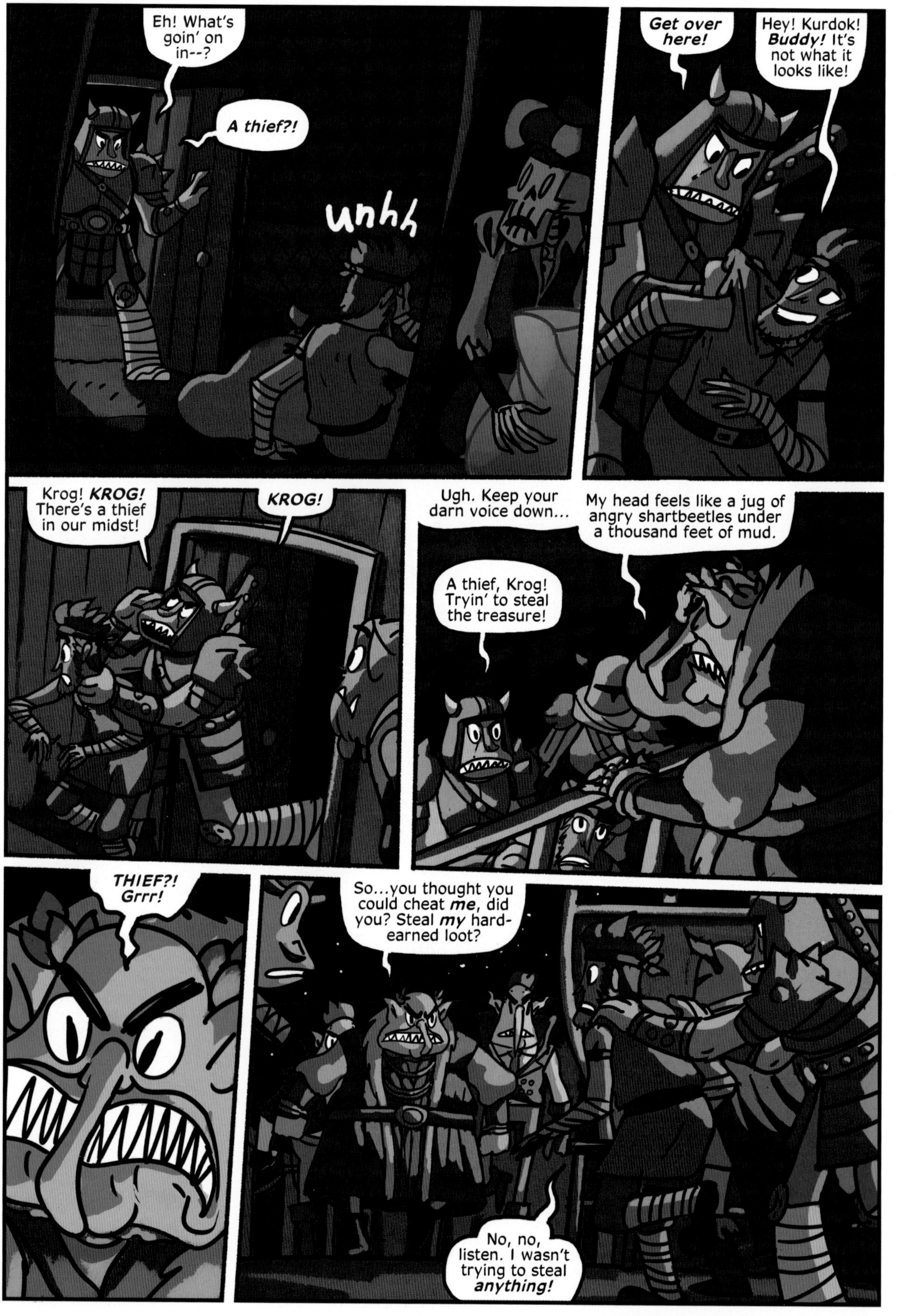

Eh! What's goin' on in--?
A thief?!
unhh
Get over here!
Hey! Kurdok! *Buddy!* It's not what it looks like!
Krog! ***KROG!*** There's a thief in our midst!
KROG!
Ugh. Keep your darn voice down...
My head feels like a jug of angry shartbeetles under a thousand feet of mud.
A thief, Krog! Tryin' to steal the treasure!
THIEF?! Grrr!
So...you thought you could cheat ***me***, did you? Steal ***my*** hard-earned loot?
No, no, listen. I wasn't trying to steal ***anything!***

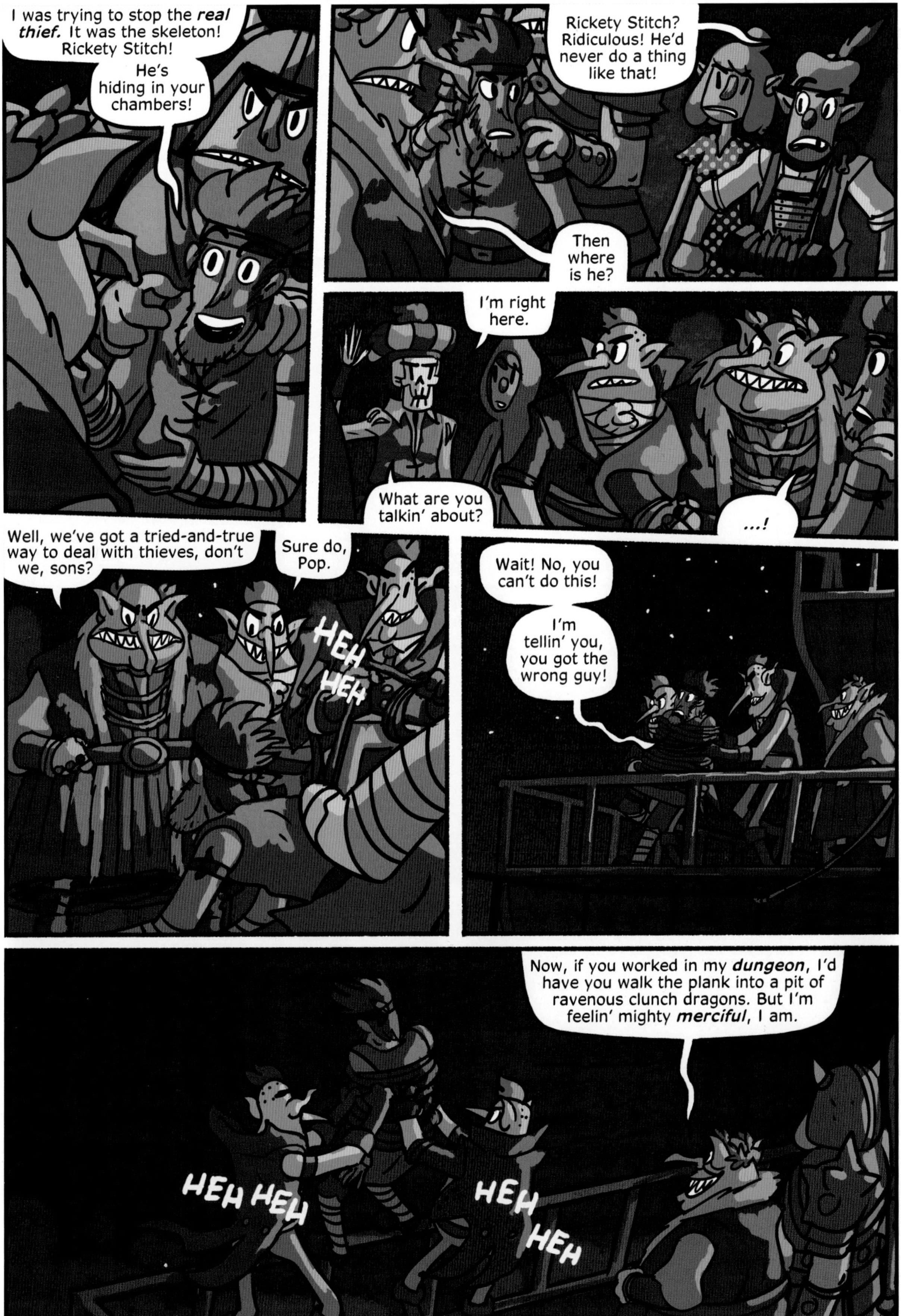

I was trying to stop the *real thief.* It was the skeleton! Rickety Stitch!
He's hiding in your chambers!
Rickety Stitch? Ridiculous! He'd never do a thing like that!
Then where is he?
I'm right here.
What are you talkin' about?
...!
Well, we've got a tried-and-true way to deal with thieves, don't we, sons?
Sure do, Pop.
HEH HEH
Wait! No, you can't do this!
I'm tellin' you, you got the wrong guy!
Now, if you worked in my *dungeon*, I'd have you walk the plank into a pit of ravenous clunch dragons. But I'm feelin' mighty *merciful*, I am.
HEH HEH
HEH HEH

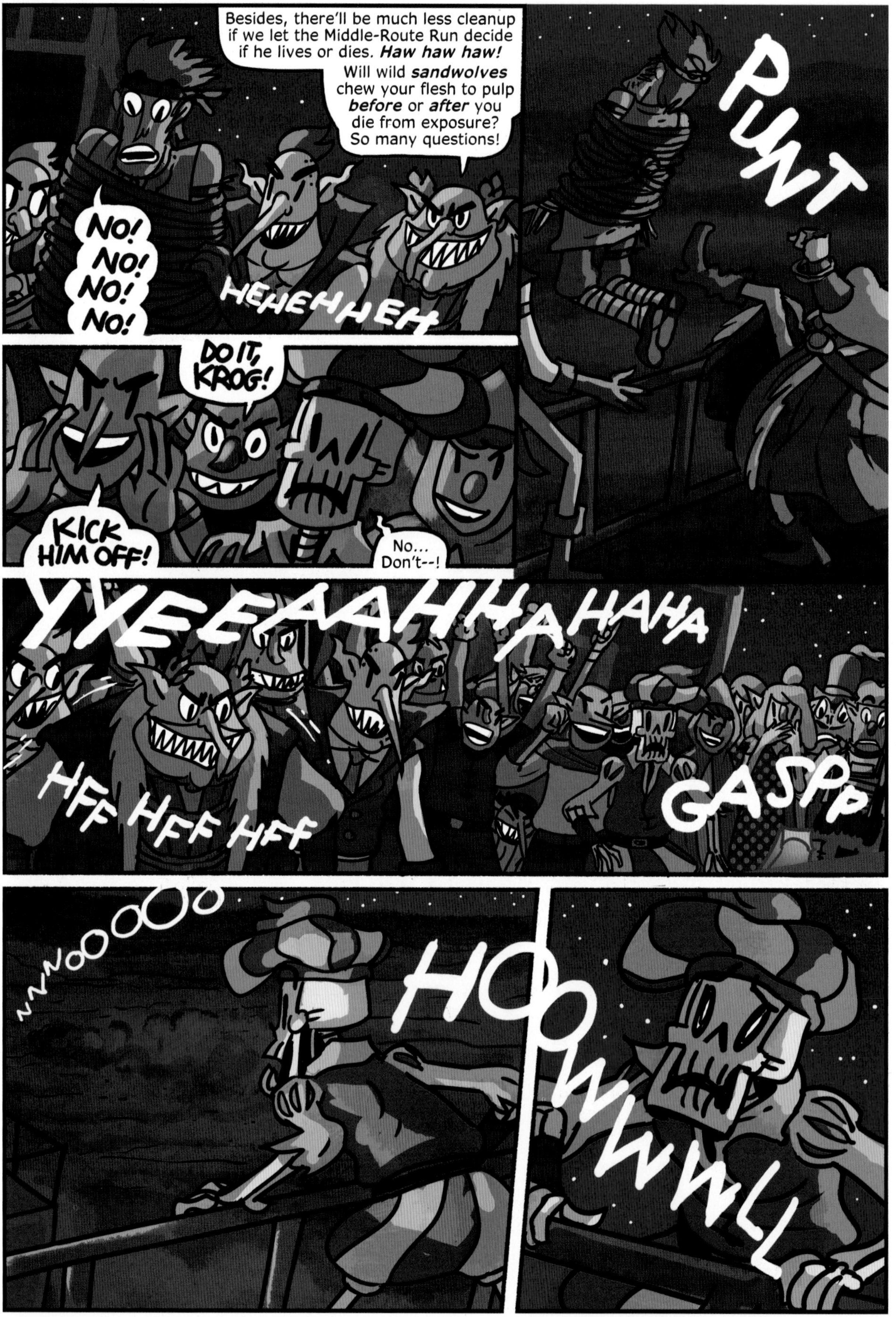

Besides, there'll be much less cleanup if we let the Middle-Route Run decide if he lives or dies. *Haw haw haw!*
Will wild *sandwolves* chew your flesh to pulp *before* or *after* you die from exposure? So many questions!
NO! NO! NO! NO!
HEHEHHEH
PUNT
DO IT, KROG!
KICK HIM OFF!
No... Don't--!
YYEEAAHHAHAHA
HFF HFF HFF
GASPP
NNNOOOOOO
HOOOWWWLL

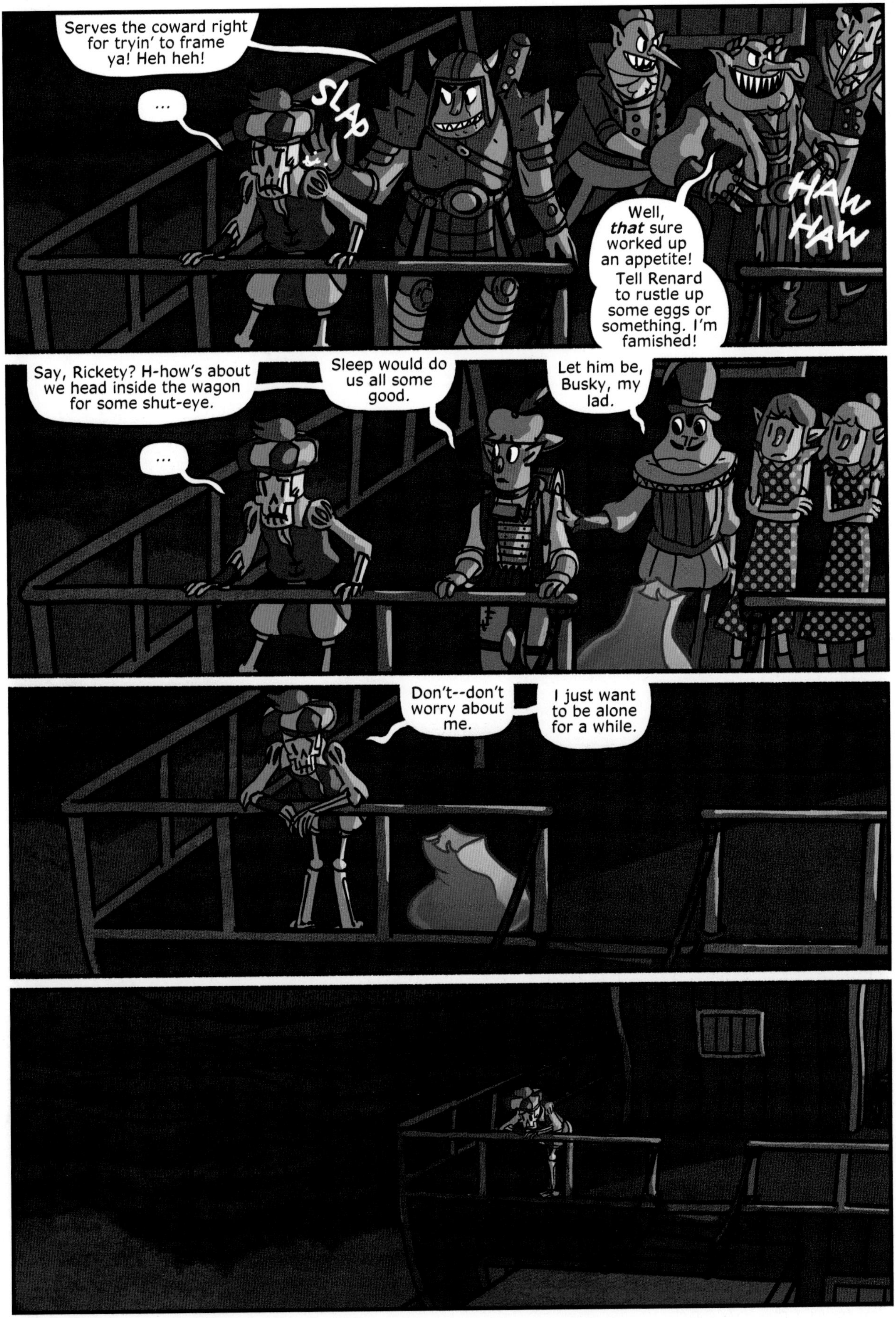

Serves the coward right for tryin' to frame ya! Heh heh!
SLAP
...
Well, *that* sure worked up an appetite!
Tell Renard to rustle up some eggs or something. I'm famished!
HAW HAW
Say, Rickety? H-how's about we head inside the wagon for some shut-eye.
Sleep would do us all some good.
Let him be, Busky, my lad.
...
Don't--don't worry about me.
I just want to be alone for a while.

Chapter 10
An Ember Burns

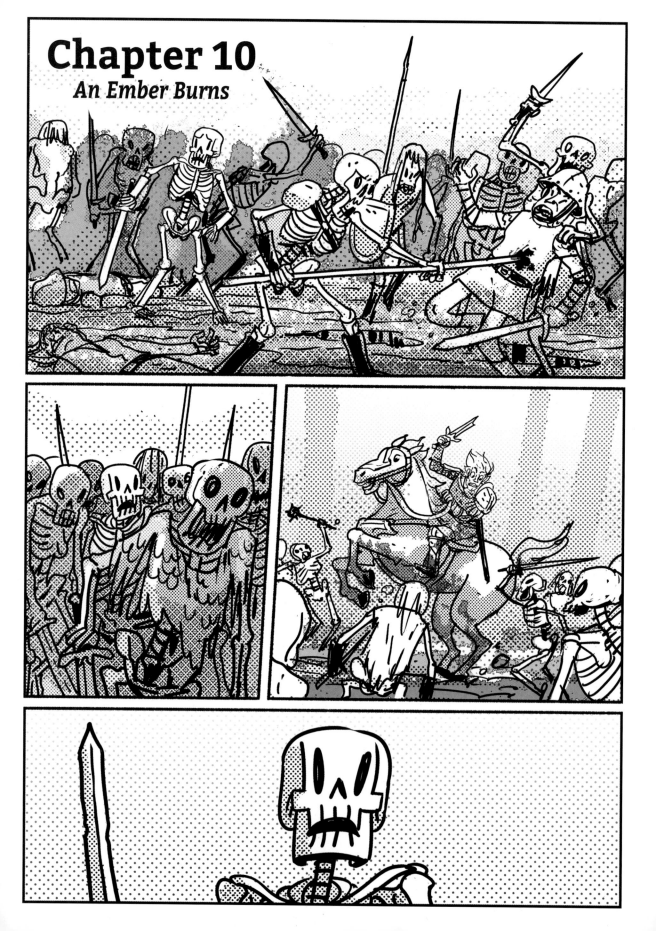

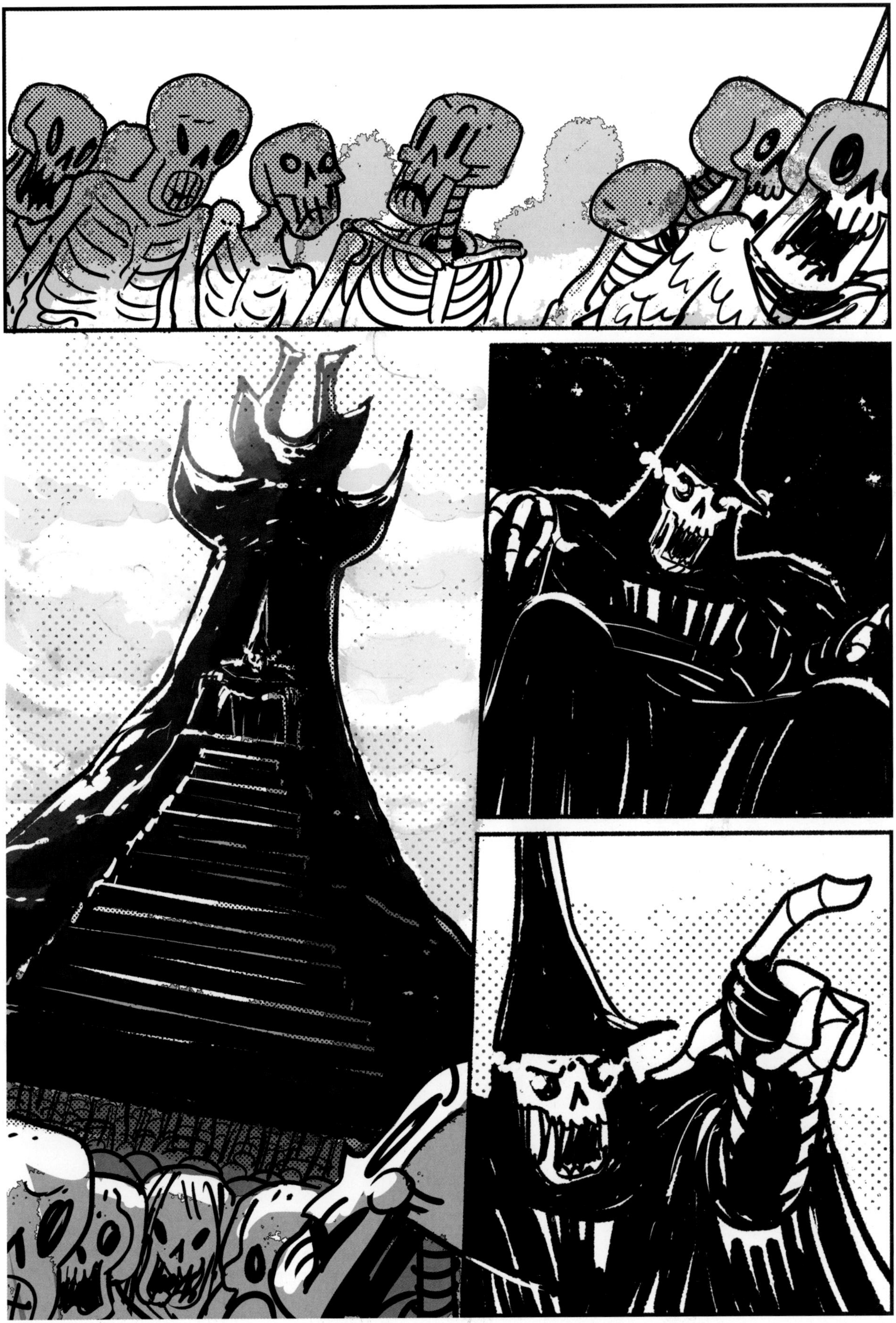

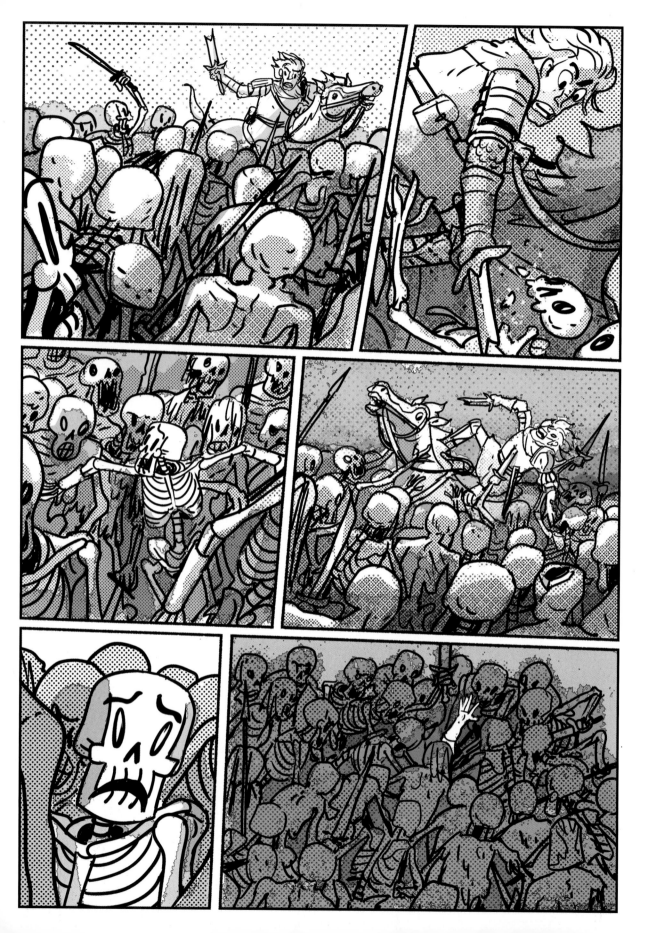

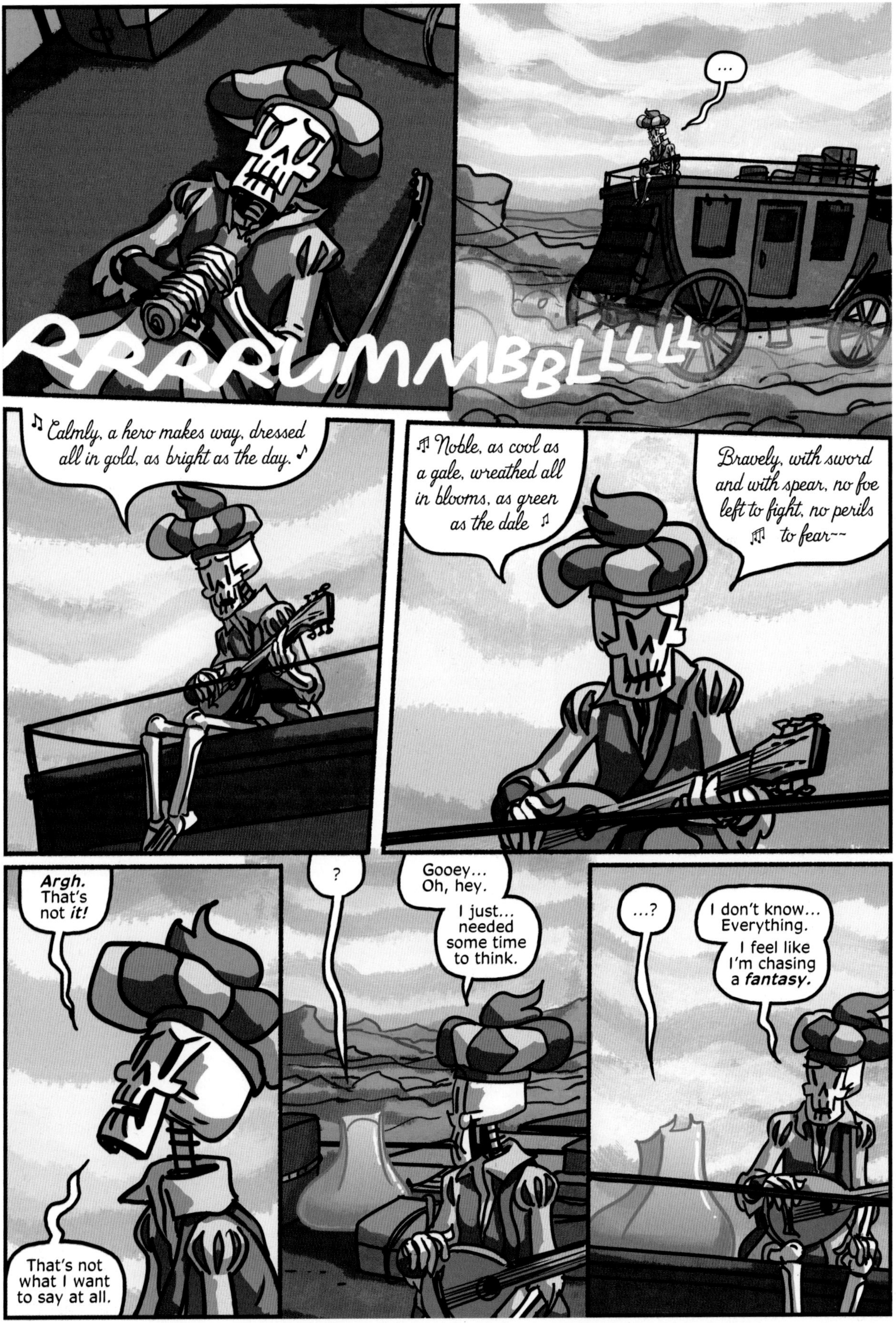
RRRRUMMBBLLLLL
...
♫ Calmly, a hero makes way, dressed all in gold, as bright as the day. ♪
♬ Noble, as cool as a gale, wreathed all in blooms, as green as the dale ♫
Bravely, with sword and with spear, no foe left to fight, no perils ♬ to fear~~
Argh. That's not it!
That's not what I want to say at all.
?
Gooey... Oh, hey.
I just... needed some time to think.
...?
I don't know... Everything.
I feel like I'm chasing a fantasy.

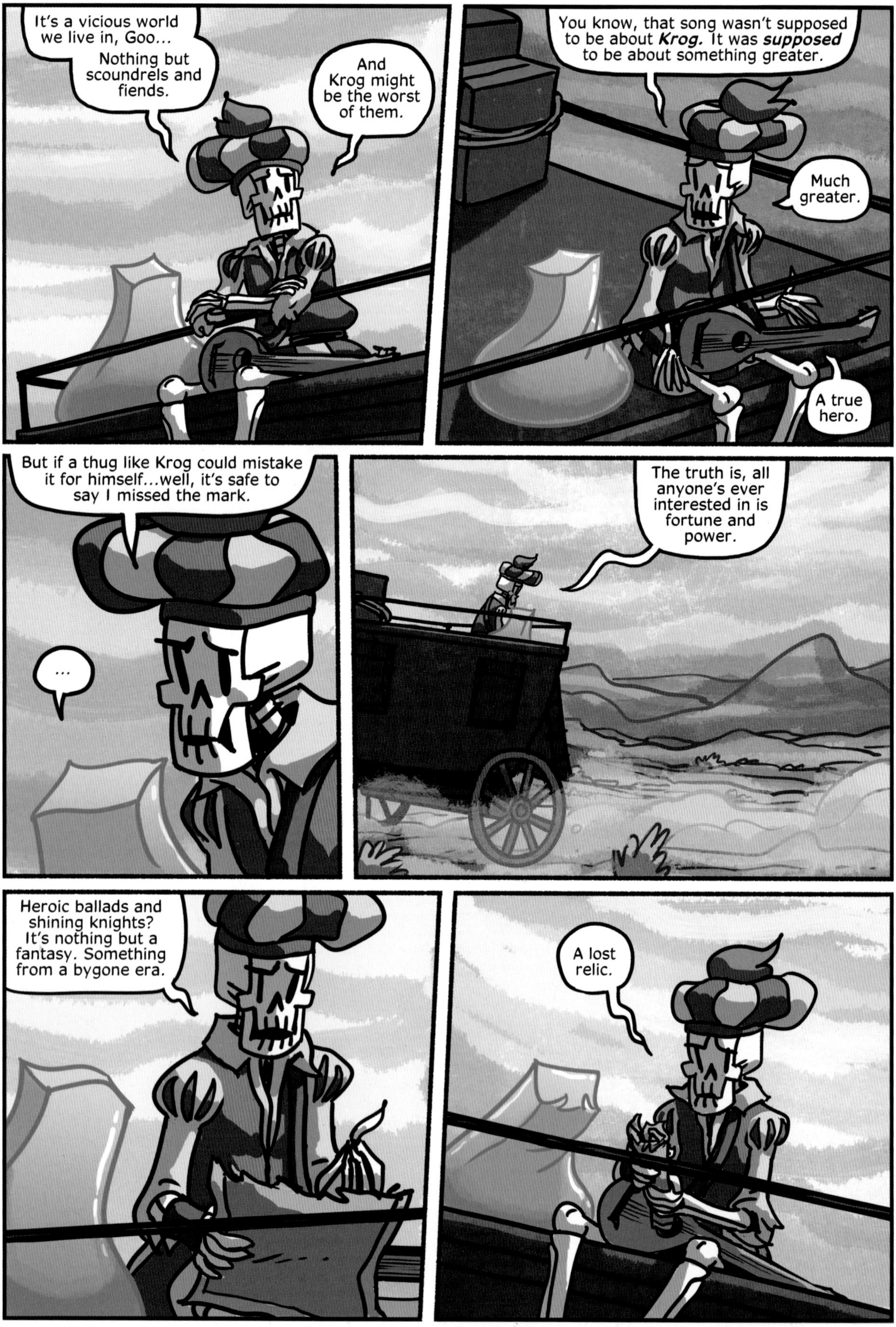
It's a vicious world we live in, Goo...
Nothing but scoundrels and fiends.
And Krog might be the worst of them.
You know, that song wasn't supposed to be about **Krog.** It was ***supposed*** to be about something greater.
Much greater.
A true hero.
But if a thug like Krog could mistake it for himself...well, it's safe to say I missed the mark.
...
The truth is, all anyone's ever interested in is fortune and power.
Heroic ballads and shining knights? It's nothing but a fantasy. Something from a bygone era.
A lost relic.

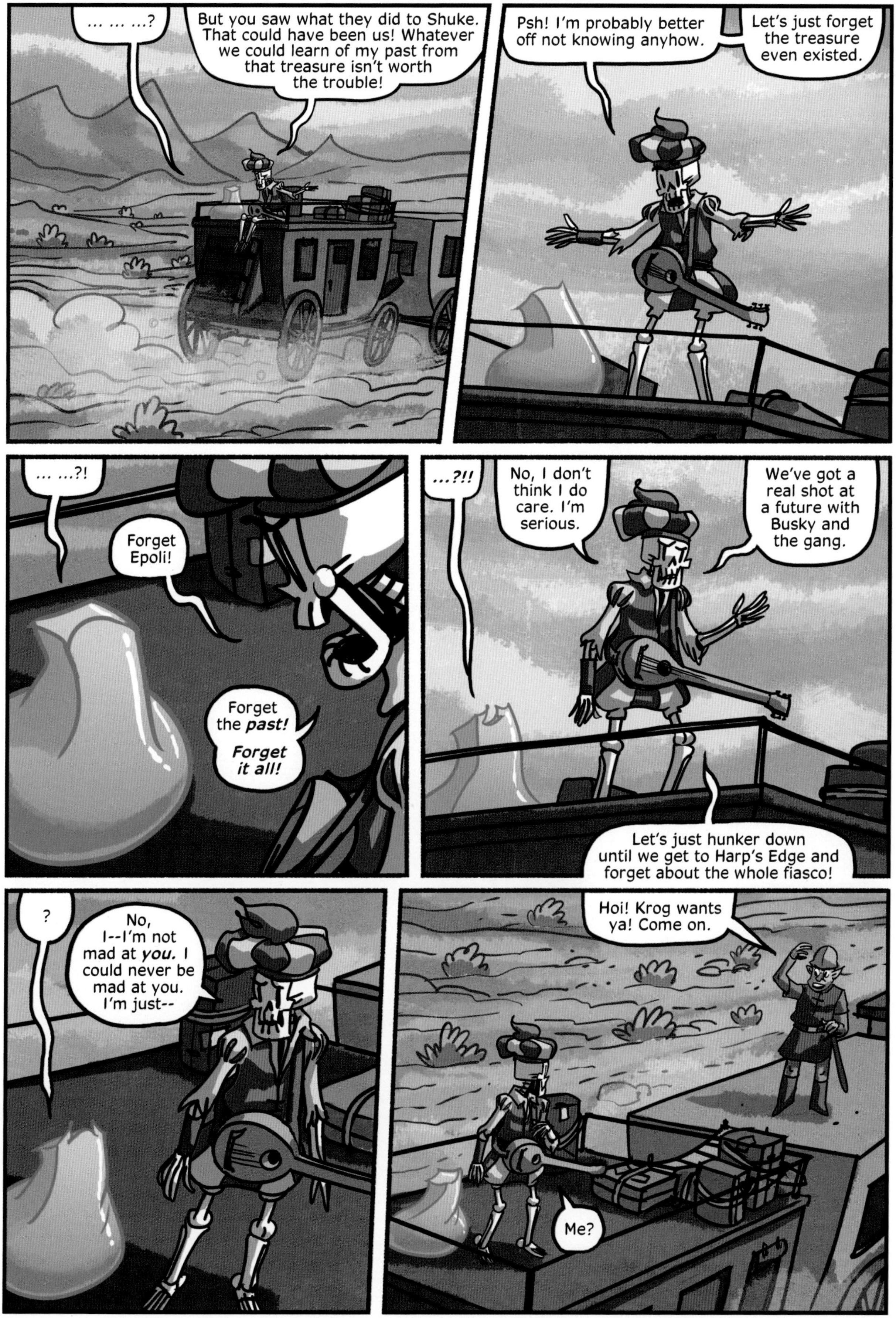
... ...?
But you saw what they did to Shuke. That could have been us! Whatever we could learn of my past from that treasure isn't worth the trouble!
Psh! I'm probably better off not knowing anyhow.
Let's just forget the treasure even existed.
... ...?!
Forget Epoli!
Forget the *past!*
Forget it all!
...?!!
No, I don't think I do care. I'm serious.
We've got a real shot at a future with Busky and the gang.
Let's just hunker down until we get to Harp's Edge and forget about the whole fiasco!
?
No, I--I'm not mad at ***you.*** I could never be mad at you. I'm just--
Hoi! Krog wants ya! Come on.
Me?

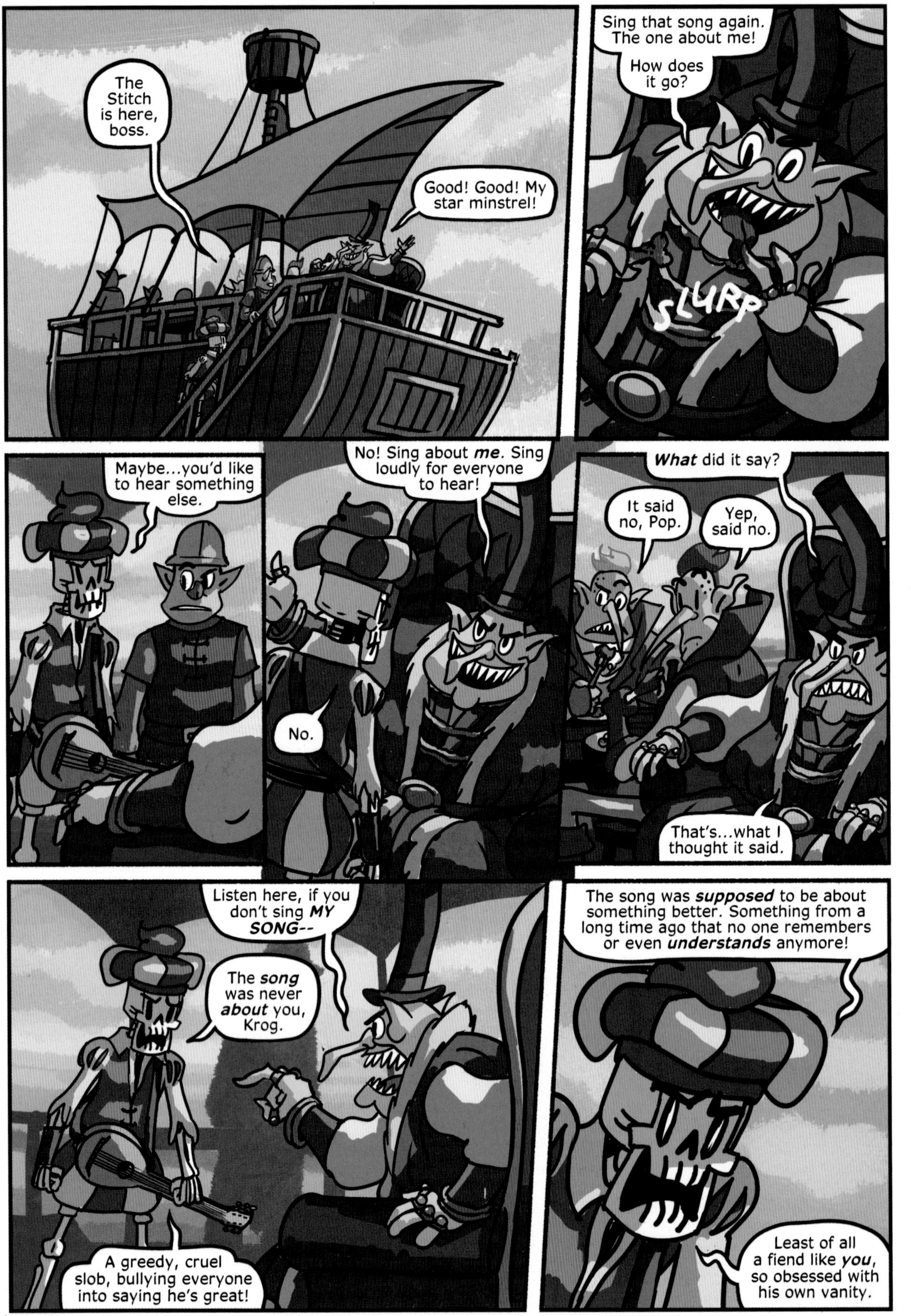

The Stitch is here, boss.
Good! Good! My star minstrel!
Sing that song again. The one about me!
How does it go?
SLURP
Maybe...you'd like to hear something else.
No! Sing about *me*. Sing loudly for everyone to hear!
No.
What did it say?
It said no, Pop.
Yep, said no.
That's...what I thought it said.
Listen here, if you don't sing ***MY SONG***--
The *song* was never *about* you, Krog.
A greedy, cruel slob, bullying everyone into saying he's great!
The song was ***supposed*** to be about something better. Something from a long time ago that no one remembers or even ***understands*** anymore!
Least of all a fiend like *you*, so obsessed with his own vanity.

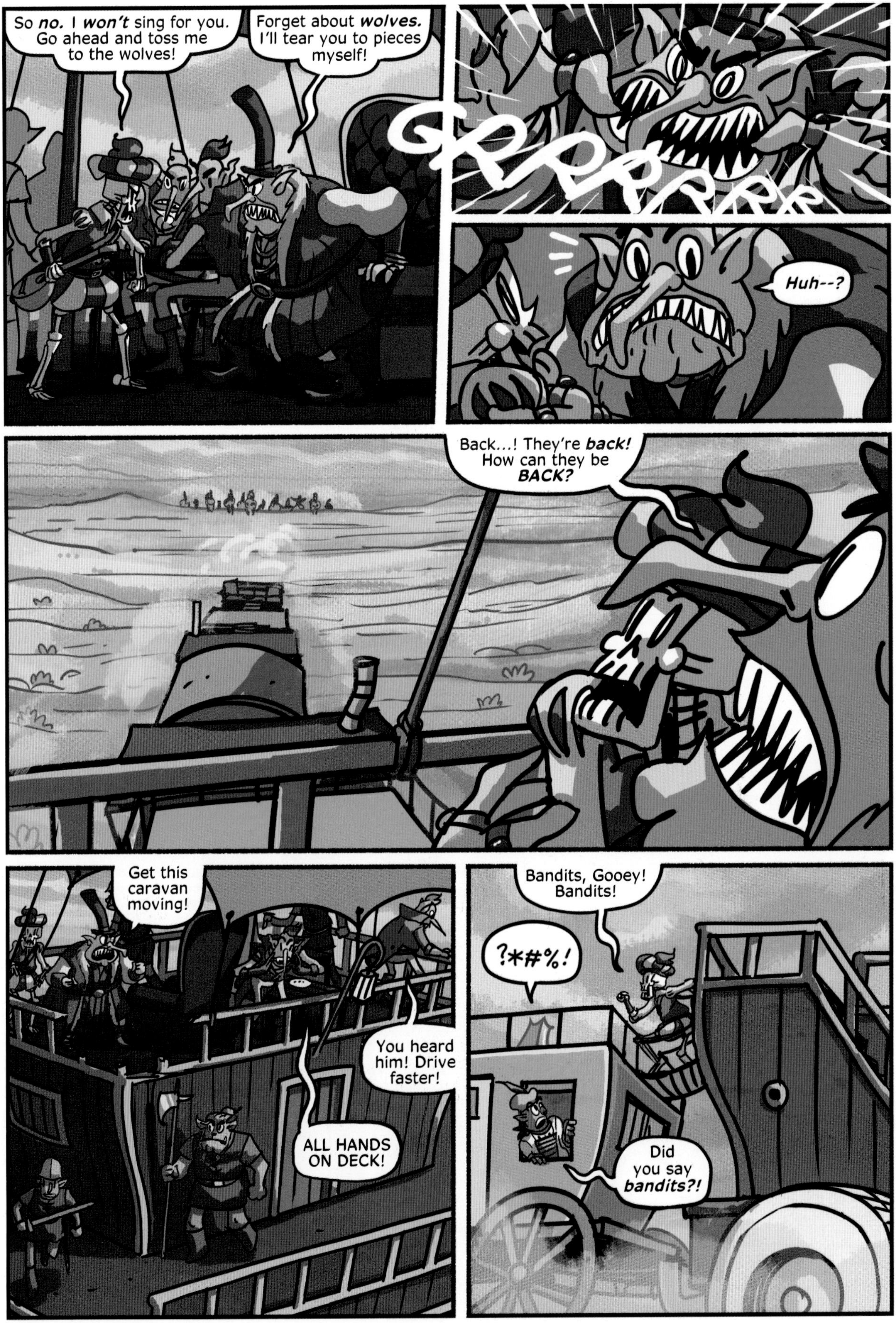
So *no.* I *won't* sing for you. Go ahead and toss me to the wolves!
Forget about *wolves.* I'll tear you to pieces myself!
GRRRRRR
Huh--?
Back...! They're *back!* How can they be *BACK?*
Get this caravan moving!
You heard him! Drive faster!
ALL HANDS ON DECK!
Bandits, Gooey! Bandits!
?*#%!
Did you say *bandits?!*

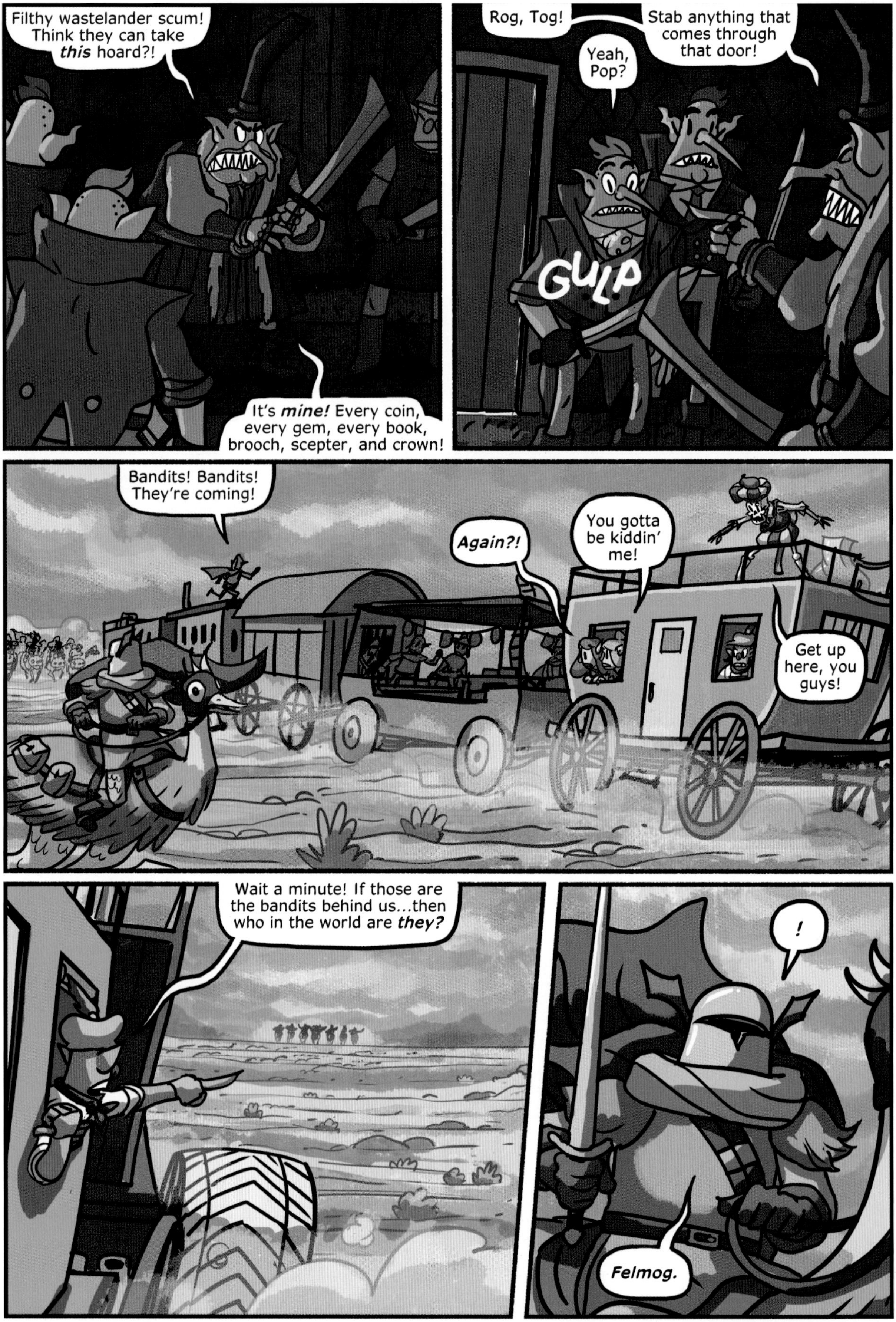
Filthy wastelander scum! Think they can take *this* hoard?!
It's *mine!* Every coin, every gem, every book, brooch, scepter, and crown!
Rog, Tog!
Yeah, Pop?
Stab anything that comes through that door!
GULP
Bandits! Bandits! They're coming!
Again?!
You gotta be kiddin' me!
Get up here, you guys!
Wait a minute! If those are the bandits behind us...then who in the world are *they?*
!
Felmog.

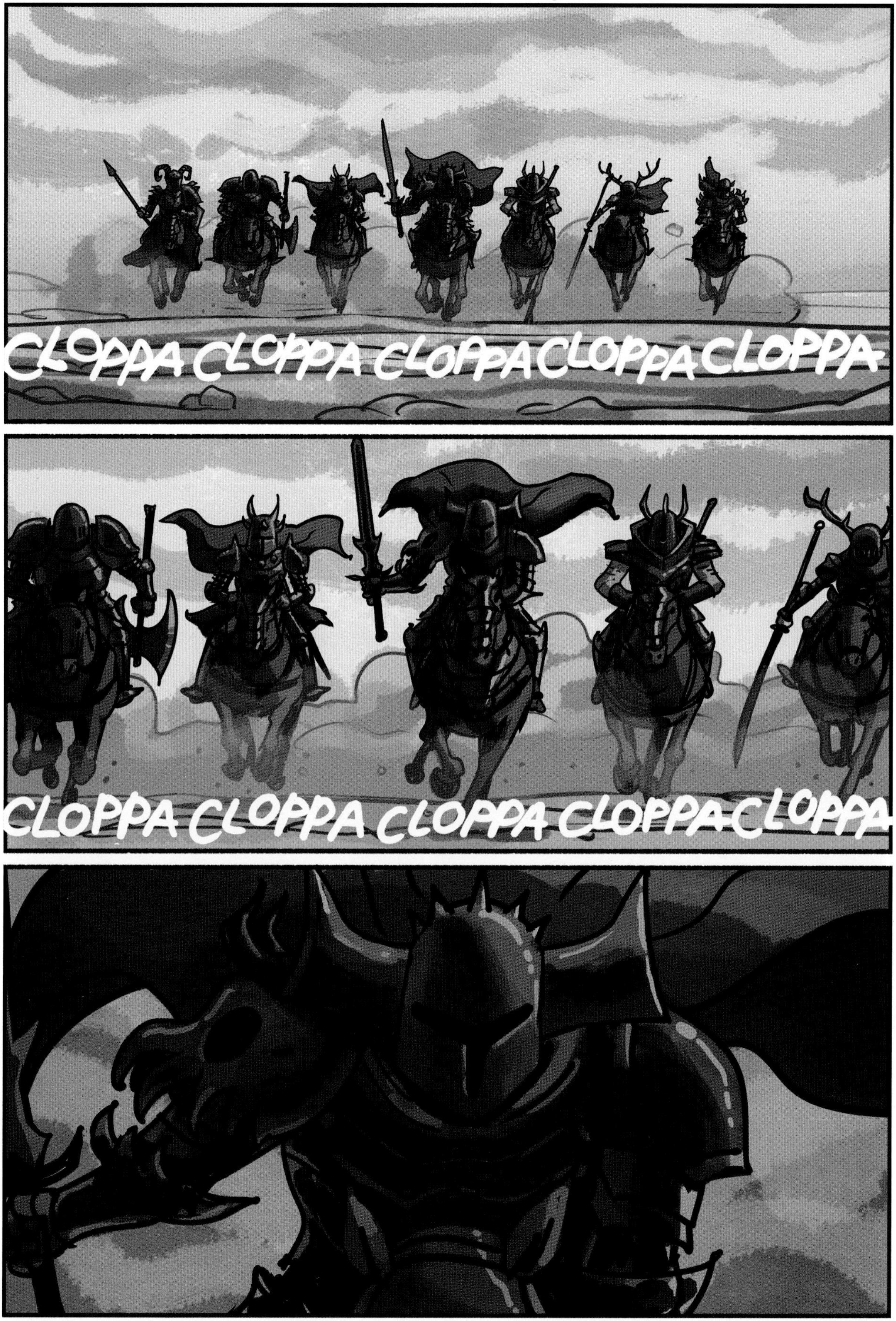
CLOPPA CLOPPA CLOPPA CLOPPA CLOPPA
CLOPPA CLOPPA CLOPPA CLOPPA CLOPPA

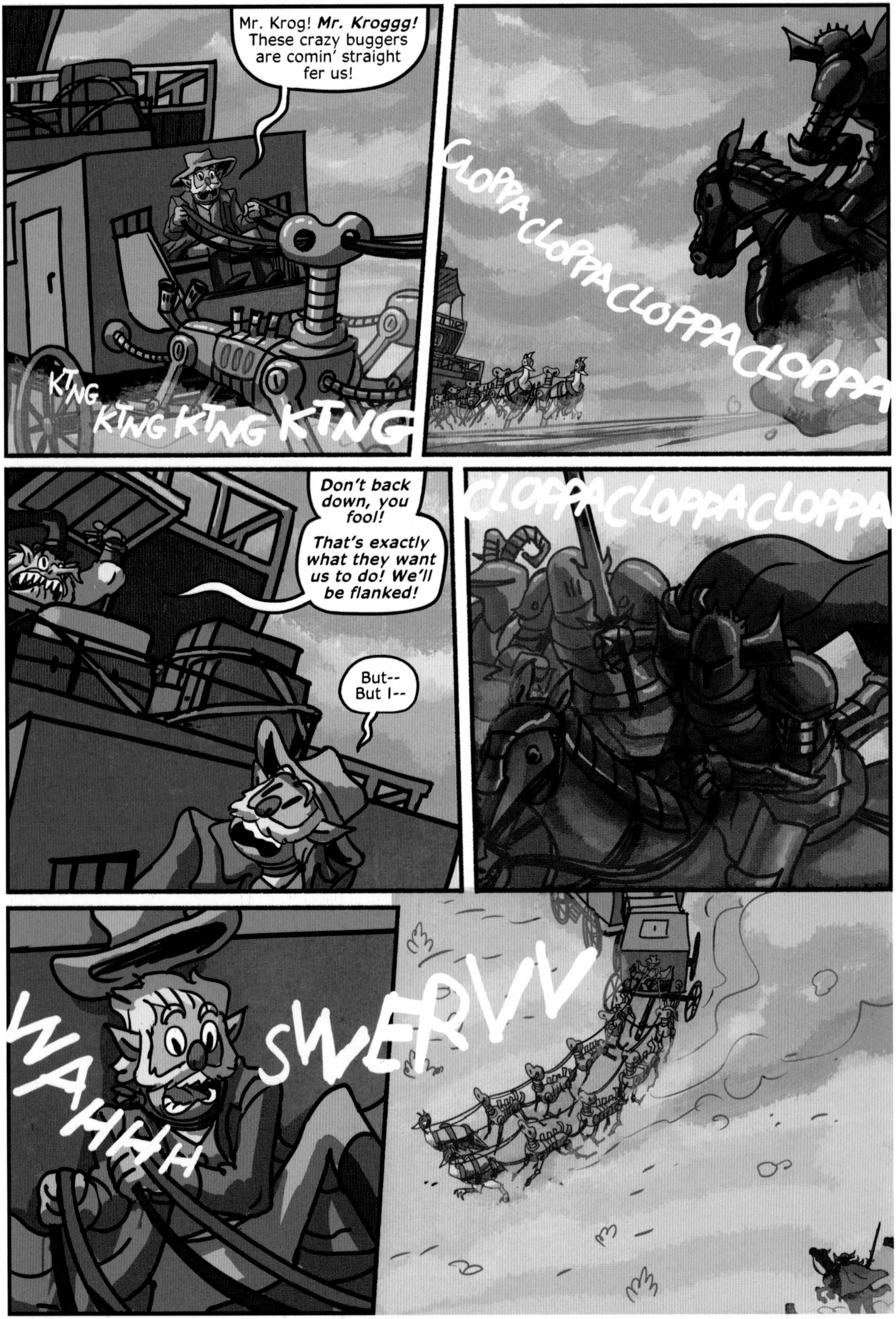

Mr. Krog! ***Mr. Kroggg!*** These crazy buggers are comin' straight fer us!
KTNG KTNG KTNG KTNG
CLOPPACLOPPACLOPPACLOPPACLOPPA
Don't back down, you fool!
That's exactly what they want us to do! We'll be flanked!
But-- But I--
CLOPPACLOPPACLOPPA
WAHHHH
SWERVV

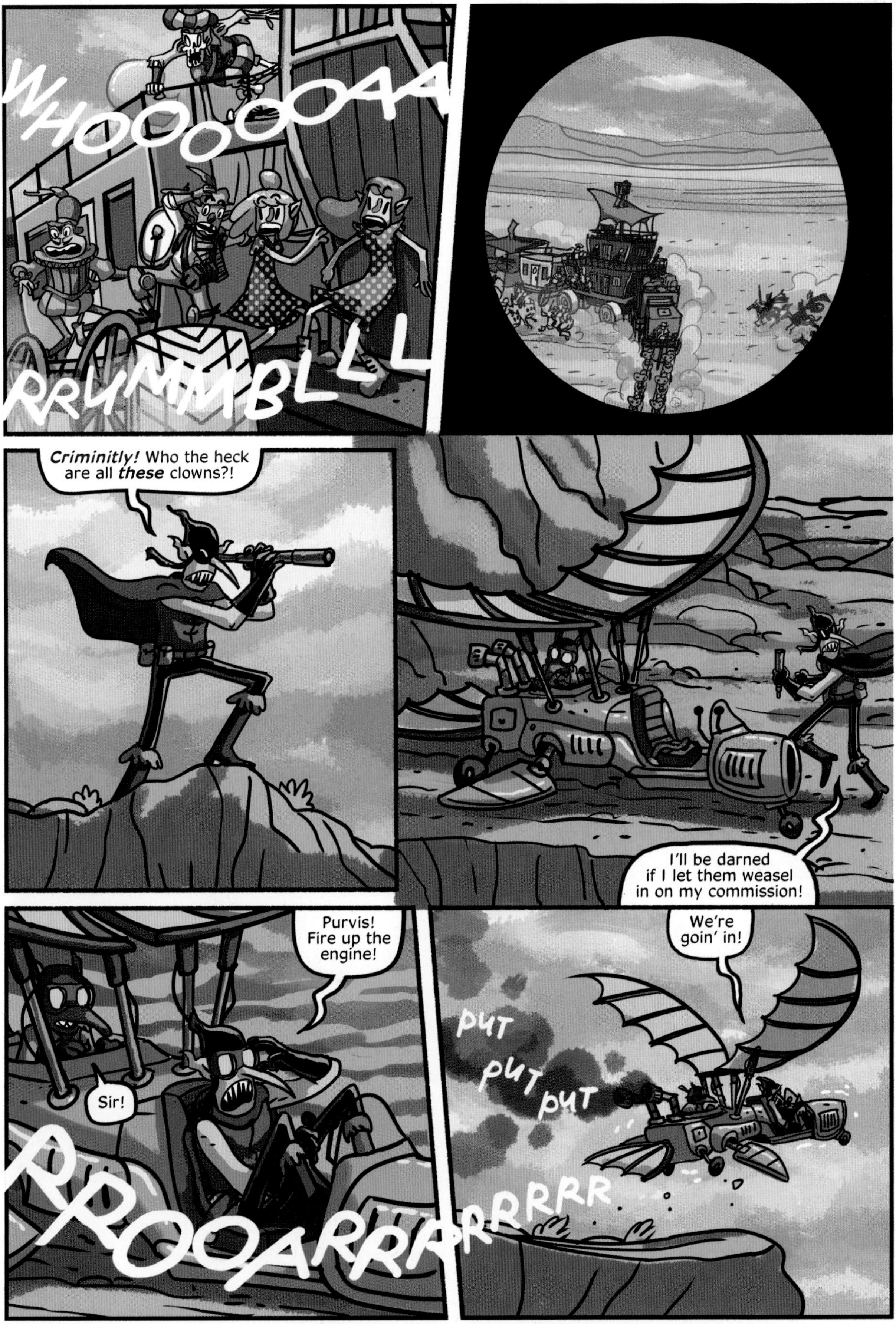
WHOOOOOAA
RRUMMBLLL
Criminitly! Who the heck are all *these* clowns?!
I'll be darned if I let them weasel in on my commission!
Purvis! Fire up the engine!
Sir!
RROOARRRRRRR
We're goin' in!
PUT
PUT PUT
PUT

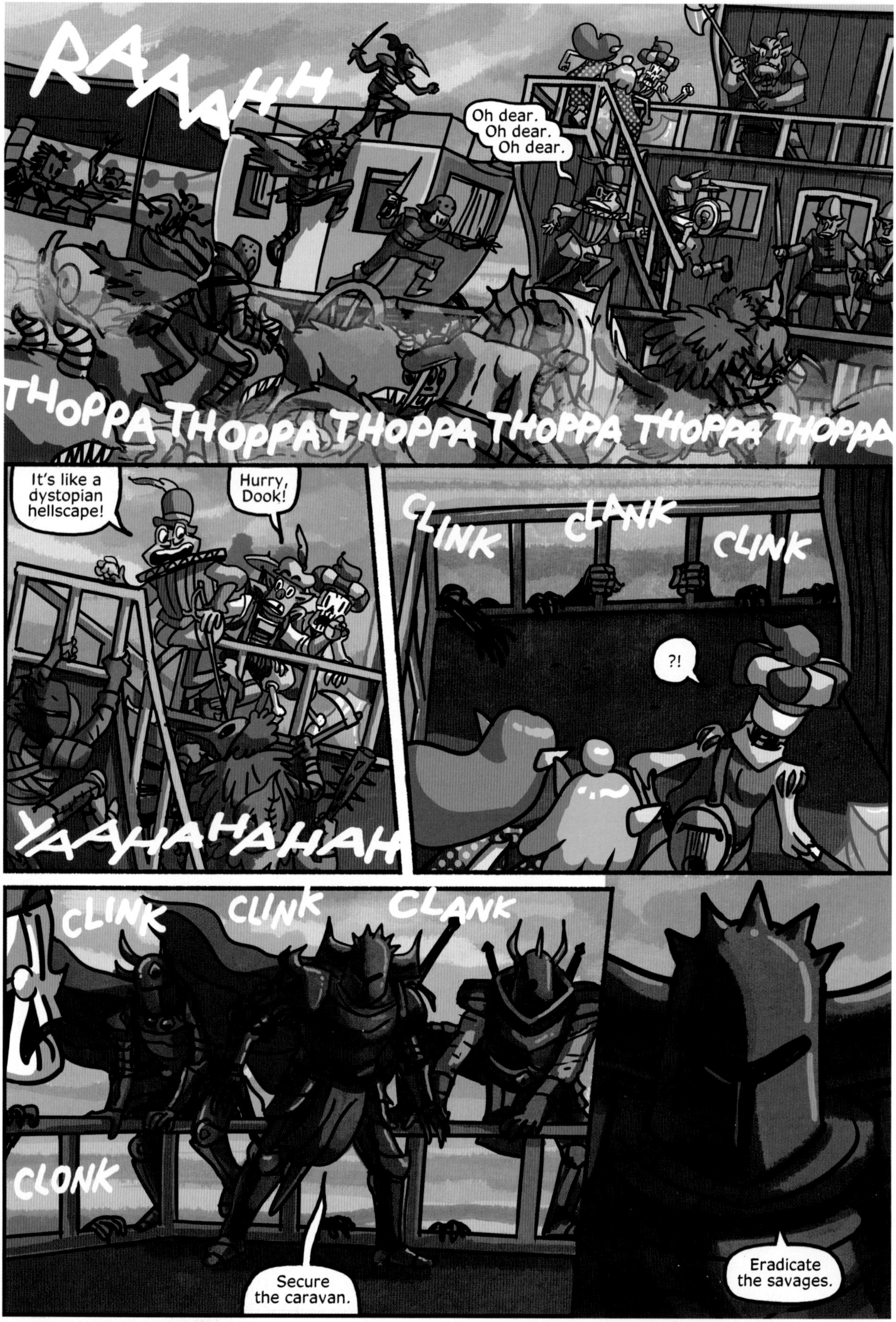
RAAAAHH
Oh dear. Oh dear. Oh dear.
THOPPA THOPPA THOPPA THOPPA THOPPA THOPPA
It's like a dystopian hellscape!
Hurry, Dook!
YAAHAHAHAH
CLINK
CLANK
CLINK
?!
CLINK
CLINK
CLANK
CLONK
Secure the caravan.
Eradicate the savages.

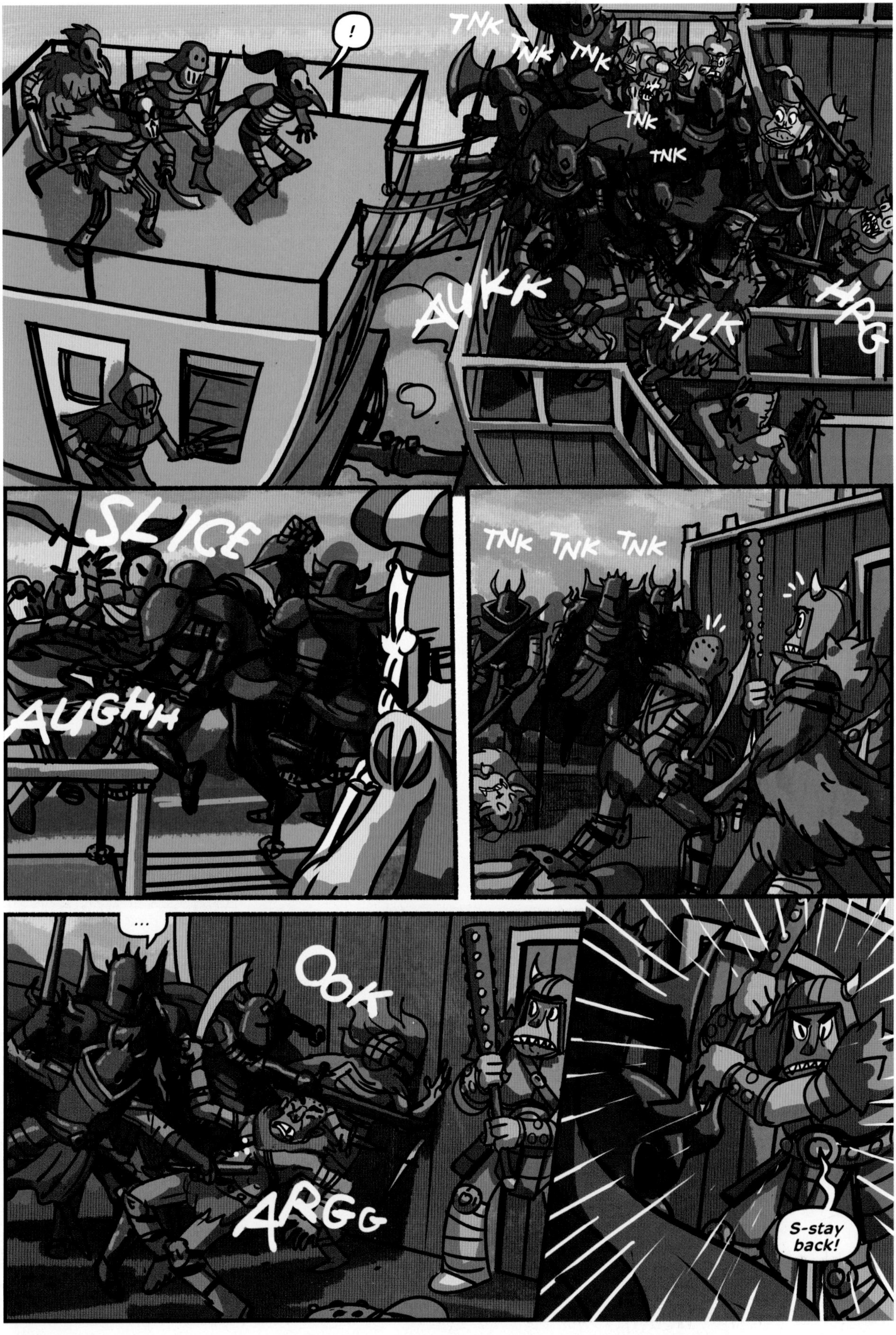
!
TNK TNK TNK
TNK
TNK
AUKK
HLK
HRG
SLICE
AUGHH
TNK TNK TNK
...
OOK
ARGG
S-stay back!

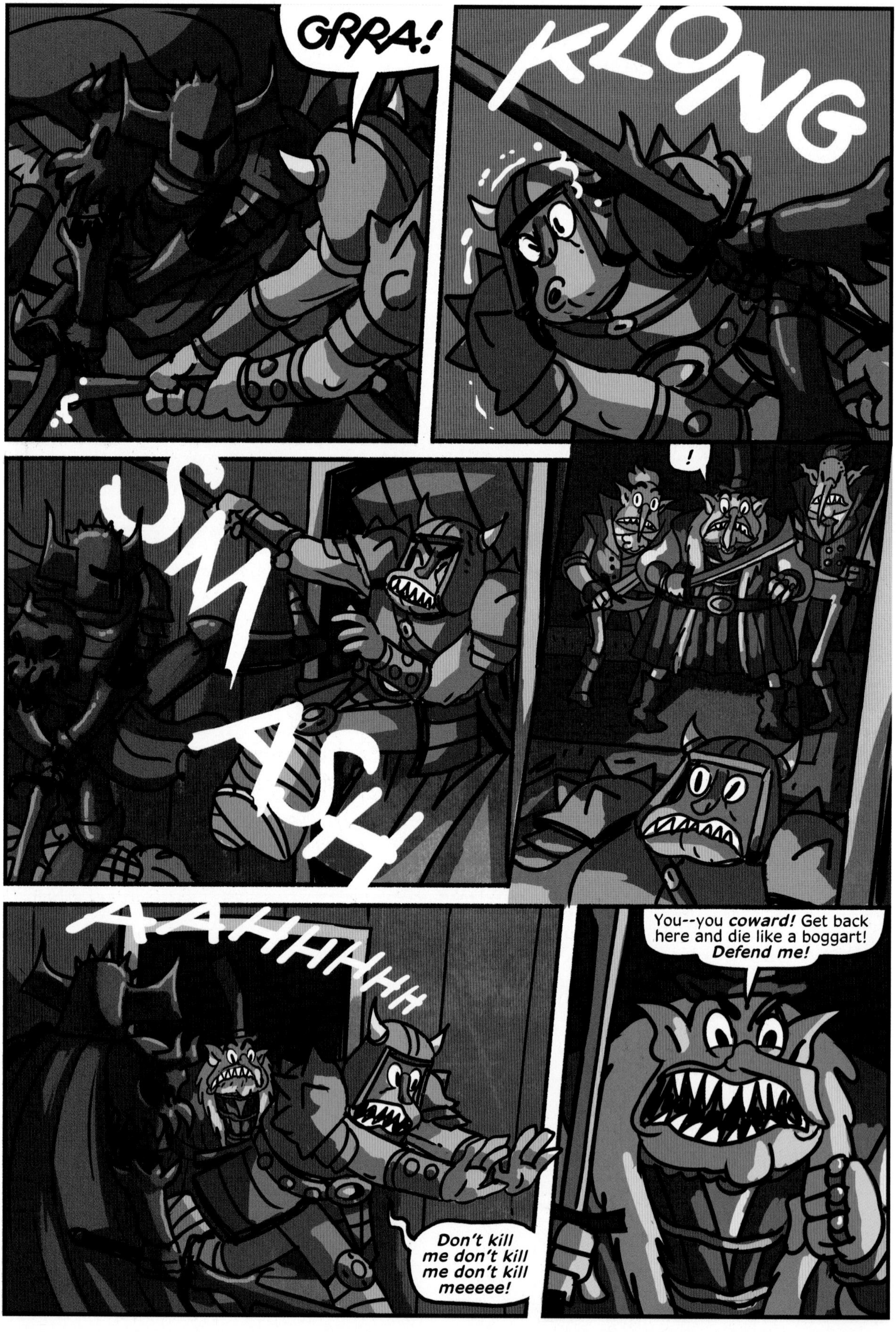
GRRA!
KLONG
SMASH
!
AAHHHHH
Don't kill me don't kill me don't kill meeeee!
You--you coward! Get back here and die like a boggart! Defend me!

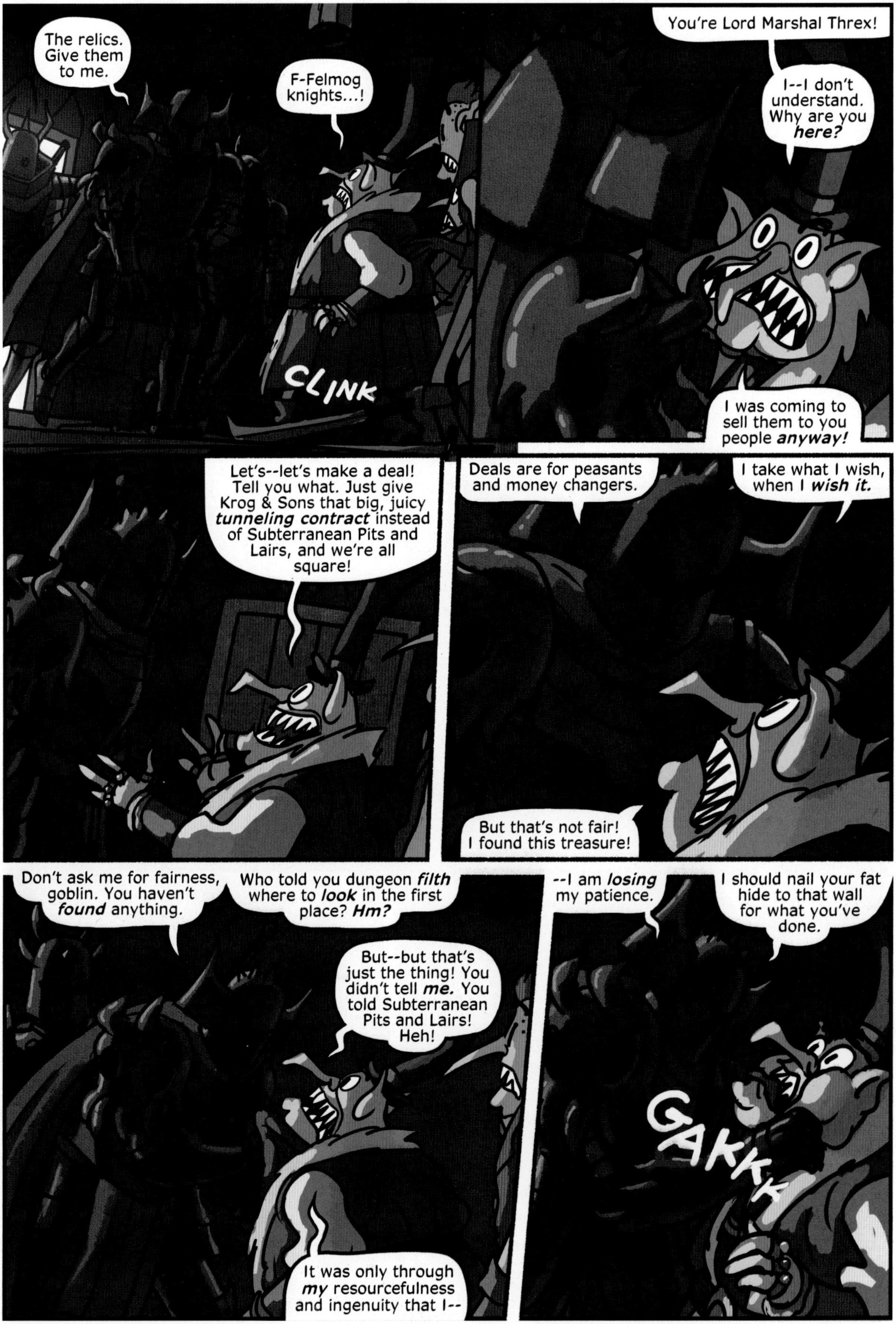
The relics. Give them to me.
F-Felmog knights...!
CLINK
You're Lord Marshal Threx!
I--I don't understand. Why are you *here?*
I was coming to sell them to you people *anyway!*
Let's--let's make a deal! Tell you what. Just give Krog & Sons that big, juicy *tunneling contract* instead of Subterranean Pits and Lairs, and we're all square!
Deals are for peasants and money changers.
I take what I wish, when I *wish it.*
But that's not fair! I found this treasure!
Don't ask me for fairness, goblin. You haven't *found* anything.
Who told you dungeon *filth* where to *look* in the first place? *Hm?*
But--but that's just the thing! You didn't tell *me.* You told Subterranean Pits and Lairs! Heh!
It was only through *my* resourcefulness and ingenuity that I--
--I am *losing* my patience.
I should nail your fat hide to that wall for what you've done.
GAKKK

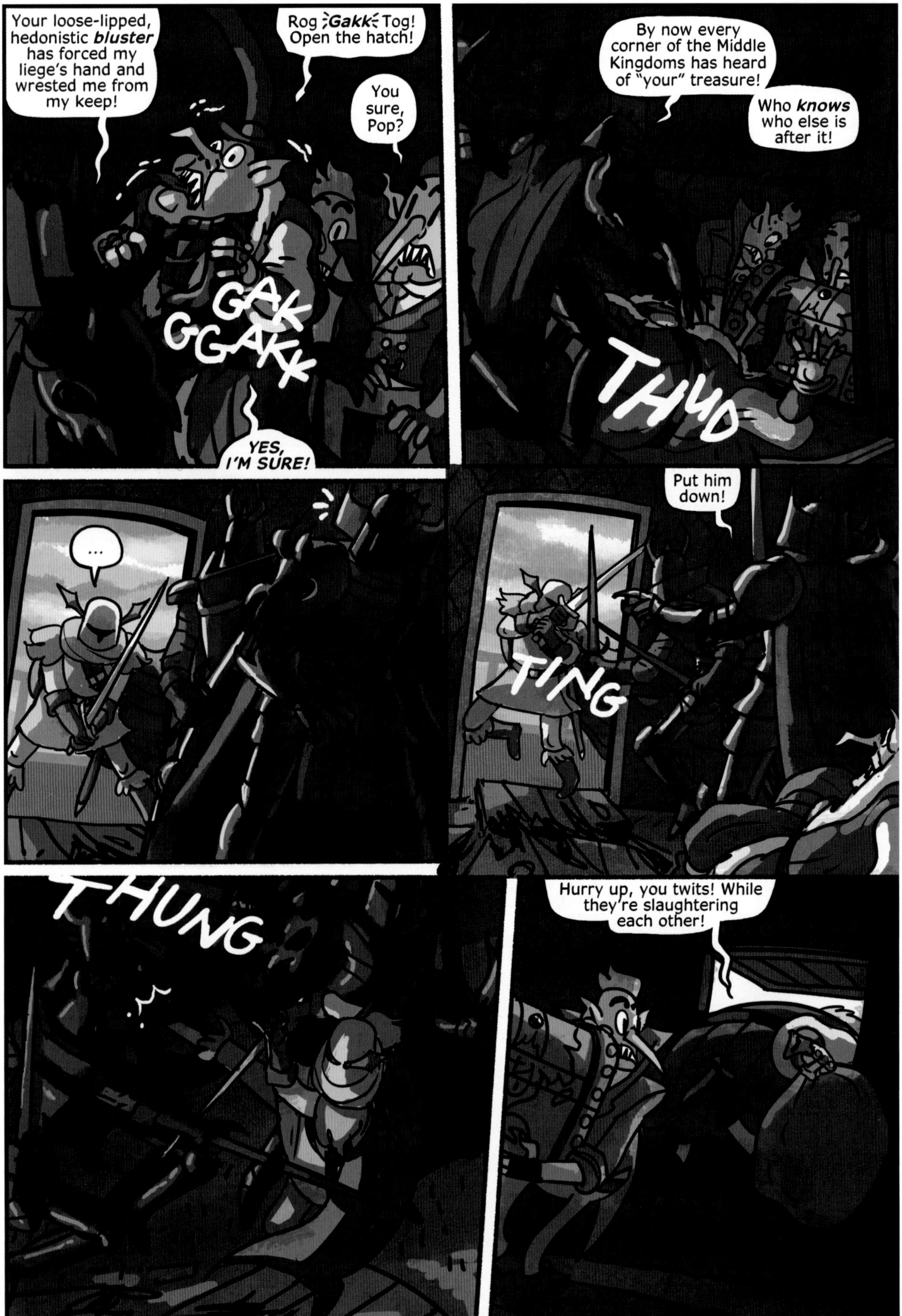
Your loose-lipped, hedonistic *bluster* has forced my liege's hand and wrested me from my keep!
Rog *Gakk* Tog! Open the hatch!
You sure, Pop?
GAK GGAKK
YES, I'M SURE!
By now every corner of the Middle Kingdoms has heard of "your" treasure!
Who *knows* who else is after it!
THUD
...
Put him down!
TING
THUNG
Hurry up, you twits! While they're slaughtering each other!

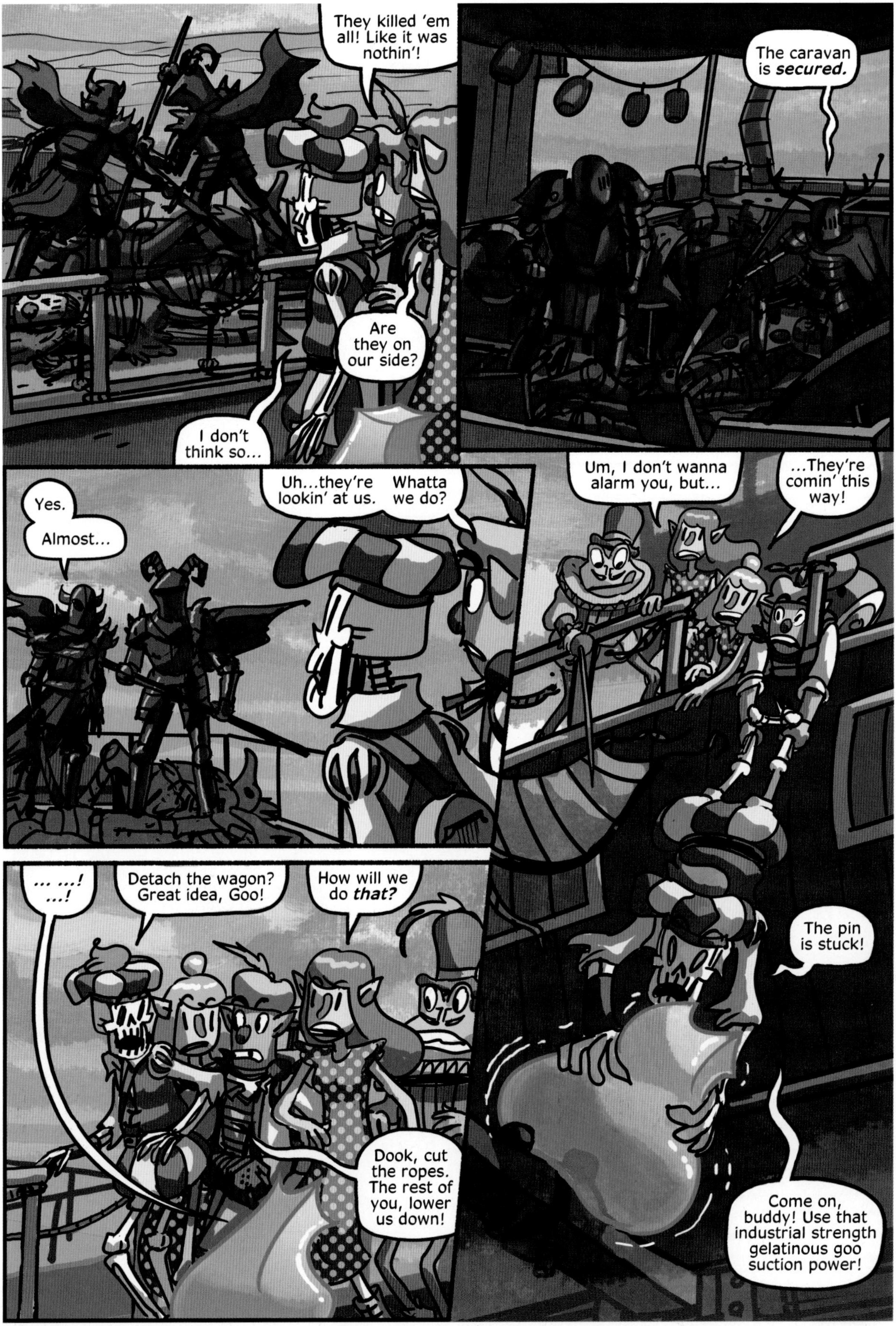
They killed 'em all! Like it was nothin'!
Are they on our side?
I don't think so...
The caravan is *secured.*
Yes.
Almost...
Uh...they're lookin' at us.
Whatta we do?
Um, I don't wanna alarm you, but...
...They're comin' this way!
... ...!
...!
Detach the wagon? Great idea, Goo!
How will we do *that?*
Dook, cut the ropes. The rest of you, lower us down!
The pin is stuck!
Come on, buddy! Use that industrial strength gelatinous goo suction power!

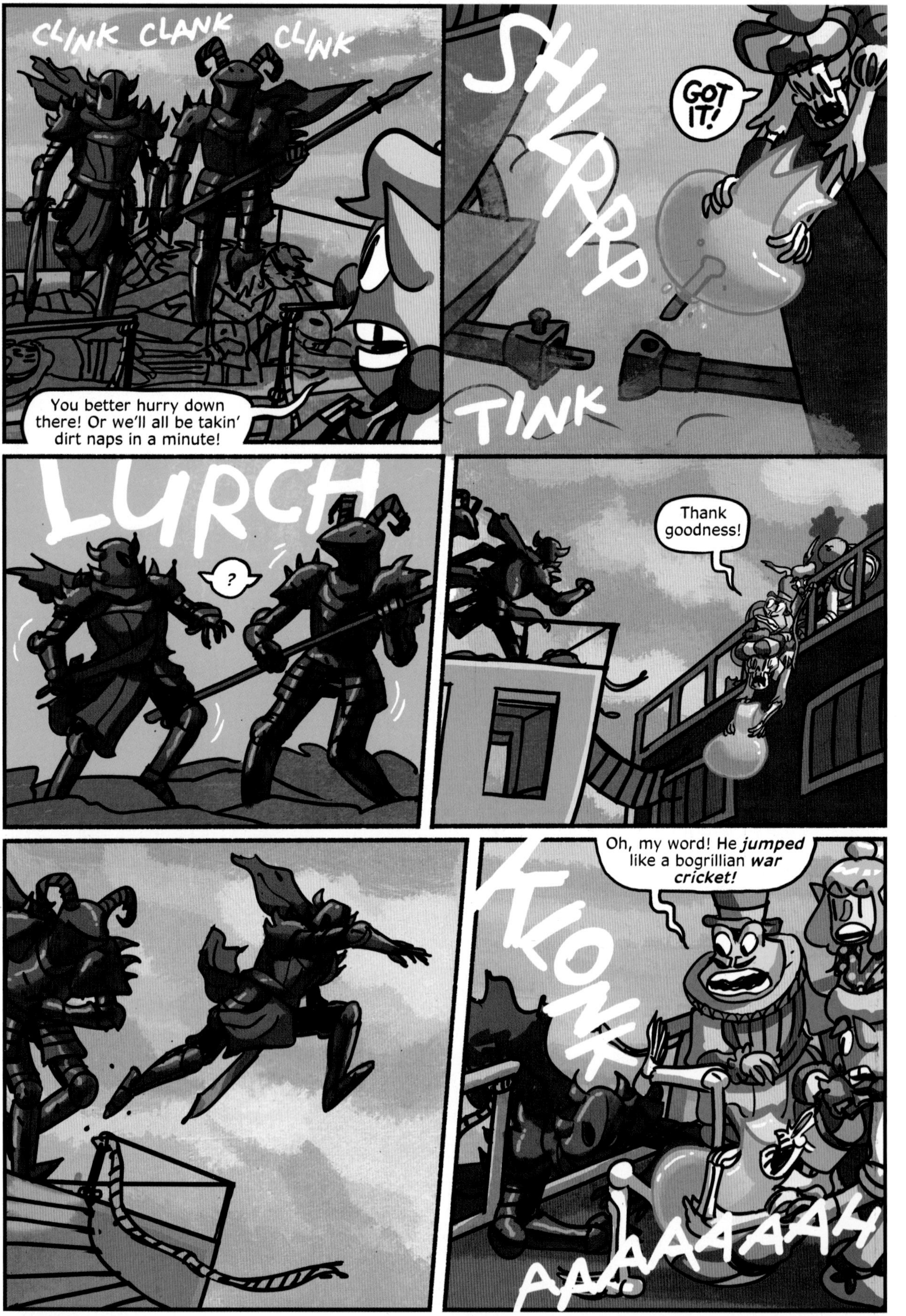
CLINK CLANK CLINK
You better hurry down there! Or we'll all be takin' dirt naps in a minute!
SHLRRP
GOT IT!
TINK
LURCH
?
Thank goodness!
Oh, my word! He *jumped* like a bogrillian *war cricket!*
KLONK
AAAAAAAAH

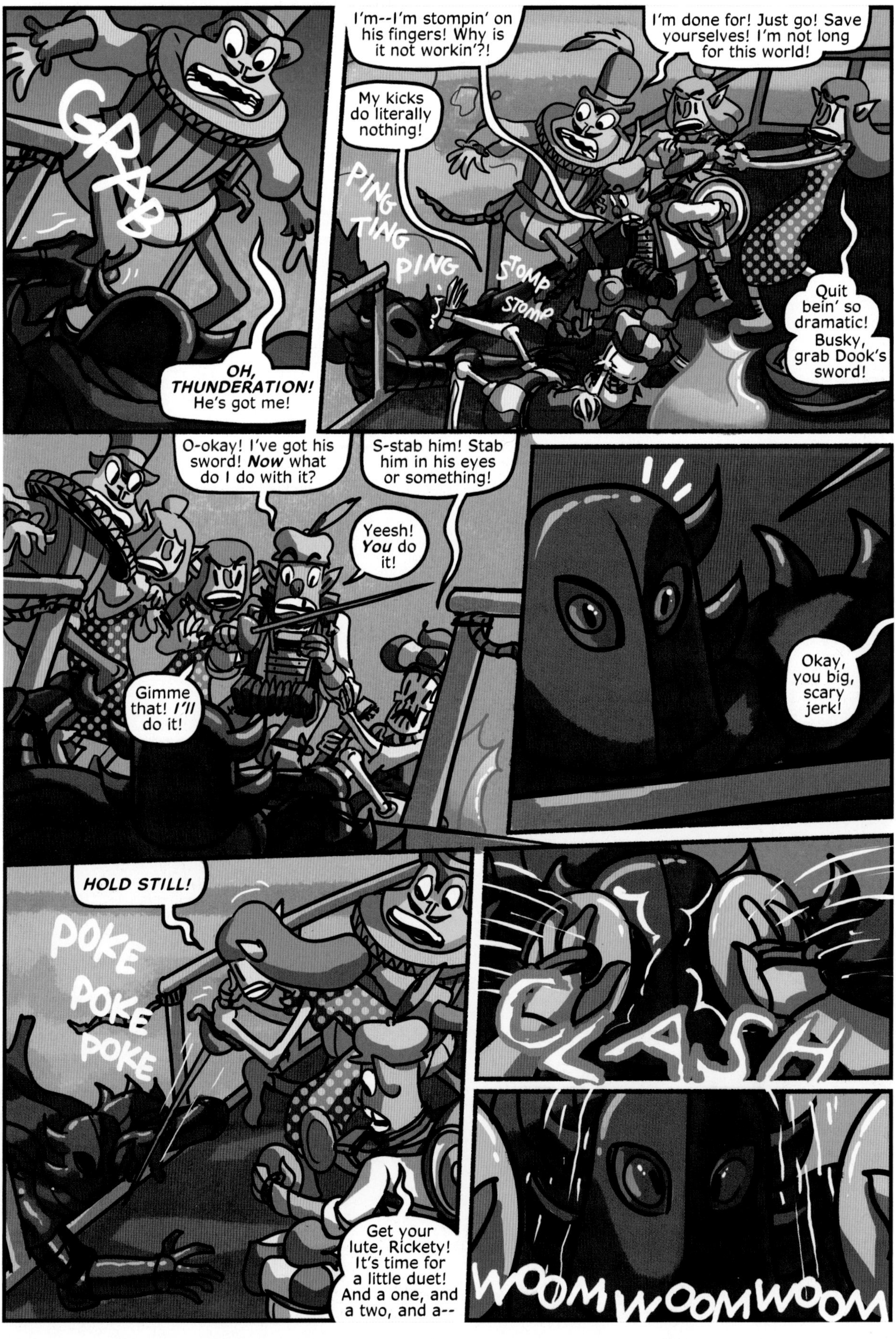
GRAB
OH, THUNDERATION! He's got me!
I'm--I'm stompin' on his fingers! Why is it not workin'?!
I'm done for! Just go! Save yourselves! I'm not long for this world!
My kicks do literally nothing!
PING TING PING
STOMP STOMP
Quit bein' so dramatic! Busky, grab Dook's sword!
O-okay! I've got his sword! Now what do I do with it?
S-stab him! Stab him in his eyes or something!
Yeesh! You do it!
Gimme that! I'll do it!
Okay, you big, scary jerk!
HOLD STILL!
POKE POKE POKE POKE
CLASH
Get your lute, Rickety! It's time for a little duet! And a one, and a two, and a--
WOOM WOOM WOOM

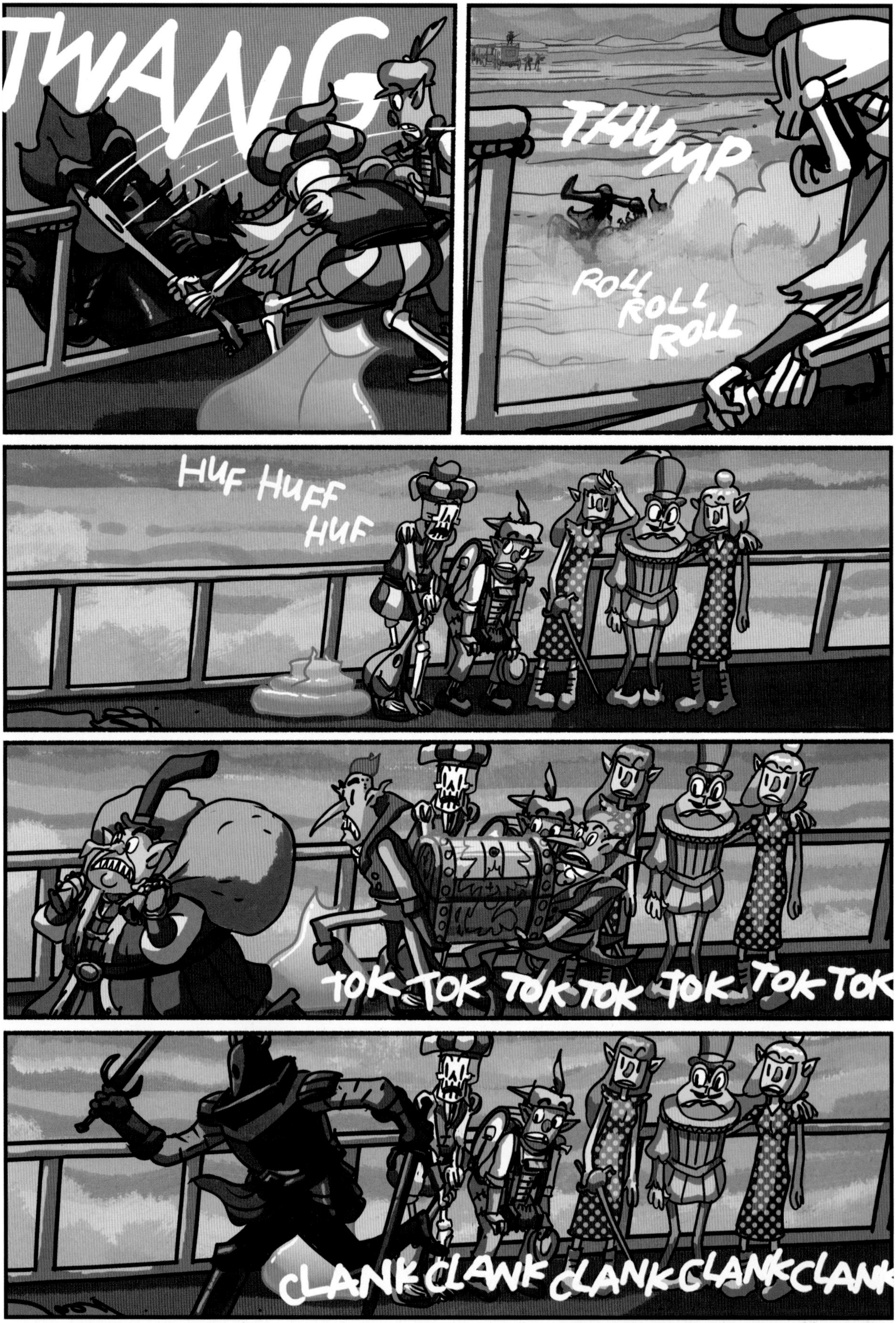
TWANG
THUMP
ROLL ROLL ROLL
HUF HUFF HUF
TOK TOK TOK TOK TOK TOK TOK
CLANK CLANK CLANK CLANK CLANK

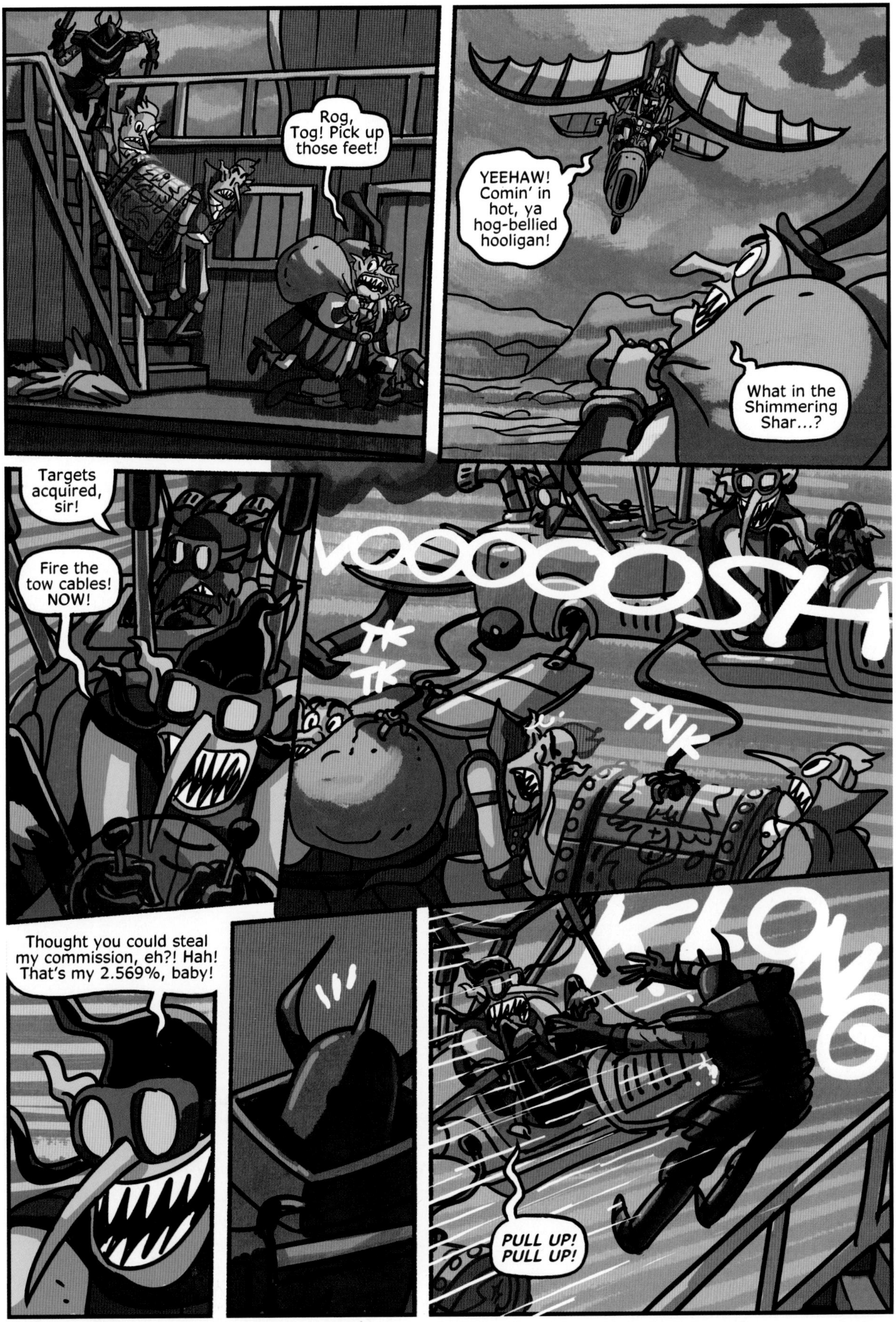
Rog, Tog! Pick up those feet!
YEEHAW! Comin' in hot, ya hog-bellied hooligan!
What in the Shimmering Shar...?
Targets acquired, sir!
Fire the tow cables! NOW!
VOOOOOOSH
TK TK
TNK
Thought you could steal my commission, eh?! Hah! That's my 2.569%, baby!
KLONG
PULL UP! PULL UP!

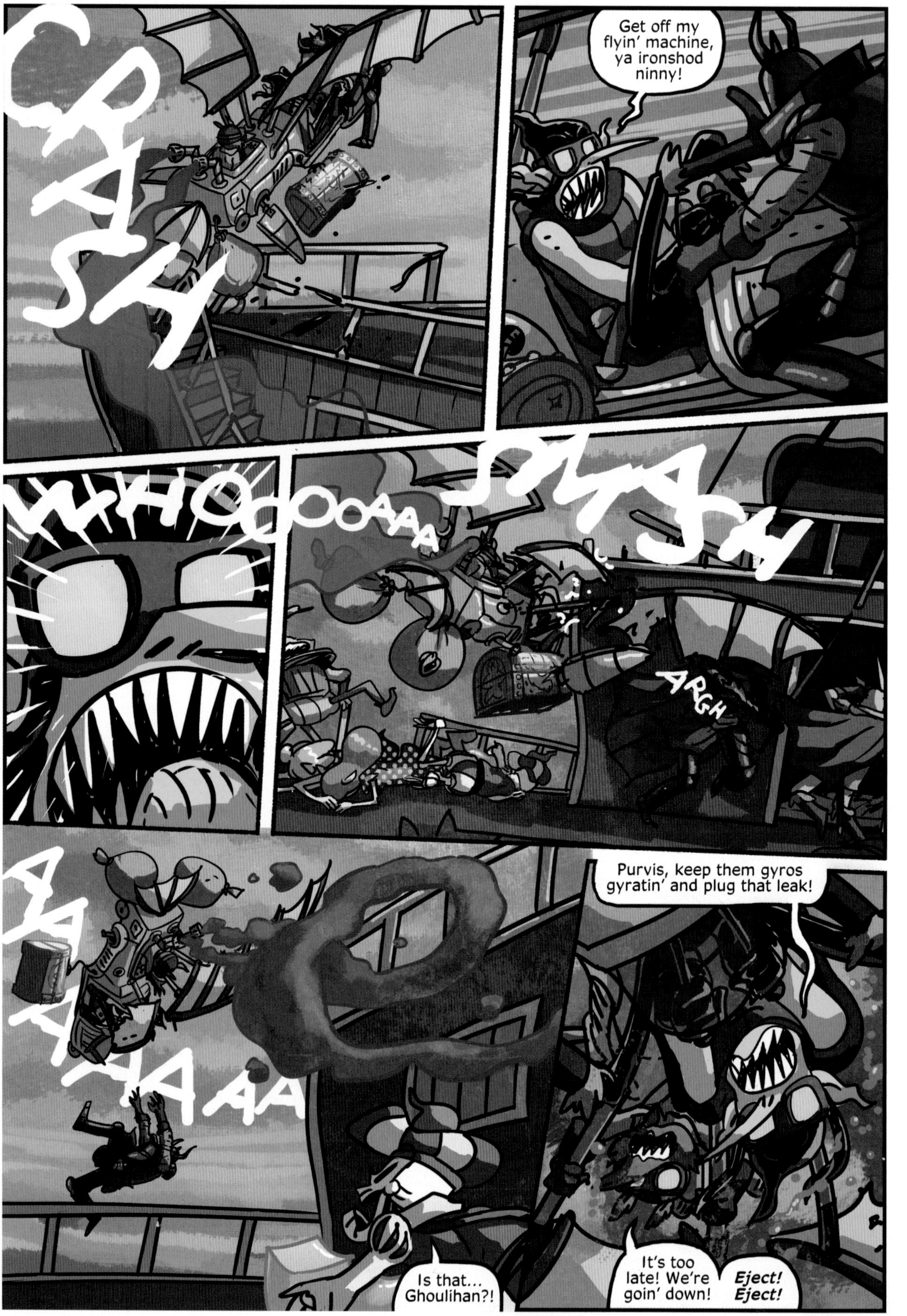
CRASH
Get off my flyin' machine, ya ironshod ninny!
WHOOOOAAA
SPLASH
ARGH
AAAAAAAAA
Purvis, keep them gyros gyratin' and plug that leak!
Is that... Ghoulihan?!
It's too late! We're goin' down!
Eject! Eject!

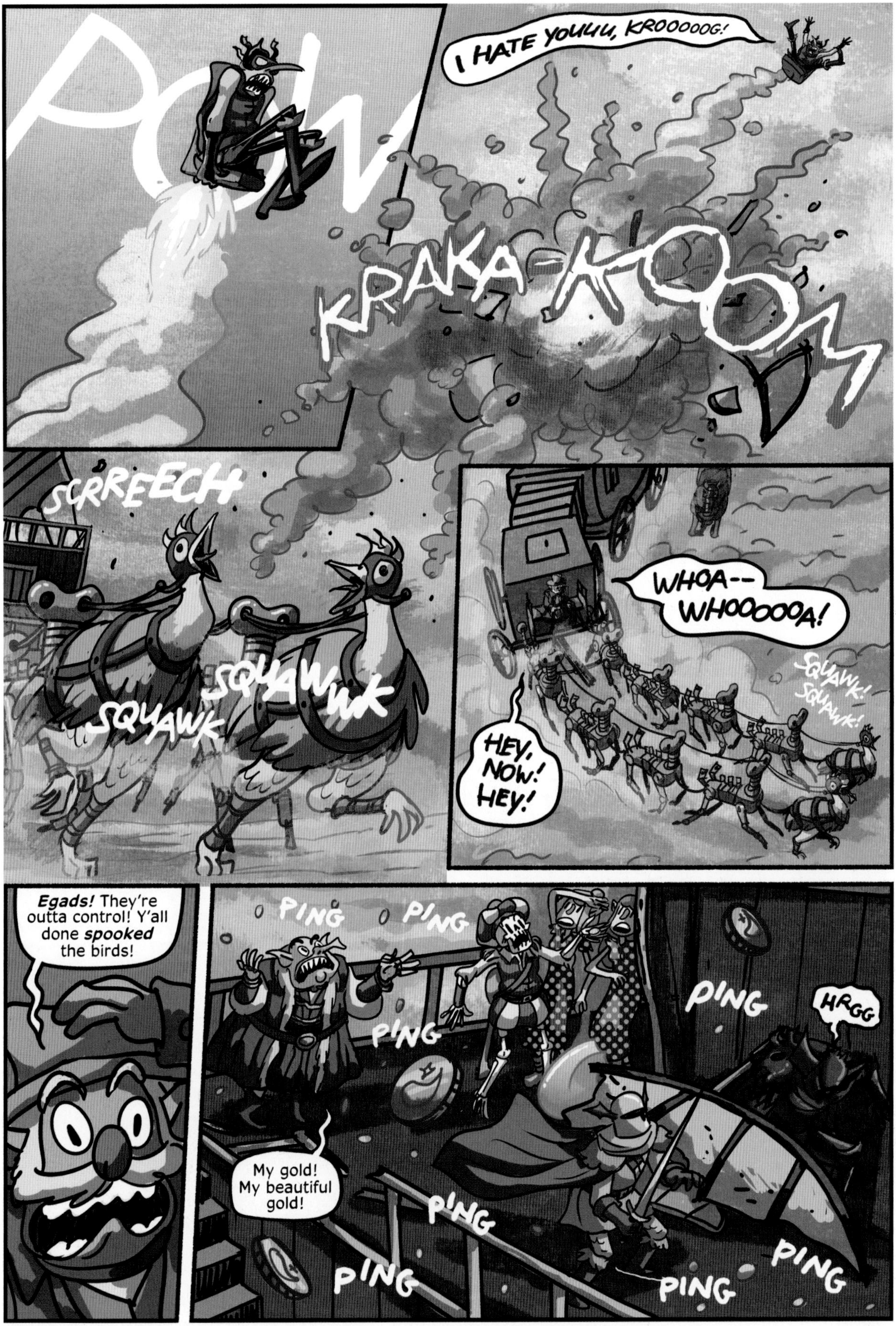
POW
I HATE YOUUU, KROOOOOG!
KRAKA-KOOM
SCRREECH
SQUAWK
SQUAWWWK
WHOA--
WHOOOOOA!
HEY, NOW! HEY!
SQUAWK! SQUAWK!
Egads! They're outta control! Y'all done spooked the birds!
PING
PING
PING
PING
HRGG
My gold! My beautiful gold!
PING
PING
PING
PING

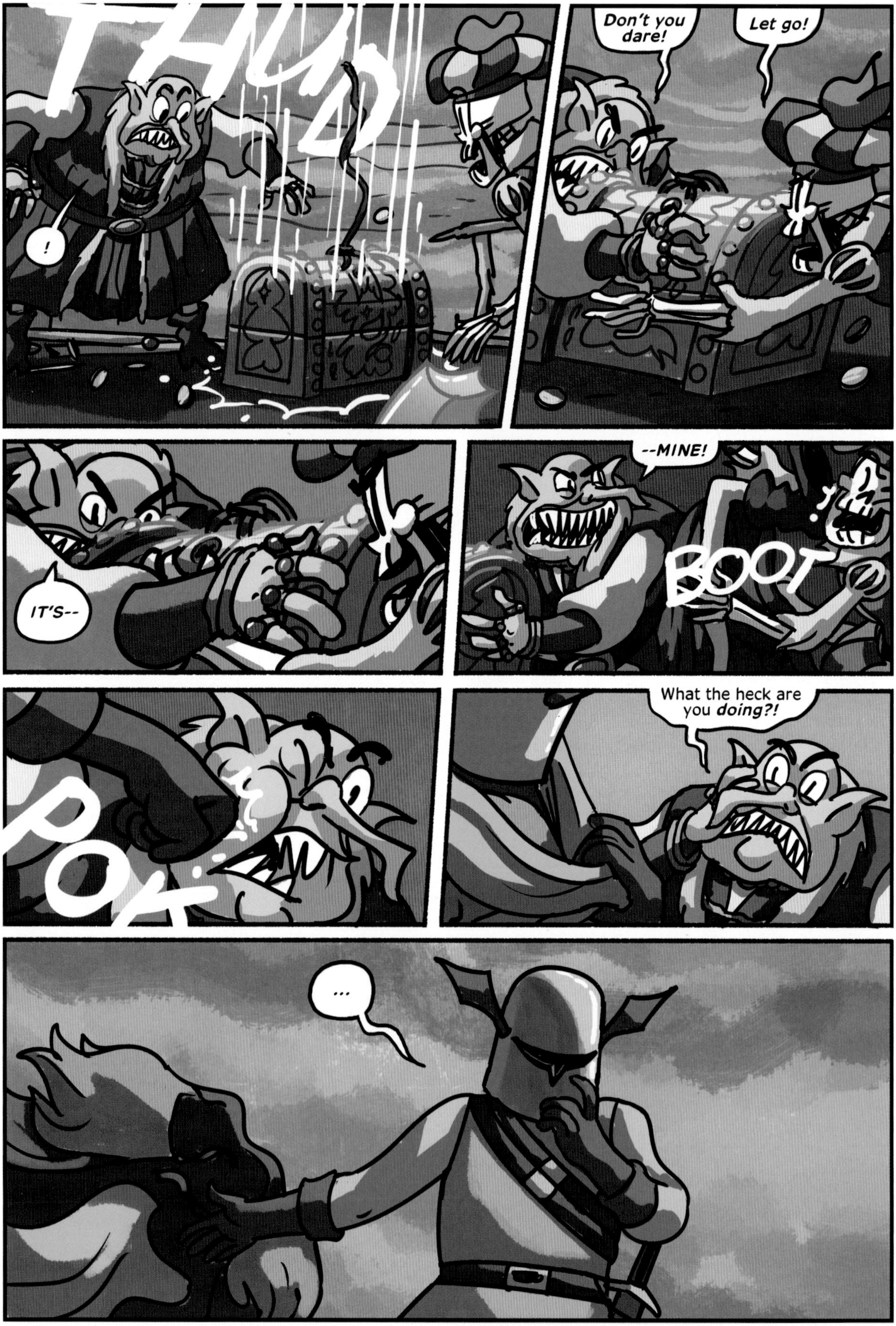
THUD
!
Don't you dare!
Let go!
IT'S--
--MINE!
BOOT
POK
What the heck are you doing?!
...

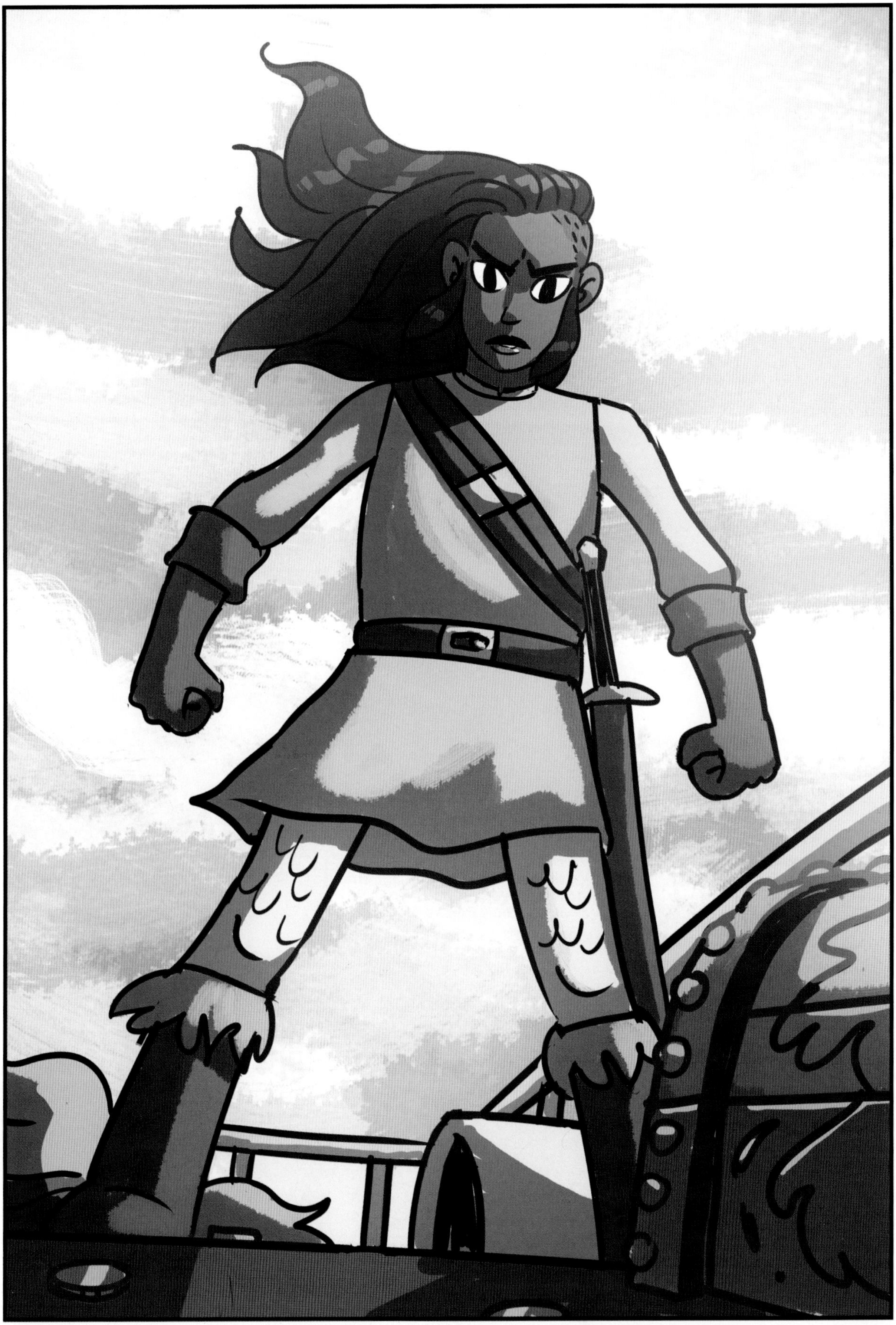

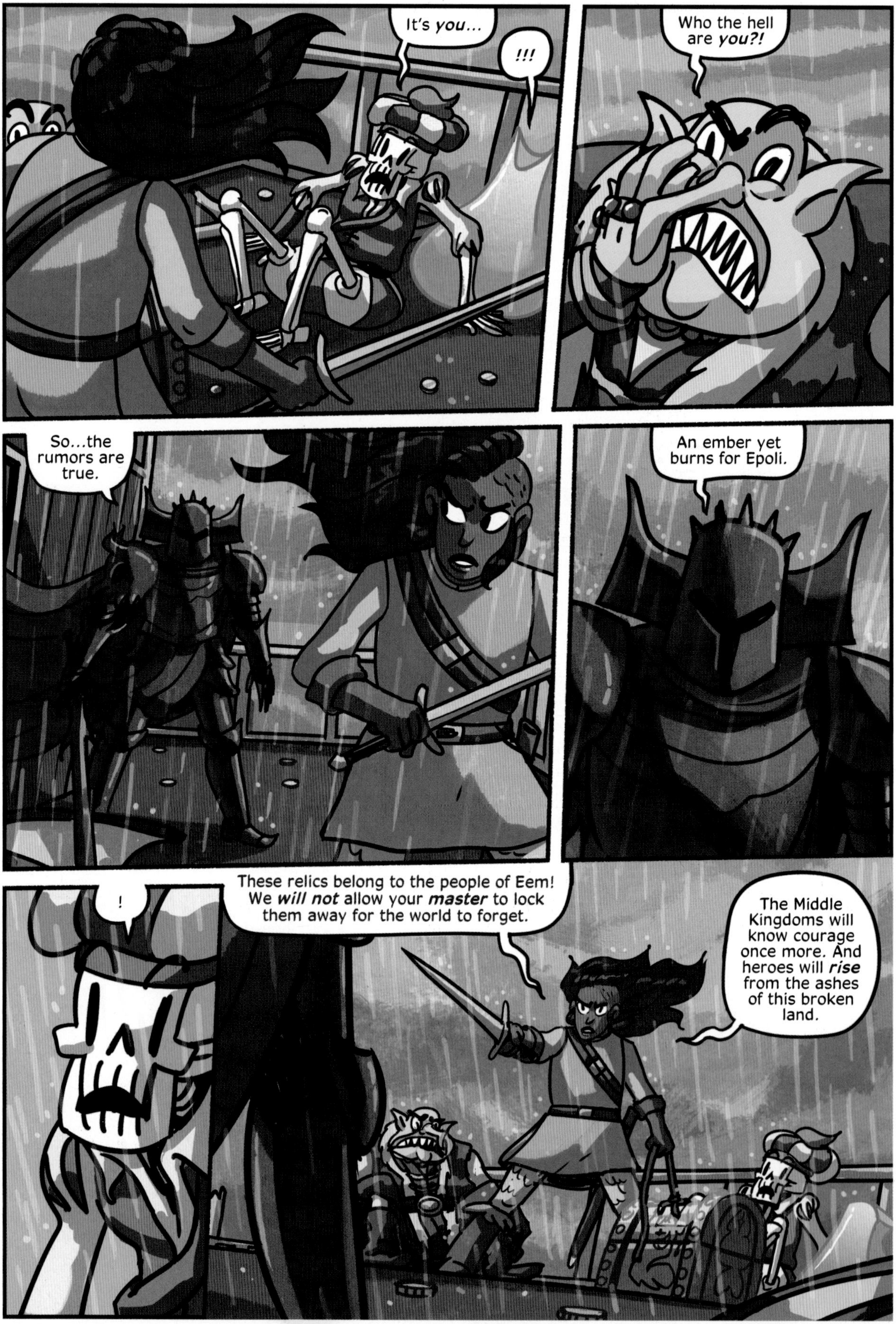
It's *you*...
!!!
Who the hell are *you?!*
So...the rumors are true.
An ember yet burns for Epoli.
!
These relics belong to the people of Eem! We ***will not*** allow your ***master*** to lock them away for the world to forget.
The Middle Kingdoms will know courage once more. And heroes will ***rise*** from the ashes of this broken land.

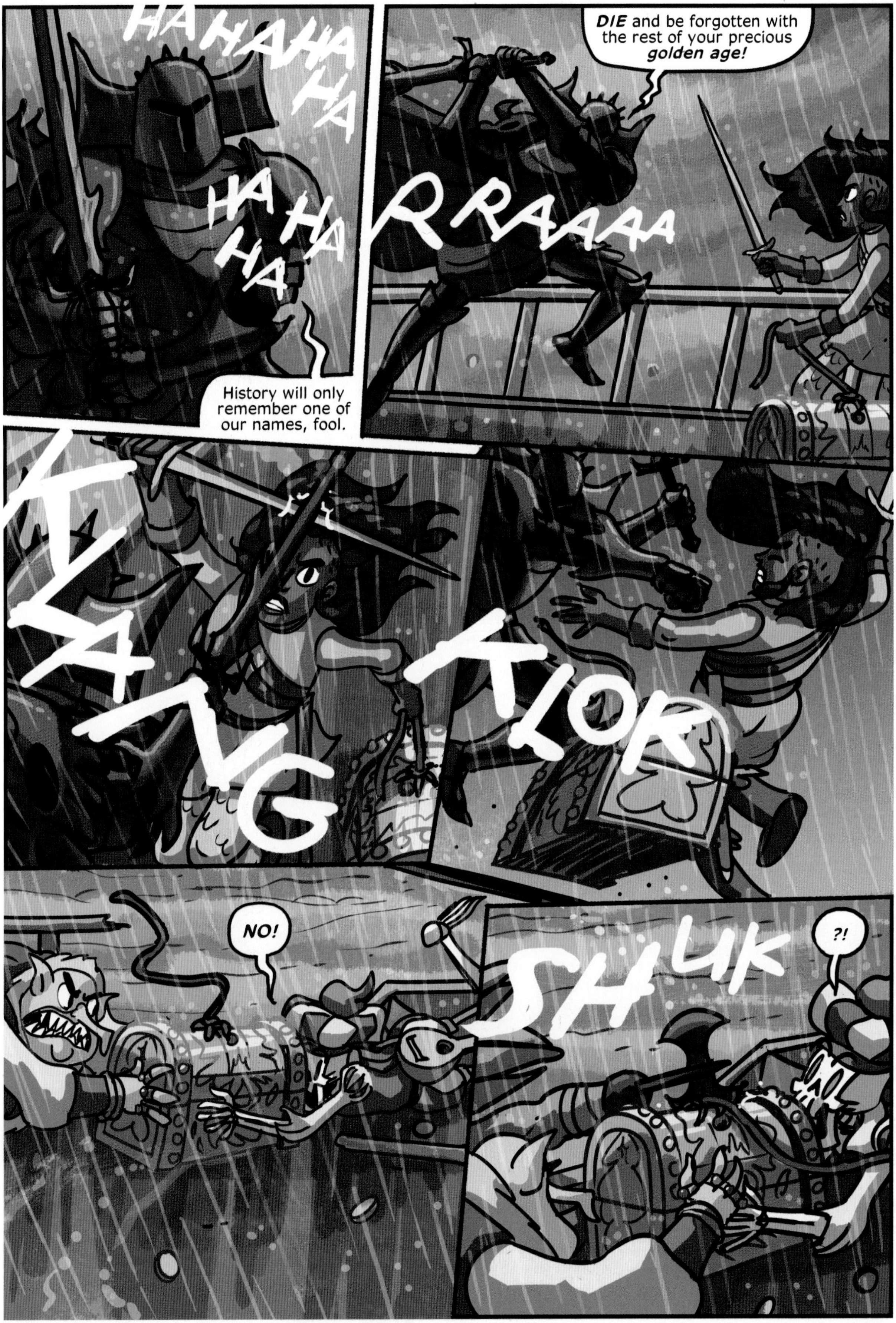
HAHAHAHA
HAHAHAHA
History will only remember one of our names, fool.
RRAAAAA
DIE and be forgotten with the rest of your precious golden age!
KLANG
KLOR
NO!
SHUK
?!

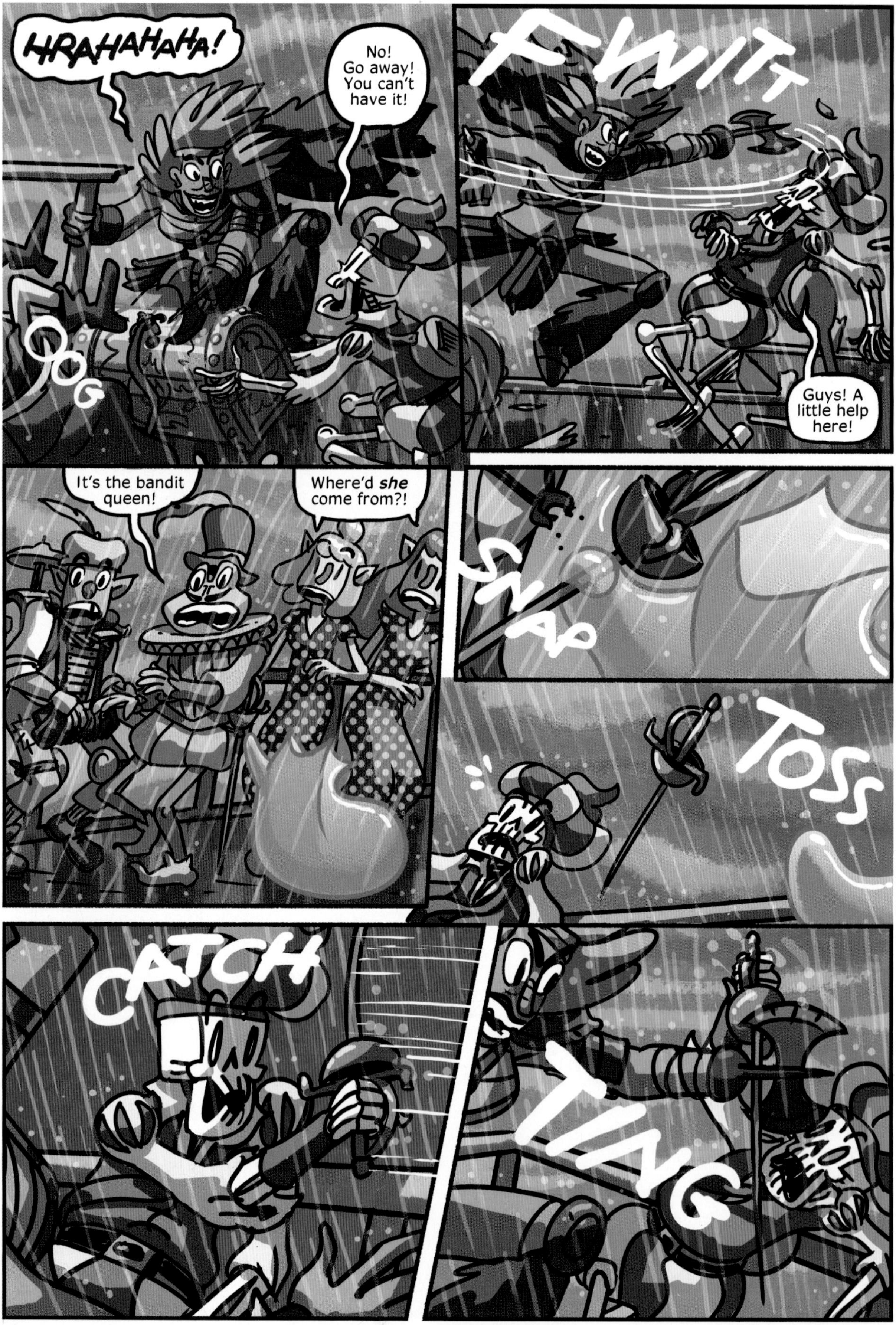
HRAHAHAHA!
No! Go away! You can't have it!
DOOG
FWITT
Guys! A little help here!
It's the bandit queen!
Where'd *she* come from?!
SNAP
TOSS
CATCH
TING

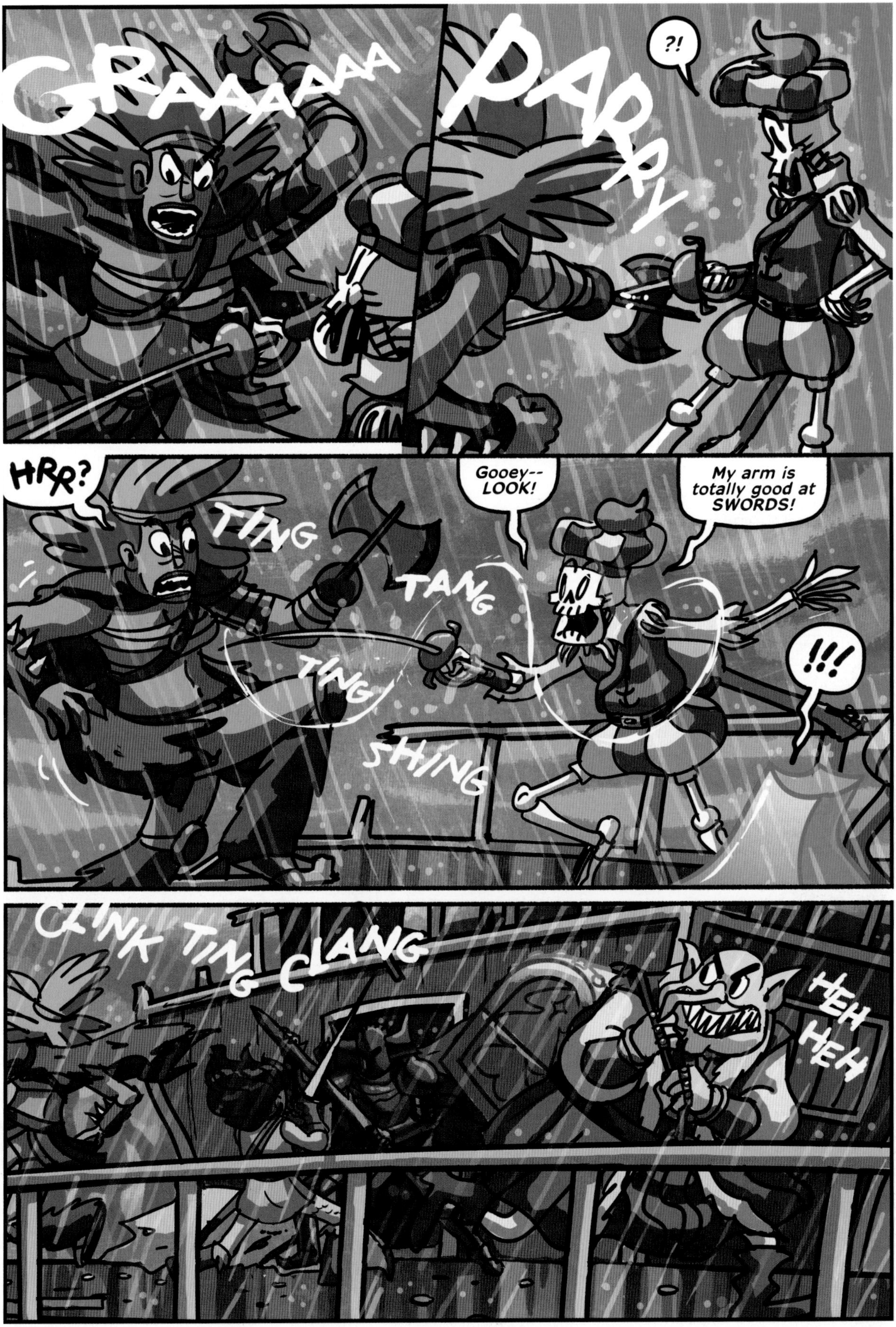
GRAAAAAA
PARRY
?!
HRR?
TING
TANG
TING
SHING
Gooey--
LOOK!
My arm is
totally good at
SWORDS!
!!!
CLINK TING CLANG
HEH HEH

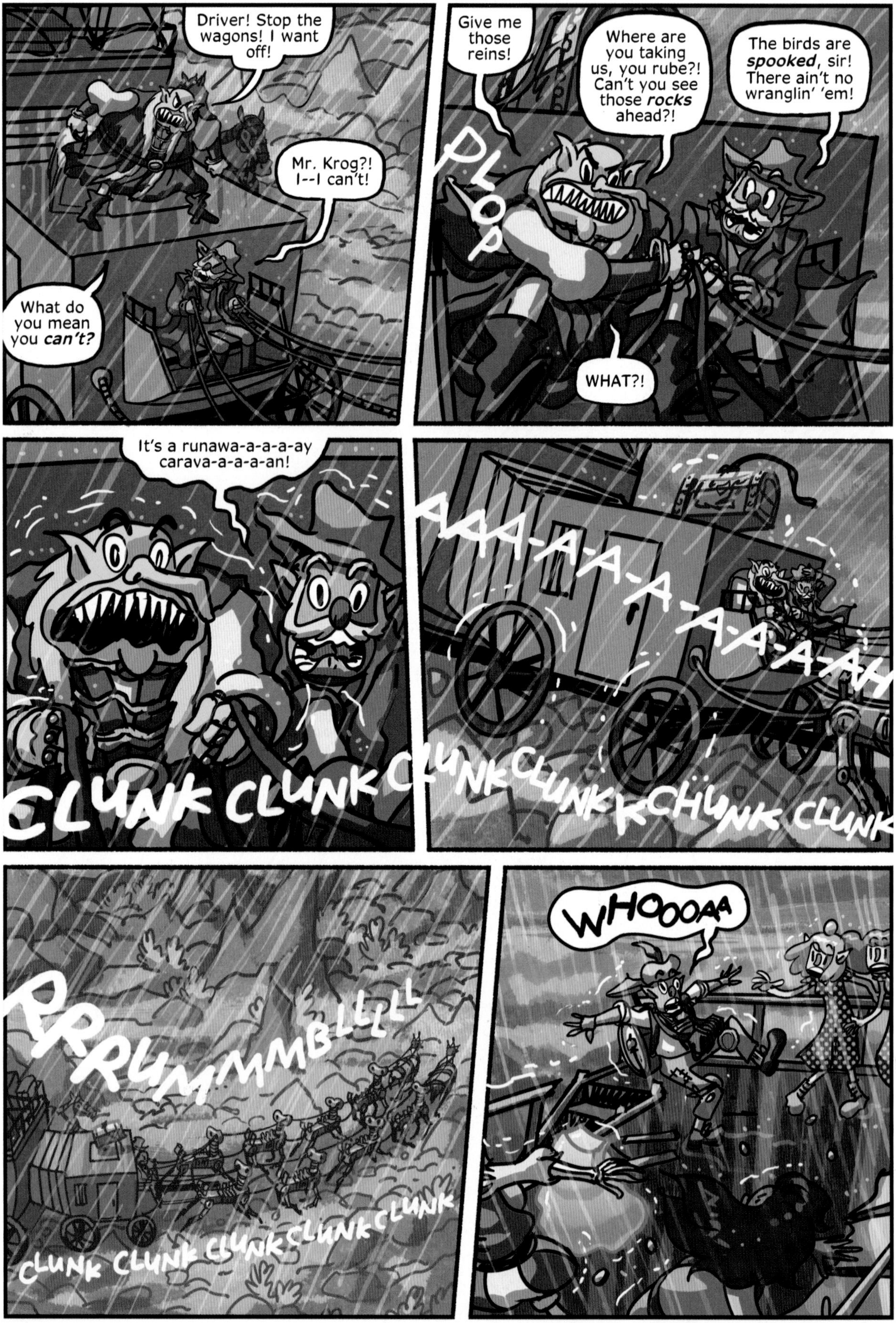

Driver! Stop the wagons! I want off!
Mr. Krog?! I--I can't!
What do you mean you *can't?*
Give me those reins!
PLOP
Where are you taking us, you rube?! Can't you see those *rocks* ahead?!
The birds are *spooked*, sir! There ain't no wranglin' 'em!
WHAT?!
It's a runawa-a-a-a-ay carava-a-a-a-an!
CLUNK CLUNK CLUNK
AAA-A-A-A-A-A-A-A-AH
CLUNK KCHUNK CLUNK
RRRUMMMBLLLL
CLUNK CLUNK CLUNK CLUNK CLUNK
WHOOOAA

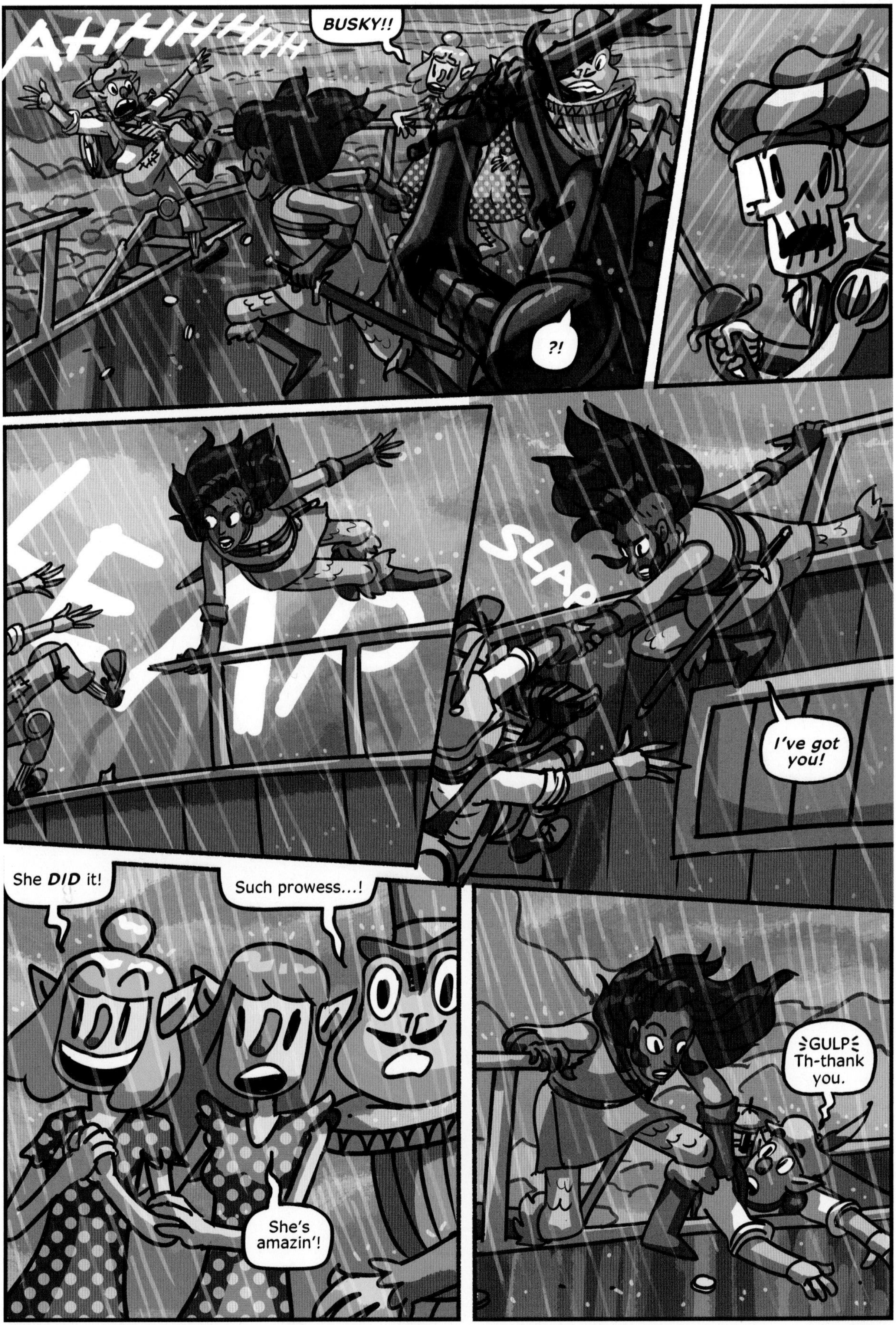
AHHHHHH
BUSKY!!
?!
LEAP
SLAP
I've got you!
She DID it!
Such prowess...!
She's amazin'!
GULP Th-thank you.

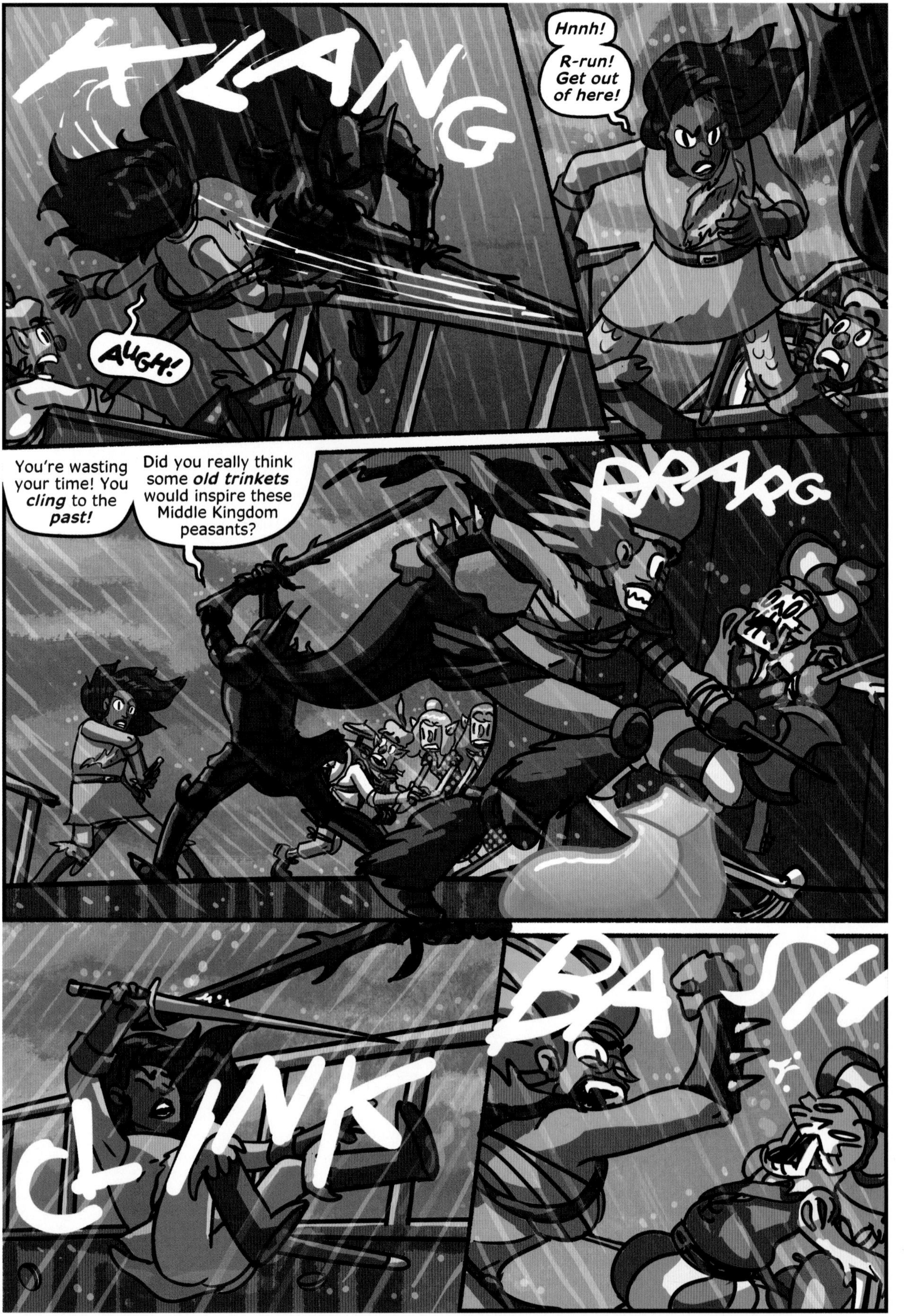
KLANG
AUGH!
Hnnh!
R-run! Get out of here!
You're wasting your time! You *cling* to the *past!*
Did you really think some ***old trinkets*** would inspire these Middle Kingdom peasants?
RRAARG
CLINK
BASH

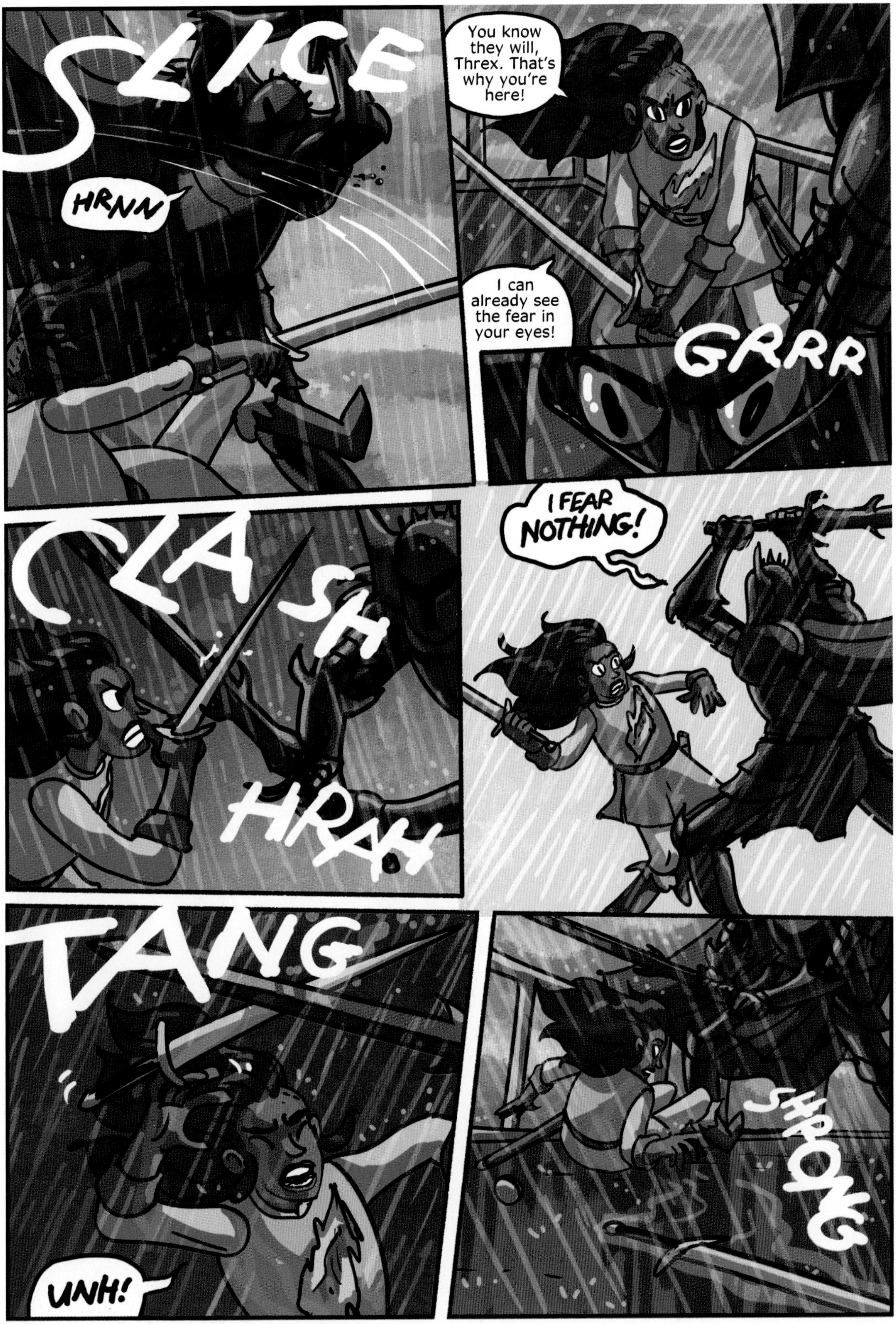
SLICE
HRNN
You know they will, Threx. That's why you're here!
I can already see the fear in your eyes!
GRRR
CLASH
HRAH
I FEAR NOTHING!
TANG
UNH!
SHRONG

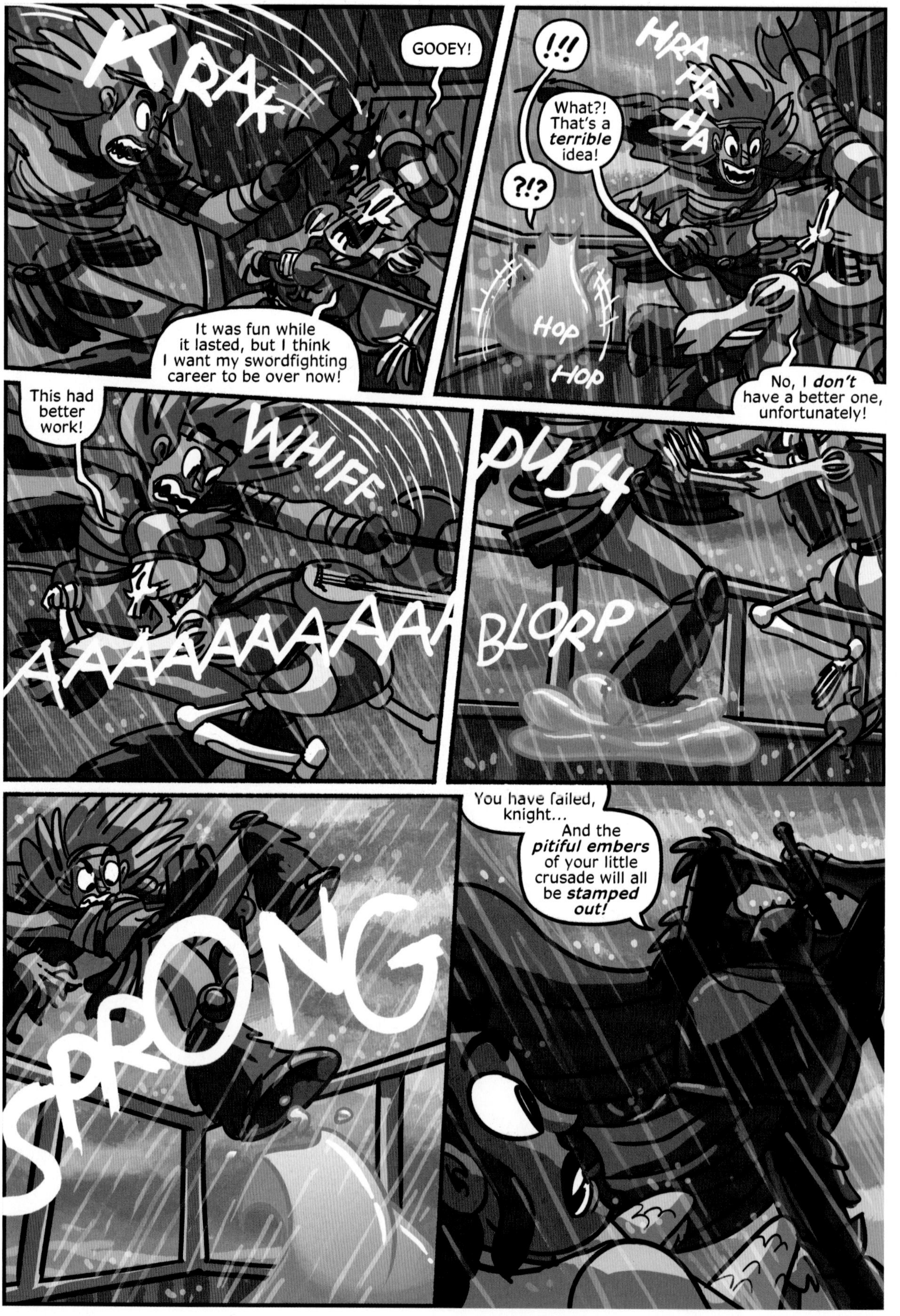
KRAK
GOOEY!
It was fun while it lasted, but I think I want my swordfighting career to be over now!
!!!
?!?
HRA HA HA HA
What?! That's a *terrible* idea!
HOP
HOP
No, I *don't* have a better one, unfortunately!
This had better work!
WHIFF
AAAAAAAAAAA
PUSH
BLORP
SPRONG
You have failed, knight...
And the *pitiful embers* of your little crusade will all be *stamped out!*

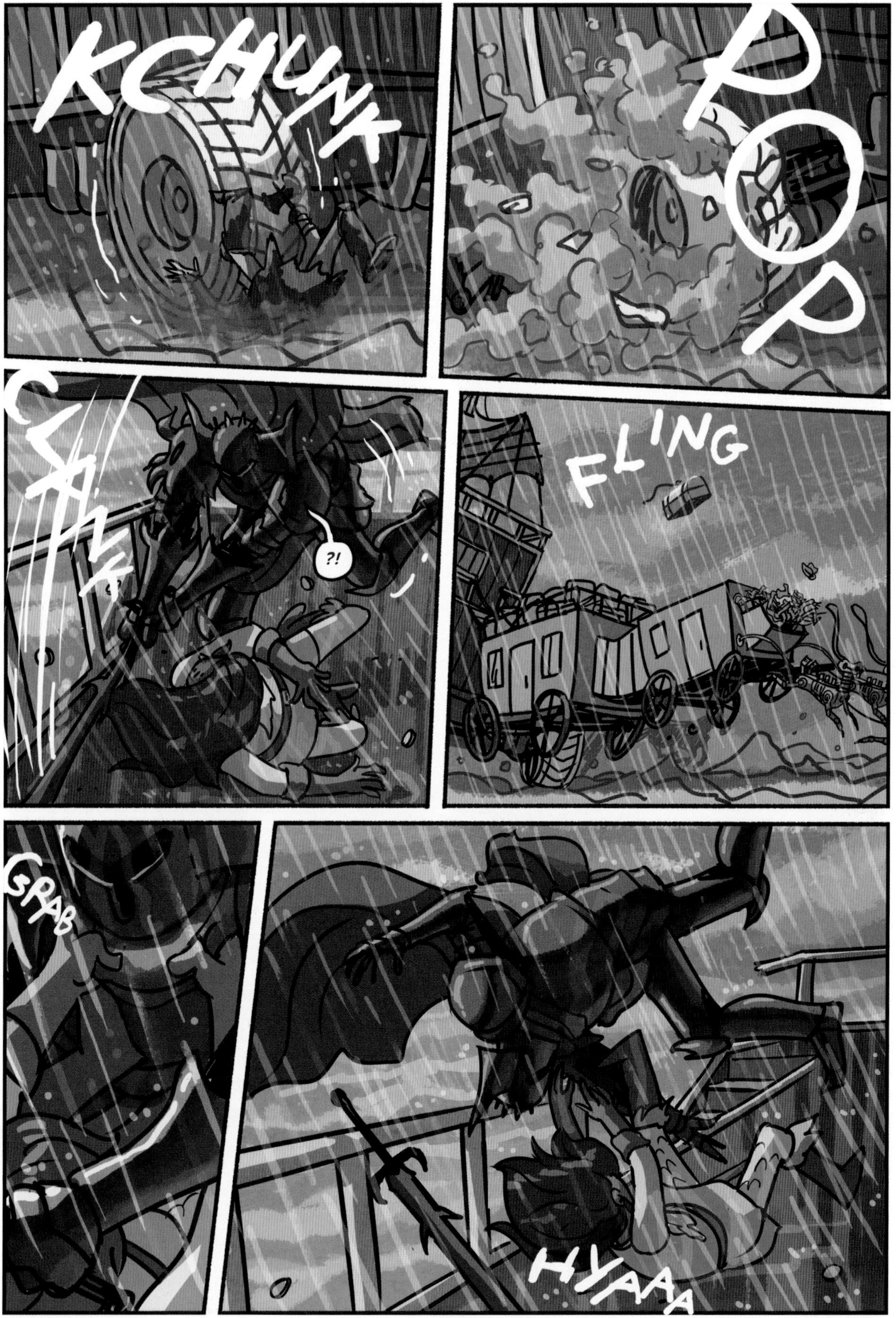
KCHUNK
POP
CLANK
?!
FLING
GRAB
HYAAA

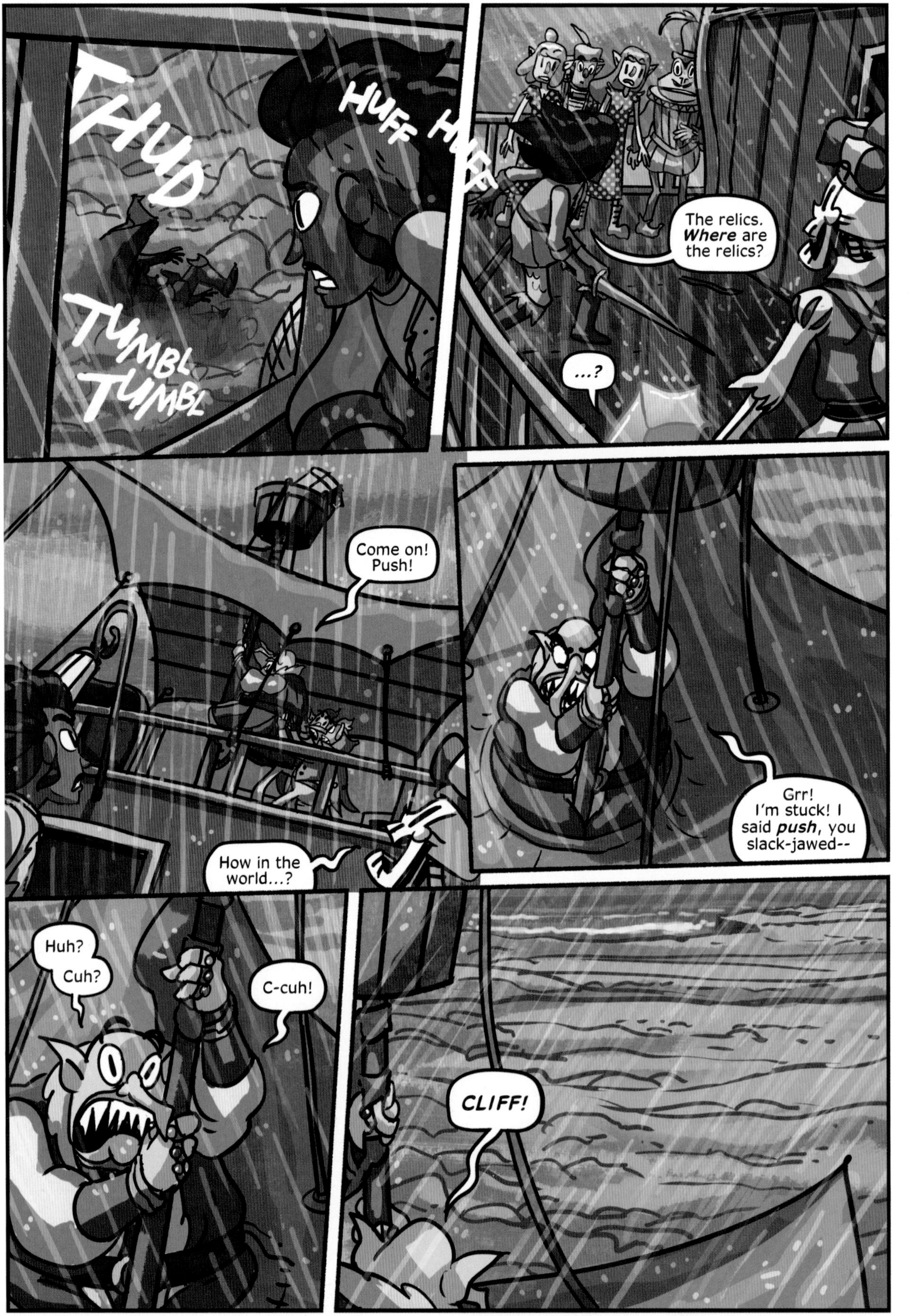
THUD
HUFF HUFF
TUMBL TUMBL
The relics. *Where* are the relics?
...?
Come on! Push!
How in the world...?
Grr! I'm stuck! I said *push*, you slack-jawed--
Huh?
Cuh?
C-cuh!
CLIFF!

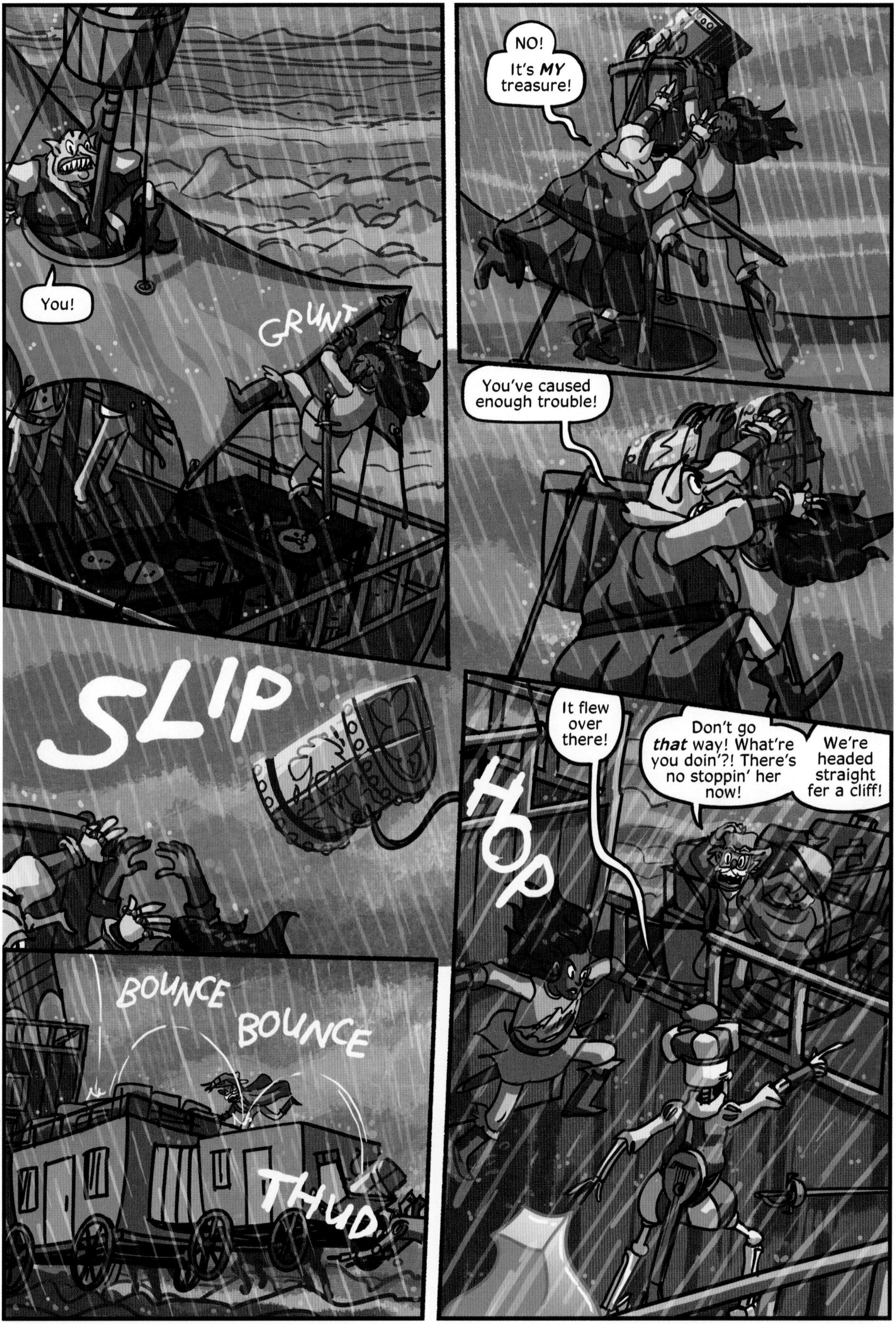
You!
GRUNT
NO!
It's *MY* treasure!
You've caused enough trouble!
SLIP
HOP
It flew over there!
Don't go *that* way! What're you doin'?! There's no stoppin' her now!
We're headed straight fer a cliff!
BOUNCE
BOUNCE
THUD

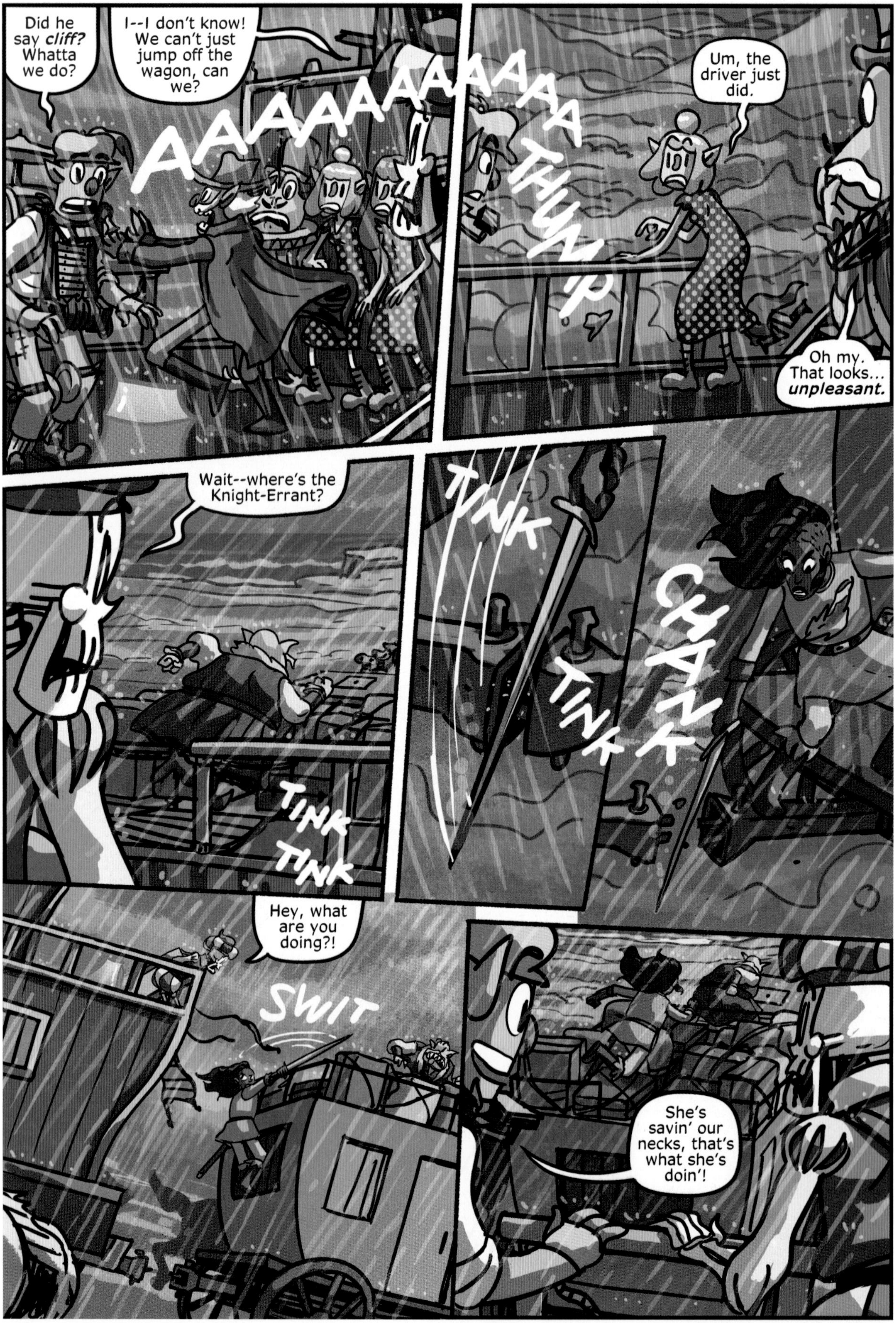
Did he say *cliff?* Whatta we do?
I--I don't know! We can't just jump off the wagon, can we?
AAAAAAAAAAAA
THUMP
Um, the driver just did.
Oh my. That looks... ***unpleasant.***
Wait--where's the Knight-Errant?
TINK TINK
TINK
CHANK
TINK
Hey, what are you doing?!
SWIT
She's savin' our necks, that's what she's doin'!

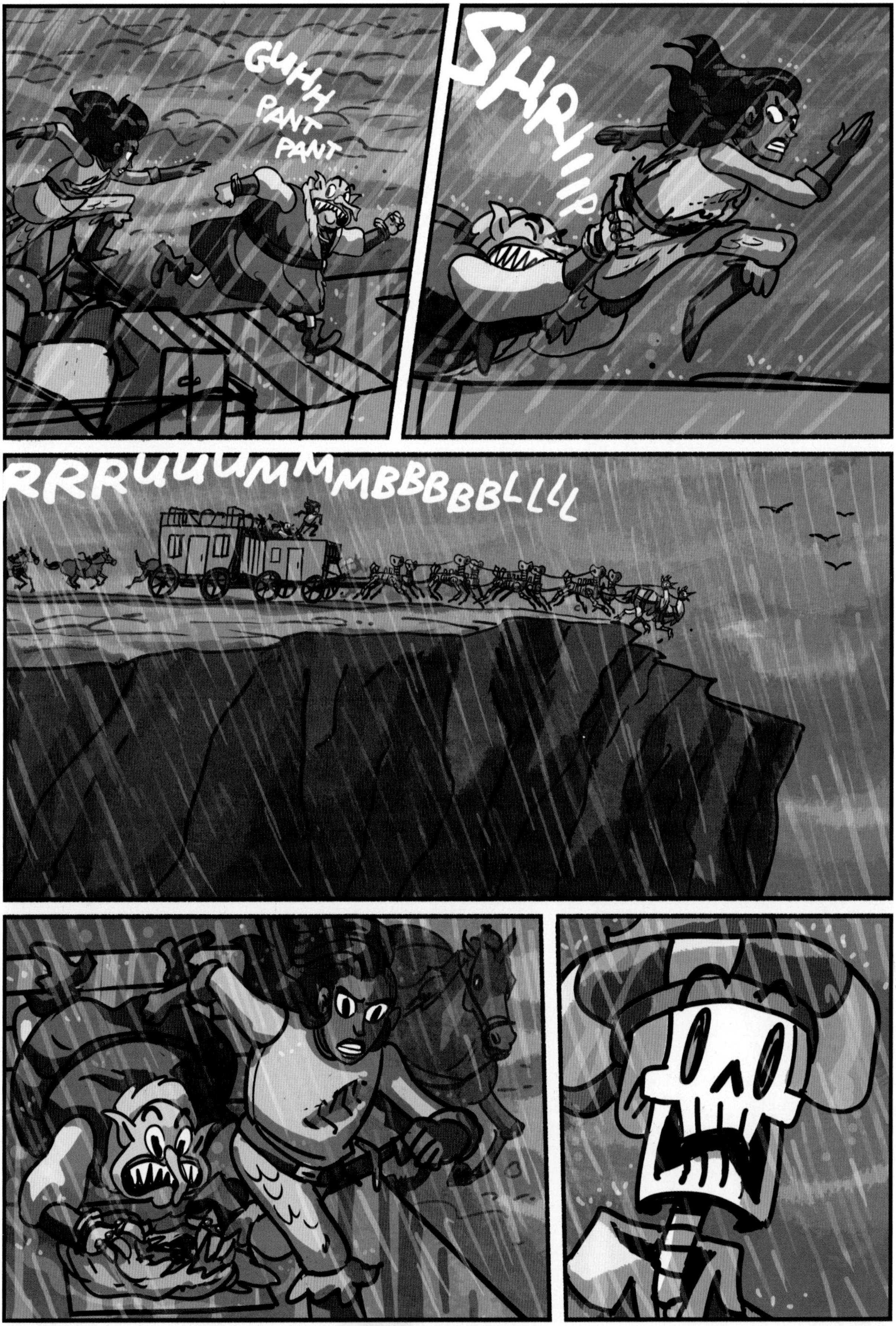
GUHH
PANT
PANT
SHRIIIP
RRRUUUMMMBBBBBLLLL

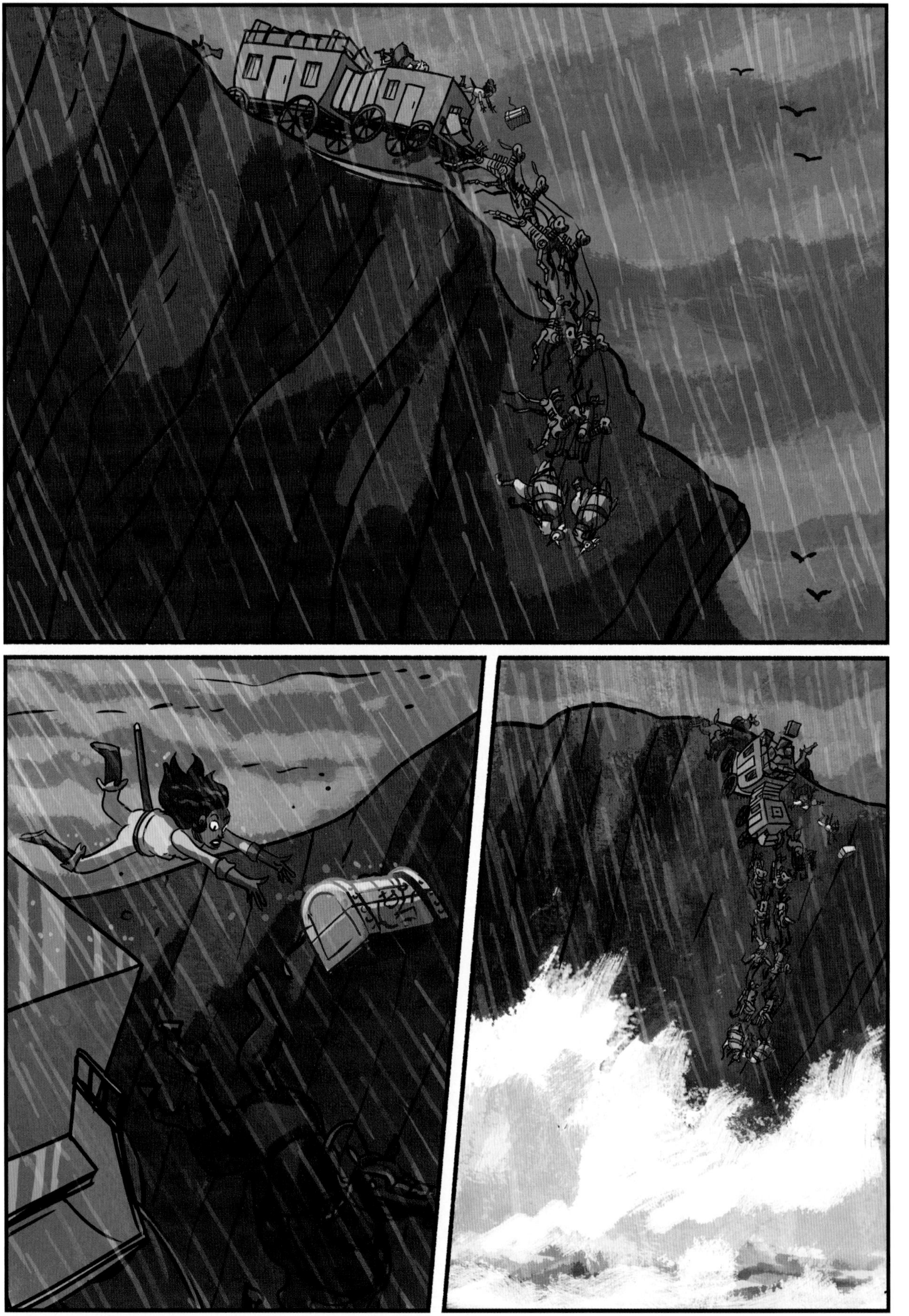

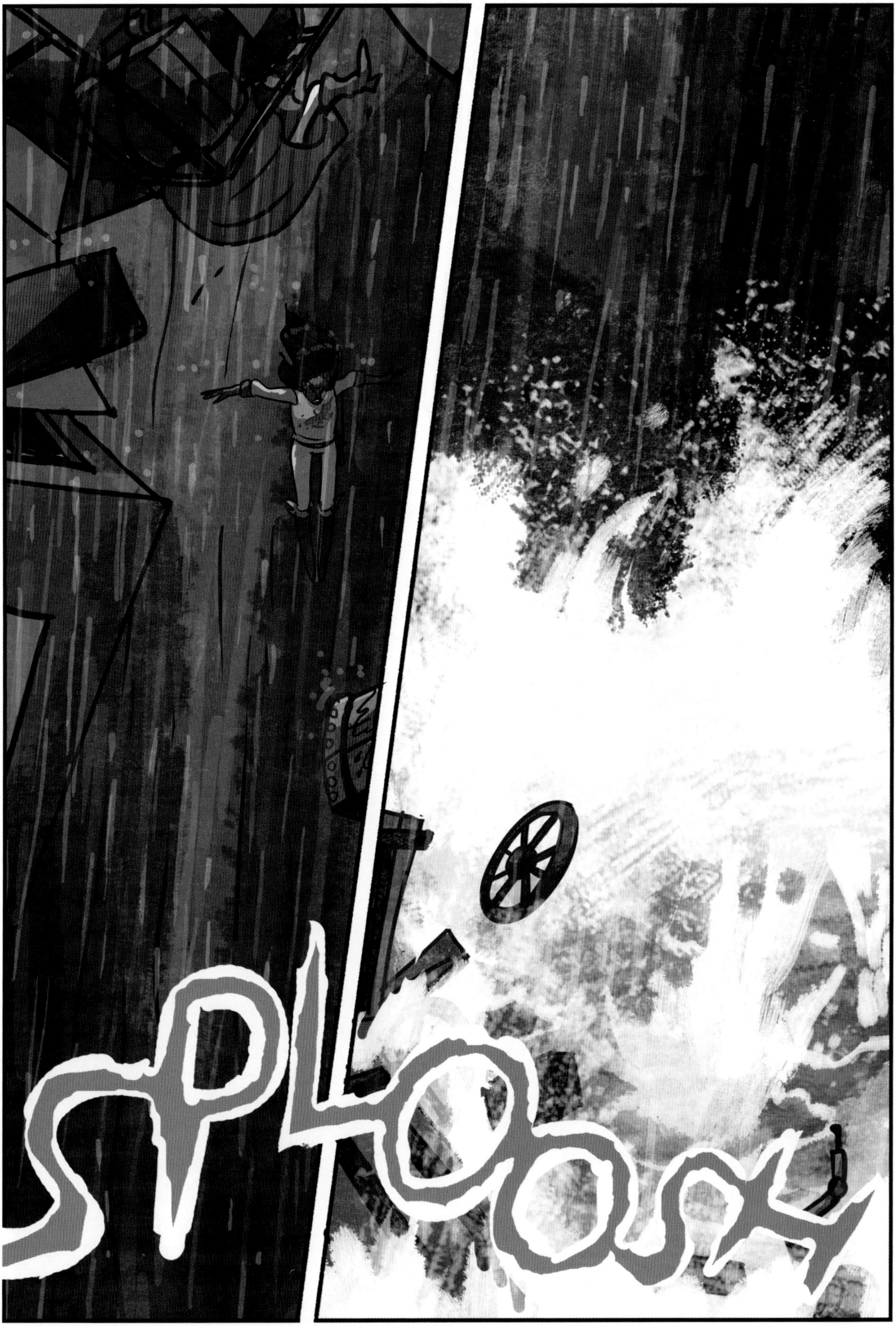
SPLOOSH

Chapter 11
Keep Singing

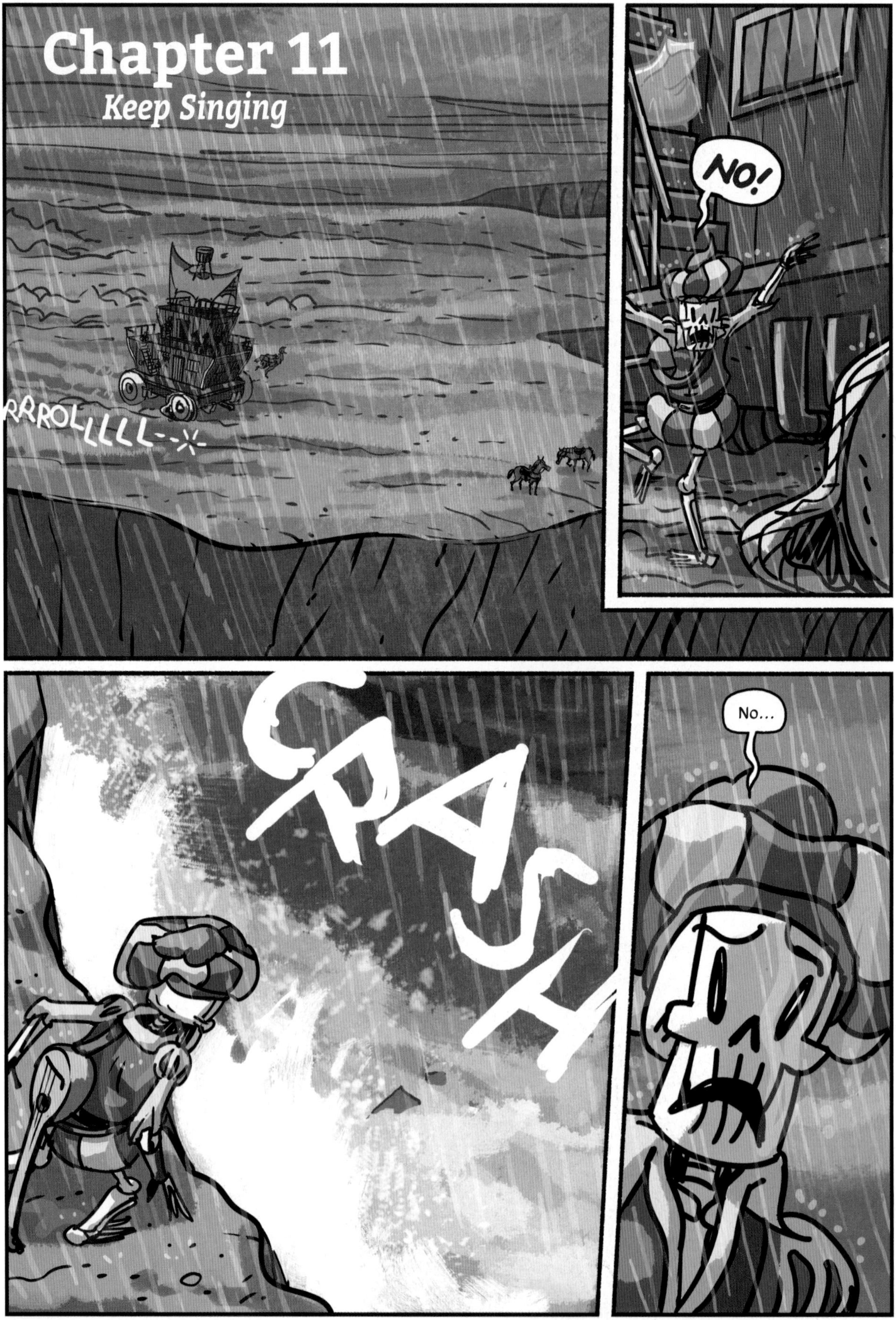
RRROLLLLLL--
NO!
CRASH
No...

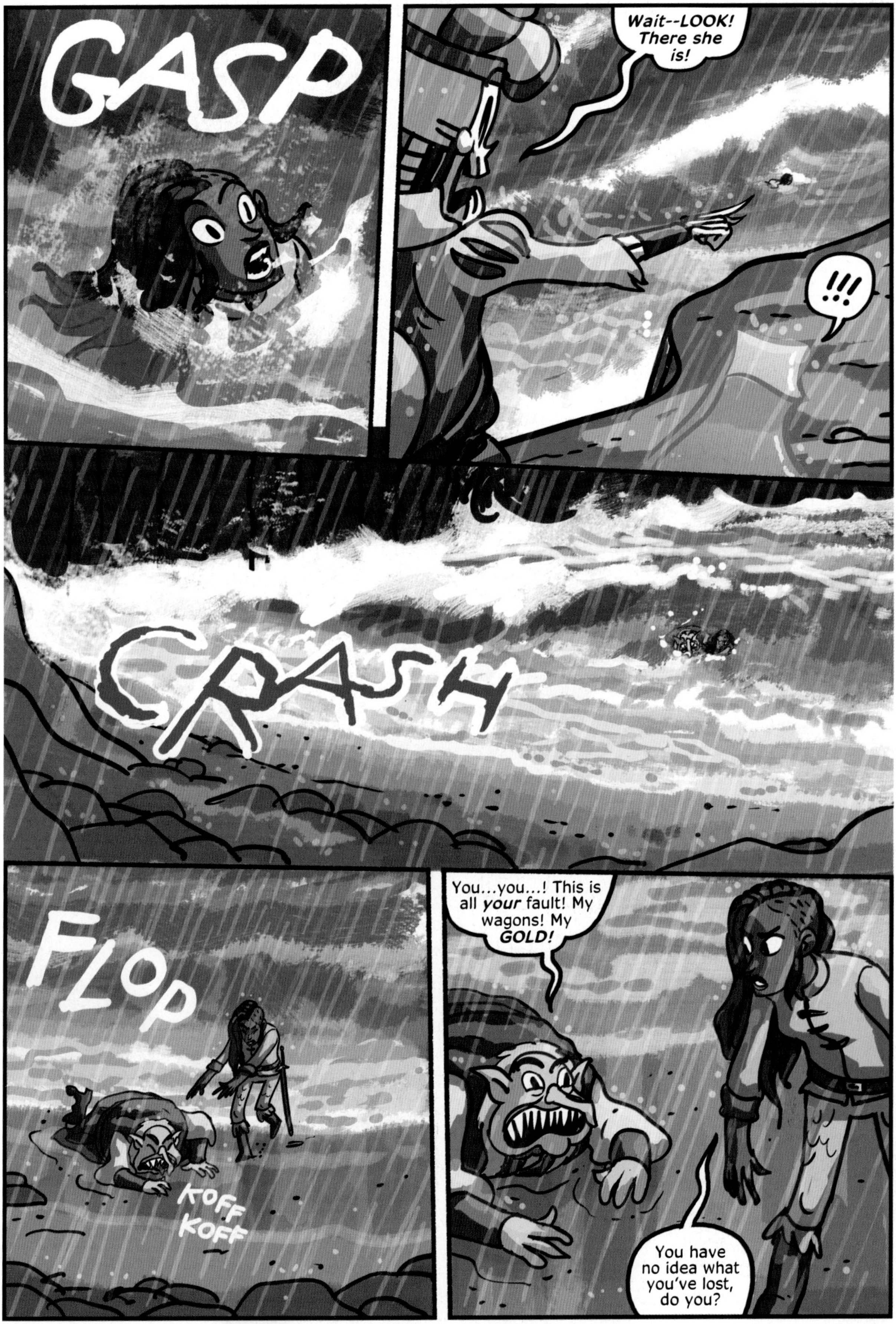
GASP
Wait--LOOK! There she is!
!!!
CRASH
FLOP
KOFF KOFF
You...you...! This is all *your* fault! My wagons! My *GOLD!*
You have no idea what you've lost, do you?

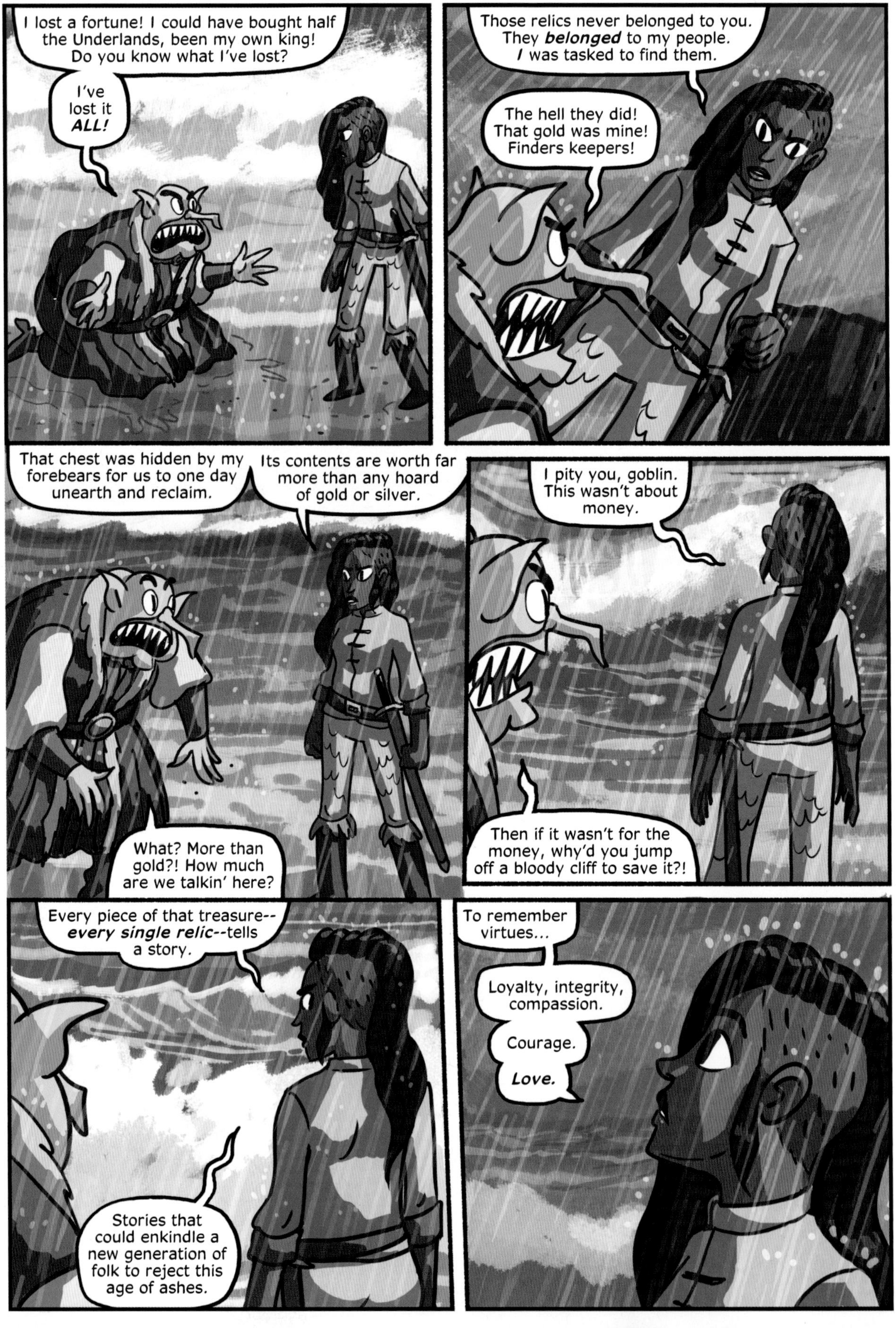
I lost a fortune! I could have bought half the Underlands, been my own king! Do you know what I've lost?
I've lost it *ALL!*
Those relics never belonged to you. They ***belonged*** to my people. *I* was tasked to find them.
The hell they did! That gold was mine! Finders keepers!
That chest was hidden by my forebears for us to one day unearth and reclaim.
Its contents are worth far more than any hoard of gold or silver.
What? More than gold?! How much are we talkin' here?
I pity you, goblin. This wasn't about money.
Then if it wasn't for the money, why'd you jump off a bloody cliff to save it?!
Every piece of that treasure--***every single relic***--tells a story.
Stories that could enkindle a new generation of folk to reject this age of ashes.
To remember virtues...
Loyalty, integrity, compassion.
Courage.
Love.

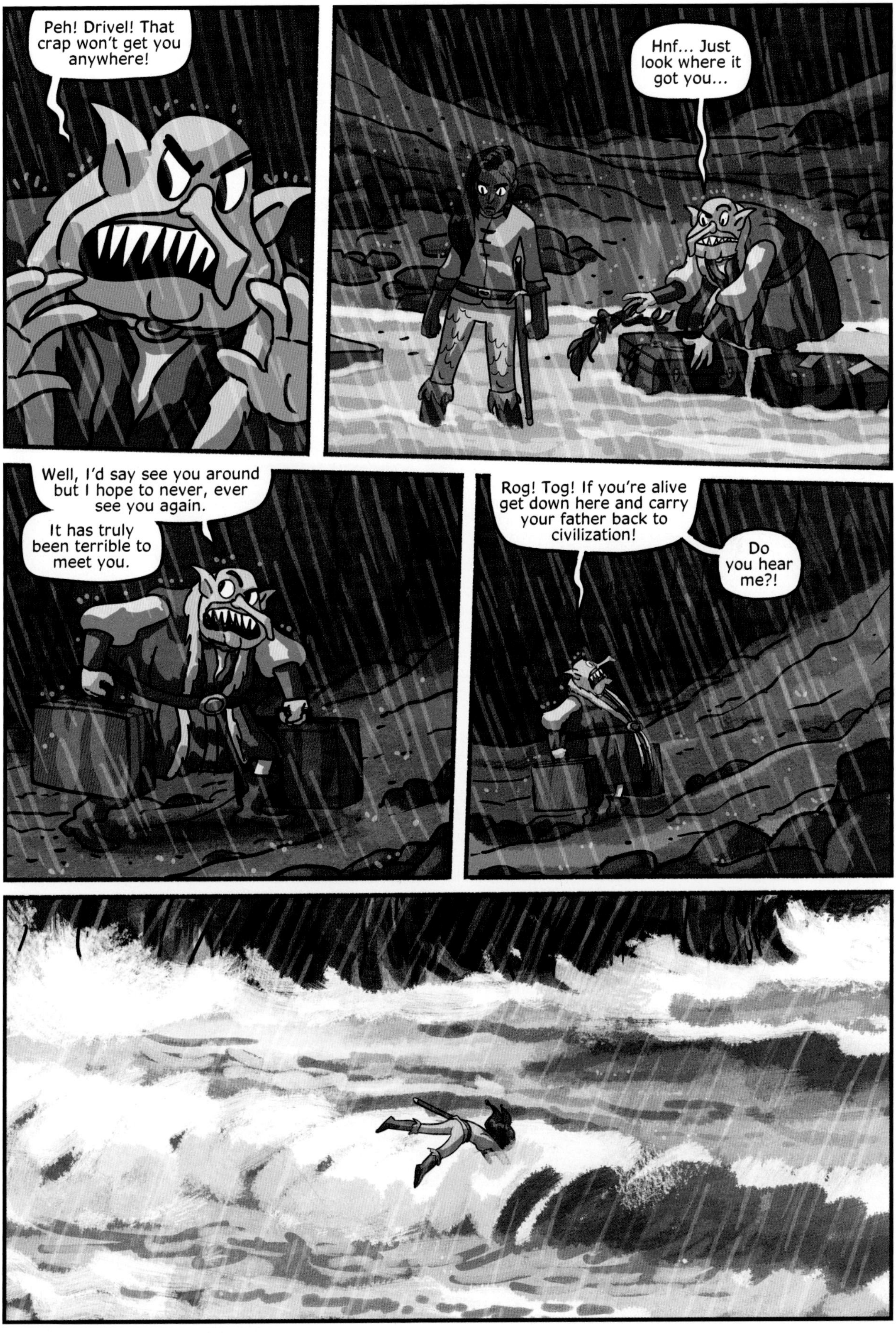
Peh! Drivel! That crap won't get you anywhere!
Hnf... Just look where it got you...
Well, I'd say see you around but I hope to never, ever see you again.
It has truly been terrible to meet you.
Rog! Tog! If you're alive get down here and carry your father back to civilization!
Do you hear me?!

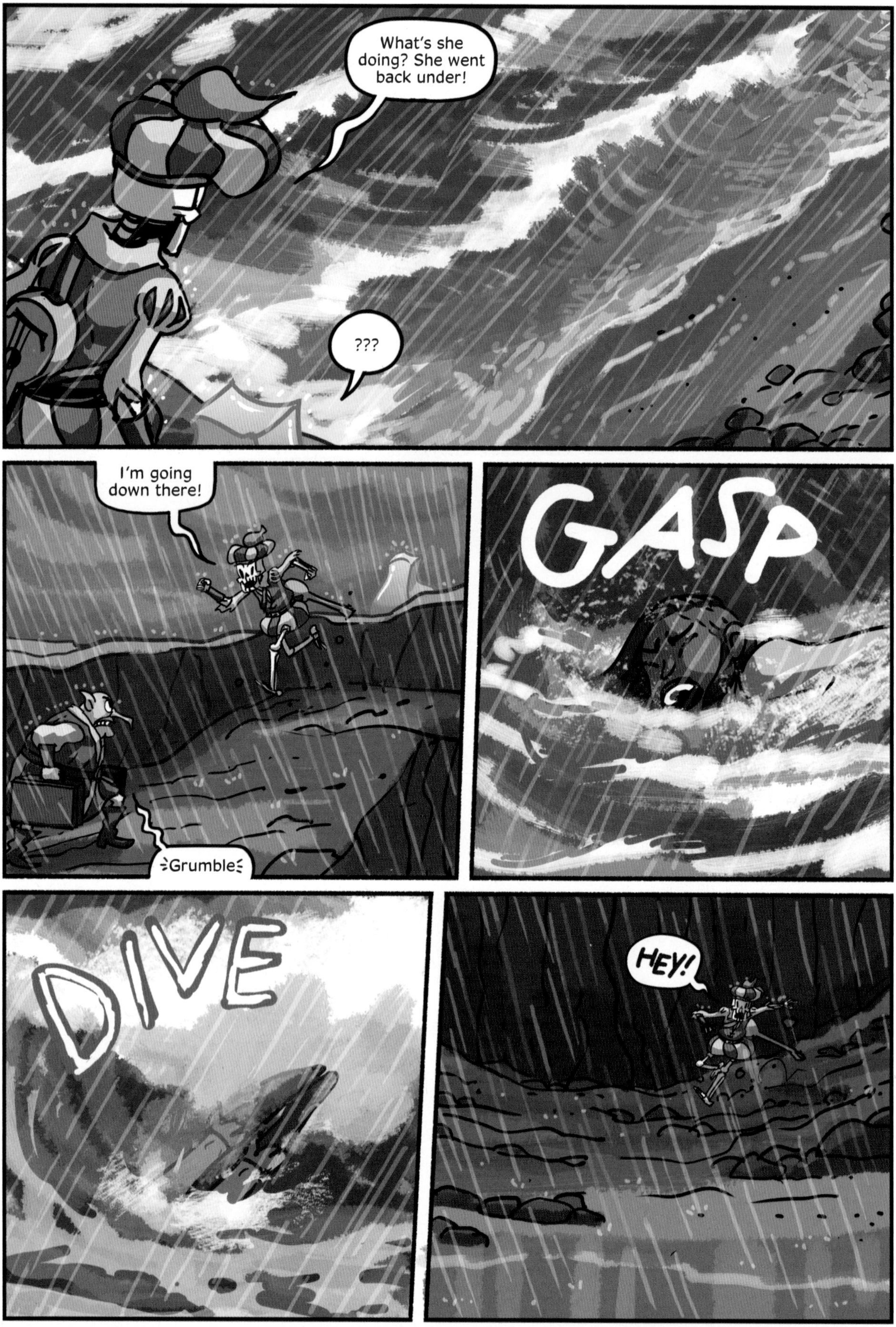
What's she doing? She went back under!
???
I'm going down there!
Grumble
GASP
DIVE
HEY!

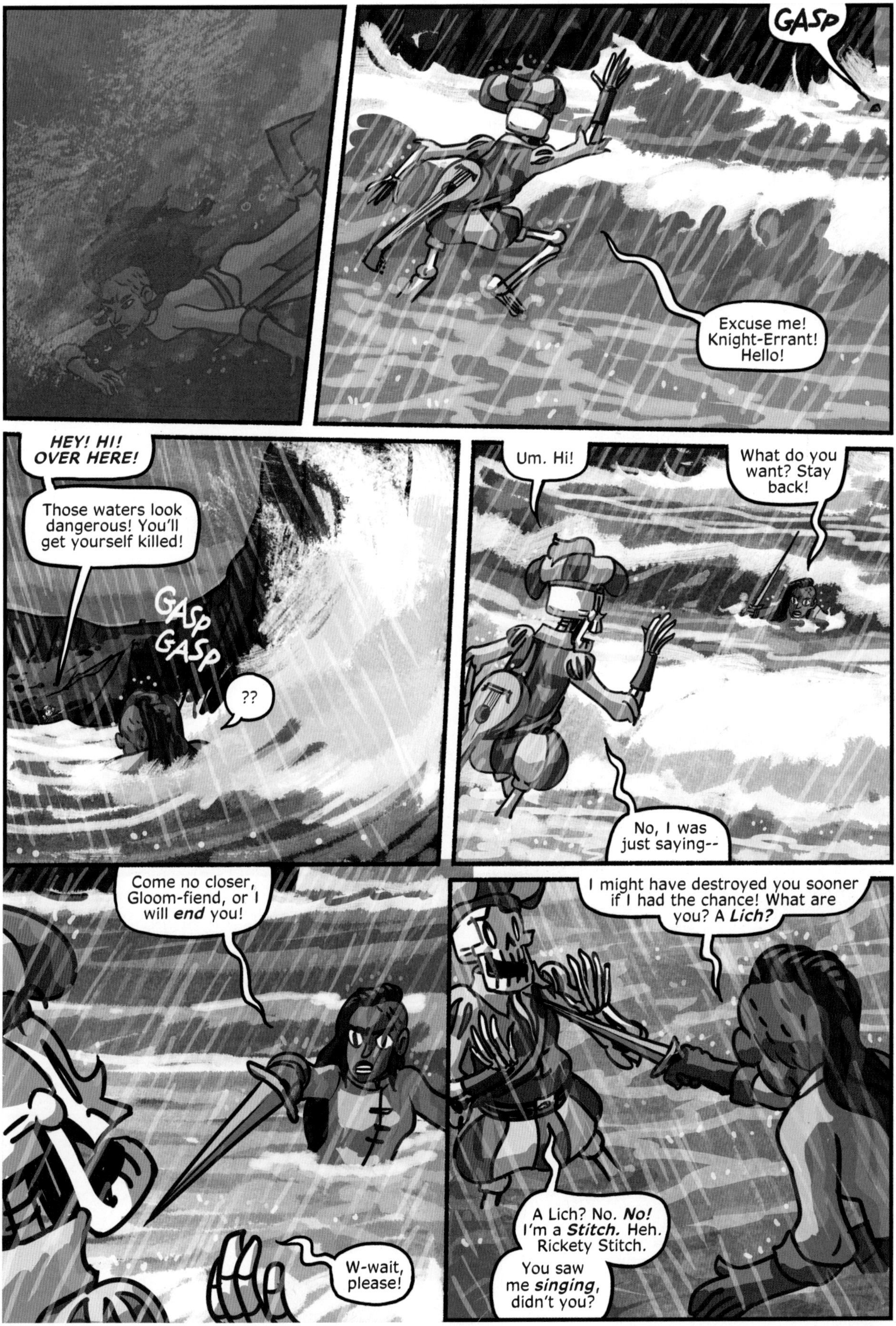

GASP
Excuse me! Knight-Errant! Hello!
HEY! HI! OVER HERE!
Those waters look dangerous! You'll get yourself killed!
GASP GASP
??
Um. Hi!
What do you want? Stay back!
No, I was just saying--
Come no closer, Gloom-fiend, or I will *end* you!
W-wait, please!
I might have destroyed you sooner if I had the chance! What are you? A *Lich?*
A Lich? No. ***No!*** I'm a ***Stitch.*** Heh. Rickety Stitch.
You saw me *singing*, didn't you?

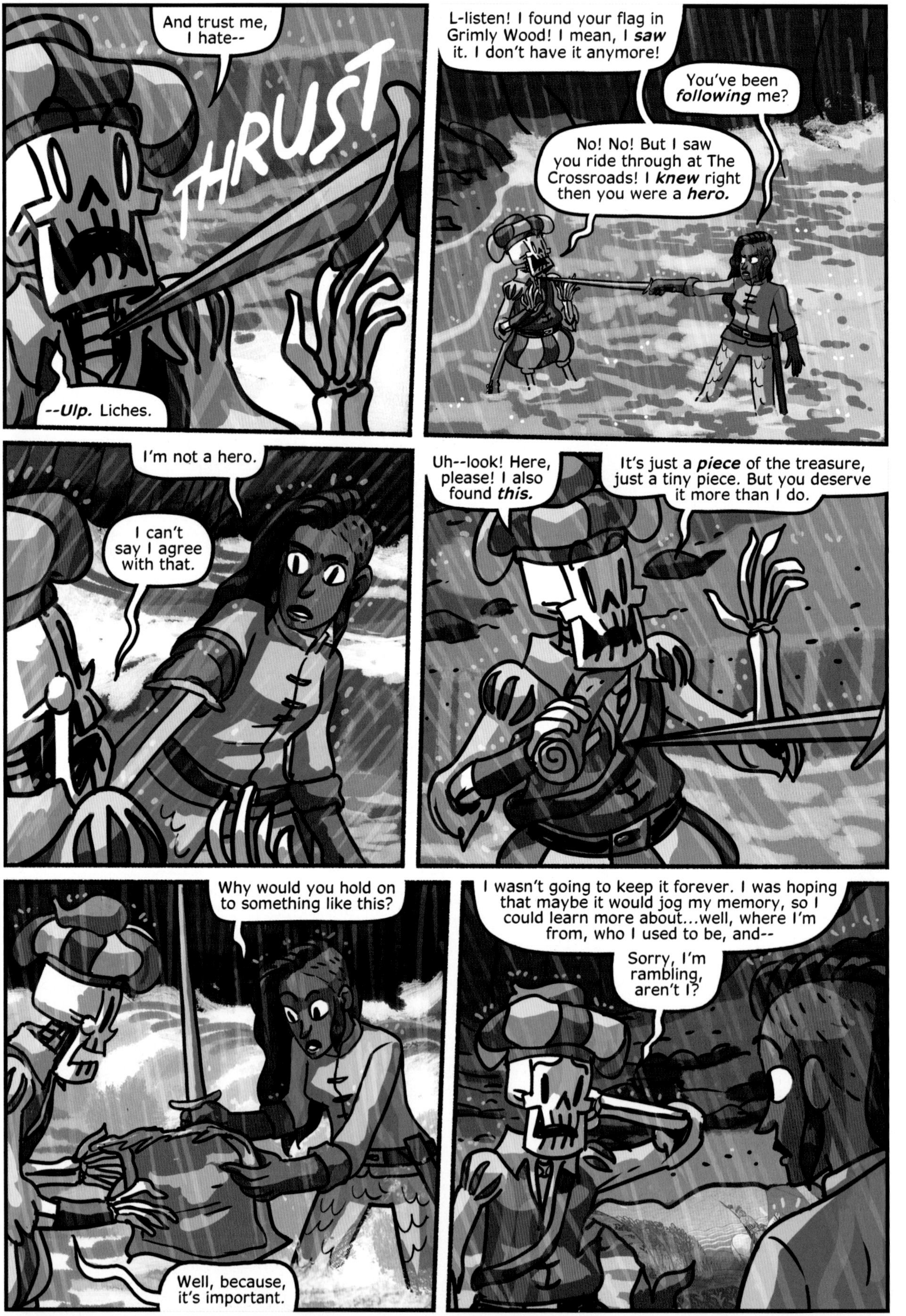
And trust me, I hate--
THRUST
--Ulp. Liches.
L-listen! I found your flag in Grimly Wood! I mean, I saw it. I don't have it anymore!
You've been following me?
No! No! But I saw you ride through at The Crossroads! I knew right then you were a hero.
I'm not a hero.
I can't say I agree with that.
Uh--look! Here, please! I also found this.
It's just a piece of the treasure, just a tiny piece. But you deserve it more than I do.
Why would you hold on to something like this?
Well, because, it's important.
I wasn't going to keep it forever. I was hoping that maybe it would jog my memory, so I could learn more about...well, where I'm from, who I used to be, and--
Sorry, I'm rambling, aren't I?

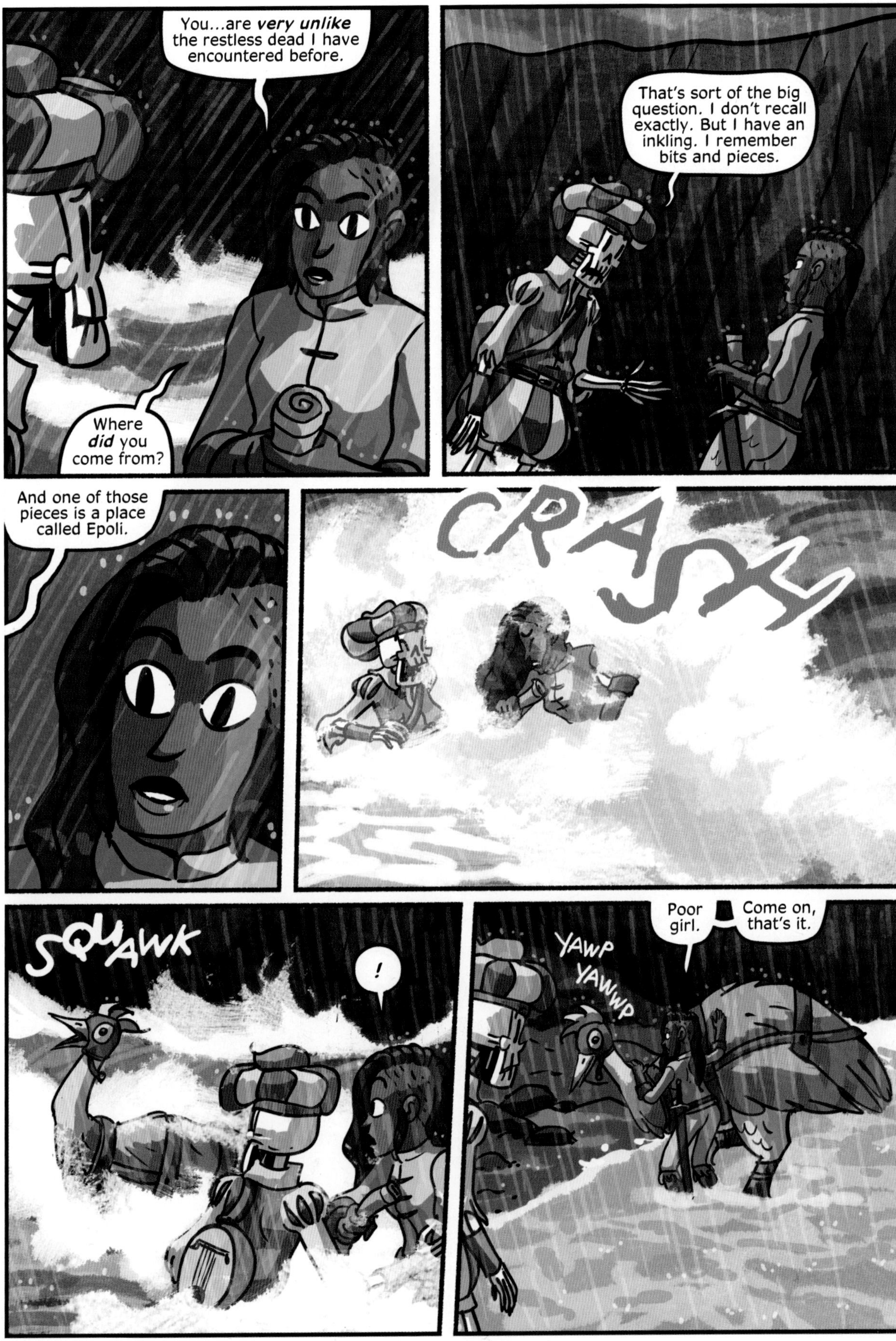

You...are *very unlike* the restless dead I have encountered before.
Where *did* you come from?
That's sort of the big question. I don't recall exactly. But I have an inkling. I remember bits and pieces.
And one of those pieces is a place called Epoli.
CRASH
SQUAWK
!
YAWP
YAWWP
Poor girl.
Come on, that's it.

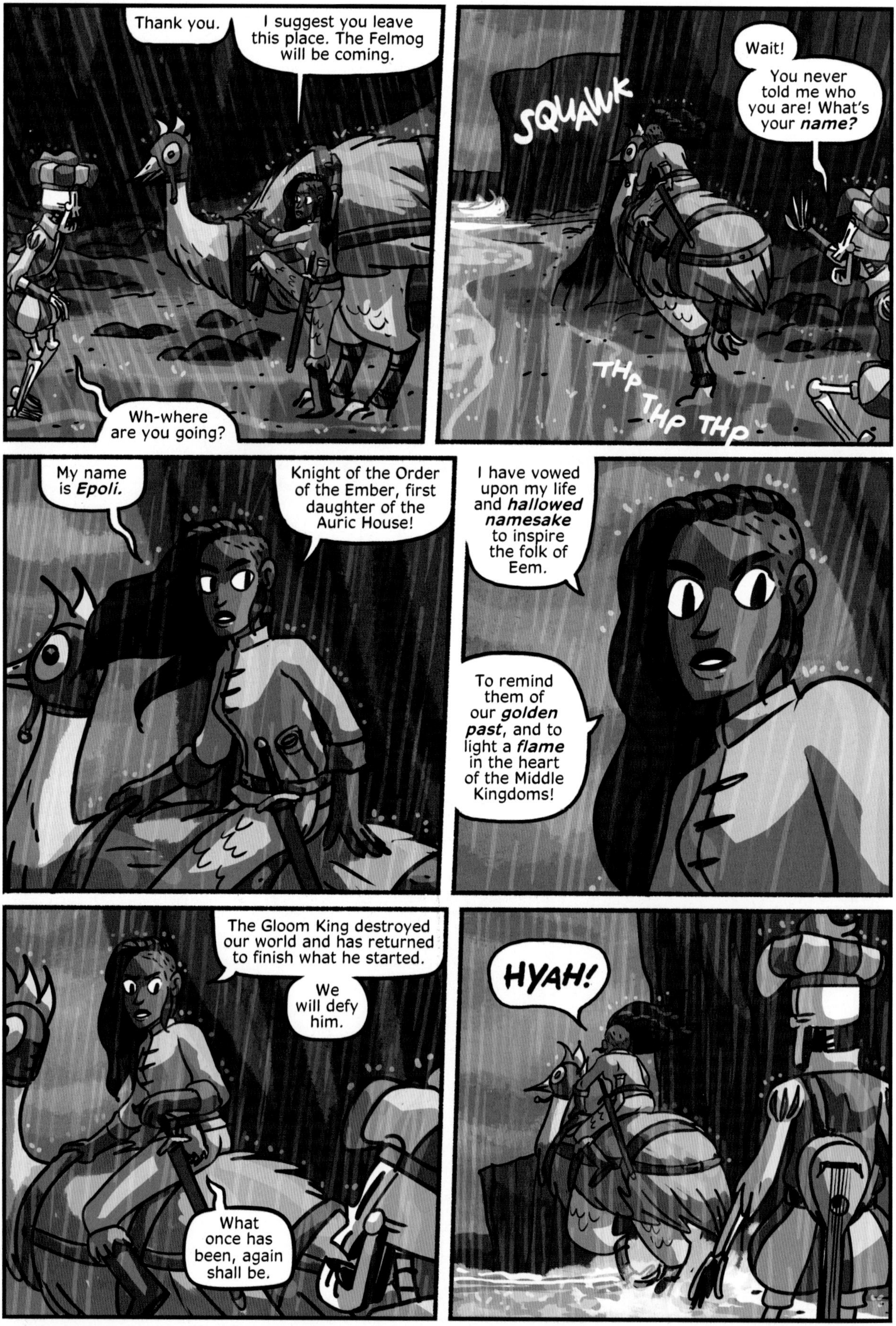

Thank you.
I suggest you leave this place. The Felmog will be coming.
Wh-where are you going?
SQUAWK
Wait!
You never told me who you are! What's your *name?*
THP THP THP
My name is *Epoli.*
Knight of the Order of the Ember, first daughter of the Auric House!
I have vowed upon my life and *hallowed namesake* to inspire the folk of Eem.
To remind them of our *golden past*, and to light a *flame* in the heart of the Middle Kingdoms!
The Gloom King destroyed our world and has returned to finish what he started.
We will defy him.
What once has been, again shall be.
HYAH!

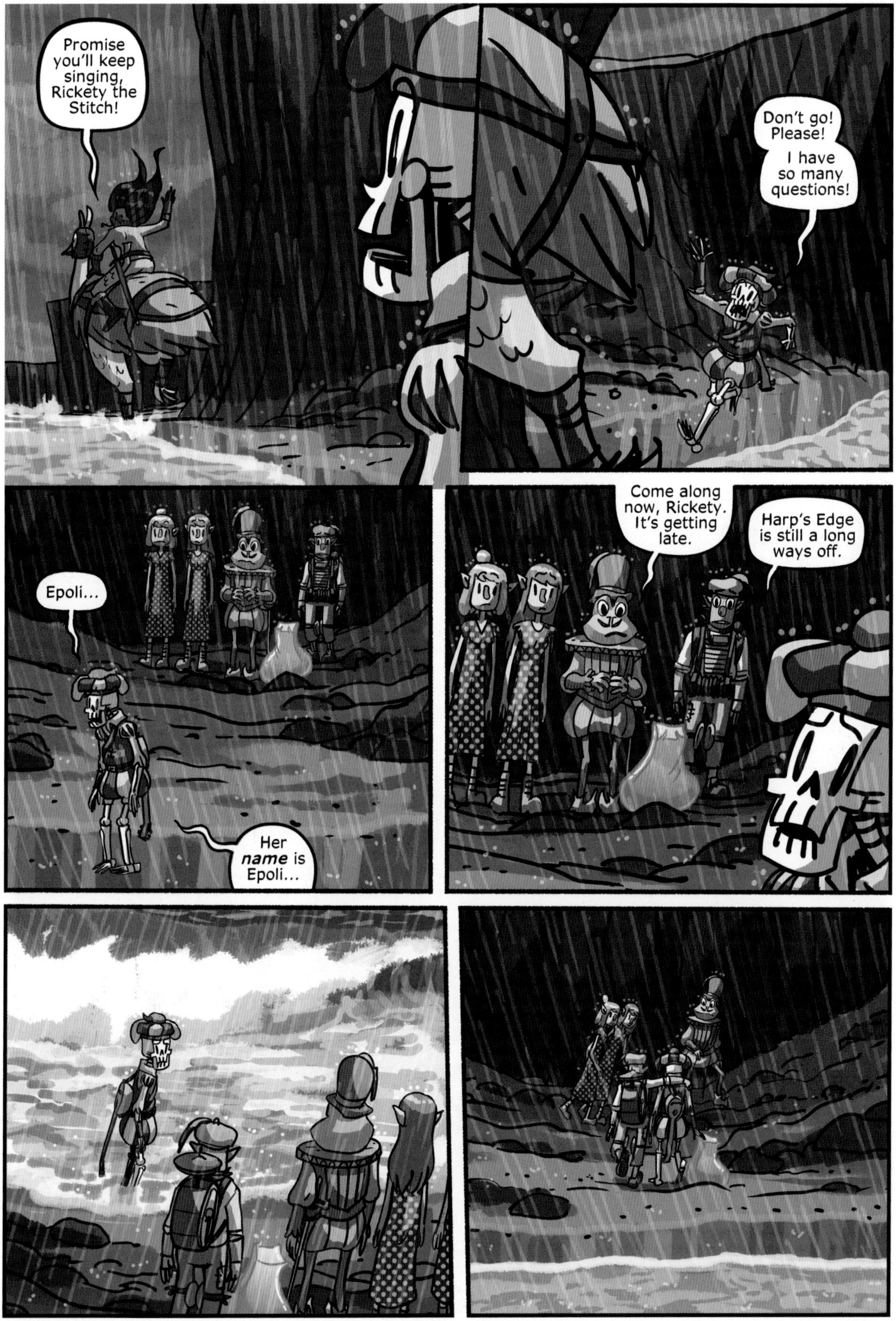
Promise you'll keep singing, Rickety the Stitch!
Don't go! Please!
I have so many questions!
Epoli...
Her *name* is Epoli...
Come along now, Rickety. It's getting late.
Harp's Edge is still a long ways off.

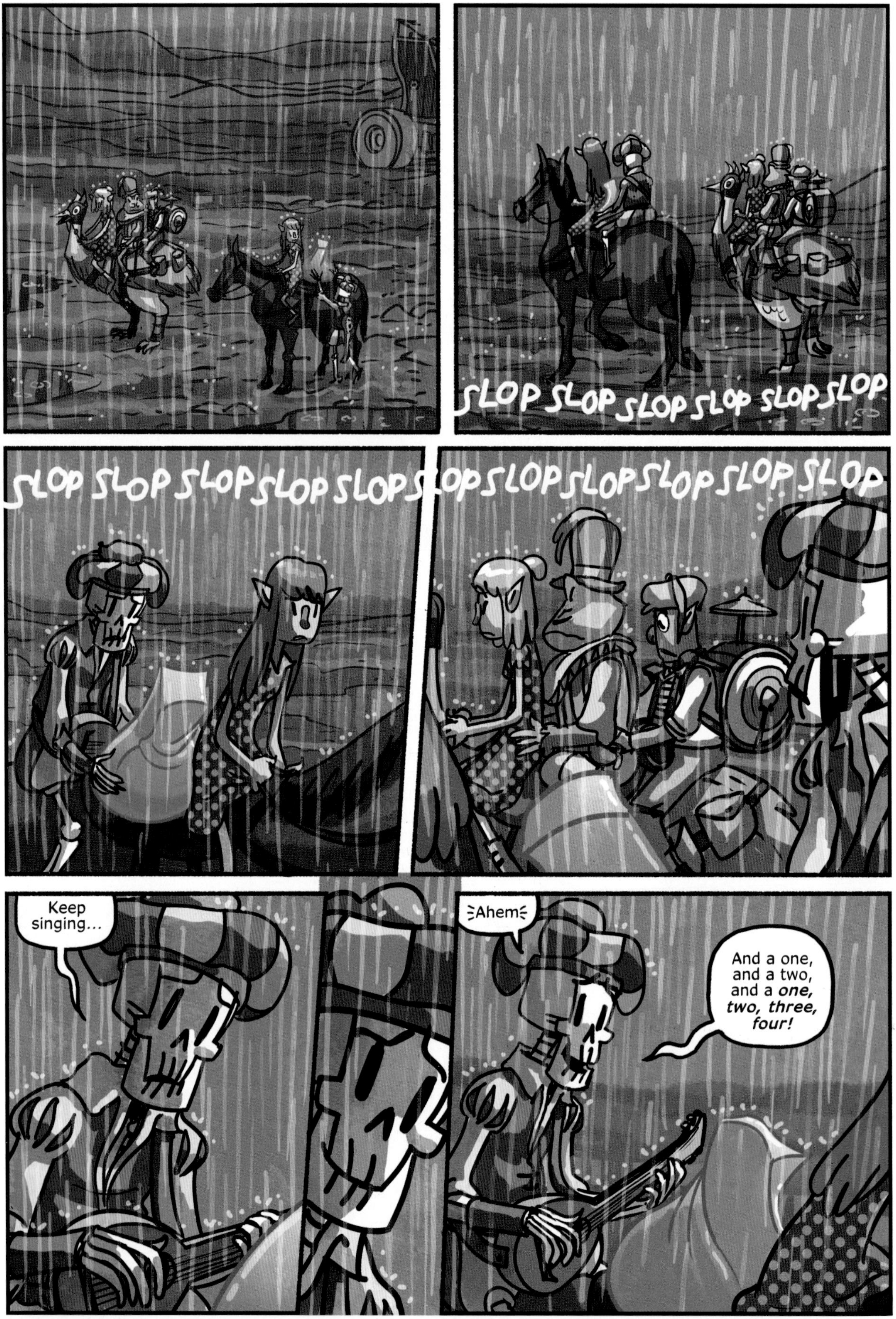

SLOP SLOP SLOP SLOP SLOP SLOP
SLOP SLOP SLOP SLOP SLOP SLOP SLOP SLOP SLOP SLOP SLOP SLOP
Keep singing...
Ahem
And a one, and a two, and a *one, two, three, four!*

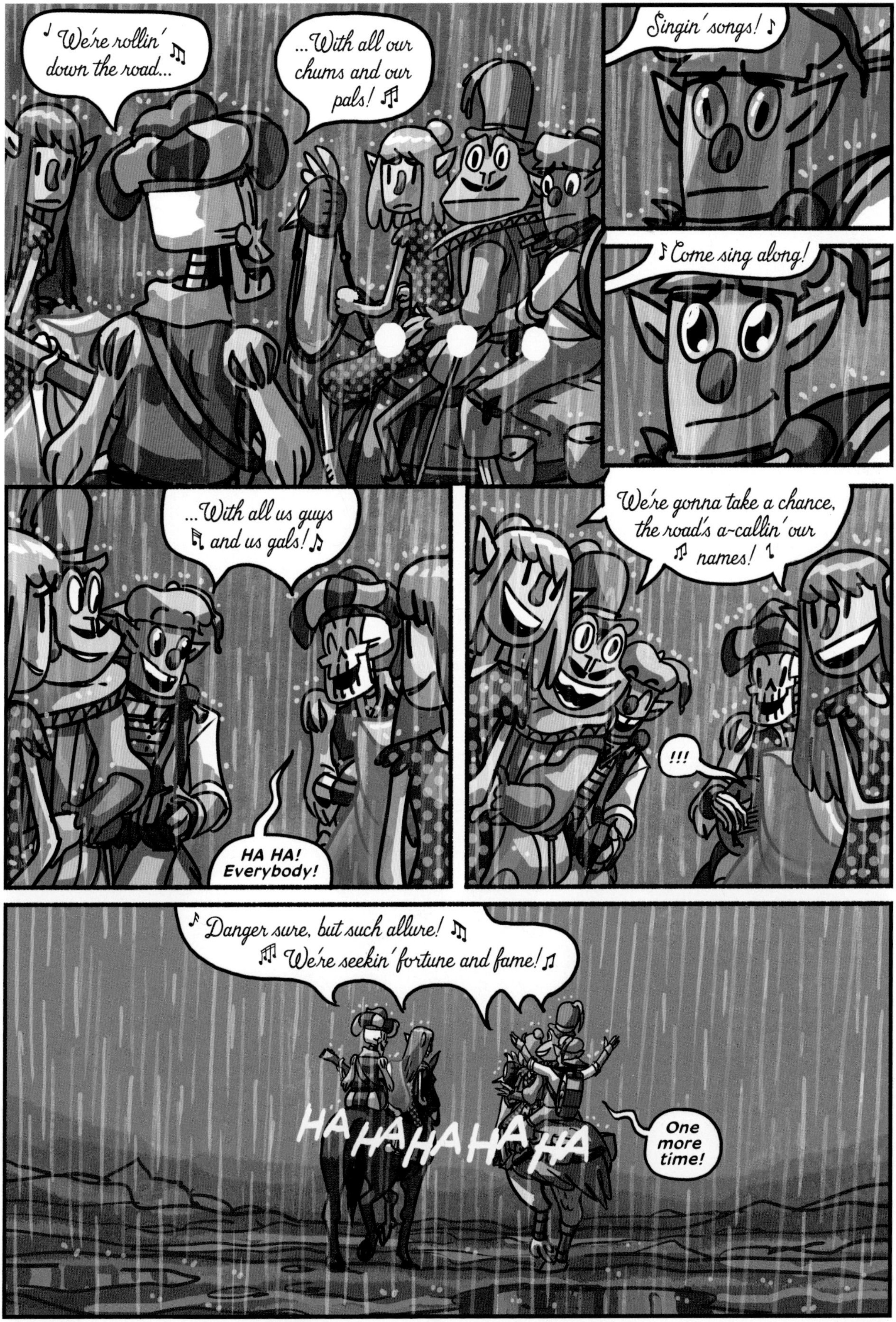
We're rollin' down the road...
...With all our chums and our pals!
Singin' songs!
Come sing along!
...With all us guys and us gals!
HA HA! Everybody!
We're gonna take a chance, the road's a-callin' our names!
!!!
Danger sure, but such allure! We're seekin' fortune and fame!
HA HA HA HA HA HA HA
One more time!

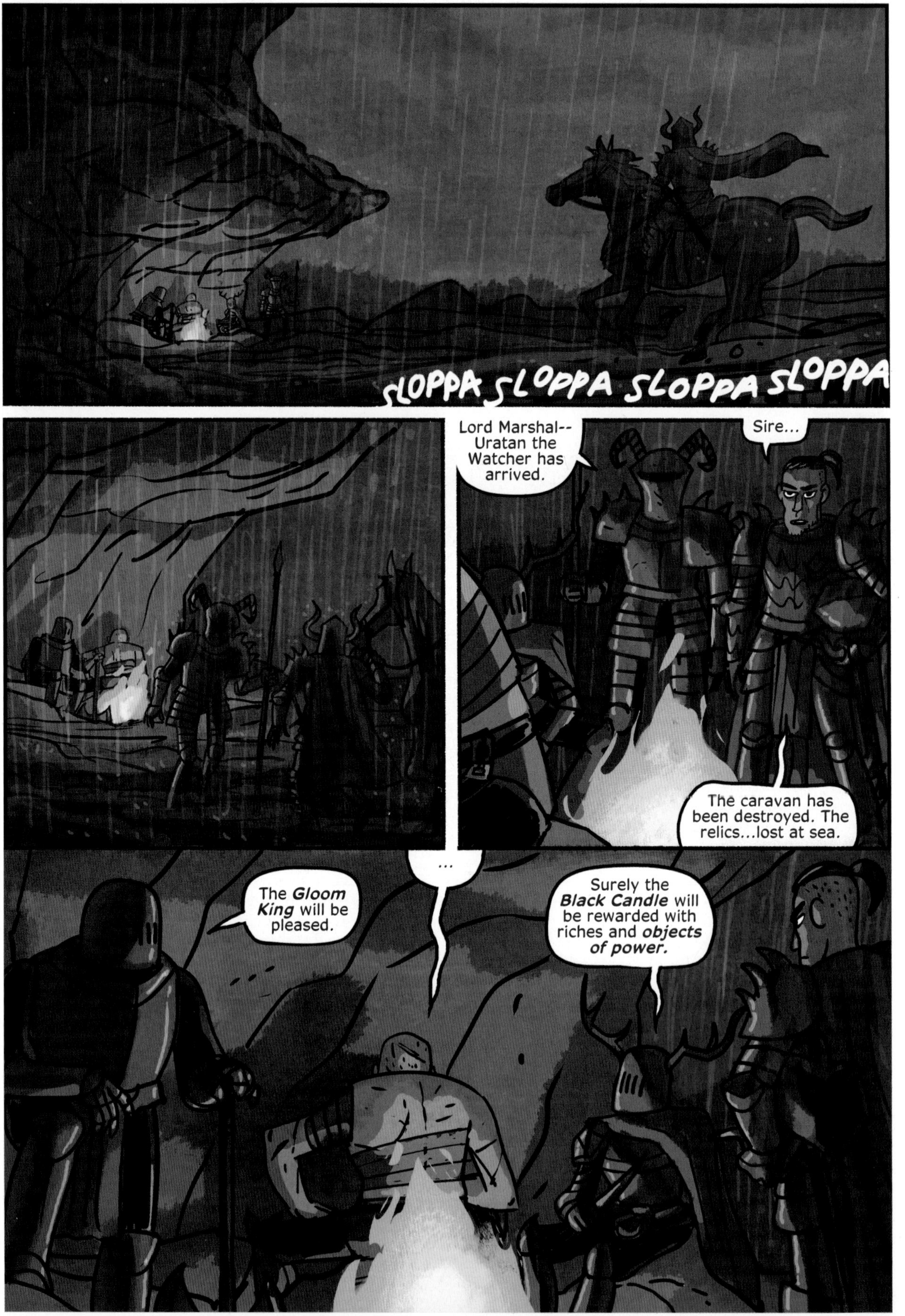
SLOPPA SLOPPA SLOPPA SLOPPA
Lord Marshal-- Uratan the Watcher has arrived.
Sire...
The caravan has been destroyed. The relics...lost at sea.
...
The *Gloom King* will be pleased.
Surely the *Black Candle* will be rewarded with riches and *objects of power.*

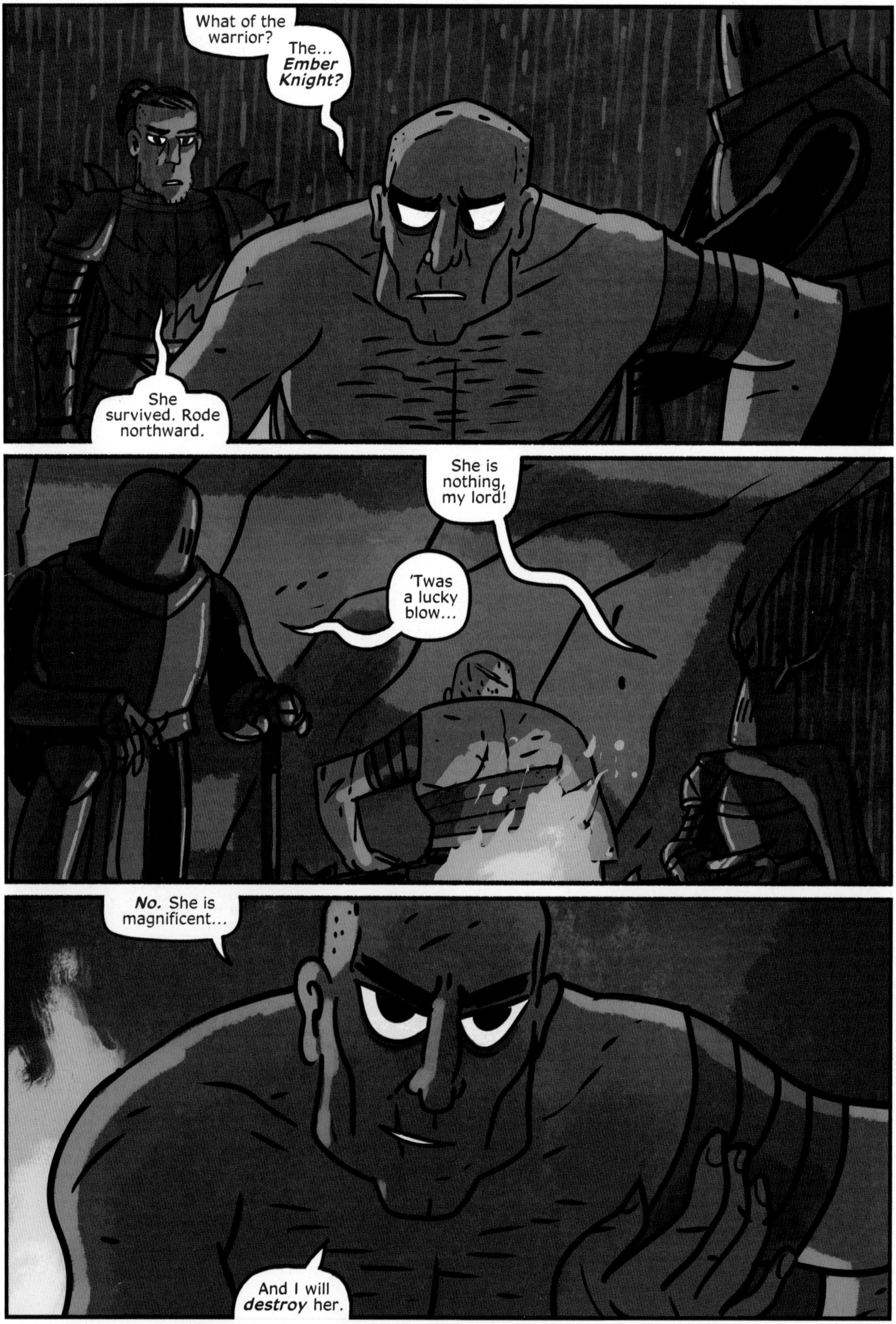
What of the warrior?
The... *Ember Knight?*
She survived. Rode northward.
She is nothing, my lord!
'Twas a lucky blow...
No. She is magnificent...
And I will *destroy* her.

A Hero in Name Only

Music written and performed by Evin Wolverton
Lyrics by Ben Costa & James Parks

Calmly
a hero makes way
dressed all in gold
as bright as the day

Noble
as cool as a gale
wreathed all in blooms
as green as the dale

Bravely
with sword and with spear
no foe left to fight
no perils to fear

Wealthy
as rich as a king
at ease in his hall
where songweavers sing

Rollin' Down the Road

Music written and performed by Evin Wolverton
Lyrics by Ben Costa & James Parks

We're rollin' down the road
with all our chums and our pals

Singin' songs, come sing along
with all us guys and us gals

We're gonna take a chance
The road's a-callin' our names

Danger, sure! But such allure
We're seekin' fortune and fame

We're rollin' down the road
Got bandits hot on our heels

But Kurdok's tough, won't take no guff
They'll eat the dust from our wheels

We're gonna take a chance
Won't nothin' stand in Krog's way

Drawin' swords and bustin' gourds
We sure did ruin their day

The Gallant Mister Krog

Music written and performed by Evin Wolverton
Lyrics by Ben Costa & James Parks

If I could travel every day, I'd take the Middle-Route Way
I'd pack my things, get up and roll!

There's a fortune to be had, and to miss it would be mad
O, there ain't no other way to go!

And there never was a friend, a finer bloke to send
Now raise that cup of glogg, here's to the Greatest Slog
And the gallant Mister Krog!

Everyone!

Now raise that cup of glogg, here's to the Greatest Slog
And the gallant Mister Krog!

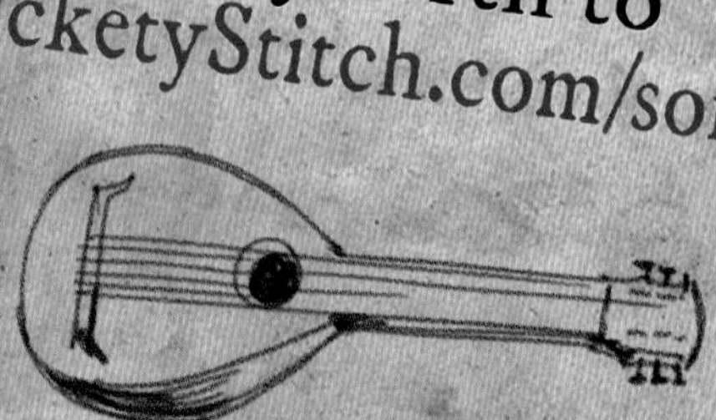

Excerpts from *The Extraordinarily Exhaustive Encyclopedia of Eem*
by P. Gandy Gandermun

Sputterhorses

The shryms of Shrym are known to be ingenious, particularly when it comes to the art and science of clockwork mechanics. Thriving in the underearth of the craggy eastern plains of Shrym, they possess quick, creative minds, which have crafted countless inventions to further their society.

One such invention is the sputterhorse, a windup beast of burden. Invented by the famed shrym machinist Izzu Winchwold, sputterhorses were originally designed to help shrym excavators haul heavy loads of ore and minerals from the shimmering depths of the Underlands. But as shrym civilization expanded into the wider world above, mastering the roads and routes that crisscross the vast geography of the Middle Kingdoms became a top priority.

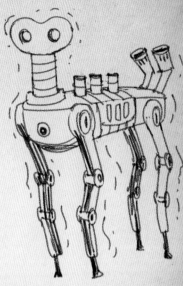

Constructed of highly dense Shar steel, and sputtering to life through a combination of torsion springs, gears, and arcane combustibles, sputterhorses generate enough power to pull loads many times their mass and weight. And they have a range of hundreds of miles before they need to be wound up again, making them a magnificent tool for crossing great distances. The only glaring drawback to their design, of course, is that they are completely mindless and require actual sentient animals to lead them in driving teams.

Along the Middle-Route Run, sputterhorses are prized, and only the wealthiest and most powerful caravan owners can afford to hitch them to their wagons. It goes without saying that any caravan boasting a complement of sputterhorses had better watch out for marauders looking for a rich score.

Thunderfoot Route-Runners

Native to the central plains and coastal regions of western Eem, thunderfoot route-runners are famed for their incredible stamina and constitution. It has been said that an adult route-runner (generally around fifty years old) can run at a sustained sprint for three days and three nights before needing rest, and a week before needing food or drink. An incredible feat, and one that has made route-runners the most prevalent mounts for those foolhardy enough to embark on a Middle-Route Run.

The thunderfoot route-runner gets its name from its powerful legs—and, of course, feet—whose stomps can be heard from miles away like rumbling thunder during a stampede on the desert plains. Much more akin to the sinewy hindquarters of an ancient lizard than a great bird, the taloned claws of a route-runner are as hard as iron and capable of enormous harm should you end up beneath them.

But to tame a route-runner is a mighty challenge that only the most experienced beast wranglers ever endeavor. Wild thunderfoots are by nature incredibly skittish, and will not hesitate to buck a rider or gore a bystander at the slightest noise or movement. It takes years of training and rearing to earn their trust and respect. But, dear, oh dear, can they ever run!

Felmog

Resting along the cold, northwestern coast, Felmog is the wealthiest country in Eem. It is a realm ruled by aristocracy, and old, chivalric orders of quest knights who have sworn to scour the world for lost relics and wonders of antiquity. Theirs is not a quest to preserve the past, but to conquer it and claim it as their own, and to immortalize their names in history.

There are three major orders of Felmog—the Iron Sun, the Cloven Tongue, and the Black Candle—all of which are ruled by a central Countship in Felmog's seaside capital of Kreeth. The Count or Countess of Felmog is generally determined by political and martial contests between the three orders, and is often passed down for generations to the firstborn of the winning house. The land is currently ruled by House Khasadar, a well-respected and particularly accomplished Black Candle family.

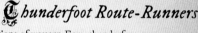

Iron Sun

Felmog maintains that their history reaches back several millennia to the Hamarung Empire, which was an ancient civilization of seafaring warlords that established a foothold along the western coast. Hamarung is credited with marvelous achievements of engineering and architecture, including the Bridge of Hamarung, which crosses the Canyons of Pim, and is the largest man-made structure in the known world.

Though Felmog is largely disinterested in the dealings of the Middle Kingdoms, its rulers have long contested the territory between its borders and the southern side of Hamarung. Many battles and skirmishes against the townships and villages speckling this area have tested the peace over the years, and driven these folk of the Middle Kingdoms further into isolation.

Cloven Tongue

Black Candle

This book is dedicated to heroes—the sung and unsung.
Those who, in uncertain times, inspire us, risk for us,
and challenge us to live as they do.

We would like to give special thanks to Ellen Ma-Parks,
Svetik Petushkova, Evin Wolverton, and Kieu Nguyen.

THIS IS A BORZOI BOOK PUBLISHED BY ALFRED A. KNOPF

Text, jacket art, and interior illustrations copyright © 2018 by Ben Costa and James Parks

All rights reserved. Published in the United States by Alfred A. Knopf, an imprint of Random House
Children's Books, a division of Penguin Random House LLC, New York.

Knopf, Borzoi Books, and the colophon are registered trademarks of Penguin Random House LLC.

Visit us on the Web! getundcrlined.com

Educators and librarians, for a variety of teaching tools, visit us at RHTeachersLibrarians.com

Library of Congress Cataloging-in-Publication Data is available upon request.
ISBN 978-0-399-55616-6 (trade) — ISBN 978-0-399-55618-0 (ebook) —
ISBN 978-0-399-55617-3 (trade pbk.)

The illustrations were created digitally.

MANUFACTURED IN CHINA
July 2018
10 9 8 7 6 5 4 3 2 1

First Edition